Stella Fregelius

Stella Fregelius

A Tale of Three Destinies

H. Rider Haggard

MINT EDITIONS

Stella Fregelius: A Tale of Three Destinies was first published in 1904.

This edition published by Mint Editions 2021.

ISBN 9781513281674 | E-ISBN 9781513286693

Published by Mint Editions®

MINT
EDITIONS

minteditionbooks.com

Publishing Director: Jennifer Newens
Design & Production: Rachel Lopez Metzger
Project Manager: Micaela Clark
Typesetting: Westchester Publishing Services

Contents

A Note From the Author

The author feels that he owes some apology to his readers for his boldness in offering to them a modest story which is in no sense a romance of the character that perhaps they expect from him; which has, moreover, few exciting incidents and no climax of the accustomed order, since the end of it only indicates its real beginning.

His excuse must be that, in the first instance, he wrote it purely to please himself and now publishes it in the hope that it may please some others. The problem of such a conflict, common enough mayhap did we but know it, between a departed and a present personality, of which the battle-ground is a bereaved human heart and the prize its complete possession; between earthly duty and spiritual desire also; was one that had long attracted him. Finding at length a few months of leisure, he treated the difficult theme, not indeed as he would have wished to do, but as best he could.

He may explain further that when he drafted this book, now some five years ago, instruments of the nature of the "aerophone" were not so much talked of as they are to-day. In fact this aerophone has little to do with his characters or their history, and the main motive of its introduction to his pages was to suggest how powerless are all such material means to bring within mortal reach the transcendental and unearthly ends which, with their aid, were attempted by Morris Monk.

These, as that dreamer learned, must be far otherwise obtained, whether in truth and spirit, or perchance, in visions only.

H. Rider Haggard, 1903

I

Morris, Mary, and the Aerophone

Above, the sky seemed one vast arc of solemn blue, set here and there with points of tremulous fire; below, to the shadowy horizon, stretched the plain of the soft grey sea, while from the fragrances of night and earth floated a breath of sleep and flowers.

A man leaned on the low wall that bordered the cliff edge, and looked at sea beneath and sky above. Then he contemplated the horizon, and murmured some line heard or learnt in childhood, ending "where earth and heaven meet."

"But they only seem to meet," he reflected to himself, idly. "If I sailed to that spot they would be as wide apart as ever. Yes, the stars would be as silent and as far away, and the sea quite as restless and as salt. Yet there must be a place where they do meet. No, Morris, my friend, there is no such place in this world, material or moral; so stick to facts, and leave fancies alone."

But that night this speculative man felt in the mood for fancies, for presently he was staring at one of the constellations, and saying to himself, "Why not? Well, why not? Granted force can travel through ether,—whatever ether is—why should it stop travelling? Give it time enough, a few seconds, or a few minutes or a few years, and why should it not reach that star? Very likely it does, only there it wastes itself. What would be needed to make it serviceable? Simply this—that on the star there should dwell an Intelligence armed with one of my instruments, when I have perfected them, or the secret of them. Then who knows what might happen?" and he laughed a little to himself at the vagary.

From all of which wandering speculations it may be gathered that Morris Monk was that rather common yet problematical person, an inventor who dreamed dreams.

An inventor, in truth, he was, although as yet he had never really invented anything. Brought up as an electrical engineer, after a very brief experience of his profession he had fallen victim to an idea and become a physicist. This was his idea, or the main point of it—for its details do not in the least concern our history: that by means of a certain machine which he had conceived, but not as yet perfected, it would be possible to complete all existing systems of aerial communication, and enormously to simplify their action and enlarge their scope. His instruments, which were wireless telephones—aerophones he called them—were to be made in pairs, twins that should talk only to each other. They required no high poles, or balloons, or any other cumbrous and expensive appliance; indeed, their size was no larger than that of a rather thick despatch box. And he had triumphed; the thing was done—in all but one or two details.

For two long years he had struggled with these, and still they eluded him. Once he had succeeded—that was the dreadful thing. Once for a while the instruments had worked, and with a space of several miles between them. But—this was the maddening part of it—he had never been able to repeat the exact conditions; or, rather, to discover precisely what they were. On that occasion he had entrusted one of his machines to his first cousin, Mary Porson, a big girl with her hair still down her back, rather idle in disposition, but very intelligent, when she chose. Mary, for the most part, had been brought up at her father's house, close by. Often, too, she stayed with her uncle for weeks at a stretch, so at that time Morris was as intimate with her as a man of eight and twenty usually is with a relative in her teens.

The arrangement on this particular occasion was that she should take the machine—or aerophone, as its inventor had named it—to her home. The next morning, at the appointed hour, as Morris had often done before, he tried to effect communication, but without result. On the following day, at the same hour, he tried again, when, to his astonishment, instantly the answer came back. Yes, as distinctly as though she were standing by his side, he heard his cousin Mary's voice.

"Are you there?" he said, quite hopelessly, merely as a matter of form—of very common form—and well-nigh fell to the ground when he received the reply:

"Yes, yes, but I have just been telegraphed for to go to Beaulieu; my mother is very ill."

"What is the matter with her?" he asked; and she replied:

"Inflammation of the lungs—but I must stop; I can't speak any more." Then came some sobs and silence.

That same afternoon, by Mary's direction, the aerophone was brought back to him in a dog-cart, and three days later he heard that her mother, Mrs. Porson, was dead.

Some months passed, and when they met again, on her return

from the Riviera, Morris found his cousin changed. She had parted from him a child, and now, beneath the shadow of the wings of grief, suddenly she had become a woman. Moreover, the best and frankest part of their intimacy seemed to have vanished. There was a veil between them. Mary thought of little, and at this time seemed to care for no one except her mother, who was dead. And Morris, who had loved the child, recoiled somewhat from the new-born woman. It may be explained that he was afraid of women. Still, with an eye to business, he spoke to her about the aerophone; and, so far as her memory served her, she confirmed all the details of their short conversation across the gulf of empty space.

"You see," he said, trembling with excitement, "I have got it at last."

"It looks like it," she answered, wearily, her thoughts already far away. "Why shouldn't you? There are so many odd things of the sort. But one can never be sure; it mightn't work next time."

"Will you try again?" he asked.

"If you like," she answered; "but I don't believe I shall hear anything now. Somehow—since that last business—everything seems different to me."

"Don't be foolish," he said; "you have nothing to do with the hearing; it is my new receiver."

"I daresay," she replied; "but, then, why couldn't you make it work with other people?"

Morris answered nothing. He, too, wondered why.

Next morning they made the experiment. It failed. Other experiments followed at intervals, most of which were fiascos, although some were partially successful. Thus, at times Mary could hear what he said. But except for a word or two, and now and then a sentence, he could not hear her whom, when she was still a child and his playmate, once he had heard so clearly.

"Why is it?" he said, a year or two later, dashing his fist upon the table in impotent rage. "It has been; why can't it be?"

Mary turned her large blue eyes up to the ceiling, and reflectively rubbed her dimpled chin with a very pretty finger.

"Isn't that the kind of question they used to ask oracles?" she asked lazily—"Oh! no, it was the oracles themselves that were so vague. Well, I suppose because 'was' is as different from 'is' as 'as' is from 'shall be.' We are changed, Cousin; that's all."

He pointed to his patent receiver, and grew angry.

"Oh, it isn't the receiver," she said, smoothing her curling hair; "it's us. You don't understand me a bit—not now—and that's why you can't hear me. Take my advice, Morris"—and she looked at him sharply—"when you find a woman whom you can hear on your patent receiver, you had better marry her. It will be a good excuse for keeping her at a distance afterwards."

Then he lost his temper; indeed, he raved, and stormed, and nearly smashed the patent receiver in his fury. To a scientific man, let it be admitted, it was nothing short of maddening to be told that the successful working of his instrument, to the manufacture of which he had given eight years of toil and study, depended upon some pre-existent sympathy between the operators of its divided halves. If that were so, what was the use of his wonderful discovery, for who could ensure a sympathetic correspondent? And yet the fact remained that when, in their playmate days, he understood his cousin Mary, and when her quiet, indolent nature had been deeply moved by the shock of the news of her mother's peril, the aerophone had worked. Whereas now, when she had become a grown-up young lady, he did not understand her any longer—he, whose heart was wrapped up in his experiments, and who by nature feared the adult members of her sex, and shrank from them; when, too, her placid calm was no longer stirred, work it would not.

She laughed at his temper; then grew serious, and said:

"Don't get angry, Morris. After all, there are lots of things that you and I can't understand, and it isn't odd that you should have tumbled across one of them. If you think of it, nobody understands anything. They know that certain things happen, and how to make them happen; but they don't know why they happen, or why, as in your case, when they ought to happen, they won't."

"It is all very well for you to be philosophical," he answered, turning upon her; "but can't you see, Mary, that the thing there is my life's work? It is what I have given all my strength and all my brain to make, and if it fails in the end—why, then I fail too, once and forever. And I have made it talk. It talked perfectly between this place and Seaview, and now you stand there and tell me that it won't work any more because I don't understand you. Then what am I to do?"

"Try to understand me, if you think it worth while, which I don't; or go on experimenting," she answered. "Try to find some substance which is less exquisitely sensitive, something a little grosser, more in key with the material world; or to discover someone whom you do understand. Don't lose heart; don't be beaten after all these years."

"No," he answered, "I don't unless I die," and he turned to go.

"Morris," she said, in a softer voice, "I am lazy, I know. Perhaps that is why I adore people who can work. So, although you don't think anything of me, I will do my honest best to get into sympathy with you again; yes, and to help in any way I can. No; it's not a joke. I would give a great deal to see the thing a success."

"Why do you say I don't think anything of you, Mary? Of course, it isn't true. Besides, you are my cousin, and we have always been good friends since you were a little thing."

She laughed. "Yes, and I suppose that as you had no brothers or sisters they taught you to pray for your cousin, didn't they? Oh, I know all about it. It is my unfortunate sex that is to blame; while I was a mere tom-boy it was different. No one can serve two masters, can they? You have chosen to serve a machine that won't go, and I daresay that you are wise. Yes, I think that it is the better part—until you find someone that will make it go—and then you would adore her—by aerophone!"

II

The Colonel and Some Reflections

Presently Morris heard a step upon the lawn, and turned to see his father sauntering towards him. Colonel Monk, C.B., was an elderly man, over sixty indeed, but still of an upright and soldierly bearing. His record was rather distinguished. In his youth he had served in the Crimea, and in due course was promoted to the command of a regiment of Guards. After this, certain diplomatic abilities caused him to be sent to one of the foreign capitals as military attache, and in reward of this service, on retiring, he was created a Companion of the Bath. In appearance he was handsome also; in fact, much better looking than his son, with his iron-grey hair, his clear-cut features, somewhat marred in effect by a certain shiftiness of the mouth, and his large dark eyes. Morris had those dark eyes also—they redeemed his face from plainness, for otherwise it showed no beauty, the features being too irregular, the brow too prominent, and the mouth too large. Yet it could boast what, in the case of a man at any rate, is better than beauty—spirituality, and a certain sympathetic charm. It was not the face which was so attractive, but rather the intelligence, the personality that shone through it, as the light shines through the horn panes of some homely, massive lantern. Speculative eyes of the sort that seem to search horizons and gather knowledge there, but shrink from the faces of women; a head of brown hair, short cut but untidy, an athletic, manlike form to which, bizarrely enough, a slight stoop, the stoop of a student, seemed to give distinction, and hands slender and shapely as those of an Eastern—such were the characteristics of Morris Monk, or at least those of them that the observer was apt to notice.

"Hullo! Morris, are you star-gazing there?" said Colonel Monk, with a yawn. "I suppose that I must have fallen asleep after dinner—that comes of stopping too long at once in the country and drinking port. I notice you never touch it, and a good thing, too. There, my cigar is out. Now's the time for that new electric lighter of yours which I can never make work."

Morris fumbled in his pocket and produced the lighter. Then he said:

"I am sorry, father; but I believe I forgot to charge it."

"Ah! that's just like you, if you will forgive my saying so. You take any amount of trouble to invent and perfect a thing, but when it comes to making use of it, then you forget," and with a little gesture of impatience the Colonel turned aside to light a match from a box which he had found in the pocket of his cape.

"I am sorry," said Morris, with a sigh, "but I am afraid it is true. When one's mind is very fully occupied with one thing—" and he broke off.

"Ah! that's it, Morris, that's it," said the Colonel, seating himself upon a garden chair; "this hobby-horse of yours is carrying you—to the devil, and your family with you. I don't want to be rough, but it is time that I spoke plain. Let's see, how long is it since you left the London firm?"

"Nine years this autumn," answered Morris, setting his mouth a little, for he knew what was coming. The port drunk after claret had upset his father's digestion and ruffled his temper. This meant that to him—Morris—Fate had appointed a lecture.

"Nine years, nine wasted years, idled and dreamt away in a village upon the eastern coast. It is a large slice out of a man's life, my boy. By the time that I was your age I had done a good deal," said his father, meditatively. When he meant to be disagreeable it was the Colonel's custom to become reflective.

"I can't admit that," answered Morris, in his light, quick voice—"I mean I can't admit that my time has either been idled away or wasted. On the contrary, father, I have worked very hard, as I did at college, and as I have always done, with results which, without boasting, I may fairly call glorious—yes, glorious—for when they are perfected they will change the methods of communication throughout the whole world." As he spoke, forgetting the sharp vexation of the moment, his face was irradiated with light—like some evening cloud on which the sun strikes suddenly.

Watching him out of the corner of his eye, even in that low moonlight, his father saw those fires of enthusiasm shine and die upon his son's face, and the sight vexed him. Enthusiasm, as he conceived, perhaps with justice, had been the ruin of Morris. Ceasing to be reflective, his tone became cruel.

"Do you really think, Morris, that the world wishes to have its methods of communication revolutionised? Aren't there enough telephones and phonograms and aerial telegraphs already? It seems to me that you merely wish to add a new terror to existence. However, there is no need to pursue an academical discussion, since this wretched machine of yours, on which you have wasted so much time, appears to be a miserable failure."

Now, to throw the non-success of his invention into the teeth of the inventor, especially when that inventor knows that it is successful really, although just at present it does not happen to work, is a very deadly insult. Few indeed could be deadlier, except, perhaps, that of the cruelty which can suggest to a woman that no man will ever look at her because of her plainness and lack of attraction; or the coarse taunt which, by shameless implication, unjustly accuses the soldier of cowardice, the diplomat of having betrayed the secrets of his country, or the lawyer of having sold his brief. All the more, therefore, was it to Morris's credit that he felt the lash sting without a show of temper.

"I have tried to explain to you, father," he began, struggling to free his clear voice from the note of indignation.

"Of course you have, Morris; don't trouble yourself to repeat that long story. But even if you were successful—which you are not—er—I cannot see the commercial use of this invention. As a scientific toy it may be very well, though, personally, I should prefer to leave it alone, since, if you go firing off your thoughts and words into space, how do you know who will answer them, or who will hear them?"

"Well, father, as you understand all about it, it is no use my explaining any further. It is pretty late; I think I will be turning in."

"I had hoped," replied the Colonel, in an aggrieved voice, "that you might have been able to spare me a few minutes' conversation. For some weeks I have been seeking an opportunity to talk to you; but somehow your arduous occupations never seem to leave you free for ordinary social intercourse."

"Certainly," replied Morris, "though I don't quite know why you should say that. I am always about the place if you want me." But in his heart he groaned, guessing what was coming.

"Yes; but you are ever working at your chemicals and machinery in the old chapel; or reading those eternal books; or wandering about rapt in contemplation of the heavens; so that, in short, I seldom like to trouble you with my mundane but necessary affairs."

Morris made no answer; he was a very dutiful son and humble-spirited. Those who pit their intelligences against the forces of Nature, and try to search out her secrets, become humble. He could not altogether respect his father; the gulf between them was too wide and deep. But even at his present age of three and thirty he considered it a duty to submit himself to him and his vagaries. Outside of other reasons, his mother had prayed him to do so almost with her last breath, and, living or dead, Morris loved his mother.

"Perhaps you are not aware," went on Colonel Monk, after a solemn pause, "that the affairs of this property are approaching a crisis."

"I know something, but no details," answered Morris. "I have not liked to interfere," he added apologetically.

"And I have not not liked to trouble you with such sordid matters," rejoined his parent, with sarcasm. "I presume, however, that you are acquainted with the main facts. I succeeded to this estate encumbered with a mortgage, created by your grandfather, an extravagant and unbusiness-like man. That mortgage I looked to your mother's fortune to pay off, but other calls made this impossible. For instance, the sea-wall here had to be built if the Abbey was to be saved, and half a mile of sea-walling costs something. Also very extensive repairs to the house were necessary, and I was forced to take three farms in hand when I retired from the army fifteen years ago. This has involved a net loss of about ten thousand pounds, while all the time the interest had to be paid and the place kept up in a humble fashion."

"I thought that my uncle Porson took over the mortgage after my mother's death," interrupted Morris.

"That is so," answered his father, wincing a little; "but a creditor remains a creditor, even if he happens to be a relative by marriage. I have nothing to say against your uncle John, who is an excellent person in his way, and well-meaning. Of course, he has been justified, perfectly justified, in using his business abilities—or perhaps I should say instincts, for they are hereditary—to his own advantage. In fact, however, directly or indirectly, he has done well out of this property and his connection with our family—exceedingly well, both financially and socially. In a time of stress I was forced to sell him the two miles of sea-frontage building-land between here and Northwold for a mere song. During the last ten years, as you know, he has cut this up into over five hundred villa sites, which he has sold upon long lease at ground-rents that to-day bring in annually as much as he paid for the whole property."

"Yes, father; but you might have done the same. He advised you to before he bought the land."

"Perhaps I might, but I am not a tradesman; I do not understand these affairs. And, Morris, I must remind you that in such matters I have had no assistance. I do not blame you any more than I blame myself—it is not in your line either—but I repeat that I have had no assistance."

Morris did not argue the point. "Well, father," he asked, "what is the upshot? Are we ruined?"

"Ruined? That is a large word, and an ugly one. No, we are no more ruined than we have been for the last half-dozen years, for, thank Heaven, I still have resources and—friends. But, of course, this place is in a way expensive, and you yourself would be the last to pretend that our burdens have been lessened by—your having abandoned the very strange profession which you selected, and devoted yourself to researches which, if interesting, must be called abstract—"

"Forgive me, father," interrupted Morris with a ring of indignation in his voice; "but you must remember that I put you to no expense. In addition to what I inherited from my mother, which, of course, under the circumstances I do not ask for, I have my fellowship, out of which I contribute something towards the cost of my living and experiments, that, by the way, I keep as low as possible."

"Of course, of course," said the Colonel, who did not wish to pursue this branch of the subject, but his son went on:

"You know also that it was at your express wish that I came to live here at Monksland, as for the purposes of my work it would have suited me much better to take rooms in London or some other scientific centre."

"Really, my dear boy, you should control yourself," broke in his father. "That is always the way with recluses; they cannot bear the slightest criticism. Of course, as you were going to devote yourself to this line of research it was right and proper that we should live together. Surely you would not wish at my age that I should be deprived of the comfort of the society of an only child, especially now that your mother has left us?"

"Certainly not, father," answered Morris, softening, as was his fashion at the thought of his dead mother.

Then came a pause, and he hoped that the conversation was at end; a vain hope, as it proved.

"My real object in troubling you, Morris," continued his father, presently, "was very different to the unnecessary discussions into which we have drifted."

His son looked up, but said nothing. Again he knew what was coming, and it was worse than anything that had gone before.

"This place seems very solitary with the two of us living in its great rooms. I, who am getting an old fellow, and you a student and a recluse—no, don't deny it, for nowadays I can barely persuade you to attend even the Bench or a lawn-tennis party. Well, fortunately, we have power to add to our numbers; or at least you have. I wish you would marry, Morris."

His son turned sharply, and answered:

"Thank you, father, but I have no fancy that way."

"Now, there's Jane Rose, or that handsome Eliza Layard," went on the Colonel, taking no notice. "I have reason to know that you might have either of them for the asking, and they are both good women without a breath against them, and, what in the state of this property is not without importance, very well to do. Jane gets fifty thousand pounds down on the day of her marriage, and as much more, together with the place, upon old Lady Rose's death; while Miss Layard—if she is not quite to the manner born—has the interest in that great colliery and a rather sickly brother. Lastly—and this is strange enough, considering how you treat them—they admire you, or at least Eliza does, for she told me she thought you the most interesting man she had ever met."

"Did she indeed!" exclaimed Morris. "Why, I have only spoken three times to her during the last year."

"No doubt, my dear boy, that is why she thinks you interesting. To her you are a mine of splendid possibilities. But I understand that you don't like either of them."

"No, not particularly—especially Eliza Layard, who isn't a lady, and has a vicious temper—nor any young woman whom I have ever met."

"Do you mean to tell me candidly, Morris, that at your age you detest women?"

"I don't say that; I only say that I never met one to whom I felt much attracted, and that I have met a great many by whom I was repelled."

"Decidedly, Morris, in you the strain of the ancestral fish is too predominant. It isn't natural; it really isn't. You ought to have been born three centuries ago, when the old monks lived here. You would have made a first-class abbot, and might have been canonised by now. Am I to understand, then, that you absolutely decline to marry?"

"No, father; I don't want you to understand anything of the sort. If I could meet a lady whom I liked, and who wouldn't expect too much, and who was foolish enough to wish to take me, of course I should marry her, as you are so bent upon it."

"Well, Morris, and what sort of a woman would fulfil the conditions, to your notion?"

His son looked about him vaguely, as though he expected to find his ideal in some nook of the dim garden.

"What sort of a woman? Well, somebody like my cousin Mary, I suppose—an easy-going person of that kind, who always looks pleasant and cool."

Morris did not see him, for he had turned his head away; but at the mention of Mary Porson's name his father started, as though someone had pricked him with a pin. But Colonel Monk had not commanded a regiment with some success and been a military attache for nothing; having filled diplomatic positions, public and private, in his time, he could keep his countenance, and play his part when he chose. Indeed, did his simpler-minded son but know it, all that evening he had been playing a part.

"Oh! that's your style, is it?" he said. "Well, at your age I should have preferred something a little different. But there is no accounting for tastes; and after all, Mary is a beautiful woman, and clever in her own way. By Jove! there's one o'clock striking, and I promised old Charters that I would always be in bed by half-past eleven. Good night, my boy. By the way, you remember that your uncle Porson is coming to Seaview to-morrow from London, and that we are engaged to dine with him at eight. Fancy a man who could build that pretentious monstrosity and call it Seaview! Well, it will condemn him to the seventh generation; but in this world one must take people as one finds them, and their houses, too. Mind you lock the garden door when you come in. Good night."

"Really," thought Colonel Monk to himself as he took off his dress-shoes and, with military precision, set them side by side beneath a chair, "it does seem a little hard on me that I should be responsible for a son who is in love with a damned, unworkable electrical machine. And with his chances—with his chances! Why he might have been a second secretary in the Diplomatic Service by now, or anything else to which interest could help him. And there he sits hour after hour gabbling down a little trumpet and listening for an answer which never comes—hour after hour, and month after month, and year after year. Is he a genius, or is he an idiot, or a moral curiosity, or simply useless?

I'm hanged if I know, but that's a good idea about Mary; though, of course, there are things against it. Curious that I should never have considered the matter seriously before—because of the cousinship, I suppose. Would she have him? It doesn't seem likely, but you can never know what a woman will or will not do, and as a child she was very fond of Morris. At any rate the situation is desperate, and if I can, I mean to save the old place, for his sake and our family's, as well as my own."

He went to the window, and, lifting a corner of the blind, looked out. "There he is, still staring at the sea and the sky, and there I daresay he will be till dawn. I bet he has forgotten all about Mary now, and is thinking of his electrical machine. What a curiosity! Good heavens; what a curiosity! Ah, I wonder what they would have made of him in my old mess five and thirty years ago?" And quite overcome by this reflection, the Colonel shook his grizzled head, put out the candle, and retired to rest.

His father was right. The beautiful September dawn was breaking over the placid sea before Morris brushed the night dew from his hair and cloak, and went in by the abbot's door.

What was he thinking of all the time? He scarcely knew. One by one, like little clouds in the summer sky, fancies arose in his mind to sail slowly across its depth and vanish upon an inconclusive and shadowy horizon. Of course, he thought about his instruments; these were never absent from his heart. His instinct flew back to them as an oasis, as an island of rest in the wilderness of this father's thorny and depressing conversation. The instruments were disappointing, it is true, at present; but, at any rate, they did not dwell gloomily upon impending ruin or suggest that it was his duty to get married. They remained silent, distressingly silent indeed.

Well, as the question of marriage had been started, he might as well face it out; that is, argue it in his mind, reduce it to its principles, follow it to its issues in a reasonable and scientific manner. What were the facts? His family, which, by tradition, was reported to be Danish in its origin, had owned this property for several hundred years, though how they came to own it remained a matter of dispute. Some said the Abbey and its lands were granted to a man of the name of Monk by Henry VIII, of course for a consideration. Others held, and evidence existed in favour of this view, that on the dissolution of the monastery the abbot of the day, a shrewd man of easy principles, managed to possess himself of the Chapter House and further extensive hereditaments, of course with the connivance of the Commissioners, and, providing himself with a wife, to exchange a spiritual for a temporal dignity. At least this remained certain, that from the time of Elizabeth onwards Morris's forefathers had been settled in the old Abbey house at Monksland; that the first of them about whom they really knew anything was named Monk, and that Monk was still the family name.

Now they were all dead and gone, and their history, which was undistinguished, does not matter. To come to the present day. His father succeeded to a diminished and encumbered estate; indeed, had it not been for the fortune of his mother, a Miss Porson and one of a middle class and business, but rather wealthy family, the property must have been sold years before. That fortune, however, had long ago been absorbed—or so he gathered—for his father, a brilliant and fashionable army officer, was not the man to stint himself or to nurse a crippled property. Indeed, it was wonderful to Morris how, without any particular change in their style of living, which, if unpretentious, was not cheap, in these bad times they had managed to keep afloat at all.

Unworldly as Morris might be, he could easily guess why his father wished that he should marry, and marry well. It was that he might bolster up the fortunes of a shattered family. Also—and this touched him, this commanded his sympathy—he was the last of his race. If he died without issue the ancient name of Monk became extinct, a consummation from which his father shrank with something like horror.

The Colonel was a selfish man—Morris could not conceal it, even from himself—one who had always thought of his own comfort and convenience first. Yet, either from idleness or pride, to advance these he had never stooped to scheme. Where the welfare of his family was concerned, however, as his son knew, he was a schemer. That desire was the one real and substantial thing in a somewhat superficial, egotistic, and finessing character.

Morris saw it all as he leaned there upon the railing, staring at the mist-draped sea, more clearly, indeed, than he had ever seen it before. He understood, moreover, what an unsatisfactory son he must be to a man like his father—if it had tried, Providence could hardly have furnished him with offspring more unsuitable. The Colonel had wished him to enter the Diplomatic Service, or the Army, or at least to get himself called to the Bar; but although a really brilliant University career and his family influence would have given him advantages in any of these professions, he had declined them all. So, following his natural bent, he became an electrician, and now, abandoning the practical side of that modest calling, he was an experimental physicist, full of deep but unremunerative lore, and—an unsuccessful inventor. Certainly he owed something to his family, and if his father wished that he should marry, well, marry he must, as a matter of duty, if for no other reason. After all, the thing was not pressing; for it it came to the point, what woman was likely to accept him? All he had done to-night was to settle the general principles in his own mind. When it became necessary—if ever—he could deal with the details.

And yet this sort of marriage which was proposed to him, was it not an unholy business? He cared little for women, having no weakness that way, probably because of the energy which other young men gave to the pursuit of them was in his case absorbed by intense and brain-exhausting study. Therefore he was not a man who if left to himself, would marry, as so many do, merely in order to be married; indeed, the idea to him was almost repulsive. Had he been a woman-hater, he might have accepted it more easily, for then to him one would have been as the other. But the trouble was that he knew and felt that a time might come when in his eyes one woman would be different from all others, a being who spoke not to his physical nature only, if at all, but to the core within him. And if that happened, what then?

Look, the sun was rising. On the eastern sky of a sudden two golden doors had opened in the canopy of night, and in and out of them seemed to pass glittering, swift-winged things, as souls might tread the Gate of Heaven. Look, too, at the little clouds that in an unending stream floated out of the gloom—travellers pressed onwards by a breath of destiny. They were leaden-hued, all of them, black, indeed, at times, until they caught the radiance, and for a while became like the pennons of an angel's wings. Then one by one the glory overtook and embraced them, and they melted into it to be seen no more.

What did the sight suggest to him? That it was worth while, perhaps, to be a mere drift of cloud, storm-driven and rain-laden in the bitter Night of Life, if the Morning of Deliverance brought such transformation on its wings. That beyond some such gates as these, gates that at times, greatly daring, he longed to tread, lay the answer to many a mystery. Amongst other things, perhaps, there he would learn the meaning of true marriage, and why it is denied to most dwellers of the earth. Without a union of the spirit was there indeed any marriage as it should be understood? And who in this world could hope to find his fellow spirit?

See, the sun had risen, the golden gates were shut. He had been dreaming, and was chilled to the bone. Wretchedness, mental and bodily, took hold of him. Well, often enough such is the fate of those who dream; those who turn from their needful, daily tasks to shape an angel out of this world's clay, trusting to some unknown god to give it life and spirit.

III

"Poor Porson"

Upon the morning following his conversation with Morris, Colonel Monk spent two hours or more in the library. Painfully did he wrestle there with balance-sheets, adding up bank books; also other financial documents.

"Phew!" he said, when at length the job was done. "It is worse than I thought, a good deal worse. My credit must be excellent, or somebody would have been down upon us before now. Well, I must talk things over with Porson. He understands figures, and so he ought, considering that he kept the books in his grandfather's shop."

Then the Colonel went to lunch less downcast than might have been expected, since he anticipated a not unamusing half-hour with his son. As he knew well, Morris detested business matters and money calculations. Still, reflected his parent, it was only right that he should take his share of the family responsibilities—a fact which he fully intended to explain to him.

But "in vain is the net spread," etc. As Morris passed the door of the library on his way to the old chapel of the Abbey, which now served him as a laboratory, he had seen his father bending over the desk and guessed his occupation. Knowing, therefore, what he must expect at lunch, Morris determined to dispense with that meal, and went out, much to the Colonel's disappointment and indignation. "I hate," he explained to his brother-in-law Porson afterwards, "yes, I hate a fellow who won't face disagreeables and shirks his responsibilities."

Between Monksland and the town of Northwold lay some four miles of cliff, most of which had been portioned off in building lots, for Northwold was what is called a "rising watering-place." About half-way between the Abbey and this town stood Mr. Porson's mansion. In fact, it was nothing but a dwelling like those about it, presenting the familiar seaside gabled roofs of red tiles, and stucco walls decorated with sham woodwork, with the difference that the house was exceedingly well built and about four times as large as the average villa.

"Great heavens! what a place!" said the Colonel to himself as he halted at the private gateway which opened on to the cliff and surveyed it affronting sea and sky in all its naked horror. "Show me the house and I will show you the man," he went on to himself; "but, after all, one mustn't judge him too hardly. Poor Porson, he did not arrange his own up-bringing or his ancestors. Hello! there he is."

"John, John, John!" he shouted at a stout little person clad in a black alpaca coat, a straw hat, and a pair of spectacles, who was engaged in sad contemplation of a bed of dying evergreens.

At the sound of that well-known voice the little man jumped as though he had trodden on a pin, and turned round slowly, muttering to himself,

"Gracious! It's him!" an ungrammatical sentence which indicated sufficiently how wide a niche in the temple of his mind was filled with the image of his brother-in-law, Colonel Monk.

John Porson was a man of about six or eight and fifty, round-faced, bald, with large blue eyes not unlike those of a china doll, and clean-shaven except for a pair of sandy-coloured mutton-chop whiskers. In expression he was gentle, even timid, and in figure short and stout. At this very moment behind a hundred counters stand a hundred replicas of that good-hearted man and worthy citizen, John Porson. Can he be described better or more briefly?

"How are you Colonel?" he said, hurrying forward. He had never yet dared to call his brother-in-law "Monk," and much less by his Christian name, so he compromised on "Colonel."

"Pretty well, thank you, considering my years and botherations. And how are you, John?"

"Not very grand, not very grand," said the little man; "my heart has been troubling me, and it was so dreadfully hot in London."

"Then why didn't you come away?"

"Really I don't know. I understood that it had something to do with a party, but I think the fact is that Mary was too lazy to look after the servants while they packed up."

"Perhaps she had some attraction there," suggested the Colonel, with an anxiety which might have been obvious to a more skilled observer.

"Attraction! What do you mean?" asked Porson.

"Mean, you old goose? Why, what should I mean? A young man, of course."

"Oh! I see. No, I am sure it was nothing of that sort. Mary won't be bothered with young men. She is too lazy; she just looks over their heads till they get tired and go away. I am sure it was the packing, or, perhaps, the party. But what are you staring at, Colonel? Is there anything wrong?"

"No, no; only that wonderful window of yours—the one filled with bottle-glass—which always reminds me of a bull's-eye lantern standing on a preserved-beef tin, or the top of a toy lighthouse."

Porson peered at the offending window through his spectacles.

"Certainly, now you mention it, it does look a little odd from here," he said; "naked, rather. You said so before, you remember, and I told them to plant the shrubs; but while I was away they let every one of the poor things die. I will ask my architect, Jenkins, if he can't do anything; it might be pulled down, perhaps."

"Better leave it alone," said the Colonel, with a sniff. "If I know anything of Jenkins he'd only put up something worse. I tell you, John, that where bricks and mortar are concerned that man's a moral monster."

"I know you don't like his style," murmured Porson; "but won't you come in, it is so hot out here in the sun?"

"Thank you, yes, but let us go to that place you call your den, not to the drawing-room. If you can spare it, I want half-an-hour with you. That's why I came over in the afternoon, before dinner."

"Certainly, certainly," murmured Porson again, as he led the way to the "den," but to himself he added: "It's those mortgages, I'll bet. Oh dear! oh dear! when shall I see the last of them?"

Presently they were established in the den, the Colonel very cool and comfortable in Mr. Porson's armchair, and Porson himself perched upon the edge of a new-looking leather sofa in an attitude of pained expectancy.

"Now I am at your service, Colonel," he said.

"Oh! yes; well, it is just this. I want you, if you will, to look through these figures for me," and he produced and handed to him a portentous document headed "List of Obligations."

Mr. Porson glanced at it, and instantly his round, simple face became clever and alert. Here he was on his own ground. In five minutes he had mastered the thing.

"Yes," he said, in a quick voice, "this is quite clear, but there is some mistake in the addition making a difference of 87 pounds 3s. 10d. in your favour. Well, where is the schedule of assets?"

"The schedule of assets, my dear John? I wish I knew. I have my pension, and there are the Abbey and estates, which, as things are, seem to be mortgaged to their full value. That's about all, I think. Unless—

unless"—and he laughed, "we throw in Morris's patent electrical machine, which won't work."

"It ought to be reckoned, perhaps," replied Mr. Porson gravely; adding in a kind of burst, with an air of complete conviction: "I believe in Morris's machine, or, at least, I believe in Morris. He has the makings of a great man—no, of a great inventor about him."

"Do you really?" replied the Colonel, much interested. "That is curious—and encouraging; for, my dear John, where business matters are concerned, I trust your judgment."

"But I doubt whether he will make any money out of it," went on Porson. "One day the world will benefit; probably he will not benefit."

The Colonel's interest faded. "Possibly, John; but, if so, perhaps for present purposes we may leave this mysterious discovery out of the question."

"I think so, I think so; but what is the point?"

"The point is that I seem to be about at the end of my tether, although, as yet, I am glad to say, nobody has actually pressed me, and I have come to you, as a friend and a relative, for advice. What is to be done? I have sold you all the valuable land, and I am glad to think that you have made a very good thing of it. Some years ago, also, you took over the two heaviest mortgages on the Abbey estate, and I am sorry to say that the interest is considerably in arrear. There remain the floating debts and other charges, amounting in all to about 7,000 pounds, which I have no means of meeting, and meanwhile, of course, the place must be kept up. Under these circumstances, John, I ask you as a business man, what is to be done?"

"And, as a business man, I say I'm hanged if I know," said Porson, with unwonted energy. "All debts, no assets—the position is impossible. Unless, indeed, something happens."

"Quite so. That's it. My only comfort is—that something might happen," and he paused.

Porson fidgeted about on the edge of the leather sofa and turned red. In his heart he was wondering whether he dared offer to pay off the debts. This he was quite able to do; more, he was willing to do, since to him, good simple man, the welfare of the ancient house of Monk, of which his only sister had married the head, was a far more important thing than parting with a certain number of thousands of pounds. For birth and station, in his plebeian humility, John Porson had a reverence which was almost superstitious. Moreover, he had loved his dead sister dearly, and, in his way, he loved her son also. Also he revered his brother-in-law, the polished and splendid-looking Colonel, although it was true that sometimes he writhed beneath his military and aristocratic heel. Particularly, indeed, did he resent, in his secret heart, those continual sarcasms about his taste in architecture.

Now, although the monetary transactions between them had been many, as luck would have it—entirely without his own design—they chanced in the main to have turned to his, Porson's, advantage. Thus, owing chiefly to his intelligent development of its possibilities, the land which he bought from the Monk estate had increased enormously in value; so much so, indeed, that, even if he lost all the other sums advanced upon mortgage, he would still be considerably to the good. Therefore, as it happened, the Colonel was really under no obligations to him. In these circumstances, Mr. Porson did not quite know how a cold-blooded offer of an advance of cash without security—in practice a gift—would be received.

"Have you anything definite in your mind?" he hesitated, timidly.

The Colonel reflected. On his part he was wondering how Porson would receive the suggestion of a substantial loan. It seemed too much to risk. He was proud, and did not like to lay himself open to the possibility of rebuff.

"I think not, John. Unless Morris should chance to make a good marriage, which is unlikely, for, as you know, he is an odd fish, I can see nothing before us except ruin. Indeed, at my age, it does not greatly matter, but it seems a pity that the old house should come to an end in such a melancholy and discreditable fashion."

"A pity! It is more than a pity," jerked out Porson, with a sudden wriggle which caused him to rock up and down upon the stiff springs of the new sofa.

As he spoke there came a knock at the door, and from the further side of it a slow, rich voice was heard, saying: "May I come in?"

"That's Mary," said Mr. Porson. "Yes, come in, dear; it's only your uncle."

The door opened, Mary came in, and, in some curious quiet way, at once her personality seemed to take possession of and dominate that shaded room. To begin with, her stature gave an idea of dominion, for, without being at all coarse, she was tall and full in frame. The face also was somewhat massive, with a rounded chin and large, blue eyes that had a trick of looking half asleep, and above a low, broad forehead grew her waving, golden hair, parted simply in the middle after the old

Greek fashion. She wore a white dress, with a silver girdle that set off the beautiful outlines of her figure to great advantage, and with her a perfume seemed to pass, perhaps from the roses on her bosom.

"A beautiful woman," thought the Colonel to himself, as she came in, and he was no mean or inexperienced judge. "A beautiful woman, but a regular lotus-eater."

"How do you do, Uncle Richard?" said Mary, pausing about six feet away and holding out her hand. "I heard you scolding my poor dad about his bow-window. In fact, you woke me up; and, do you know, you used exactly the same words as you did at your visit after we came down from London last year."

"Bless me, my dear," said the Colonel, struggling to his feet, and kissing his niece upon the forehead, "what a memory you have got! It will get you into trouble some day."

"I daresay—me, or somebody else. But history repeated itself, uncle, that is all. The same sleepy Me in a lounge-chair, the same hot day, the same blue-bottle, and the same You scolding the same Daddy about the same window. Though what on earth dad's window can matter to anyone except himself, I can't understand."

"I daresay not, my dear; I daresay not. We can none of us know everything—not even latter day young ladies—but I suggest that a few hours with Fergussen's 'Handbook of Architecture' might enlighten you on the point."

Mary reflected, but the only repartee that she could conjure at the moment was something about ancient lights which did not seem appropriate. Therefore, as she thought that she had done enough for honour, and to remind her awe-inspiring relative that he could not suppress her, suddenly she changed the subject.

"You are looking very well, uncle," she said, surveying him calmly; "and younger than you did last year. How is my cousin Morris? Will the aerophone talk yet?"

"Be careful," said the Colonel, gallantly. "If even my grey hairs can provoke a compliment, what homage is sufficient for a Sleeping Beauty? As for Morris, he is, I believe, much as usual; at least he stood this morning till daybreak staring at the sea. I understand, however—if he doesn't forget to come—that you are to have the pleasure of seeing him this evening, when you will be able to judge for yourself."

"Now, don't be sarcastic about Morris, uncle; I'd rather you went on abusing dad's window."

"Certainly not, my dear, if it displeases you. But may I ask why he is to be considered sacred?"

"Why?" she answered, and a genuine note crept into her bantering voice. "Because he is one of the few men worth anything whom I ever chanced to meet—except dad there and—"

"Spare me," cut in the Colonel, with admirable skill, for well he knew that his name was not upon the lady's lips. "But would it be impertinent to inquire what it is that constitutes Morris's preeminent excellence in your eyes?"

"Of course not; only it is three things, not one. First, he works harder than any man I know, and I think men who work adorable, because I am so lazy myself. Secondly, he thinks a great deal, and very few people do that to any purpose. Thirdly, I never feel inclined to go to sleep when he takes me in to dinner. Oh! you may laugh if you like, but ask dad what happened to me last month with that wretched old member of the Government, and before the sweets, too!"

"Please, please," put in Mr. Porson, turning pink under pressure of some painful recollection. "If you have finished sparring with your uncle, isn't there any tea, Mary?"

"I believe so," she said, relapsing into a state of bland indifference. "I'll go and see. If I don't come back, you'll know it is there," and Mary passed through the door with that indolent, graceful walk which no one could mistake who once had seen her.

Both her father and her uncle looked after her with admiration. Mr. Porson admired her because the man or woman who dared to meet that domestic tyrant his brother-in-law in single combat, and could issue unconquered from the doubtful fray, was indeed worthy to be honoured. Colonel Monk for his part hastened to do homage to a very pretty and charming young lady, one, moreover, who was not in the least afraid of him.

Mary had gone, and the air from the offending window, which was so constructed as to let in a maximum of draught, banged the door behind her. The two men looked at each other. A thought was in the mind of each; but the Colonel, trained by long experience, and wise in his generation, waited for Mr. Porson to speak. Many and many a time in the after days did he find reason to congratulate himself upon this superb reticence—for there are occasions when discretion can amount almost to the height of genius. Under their relative circumstances, if it had been he who first suggested this alliance, he and his family must have remained at the gravest disadvantage, and as for stipulations, well, he could have made none. But as it chanced it was from poor Porson's lips that the suggestion came.

Mr. Porson cleared this throat—once, twice, thrice. At the third rasp, the Colonel became very attentive. He remembered that his brother-in-law had done exactly the same thing at the very apex of a long-departed crisis; indeed, just before he offered spontaneously to take over the mortgages on the Abbey estate.

"You were talking, Colonel," he began, "when Mary came in," and he paused.

"I daresay," replied the Colonel indifferently, fixing a contemptuous glance upon some stone mullions of atrocious design.

"About Morris marrying?"

"Oh, yes, so I was! Well?"

"Well—she seems to like him. I know she does indeed. She never talks of any other young man."

"She? Who?"

"My daughter, Mary; and—so—why shouldn't they—you know?"

"Really, John, I must ask you to be a little more explicit. It's no good your addressing me in your business ciphers."

"Well—I mean—why shouldn't he marry her? Morris marry Mary? Is that plain enough?" he asked in desperation.

For a moment a mist gathered before the Colonel's eyes. Here was salvation indeed, if only it could be brought about. Oh! if only it could be brought about.

But the dark eyes never changed, nor did a muscle move upon that pale, commanding countenance.

"Morris marry Mary," he repeated, dwelling on the alliterative words as though to convince himself that he had heard them aright. "That is a very strange proposition, my dear John, and sudden, too. Why, they are first cousins, and for that reason, I suppose, the thing never occurred to me—till last night," he added to himself.

"Yes, I know, Colonel; but I am not certain that this first cousin business isn't a bit exaggerated. The returns of the asylums seem to show it, and I know my doctor, Sir Henry Andrews, says it's nonsense. You'll admit that he is an authority. Also, it happened in my own family, my father and mother were cousins, and we are none the worse."

On another occasion the Colonel might have been inclined to

comment on this statement—of course, most politely. Now, however, he let it pass.

"Well, John," he said, "putting aside the cousinship, let me hear what your idea is of the advantages of such a union, should the parties concerned change to consider it suitable."

"Quite so, quite so, that's business," said Mr. Porson, brightening up at once. "From my point of view, these would be the advantages. As you know, Colonel, so far as I am concerned my origin, for the time I have been able to trace it—that's four generations from old John Porson, the Quaker sugar merchant, who came from nobody knows where—although honest, is humble, and until my father's day all in the line of retail trade. But then my dear wife came in. She was a governess when I married her, as you may have heard, and of a very good Scotch family, one of the Camerons, so Mary isn't all of our cut—any more," he added with a smile, "than Morris is all of yours. Still for her to marry a Monk would be a lift up—a considerable lift up, and looked at from a business point of view, worth a deal of money.

"Also, I like my nephew Morris, and I am sure that Mary likes him, and I'd wish the two of them to inherit what I have got. They wouldn't have very long to wait for it, Colonel, for those doctors may say what they will, but I tell you," he added, pathetically, tapping himself over the heart—"though you don't mention it to Mary—I know better. Oh! yes, I know better. That's about all, except, of course, that I should wish to see her settled before I'm gone. A man dies happier, you understand, if he is certain whom his only child is going to marry; for when he is dead I suppose that he will know nothing of what happens to her. Or, perhaps," he added, as though by an afterthought, "he may know too much, and not be able to help; which would be painful, very painful."

"Don't get into those speculations, John," said the Colonel, waving his hand. "They are unpleasant, and lead nowhere—sufficient to the day is the evil thereof."

"Quite so, quite so. Life is a queer game of blind-man's buff, isn't it; played in a mist on a mountain top, and the players keep dropping over the precipices. But nobody heeds, because there are always plenty more, and the game goes on forever. Well, that's my side of the case. Do you wish me to put yours?"

"I should like to hear your view of it."

"Very good, it is this. Here's a nice girl, no one can deny that, and a nice man, although he's odd—you will admit as much. He's got name, and he will have fame, or I am much mistaken. But, as it chances, through no fault of his, he wants money, or will want it, for without money the old place can't go on, and without a wife the old race can't go on. Now, Mary will have lots of money, for, to tell the truth, it keeps piling up until I am sick of it. I've been lucky in that way, Colonel, because I don't care much about it, I suppose. I don't think that I ever yet made a really bad investment. Just look. Two years ago, to oblige an old friend who was in the shop with me when I was young, I put 5,000 pounds into an Australian mine, never thinking to see it again. Yesterday I sold that stock for 50,000 pounds."

"Fifty thousand pounds!" exclaimed the Colonel, astonished into admiration.

"Yes, or to be accurate, 49,375 pounds, 3s., 10d., and—that's where the jar comes in—I don't care. I never thought of it again since I got the broker's note till this minute. I have been thinking all day about my heart, which is uneasy, and about what will happen to Mary when I am gone. What's the good of this dirty money to a dying man? I'd give it all to have my wife and the boy I lost back for a year or two; yes, I would go into a shop again and sell sugar like my grandfather, and live on the profits from the till and the counter. There's Mary calling. We must tell a fib, we must say that we thought she was to come to fetch us; don't you forget. Well, there it is, perhaps you'll think it over at your leisure."

"Yes, John," replied the Colonel, solemnly; "certainly I will think it over. Of course, there are pros and cons, but, on the whole, speaking offhand, I don't see why the young people should not make a match. Also you have always been a good relative, and, what is better, a good friend to me, so, of course, if possible I should like to fall in with your wishes."

Mr. Porson, who was advancing towards the door, wheeled round quickly.

"Thank you, Colonel," he said, "I appreciate your sentiments; but don't you make any mistake. It isn't my wishes that have to be fallen in with—or your wishes. It's the wishes of your son, Morris, and my daughter, Mary. If they are agreeable I'd like it well; if not, all the money in the world, nor all the families in the world, wouldn't make me have anything to do with the job, or you either. Whatever our failings, we are honest men—both of us, who would not sell our flesh and blood for such trash as that."

IV

Mary Preaches
and the Colonel Prevails

A fortnight had gone by, and during this time Morris was a frequent visitor at Seaview. Also his Cousin Mary had come over twice or thrice to lunch, with her father or without him. Once, indeed, she had stopped all the afternoon, spending most of it in the workshop with Morris. This workshop, it may be remembered, was the old chapel of the Abbey, a very beautiful and still perfect building, finished in early Tudor times, in which, by good fortune, the rich stained glass of the east window still remained. It made a noble and spacious laboratory, with its wide nave and lovely roof of chestnut wood, whereof the corbels were seraphs, white-robed and golden-winged.

"Are you not afraid to desecrate such a place with your horrid vices—I mean the iron things—and furnace and litter?" asked Mary. She had sunk down upon an anvil, on which lay a newspaper, the first seat that she could find, and thence surveyed the strange, incongruous scene.

"Well, if you ask, I don't like it," answered Morris. "But there is no other place that I can have, for my father is afraid of the forge in the house, and I can't afford to build a workshop outside."

"It ought to be restored," said Mary, "with a beautiful organ in a carved case and a lovely alabaster altar and one of those perpetual lamps of silver—the French call them 'veilleuses', don't they?—and the Stations of the Cross in carved oak, and all the rest of it."

Mary, it may be explained, had a tendency to admire the outward adornments of ritualism if not its doctrines.

"Quite so," answered Morris, smiling. "When I have from five to seven thousand to spare I will set about the job, and hire a high-church chaplain with a fine voice to come and say Mass for your benefit. By the way, would you like a confessional also? You omitted it from the list."

"I think not. Besides, what on earth should I confess, except being always late for prayers through oversleeping myself in the morning, and general uselessness?"

"Oh, I daresay you might find something if you tried," suggested Morris.

"Speak for yourself, please, Morris. To begin with your own account, there is the crime of sacrilege in using a chapel as a workshop. Look, those are all tombstones of abbots and other holy people, and under each tombstone one of them is asleep. Yet there you are, using strong language and whistling and making a horrible noise with hammers just above their heads. I wonder they don't haunt you; I would if I were they."

"Perhaps they do," said Morris, "only I don't see them."

"Then they can't be there."

"Why not? Because things are invisible and intangible it does not follow that they don't exist, as I ought to know as much as anyone."

"Of course; but I am sure that if there were anything of that sort about you would soon be in touch with it. With me it is different; I could sleep sweetly with ghosts sitting on my bed in rows."

"Why do you say that—about me, I mean?" asked Morris, in a more earnest voice.

"Oh, I don't know. Go and look at your own eyes in the glass—but I daresay you do often enough. Look here, Morris, you think me very silly—almost foolish—don't you?"

"I never thought anything of the sort. As a matter of fact, if you want to know, I think you a young woman rather more idle than most, and with a perfect passion for burying your talent in very white napkins."

"Well, it all comes to the same thing, for there isn't much difference between fool-born and fool-manufactured. Sometimes I wake up, however, and have moments of wisdom—as when I made you hear that thing, you know, thereby proving that it is all right, only useless—haven't I?"

"I daresay; but come to the point."

"Don't be in a hurry. It is rather hard to express myself. What I mean is that you had better give up staring."

"Staring? I never stared at you or anyone else, in my life!"

"Stupid Morris! By staring I mean star-gazing, and by star-gazing I mean trying to get away from the earth—in your mind, you know."

Morris ran his fingers through his untidy hair and opened his lips to answer.

"Don't contradict me," she interrupted in a full steady voice. "That's what you are thinking of half the day, and dreaming about all the night."

"What's that?" he exclaimed.

"I don't know," she answered, with a sudden access of indifference. "Do you know yourself?"

"I am waiting for instruction," said Morris, sarcastically.

"All right, then, I'll try. I mean that you are not satisfied with this world and those of us who live here. You keep trying to fashion another—oh! yes, you have been at it from a boy, you see I have got a good memory, I remember all your 'vision stories'—and then you try to imagine its inhabitants."

"Well," said Morris, with the sullen air of a convicted criminal, "without admitting one word of this nonsense, what if I do?"

"Only that you had better look out that you don't *find* whatever it is you seek. It's a horrible mistake to be so spiritual, at least in that kind of way. You should eat and drink, and sleep ten hours as I do, and not go craving for vision till you can see, and praying for power until you can create."

"See! Create! Who? What?"

"The inhabitant, or inhabitants. Just think, you may have been building her up all this time, imagination by imagination, and thought by thought. Then her day might come, and all that you have put out piecemeal will return at once. Yes, she may appear, and take you, and possess you, and lead you—"

"She? Why she? and where?"

"To the devil, I imagine," answered Mary composedly, "and as you are a man one can guess the guide's sex. It's getting dark, let us go out. This is such a creepy place in the dark that it actually makes me understand what people mean by nerves. And, Morris, of course you understand that I have only been talking rubbish. I always liked inventing fairy tales; you taught me; only this one is too grown up—disagreeable. What I really mean is that I do think it might be a good thing if you wouldn't live quite so much alone, and would go out a bit more. You are getting quite an odd look on your face; you are indeed, not like other men at all. I believe that it comes from your worrying about this wretched invention until you are half crazy over the thing. Any change there?"

He shook his head. "No, I can't find the right alloy—not one that can be relied upon. I begin to doubt whether it exists."

"Why don't you give it up—for a while at any rate?"

"I have. I made a novel kind of electrical hand-saw this spring, and sold the patent for 100 pounds and a royalty. There's commercial success for you, and now I am at work on a new lamp of which I have the idea."

"I am uncommonly glad to hear it," said Mary with energy. "And, I say, Morris, you are not offended at my silly parables, are you? You know what I mean."

"Not a bit. I think it is very kind of you to worry your head about an impossible fellow like me. And look here, Mary, I have done some dreaming in my time, it is true, for so far the world has been a place of tribulation to me, and it is sick hearts that dream. But I mean to give it up, for I know as well as you do that there is only one end to all these systems of mysticism." Mary looked up.

"I mean," he went on, correcting himself, "to the mad attempt unduly and prematurely to cultivate our spiritual natures that we may live to and for them, and not to and for our natural bodies."

"Exactly my argument, put into long words," said Mary. "There will be plenty of time for that when we get down among those old gentlemen yonder—a year or two hence, you know. Meanwhile, let us take the world as we find it. It isn't a bad place, after all, at times, and there are several things worth doing for those who are not too lazy.

"Good-bye, I must be off; my bicycle is there against the railings. Oh, how I hate that machine! Now, listen, Morris; do you want to do something really useful, and earn the blessings of an affectionate relative? Then invent a really reliable electrical bike, that would look nice and do all the work, so that I could sit on it comfortably and get to a place without my legs aching as though I had broken them, and a red face, and no breath left in my body."

"I will think about it," he said; "indeed, I have thought of it already but the accumulators are the trouble."

"Then go on thinking, there's an angel; think hard and continually until you evolve that blessed instrument of progression. I say, I haven't a lamp."

"I'll lend you mine," suggested Morris.

"No; other people's lamps always go out with me, and so do my own, for that matter. I'll risk it; I know the policeman, and if we meet I will argue with him. Good-bye; don't forget we are coming to dinner to-morrow night. It's a party, isn't it?"

"I believe so."

"What a bore, I must unpack my London dresses. Well, good-bye again."

"Good-bye, dear," answered Morris, and she was gone.

"'Dear,'" thought Mary to herself; "he hasn't called me that since I was sixteen. I wonder why he does it now? Because I have been scolding him, I suppose; that generally makes men affectionate."

For a while she glided forward through the grey twilight, and then began to think again, muttering to herself:

"You idiot, Mary, why should you be pleased because he called you 'dear'? He doesn't really care two-pence about you; his blood goes no quicker when you pass by and no slower when you stay away. Why do you bother about him? and what made you talk all that stuff this afternoon? Because you think he is in a queer way, and that if he goes on giving himself up to his fancies he will become mad—yes, mad—because—Oh! what's the use of making excuses—because you are fond of him, and always have been fond of him from a child, and can't help it. What a fate! To be fond of a man who hasn't the heart to care for you or for any other woman. Perhaps, however, that's only because he hasn't found the right one, as he might do at any time, and then—"

"Where are you going to, and where's your light?" shouted a hoarse voice from the pathway on which she was unlawfully riding.

"My good man, I wish I knew," answered Mary, blandly.

Morris, for whom the day never seemed long enough, was a person who breakfasted punctually at half-past eight, whereas Colonel Monk, to whom—at any rate at Monksland—the day was often too long, generally breakfasted at ten. To his astonishment, however, on entering the dining-room upon the morrow of his interview in the workshop with Mary, he found his father seated at the head of the table.

"This means a 'few words' with me about something disagreeable," thought Morris to himself as he dabbed viciously at an evasive sausage. He was not fond of these domestic conversations. Nor was he in the least reassured by his father's airy and informed comments upon the contents of the "Globe," which always arrived by post, and the marvel of its daily "turnover" article, whereof the perpetual variety throughout the decades constituted, the Colonel was wont to say, the eighth wonder of the world. Instinct, instructed by experience, assured him that these were but the first moves in the game.

Towards the end of the meal he attempted retreat, pretending that he wanted to fetch something, but the Colonel, who was watching him over the top of the pink page of the "Globe," intervened promptly.

"If you have a few minutes to spare, my dear boy, I should like to have a chat with you," he said.

"Certainly, father," answered the dutiful Morris; "I am at your service."

"Very good; then I will light my cigar, and we might take a stroll on the beach, that is, after I have seen the cook about the dinner to-night. Perhaps I shall find you presently by the steps."

"I will wait for you there," answered Morris. And wait he did, for a considerable while, for the interview with the cook proved lengthy. Moreover, the Colonel was not a punctual person, or one who set an undue value upon his own or other people's time. At length, just as Morris was growing weary of the pristine but enticing occupation of making ducks and drakes with flat pebbles, his father appeared. After "salutations," as they say in the East, he wasted ten more minutes in abusing the cook, ending up with a direct appeal for his son's estimate of her capacities.

"She might be better and she might be worse," answered Morris, judicially.

"Quite so," replied the Colonel, drily; "the remark is sound and applies to most things. At present, however, I think that she is worse; also I hate the sight of her fat red face. But bother the cook, why do you think so much about her; I have something else to say."

"I don't think," said Morris. "She doesn't excite me one way or the other, except when she is late with my breakfast."

Then, as he expected, after the cook came the crisis.

"You will remember, my dear boy," began the Colonel, affectionately, "a little talk we had a while ago."

"Which one, father?"

"The last of any importance, I believe. I refer to the occasion when you stopped out all night contemplating the sea; an incident which impressed it upon my memory."

Morris looked at him. Why was the old gentleman so inconveniently observant?

"And doubtless you remember the subject?"

"There were a good many subjects, father; they ranged from mortgages to matrimony."

"Quite so, to matrimony. Well, have you thought any more about it?"

"Not particularly, father. Why should I?"

"Confound it, Morris," exclaimed the Colonel, losing patience; "don't chop logic like a petty sessions lawyer. Let's come to the point."

"That is my desire," answered Morris; and quite clearly there rose up before him an inconsequent picture of his mother teaching him the Catechism many, many years ago. Thereat, as was customary with his mind when any memory of her touched it, his temper softened like iron beneath the influence of fire.

"Very good, then what do you think of Mary as a wife?"

"How should I know under the circumstances?"

The Colonel fumed, and Morris added, "I beg your pardon, I understand what you mean."

Then his father came to the charge.

"To be brief, will you marry her?"

"Will she marry me?" asked Morris. "Isn't she too sensible?"

His father's eye twinkled, but he restrained himself. This, he felt, was not an occasion upon which to indulge his powers of sarcasm.

"Upon my word, if you want my opinion, I believe she will; but you have to ask her first. Look here, my boy, be advised by me, and do it as soon as possible. The notion is rather new to me, I admit; but, taking her all round, where would you find a better woman? You and I don't always agree about things; we are of a different generation, and look at the world from different standpoints. But I think that at the bottom we respect each other, and I am sure," he added with a touch of restrained dignity, "that we are naturally and properly attached to each other. Under these circumstances, and taking everything else into consideration, I am convinced also that you will give weight to my advice. I assure you that I do not offer it lightly. It is that you should marry your cousin Mary."

"There is her side of the case to be considered," suggested Morris.

"Doubtless, and she is a very shrewd and sensible young woman under all her 'dolce far niente' air, who is quite capable of consideration."

"I am not worthy of her," his son broke in passionately.

"That is for her to decide. I ask you to give her an opportunity of expressing an opinion."

Morris looked at the sea and sky, then he looked at his father standing before him in an attitude that was almost suppliant, with head bowed, hands clasped, and on his clear-cut face an air of real sincerity. What right had he to resist this appeal? He was heart-whole, without any kind of complication, and for his cousin Mary he had true affection and respect. Moreover, they had been brought up together. She understood him, and in the midst of so much that was uncertain and bewildering she seemed something genuine and solid, something to which a man could cling. It may not have been a right spirit in which to approach this question of marriage, but in the case of a young man like Morris, who was driven forward by no passion, by no scheme even of personal advancement, this substitution of reason for impulse and instinct was perhaps natural.

"Very well, I will," he answered; "but if she is wise, she won't."

His father turned his head away and sighed softly, and that sigh seemed to lift a ton's weight off his heart.

"I am glad to hear it," he answered simply, "the rest must settle itself. By the way, if you are going up to the house, tell the cook that I have changed my mind, we will have the soles fried with lemon; she always makes a mess of them 'au maitre d'hotel.'"

V

A Proposal and a Promise

Although it consisted of but a dozen people, the dinner-party at the Abbey that night was something of a function. To begin with, the old refectory, with its stone columns and arches still standing as they were in the pre-Reformation days, lit with cunningly-arranged and shaded electric lights designed and set up by Morris, was an absolutely ideal place in which to dine. Then, although the Monk family were impoverished, they still retained the store of plate accumulated by past generations. Much of this silver was old and very beautiful, and when set out upon the great side-boards produced an affect well suited to that chamber and its accessories. The company also was pleasant and presentable. There were the local baronet and his wife; the two beauties of the neighbourhood, Miss Jane Rose and Miss Eliza Layard, with their respective belongings; the clergyman of the parish, a Mr. Tomley, who was leaving the county for the north of England on account of his wife's health; and a clever and rising young doctor from the county town. These, with Mr. Porson and his daughter, made up the number who upon this particular night with every intention of enjoying themselves, sat down to that rather rare entertainment in Monksland, a dinner-party.

Colonel Monk had himself very carefully placed the guests. As a result, Morris, to whose lot it had fallen to take in the wealthy Miss Layard, a young lady of handsome but somewhat ill-tempered countenance, found himself at the foot of the oblong table with his partner on one side and his cousin on the other. Mary, who was conducted to her seat by Mr. Layard, the delicate brother, an insignificant, pallid-looking specimen of humanity, for reasons of her own, not unconnected perhaps with the expected presence of the Misses Layard and Rose, had determined to look and dress her best that night. She wore a robe of some rich white silk, tight fitting and cut rather low, and upon her neck a single row of magnificent diamonds. The general effect of her sheeny dress, snow-like skin, and golden, waving hair, as she glided into the shaded room, suggested to Morris's mind a great white lily floating down the quiet water of some dark stream, and, when presently the light fell on her, a vision of a silver, mist-laden star lying low upon the ocean at the break of dawn. Later, after she became acquainted with these poetical imaginings, Mary congratulated herself and her maid very warmly on the fact that she had actually summoned sufficient energy to telegraph to town for this particular dress.

Of the other ladies present, Miss Layard was arrayed in a hot-looking red garment, which she imagined would suit her dark eyes and complexion. Miss Rose, on the contrary, had come out in the virginal style of muslin and blue bows, whereof the effect, unhappily, was somewhat marred by a fiery complexion, acquired as the result of three days' violent play at a tennis tournament. To this unfortunate circumstance Miss Layard, who had her own views of Miss Rose, was not slow in calling attention.

"What has happened to poor Jane?" she said, addressing Mary. "She looks as though she had been red-ochred down to her shoulders."

"Who is poor Jane?" asked that young lady languidly. "Oh! you mean Miss Rose. I know, she has been playing in that tennis tournament at—what's the name of the place? Dad would drive me there this afternoon, and it made me quite hot to look at her, jumping and running and hitting for hour after hour. But she's awfully good at it; she won the prize. Don't you envy anybody who can win a prize at a tennis tournament, Miss Layard?"

"No," she answered sharply, for Miss Layard did not shine at Tennis. "I dislike women who go about what my brother calls 'pot-hunting' just as if they were professionals."

"Oh, do you? I admire them. It must be so nice to be able to do anything well, even if it's only lawn tennis. It's the poor failures like myself for whom I am so sorry."

"I don't admire anybody who can come to out to a dinner party with a head and neck like that," retorted Eliza.

"Why not? You can't burn, and that should make you more charitable. And I tie myself up in veils and umbrellas, which is absurd. Besides, what does it matter? You see, it is different with most of us; Miss Rose is so good-looking that she can afford herself these little luxuries."

"That is a matter of opinion," replied Miss Layard.

"Oh! I don't think so; at least, the opinion is all one way. Don't you think Miss Rose beautiful, Mr. Layard?" she said, turning to her companion.

"Ripping," said that gentleman, with emphasis. "But I wish she wouldn't beat one at tennis; it is an insult to the stronger sex."

Mary looked at him reflectively. His sister looked at him also.

"And I am sure that you think her beautiful, don't you, Morris?" went on the imperturbable Mary.

"Certainly, of course; lovely," he replied, with a vacuous stare at the elderly wife of the baronet.

"There, Miss Layard, now you collect the opinions of the gentlemen all along your side." And Mary turned away, ostensibly to talk to her cavalier; but really to find out what could possibly interest Morris so deeply in the person or conversation of Lady Jones.

Lady Jones was talking across the table to Mr. Tomley, the departing rector, a benevolent-looking person, with a broad forehead adorned like that of Father Time by a single lock of snowy hair.

"And so you are really going to the far coast of Northumberland, Mr. Tomley, to exchange livings with the gentleman with the odd name? How brave of you!"

Mr. Tomley smiled assent, adding: "You can imagine what a blow it is to me, Lady Jones, to separate myself from my dear parishioners and friends"—here he eyed the Colonel, with whom he had waged a continual war during his five years of residence in the parish, and added: "But we must all give way to the cause of duty and the necessities of health. Mrs. Tomley says that this part of the country does not agree with her, and is quite convinced that unless she is taken back to her native Northumberland air the worst may be expected."

"I fancy that it has arrived in that poor man's case," thought Mary to herself. Lady Jones, who also knew Mrs. Tomley and the power of her tongue, nodded her head sympathetically and said:

"Of course, of course. A wife's health must be the first consideration of every good man. But isn't it rather lonely up there, Mr. Tomley?"

"Lonely, Lady Jones?" the clergyman replied with energy, and shaking his white lock. "I assure you that the place is a howling desert; a great moor behind, and the great sea in front, and some rocks and the church between the two. That's about all, but my wife likes it because she used to stay at the rectory when she was a little girl. Her uncle was the incumbent there. She declares that she has never been well since she left the parish."

"And what did you say is the name of the present inhabitant of this earthly paradise, the man with whom you have exchanged?" interrupted the Colonel.

"Fregelius—the Reverend Peter Fregelius."

"What an exceedingly odd name! Is he an Englishman?"

"Yes; but I think that his father was a Dane, and he married a Danish lady."

"Indeed! Is she living?"

"Oh, no. She died a great many years ago. The old gentleman has only one child left—a girl."

"What is her name?" asked someone idly, in a break of the general conversation, so that everybody paused to listen to his reply.

"Stella—Stella Fregelius; a very unusual girl."

Then the conversation broke out again with renewed vigour, and all that those at Morris's end of the table could catch were snatches such as: "Wonderful eyes;" "Independent young person"; "Well read and musical;" "Oh, yes! poor as church mice, that's why he accepted my offer."

At this point the Doctor began a rather vehement argument with Mr. Porson as to the advisability of countervailing duties to force foreign nations to abandon the sugar bounties, and no more was heard of Mr. Tomley and his plans.

On the whole, Mary enjoyed that dinner-party. Miss Layard, somewhat sore after her first encounter, attempted to retaliate later.

But by this time Mary's argumentative energy had evaporated. Therefore, adroitly appealing to Mr. Layard to take her part, she retired from the fray till, seeing that it grew acrimonious, for this brother and sister did not love each other, she pretended to hear no more.

"Have you been stopping out all night again and staring at the sea, Morris?" she inquired; "because I understand it is a habit of yours. You seem so sleepy. I know that I must have looked just like you when that old political gentleman took me in to dinner, and I made an exhibition of myself."

"What was that?" asked Morris.

So she told him the story of her unlawful slumbers, and so amusingly that he burst out laughing and remained in an excellent mood for the rest of the feast, or at any rate until the ladies had departed. After this event once more he became somewhat silent and distant.

It was not wonderful. To most men, except the very experienced, proposals are terrifying ordeals, and Morris had made up his mind, if he could find a chance, to propose to Mary that night. The thing was to be done, so the sooner he did it the better.

Then it would be over, one way or the other. Besides, and this was strange and opportune enough, never had he felt so deeply and truly attracted to Mary. Whether it was because her soft, indolent beauty showed at its best this evening in that gown and setting, or because her conversation, with its sub-acid tinge of kindly humour amused him, or—and this seemed more probable—because her whole attitude towards himself was so gentle and so full of sweet benevolence, he could not say. At any rate, this remained true, she attracted him more than any woman he had ever met, and sincerely he hoped and prayed that when he asked her to be his wife she might find it in her heart to say Yes.

The rest of the entertainment resembled that of most country dinner-parties. Conducted to the piano by the Colonel, who understood music very well, the talented ladies of the party, including Miss Rose, sang songs with more or less success, while Miss Layard criticised, Mary was appreciative, and the men talked. At length the local baronet's wife looked at the local baronet, who thereupon asked leave to order the carriage. This example the rest of the company followed in quick succession until all were gone except Mr. Porson and his daughter.

"Well, my dear," said Mr. Porson, "I suppose that we had better be off too, or you won't get your customary nine hours."

Mary yawned slightly and assented, asserting that she had utterly exhausted herself in defending Miss Rose from the attacks of her rival, Miss Layard.

"No, no," broke in the Colonel, "come and have a smoke first, John. I've got that old map of the property unrolled on purpose to show you, and I don't want to keep it about, for it fills up the whole place. Morris will look after Mary for half an hour, I daresay."

"Certainly," said Morris, but the heart within him sank to the level of his dress-shoes. Here was the opportunity for which he had wished, but as he could not be called a forward, or even a pushing lover, he was alarmed at its very prompt arrival. This answer to his prayers was somewhat too swift and thorough. There is a story of an enormously fat old Boer who was seated on the veld with his horse at his side, when suddenly a band of armed natives rushed to attack him. "Oh, God, help!" he cried in his native *taal*, as he prepared to heave his huge form into the saddle. Having thus invoked divine assistance, this Dutch Falstaff went at the task with such a will that in a trice he found himself not on the horse, but over it, lying upon his back, indeed, among the grasses. "O God!" that deluded burgher exclaimed, reproachfully, as the Kaffirs came up and speared him, "Thou hast helped a great deal too much!"

At this moment Morris felt very much like this stout but simple dweller in the wilderness. He would have preferred to coquet with the enemy for a while from the safety of his saddle. But Providence willed it otherwise.

"Won't you come out, Mary?" he said, with the courage which inspires men in desperate situations. He felt that it would be impossible to say those words with the electric lights looking at him like so many eyes. The thought of it, even, made him warm all over.

"I don't know; it depends. Is there anything comfortable to sit on?"

"The deck chair," he suggested.

"That sounds nice. I have slumbered for hours in deck chairs. Look, there's a fur rug on that sofa, and here's my white cape; now you get your coat, and I'll come."

"Thank you, no; I don't want any coat; I am hot enough already."

Mary turned and looked him up and down with her wondering blue eyes.

"Do you really think it safe," she said, "to expose yourself to all sorts of unknown dangers in this unprotected condition?"

"Of course," he answered. "I am not afraid of the night air even in October."

"Very well, very well, Morris," she went on, and there was meaning in her voice; "then whatever happens don't blame me. It's so easy to be rash and thoughtless and catch a chill, and then you may become an invalid for life, or die, you know. One can't get rid of it again—at least, not often."

Morris looked at her with a puzzled air, and stepped through the window which he had opened, on to the lawn, whither, with a quaint little shrug of her shoulders, Mary followed him, muttering to herself:

"Now if he takes cold, it won't be *my* fault." Then she stopped, clasped her hands, and said, "Oh! what a lovely night. I am glad that we came out here."

She was right, it was indeed lovely. High in the heavens floated a bright half-moon, across whose face the little white-edged clouds drifted in quick succession, throwing their gigantic shadows to the world beneath. All silver was the sleeping sea where the moonlight fell upon it, and when this was eclipsed, then it was all jet. To the right and left, up to the very borders of the cliff, lay the soft wreaths of roke or land-fog, covering the earth as with a cloak of down, but pierced here and there by the dim and towering shapes of trees. Yet although these

H. RIDER HAGGARD

curling wreaths of mist hung on the edges of the cliff like white water about to fall, they never fell, since clear to the sight, though separated from them by a gulf of translucent blackness, lay the yellow belt of sand up which, inch by inch, the tide was creeping.

And the air—no wind stirred it, though the wind was at work aloft—it was still and bright as crystal, and crisp and cold as new-iced wine, for the first autumn frost was falling.

They stood for a few moments looking at all these wonderful beauties of the mysterious night—which dwellers in the country so rarely appreciate, because to them they are common, daily things—and listening to the soft, long-drawn murmuring of the sea upon the shingle. Then they went forward to the edge of the cliff, but although Morris threw the fur rug over it Mary did not seat herself in the comfortable-looking deck chair. Her desire for repose had departed. She preferred to lean upon the low grey wall in whose crannies grew lichens, tiny ferns, and, in their season, harebells and wallflowers. Morris came and leant at her side; for a while they both stared at the sea.

"Pray, are you making up poetry?" she inquired at last.

"Why do you ask such silly questions?" he answered, not without indignation.

"Because you keep muttering to yourself, and I thought that you were trying to get the lines to scan. Also the sea, and the sky, and the night suggest poetry, don't they?"

Morris turned his head and looked at her.

"*You* suggest it," he said, with desperate earnestness, "in all that shining white, especially when the moon goes in. Then you look like a beautiful spirit new lit upon the edge of the world."

At first Mary was pleased, the compliment was obvious, and, coming from Morris, great. She had never heard him say so much as that before. Then she thought an instant, and the echo of the word "spirit" came back to her mind, and jarred upon it with a little sudden shock. Even when he had a lovely woman at his side must his fancy be wandering to these unearthly denizens and similes.

"Please, Morris," she said almost sharply, "do not compare me to a spirit. I am a woman, nothing more, and if it is not enough that I should be a woman, then—" she paused, to add, "I beg your pardon, I know you meant to be nice, but once I had a friend who went in for spirits—table-turning ones I mean—with very bad results, and I detest the name of them."

Morris took this rebuff better than might have been expected.

"Would you object if one ventured to call you an angel?" he asked.

"Not if the word was used in a terrestrial sense. It excites a vision of possibilities, and the fib is so big that anyone must pardon it."

"Very well, then; I call you that."

"Thank you, I should be delighted to return the compliment. Can you think of any celestial definition appropriate to a young gentleman with dark eyes?"

"Oh! Mary, please stop making fun of me," said Morris, with something like a groan.

"Why?" she asked innocently. "Besides I wasn't making fun. It's only my way of carrying on conversation; they taught it me at school, you know."

Morris made no answer; in fact, he did not know what on earth to say, or rather how to find the fitting words. After all, it was an accident and not his own intelligence that freed him from his difficulty. Mary moved a little, causing the white cloak, which was unfastened, to slip from her shoulders. Morris put out his hand to catch it, and met her hand. In another instant he had thrown his arm round her, drawn her to him, and kissed her on the lips. Then, abashed at what he had done, he let her go and picked up the cloak.

"Might I ask?" began Mary in her usual sweet, low tones. Then her voice broke, and her blue eyes filled with tears.

"I beg your pardon; I am a brute," began Morris, utterly abased by the sight of these tears, which glimmered like pearls in the moonlight, "but, of course, you know what I mean."

Mary shook her head vacantly. Apparently she could not trust herself to speak.

"Dear, will you take me?"

She made no answer; only, after pausing for some few seconds as though lost in thought, with a little action more eloquent than any speech, she leant herself ever so slightly towards him.

Afterwards, as she lay in his arms, words came to him readily enough:

"I am not worth your having," he said. "I know I am an odd fellow, not like other men; my very failings have not been the same as other men's. For instance—before heaven it is true—you are the first woman whom I ever kissed, as I swear to you that you shall be the last. Then, what else am I? A failure in the very work that I have chosen, and the heir to a bankrupt property! Oh! it is not fair; I have no right to ask you!"

"I think it quite fair, and here I am the judge, Morris." Then, sentence by sentence, she went on, not all at once, but with breaks and pauses.

"You asked me just now if I loved you, and I told you—Yes. But you did not ask me when I began to love you. I will tell you all the same. I can't remember a time when I didn't; no, not since I was a little girl. It was you who grew away from me, not me from you, when you took to studying mysticism and aerophones, and were repelled by all women, myself included."

"I know, I know," he said. "Don't remind me of my dead follies. Some things are born in the blood."

"Quite so, and they remain in the bone. I understand. Morris, unless you maltreat me wilfully—which I am sure you would never do—I shall always understand."

"What are you afraid of?" he asked in a shaken voice. "I feel that you are afraid."

"Oh, one or two things; that you might overwork yourself, for instance. Or, lest you should find that after all you are more human than you imagine, and be taken possession of by some strange Stella coming out of nowhere."

"What do you mean, and why do you use that name?" he said amazed.

"What I say, dear. As for that name, I heard it accidentally at table to-night, and it came to my lips—of itself. It seemed to typify what I meant, and to suggest a wandering star—such as men like you are fond of following."

"Upon my honour," said Morris, "I will do none of these things."

"If you can help it, you will do none of them. I know it well enough. I hope and believe that there will never be a shadow between us while we live. But, Morris, I take you, risks and all, because it has been my chance to love you and nobody else. Otherwise, I should think twice; but love doesn't stop at risks."

"What have I done to deserve this?" groaned Morris.

"I cannot see. I should very much like to know," replied Mary, with a touch of her old humour.

It was at this moment that Colonel Monk, happening to come round the corner of the house, walking on the grass, and followed by Mr. Porson, saw a sight which interested him. With one hand he pointed it out to Porson, at the same moment motioning him to silence with the other. Then, taking his brother-in-law by the arm, he dragged him back round the corner of the house.

"They make a pretty picture there in the moonlight, don't they, John, my boy?" he said. "Come, we had better go back into the study and talk over matters till they have done. Even the warmth of their emotions won't keep out the night air for ever."

VI

The Good Old Days

For the next month, or, to be accurate, the next five weeks, everything went merrily at Monk's Abbey. It was as though some cloud had been lifted off the place and those who dwelt therein. No longer did the Colonel look solemn when he came down in the morning, and no longer was he cross after he had read his letters. Now his interviews with the steward in the study were neither prolonged nor anxious; indeed, that functionary emerged thence on Saturday mornings with a shining countenance, drying the necessary cheque, heretofore so difficult to extract, by waving it ostentatiously in the air. Lastly, the Colonel did not seem to be called upon to make such frequent visits to his man of business, and to tarry at the office of the bank manager in Northwold. Once there was a meeting, but, contrary to the general custom, the lawyer and the banker came to see him in company, and stopped to luncheon. At this meal, moreover, the three of them appeared to be in the best of spirits.

Morris noted all these things in his quiet, observant way, and from them drew certain conclusions of his own. But he shrank from making inquiries, nor did the Colonel offer any confidences. After all, why should he, who had never meddled with his father's business, choose this moment to explore it, especially as he knew from previous experience that such investigations would not be well received? It was one of the Colonel's peculiarities to keep his affairs to himself until they grew so bad that circumstances forced him to seek the counsel or the aid of others. Still, Morris could well guess from what mine the money was digged that caused so comfortable a change in their circumstances, and the solution of this mystery gave him little joy. Cash in consideration of an unconcluded marriage; that was how it read. To his sensitive nature the transaction seemed one of doubtful worth.

However, no one else appeared to be troubled, if, indeed, these things existed elsewhere than in his own imagination. This, Morris admitted, was possible, for their access of prosperity might, after all, be no more than a resurrection of credit, vivified by the news of his engagement with the only child of a man known to be wealthy. His uncle Porson, with a solemnity that was almost touching, had bestowed upon Mary and himself a jerky but earnest blessing before he drove home on the night of the dinner-party. He went so far, indeed, as to kiss them both; an example which the Colonel followed with a more finished but equally heartfelt grace.

Now his uncle John beamed upon him daily like the noonday sun. Also he began to take him into his confidence, and consult him as to the erection of houses, affairs of business, and investments. In the course of these interviews Morris was astonished, not to say dismayed, to discover how large were the sums of money as to the disposal of which he was expected to express opinions.

"You see, it will all be yours, my boy," said Mr. Porson one day, in explanation; "so it is best that you should know something of these affairs. Yes, it will all be yours, before very long," and he sighed.

"I trust that I shall have nothing to do with it for many years," blurted out Morris.

"Say months, say months," answered his uncle, stretching out his hands as though to push something from him. Then, to all appearances overcome by a sudden anguish, physical or mental, he turned and hurried from the room.

Taking them all together, those five weeks were the happiest that Morris had ever known. No longer was he profoundly dissatisfied with things in general, no longer ravaged by that desire of the moth for the star which in some natures is almost a disease. His outlook upon the world was healthier and more hopeful; for the first time he saw its wholesome, joyous side. Had he failed to do so, indeed, he must have been a very strange man, for he had much to make the poorest heart rejoice.

Thus Mary, always a charming woman, since her engagement had become absolutely delightful; witter, more wideawake, more beautiful. Morris could look forward to the years to be spent in her company not only without misgiving, but with a confidence that a while ago he would have thought impossible. Moreover, as good fortunes never come singly, his were destined to be multiplied. It was in those days after so many years of search and unfruitful labour that at last he discovered a clue which in the end resulted in the perfection of the instrument that was the parent of the aerophone of commerce, and gave him a name among the inventors of the century which will not easily be forgotten.

Strangely enough it was Morris's good genius, Mary, who suggested the substance, or, rather, the mixture of substances, whereof that portion of the aerophone was finally constructed which is still known as the Monk Sound Waves Receiver. Whether, as she alleged, she made this discovery by pure accident, or whether, as seems possible, she had thought the problem out in her own feminine fashion with results that proved excellent, does not matter in the least. The issue remains the same. An apparatus which before would work only on rare occasions— and then without any certitude—between people in the highest state of sympathy or nervous excitement, has now been brought to such a stage of perfection that by its means anybody can talk to anybody, even if their interests are antagonistic, or their personal enmity bitter.

After the first few experiments with this new material Morris was not slow to discover that although it would need long and careful testing and elaboration, for him it meant, in the main, the realisation of his great dream, and success after years of failure. And—that was the strange part of it—this realisation and success he owed to no effort of his own, but to some chance suggestion made by Mary. He told her this, and thanked her as a man thanks one through whom he has found salvation. In answer she merely laughed, saying that she was nothing but the wire along which a happy inspiration had reached his brain, and that more than this she neither wished, nor hoped, nor was capable of being.

Then suddenly on this happy, tranquil atmosphere which wrapped them about—like the sound of a passing bell at a child's feast—floated the first note of impending doom and death.

The autumn held fine and mild, and Mary, who had been lunching at the Abbey, was playing croquet with Morris upon the side lawn. This game was the only one for which she chanced to care, perhaps because it did not involve much exertion. Morris, who engaged in the pastime with the same earnestness that he gave to every other pursuit in which he happened to be interested, was, as might be expected, getting the best of the encounter.

"Won't you take a couple of bisques, dear?" he asked affectionately, after a while. "I don't like always beating you by such a lot."

"I'd die first," she answered; "bisques are the badge of advertised inferiority and a mark of the giver's contempt."

"Stuff!" said Morris.

"Stuff, indeed! As though it wasn't bad enough to be beaten at all; but to be beaten with bisques!"

"That's another argument," said Morris. "First you say you are too proud to accept them, and next that you won't accept them because it is worse to be defeated with points than without them."

"Anyway, if you had the commonest feelings of humanity you wouldn't beat me," replied Mary, adroitly shifting her ground for the third time.

"How can I help it if you won't have the bisques?"

"How? By pretending that you were doing your best, and letting me win all the same, of course; though if I caught you at it I should be furious. But what's the use of trying to teach a blunt creature like you tact? My dear Morris, I assure you I do not believe that your efforts at deception would take in the simplest-minded cow. Why, even Dad sees through you, and the person who can't impose upon my Dad—. Oh!" she added, suddenly, in a changed voice, "there is George coming through the gate. Something has happened to my father. Look at his face, Morris; look at his face!"

In another moment the footman stood before them.

"Please, miss, the master," he began, and hesitated.

"Not dead?" said Mary, in a slow, quiet voice. "Do not say that he is dead!"

"No, miss, but he has had a stroke of the heart or something, and the doctor thought you had better be fetched, so I have brought the carriage."

"Come with me, Morris," she said, as, dropping the croquet mallet, she flew rather than ran to the brougham.

Ten minutes later they were at Seaview. In the hall they met Mr. Charters, the doctor. Why was he leaving? Because—

"No, no," he said, answering their looks; "the danger is past. He seems almost as well as ever."

"Thank God!" stammered Mary. Then a thought struck her, and she looked up sharply and asked, "Will it come back again?"

"Yes," was his straightforward answer.

"When?"

"From time to time, at irregular periods. But in its fatal shape, as I hope, not for some years."

"The verdict might have been worse, dear," said Morris.

"Yes, yes, but to think that *it* has passed so near to him, and he quite alone at the time. Morris," she went on, turning to him with an energy that was almost fierce, "if you won't have my father to live with us, I won't marry you. Do you understand?"

"Perfectly, dear, you leave no room for misconception. By all means let him live with us—if he can get on with my father," he added meaningly.

"Ah!" she replied, "I never thought of that. Also I should not have spoken so roughly, but I have had such a shock that I feel inclined to treat you like—like—a toad under a harrow. So please be sympathetic, and don't misunderstand me, or I don't know what I shall say." Then by way of making amends, Mary put her arms round his neck and gave him a kiss "all of her own accord," saying, "Morris, I am afraid—I am afraid. I feel as if our good time was done."

After this the servant came to say that she might go up to her father's room, and that scene of our drama was at an end.

Mr. Porson owned a villa at Beaulieu, in the south of France, which he had built many years before as a winter house for his wife, whose chest was weak. Here he was in the habit of spending the spring months, more, perhaps, because of the associations which the place possessed for him than of any affection for foreign lands. Now, however, after this last attack, three doctors in consultation announced that it would be well for him to escape from the fogs and damp of England. So to Beaulieu he was ordered.

This decree caused consternation in various quarters. Mr. Porson did not wish to go; Mary and Morris were cast down for simple and elementary reasons; and Colonel Monk found this change of plan— it had been arranged that the Porsons should stop at Seaview till the New Year, which was to be the day of the marriage—inconvenient, and, indeed, disturbing. Once those young people were parted, reflected the Colonel in his wisdom, who could tell what might or might not happen?

In this difficulty he found an inspiration. Why should not the wedding take place at once? Very diplomatically he sounded his brother-in-law, to find that he had no opposition to fear in this quarter provided that Mary and her husband would join him at Beaulieu after a week or two of honeymoon. Then he spoke to Morris, who was delighted with the idea. For Morris had come to the conclusion that the marriage state would be better and more satisfactory than one of prolonged engagement.

It only remained, therefore, to obtain the consent of Mary, which would perhaps, have been given without much difficulty had her uncle been content to leave his son or Mr. Porson to ask it of her. As it chanced, this he was not willing to do. Porson, he was sure, would at once give way should his daughter raise any objection, and in Morris's tact and persuasive powers the Colonel had no faith.

In the issue, confident in his own diplomatic abilities, he determined to manage the affair himself and to speak to his niece. The mistake was grave, for whereas she was as wax to her father or her lover, something in her uncle's manner, or it may have been his very personality, always aroused in Mary a spirit of opposition. On this occasion, too, that manner was not fortunate, for he put the proposal before her as a thing already agreed upon by all concerned, and one to which her consent was asked as a mere matter of form.

Instantly Mary became antagonistic. She pretended not to understand; she asked for reasons and explanations. Finally, she announced in idle words, beneath which ran a current of determination, that neither her father nor Morris could really wish this hurried marriage, since had they done so one or other of them would have spoken to her on the subject. When pressed, she intimated very politely, but in language whereof the meaning could hardly be mistaken, that she held this fixing of the date to be peculiarly her own privilege; and when still further pressed said plainly that she considered her father too ill for her to think of being married at present.

"But they both desire it," expostulated the Colonel.

"They have not told me so," Mary answered, setting her red lips.

"If that is all, they will tell you so soon enough, my dear girl."

"Perhaps, uncle, after they have been directed to do so, but that is not quite the same thing."

The Colonel saw that he had made a mistake, and too late changed his tactics.

"You see, Mary, your father's state of health is precarious; he might grow worse."

She tapped her foot upon the ground. Of these allusions to the possible, and, indeed, the certain end of her beloved father's illness, she had a kind of horror.

"In that event, that dreadful event," she answered, "he will need me, my whole time and care to nurse him. These I might not be able to give if I were already married. I love Morris very dearly. I am his for whatever I may be worth; but I was my father's before Morris came into my life, and he has the first claim upon me."

"What, then, do you propose?" asked the Colonel curtly, for opposition and argument bred no meekness in his somewhat arbitrary breast.

"To be married on New Year's Day, wherever we are, if Morris wishes it and the state of my father's health makes it convenient. If not, Uncle Richard, to wait till a more fitting season." Then she rose—for this conversation took place at Seaview—saying that it was time she should give her father his medicine.

Thus the project of an early marriage fell through; for, having once been driven into announcing her decision in terms so open and unmistakable, Mary would not go back on her word.

Morris, who was much disappointed, pleaded with her. Her father also spoke upon the subject, but though the voice was the voice of Mr. Porson, the arguments, she perceived, were the arguments of Colonel Monk. Therefore she hardened her heart and put the matter by, refusing, indeed, to discuss it at any length. Yet—and it is not the first time that a woman has allowed her whims to prevail over her secret wishes—in truth she desired nothing more than to be married to Morris so soon as it was his will to take her.

Finally, a compromise was arranged. There was to be no wedding at present, but the whole party were to go together to Beaulieu, there to await the development of events. It was arranged, moreover, by all concerned, that unless something unforeseen occurred to prevent it, the marriage should be celebrated upon or about New Year's Day.

VII

Beaulieu

Beautiful as it might be and fashionable as it might be, Morris did not find Beaulieu very entertaining; indeed, in an unguarded moment he confessed to Mary that he "hated the hole." Even the steam launch in which they went for picnics did not console him, fond though he was of the sea; while as for Monte Carlo, after his third visit he was heard to declare that if they wanted to take him there again it must be in his coffin.

The Colonel did not share these views. He was out for a holiday, and he meant to enjoy himself. To begin with, there was the club at Nice, where he fell in with several old comrades and friends. Then, whom should he meet but Lady Rawlins: once, for a little while in the distant past, they had been engaged; until suddenly the young lady, a beauty in her day, jilted him in favour of a wealthy banker of Hebraic origin. Now, many years after, the banker was aged, violent, and uncomely, habitually exceeded in his cups, and abused his wife before the servants. So it came about that to the poor woman the Colonel's courteous, if somewhat sarcastic, consolations were really very welcome. It pleased him also to offer them. The jilting he had long ago forgiven indeed, he blessed her nightly for having taken that view of her obligations, seeing that Jane Millet, as she was then, however pretty her face may once have been, had neither fortune nor connections.

"Yes, my dear Jane," he said to her confidentially one afternoon, "I assure you I often admire your foresight. Now, if you had done the other thing, where should we have been to-day? In the workhouse, I imagine."

"I suppose so," answered Lady Rawlins, meekly, and suppressing a sigh, since for the courtly and distinguished Colonel she cherished a sentimental admiration which actually increased with age; "but you didn't always think like that, Richard." Then she glanced out of the window, and added: "Oh, there is Jonah coming home, and he looks so cross," and the poor lady shivered.

The Colonel put up his eyeglass and contemplated Jonah through the window. He was not a pleasing spectacle. A rather low-class

Hebrew who calls himself a Christian, of unpleasant appearance and sinister temper, suffering from the effects of lunch, is not an object to be loved.

"Ah, I see," said the Colonel. "Yes, Sir Jonah ages, doesn't he? as, indeed, we do all of us," and he glanced at the lady's spreading proportions. Then he went on. "You really should persuade him to be tidier in his costume, Jane; his ancestral namesake could scarcely have looked more dishevelled after his sojourn with the whale. Well, it is a small failing; one can't have everything, and on the whole, with your wealth and the rest, you have been a very fortunate woman."

"Oh, Richard, how can you say so?" murmured the wretched Lady Rawlins, as she took the hand outstretched in farewell. For Jonah in large doses was more than the Colonel could stomach.

Indeed, as the door closed behind him she wiped away a tear, whispering to herself: "And to think that I threw over dear Richard in order to marry that—that—yes, I will say it—that horror!"

Meanwhile, as he strolled down the street, beautifully dressed, and still looking very upright and handsome—for he had never lost his figure—the Colonel was saying to himself:

"Silly old woman! Well, I hope that by now she knows the difference between a gentleman and a half-Christianised, money-hunting, wine-bibbing Jew. However, she's got the fortune, which was what she wanted, although she forgets it now, and he's got a lachrymose, stout, old party. But how beautiful she used to be! My word, how beautiful she used to be! To go to see her now is better than any sermon; it is an admirable moral exercise."

To Lady Rawlins also the Colonel's visits proved excellent moral exercises tinged with chastenings. Whenever he went away he left behind him some aphorism or reflection filled with a wholesome bitter. But still she sought his society and, in secret, adored him.

In addition to the club and Lady Rawlins there were the tables at Monte Carlo, with their motley company, which to a man of the world could not fail to be amusing. Besides, the Colonel had one weakness—sometimes he did a little gambling, and when he played he liked to play fairly high. Morris accompanied him once to the "Salles de jeu," and—that was enough. What passed there exactly, could never be got out of him, even by Mary, whose sense of humour was more than satisfied with the little comedies in progress about her, no single point of which did she ever miss.

Only, funny as she might be in her general feebleness, and badly as she might have behaved in some distant past, for Lady Rawlins she felt sorry. Her kind heart told Mary that this unhappy person also possessed a heart, although she was now stout and on the wrong side of middle age. She was aware, too, that the Colonel knew as much, and his scientific pin-pricks and searings of that guileless and unprotected organ struck her as little short of cruel. None the less so, indeed, because the victim at the stake imagined that they were inflicted in kindness by the hand of a still tender and devoted friend.

"I hope that I shan't quarrel with my father-in-law," reflected Mary to herself, after one of the best of these exhibitions; "he's got an uncommonly long memory, and likes to come even. However, I never shall, because he's afraid of me and knows that I see through him."

Mary was right. A very sincere respect for her martial powers when roused ensured perfect peace between her and the Colonel. With his son, however, it was otherwise. Even in this age of the Triumph of the Offspring parents do exist who take advantage of their sons' strict observance of the Fifth Commandment. It is easy to turn a man into a moral bolster and sit upon him if you know that an exaggerated sense of filial duty will prevent him from stuffing himself with pins. So it came about that Morris was sometimes sat upon, especially when the Colonel was suffering from a bad evening at the tables; well out of sight and hearing of Mary, be it understood, who on such occasions was apt to develop a quite formidable temper.

It is over this question of the tables that one of these domestic differences arose which in its results brought about the return of the Monks to Monksland. Upon a certain afternoon the Colonel asked his son to accompany him to Monte Carlo. Morris refused, rather curtly, perhaps.

"Very well," replied the Colonel in his grandest manner. "I am sure I do not wish for an unwilling companion, and doubtless your attention is claimed by affairs more important than the according of your company to a father."

"No," replied Morris, with his accustomed truthfulness; "I am going out sea-fishing, that is all."

"Quite so. Allow me then to wish good luck to your fishing. Does Mary accompany you?"

"No, I think not; she says the boat makes her sick, and she can't bear eels."

"So much the better, as I can ask for the pleasure of her society this afternoon."

"Yes, you can ask," said Morris, suddenly turning angry.

"Do you imply, Morris, that the request will be refused?"

"Certainly, father; if I have anything to do with it."

"And might I inquire why?"

"Because I won't have Mary taken to that place to mix with the people who frequent it."

"I see. This is exclusiveness with a vengeance. Perhaps you consider that those unholy doors should be shut to me also."

"I have no right to express an opinion as to where my father should or should not go; but if you ask me, I think that, under all the circumstances, you would do best to keep away."

"The circumstances! What circumstances?"

"Those of our poverty, which leaves us no money to risk in gambling."

Then the Colonel lost all control of his temper, as sometimes happened to him, and became exceedingly violent and unpleasant. What he said does not matter; let it suffice that the remarks were of a character which even headstrong men are accustomed to reserve for the benefit of their women-folk and other intimate relations.

Attracted by the noise, which was considerable, Mary came in to find her uncle marching up and down the room vituperating Morris, who, with quite a new expression upon his face—a quiet, dogged kind of expression—was leaning upon the mantel-piece and watching him.

"Uncle," began Mary, "would you mind being a little quieter? My father is asleep upstairs, and I am afraid that you will wake him."

"I am sorry, my dear, very sorry, but there are some insults that no man with self-respect can submit to, even from a son."

"Insults! insults!" Mary repeated, opening her blue eyes; then, looking at him with a pained air: "Morris, why do you insult your father?"

"Insult?" he replied. "Then I will tell you how. My father wanted to take you to play with him at Monte Carlo this afternoon and I said that you shouldn't go. That's the insult."

"You observe, my dear," broke in the Colonel, "that already he treats you as one having authority."

"Yes," said Mary, "and why shouldn't he? Now that my father is so weak who am I to obey if not Morris?"

"Oh, well, well," said the Colonel, diplomatically beginning to cool, for he could control his temper when he liked. "Everyone to their taste;

but some matters are so delicate that I prefer not to discuss them," and he looked round for his hat.

By this time, however, the cyclonic condition of things had affected Mary also, and she determined that he should not escape so easily.

"Before you go," she went on in her slow voice, "I should like to say, uncle, that I quite agree with Morris. I don't think those tables are quite the place to take young ladies to, especially if the gentleman with them is much engaged in play."

"Indeed, indeed; then you are both of a mind, which is quite as it should be. Of course, too, upon such matters of conduct and etiquette we must all bow to the taste and the experience of the young—even those of us who have mixed with the world for forty years. Might I ask, my dear Mary, if you have any further word of advice for me before I go?"

"Yes, uncle," replied Mary quite calmly. "I advise you not to lose so much of—of your money, or to sit up so late at night, which, you know, never agrees with you. Also, I wish you wouldn't abuse Morris for nothing, because he doesn't deserve it, and I don't like it; and if we are all to live together after I am married, it will be so much more comfortable if we can come to an understanding first."

Then muttering something beneath his breath about ladies in general and this young lady in particular, the Colonel departed with speed.

Mary sat down in an armchair, and fanned herself with a pocket-handkerchief.

"Thinking of the right thing to say always makes me hot," she remarked.

"Well, if by the right thing you mean the strong thing, you certainly discovered it," replied Morris, looking at her with affectionate admiration.

"I know; but it had to be done, dear. He's losing a lot of money, which is mere waste"—here Morris groaned, but asked no questions—"besides," and her voice became earnest, "I will not have him talking to you like that. The fact that one man is the father of another man doesn't give him the right to abuse him like a pickpocket. Also, if you are so good that you put up with it, I have myself to consider—that is, if we are all to live as a happy family. Do you understand?"

"Perfectly," said Morris. "I daresay you are right, but I hate rows."

"So do I, and that is why I have accepted one or two challenges to single combat quite at the beginning of things. You mark my words, he will be like a lamb at breakfast to-morrow."

"You shouldn't speak disrespectfully of my father; at any rate, to me," suggested the old-fashioned Morris, rather mildly.

"No, dear, and when I have learnt to respect him I promise you that I won't. There, don't be vexed with me; but my uncle Richard makes me cross, and then I scratch. As he said the other day, all women are like cats, you know. When they are young they play, when they get old they use their claws—I quote uncle Richard—and although I am not old yet, I can't help showing the claws. Dad is ill, that is the fact of it, Morris, and it gets upon my nerves."

"I thought he was better, love."

"Yes, he is better; he may live for years; I hope and believe that he will, but it is terribly uncertain. And now, look here, Morris, why don't you go home?"

"Do you want to get rid of me, love?" he asked, looking up.

"No, I don't. You know that, I am sure. But what is the use of your stopping here? There is nothing for you to do, and I feel that you are wasting your time and that you hate it. Tell the truth. Don't you long to be back at Monksland, working at that aerophone?"

"I should be glad to get on with my experiments, but I don't like leaving you," he answered.

"But you had better leave me for a while. It is not comfortable for you idling here, particularly when your father is in this uncertain temper. If all be well, in another couple of months or so we shall come together for good, and be able to make our own arrangements, according to circumstances. Till then, if I were you, I should go home, especially as I find that I can get on with my uncle much better when you are not here."

"Then what is to happen after we marry, and I can't be sent away."

"Who knows? But if we are not comfortable at Monk's Abbey, we can always set up for ourselves—with Dad at Seaview, for instance. He's peaceable enough; besides, he must be looked after; and, to be frank, my uncle hectors him, poor dear."

"I will think it over," said Morris. "And now come for a walk on the beach, and we will forget all these worries."

Next morning the Colonel appeared at breakfast in a perfectly angelic frame of mind, having to all appearance utterly forgotten the "contretemps" of the previous afternoon. Perhaps this was policy, or perhaps the fact of his having won several hundred pounds the night before mollified his mood. At least it had become genial, and he proved a most excellent companion.

"Look here, old fellow," he said to Morris, throwing him a letter across the table; "if you have nothing to do for a week or so, I wish you would save an aged parent a journey and settle up this job with Simpkins."

Morris read the letter. It had to do with the complete reerection of a set of buildings on the Abbey farm, and the putting up of a certain drainage mill. Over this question differences had arisen between the agent Simpkins and the rural authorities, who alleged that the said mill would interfere with an established right of way. Indeed, things had come to such a point that if a lawsuit was to be avoided the presence of a principal was necessary.

"Simpkins is a quarrelsome ass," explained the Colonel, "and somebody will have to smooth those fellows down. Will you go? because if you won't I must, and I don't want to break into the first pleasant holiday I have had for five years—thanks to your kindness, my dear John."

"Certainly I will go, if necessary," answered Morris. "But I thought you told me a few months ago that it was quite impossible to execute those alterations, on account of the expense."

"Yes, yes; but I have consulted with your uncle here, and the matter has been arranged. Hasn't it, John?"

Mr. Porson was seated at the end of the table, and Morris, looking at him, noticed with a shock how old he had suddenly become. His plump, cheerful face had fallen in; the cheeks were quite hollow now; his jaws seemed to protrude, and the skin upon his bald head to be drawn quite tight like the parchment on a drum.

"Of course, of course, Colonel," he answered, lifting his chin from his breast, upon which it was resting, "arranged, quite satisfactorily arranged." Then he looked about rather vacantly, for his mind, it was clear, was far away, and added, "Do you want: I mean, were you talking about the new drainage mill for the salt marshes?" Mary interrupted and explained.

"Yes, yes; how stupid of me! I am afraid I am getting a little deaf, and this air makes me so sleepy in the morning. Now, just tell me again, what is it?"

Mary explained further.

"Morris to go and see about it. Well, why shouldn't he? It doesn't take long to get home nowadays. Not but that we shall be sorry to lose you, my dear boy; or, at least, one of us will be sorry," and he tried to wink in his old jovial fashion, and chuckled feebly.

Mary saw and sighed; while the Colonel shook his head portentously. Nobody could play the part of Job's comforter to greater perfection.

The end of it was that, after a certain space of hesitation, Morris agreed to go. This "menage" at Beaulieu oppressed him, and he hated the place. Besides, Mary, seeing that he was worried, almost insisted on his departure.

"If I want you back I will send for you," she said. "Go to your work, dear; you will be happier."

So he kissed her fondly and went—as he was fated to go.

"Good-bye, my dear son," said Mr. Porson—sometimes he called him his son, now. "I hope that I shall see you again soon, and if I don't, you will be kind to my daughter Mary, won't you? You understand, everybody else is dead—my wife is dead, my boy is dead, and soon I shall be dead. So naturally I think a good deal about her. You will be kind to her, won't you? Good-bye, my son, and don't trouble about money; there's plenty."

VIII

THE SUNK ROCKS AND THE SINGER

Morris arrived home in safety, and speedily settled the question of the drainage mill to the satisfaction of all concerned. But he did not return to Beaulieu. To begin with, although the rural authorities ceased to trouble them, his father was most urgent that he should stay and supervise the putting up of the new farm buildings, and wrote to him nearly every day to this effect. It occurred to his son that under the circumstances he might have come to look after the buildings himself; also, that perhaps he found the villa at Beaulieu more comfortable without his presence; a conjecture in which he was perfectly correct.

Upon the first point, also, letters from Mary soon enlightened him. It appeared that shortly after his departure Sir Jonah, in a violent fit of rage, brought on by drink and a remark of his wife's that had she married Colonel Monk she "would have been a happy woman," burst a small blood-vessel in his head, with the strange result that from a raging animal of a man he had been turned into an amiable and perfectly harmless imbecile. Under so trying a domestic blow, naturally, Mary explained, Colonel Monk felt it to be his duty to support and comfort his old friend to the best of his ability. "This," added Mary, "he does for about three hours every day. I believe, indeed, that a place is always laid for him at meals, while poor Sir Jonah, for whom I feel quite sorry, although he was such a horrid man, sits in an armchair and smiles at him continually."

So Morris determined to take the advice which Mary gave him very plainly, and abandoned all idea of returning to Beaulieu, at any rate, on this side of Christmas. His plans settled, he went to work with a will, and was soon deeply absorbed in the manufacture of experimental receivers made from the new substance. So completely, indeed, did these possess his mind that, as Mary at last complained, his letters to her might with equal fitness have been addressed to an electrical journal, since from them even diagrams were not lacking.

So things went on until the event occurred which was destined profoundly and mysteriously to affect the lives of Morris and his affianced wife. That event was the shipwreck of the steam tramp, Trondhjem, upon the well-known Sunk Rocks outside the Sands which run parallel to the coast at a distance of about five knots from the Monksland cliff. In this year of our story, about the middle of November, the weather set in very mild and misty. It was the third of these "roky" nights, and the sea-fog poured along the land like vapour from an opened jar of chemicals. Morris was experimenting at the forge in his workshop very late—or, rather early, for it was near to two o'clock in the morning—when of a sudden through the open window, rising from the quiet sea beneath, he heard the rattle of oars in rowlocks. Wondering what a boat could be doing so near inshore at a season when there was no night fishing, he went to the window to listen. Presently he caught the sound of voices shouting in a tongue with which he was unacquainted, followed by another sound, that of a boat being beached upon the shingle immediately below the Abbey. Now guessing that something unusual must have happened, Morris took his hat and coat, and, unlocking the Abbot's door, lit a lantern, and descended the cement steps to the beach. Here he found himself in the midst of ten or twelve men, most of them tall and bearded, who were gathered about a ship's boat which they had dragged up high and dry. One of these men, who from his uniform he judged to be the captain, approached and addressed him in a language that he did not understand, but imagined must be Danish or Norwegian.

Morris shook his head to convey the blankness of his ignorance, whereupon other men addressed him, also in northern tongues. Then, as he still shook his head, a lad of about nineteen came forward and spoke in broken and barbarous French.

"Naufrage la bas," he said; "bateau a vapeur, naufrage sur les rochers—brouillard. Nouse echappe."

"Tous?" asked Morris.

The young man shrugged his shoulders as though he were doubtful on the point, then added, pointing to the boat:

"Homme beaucoup blesse, pasteur anglais."

Morris went to the cutter, and, holding up the lantern, looked down, to find an oldish man with sharp features, dark eyes, and grizzled beard, lying under a tarpaulin in the bottom of the boat. He was clothed only in a dressing gown and a blood-stained nightshirt, groaning and semi-unconscious.

"Jambe casse, beaucoup mal casse," explained the French scholar.

"Apportez-le vite apres moi," said Morris. This order having been translated by the youth, several stalwart sailors lifted up the injured man, and, placing the tarpaulin beneath him, took hold of it by the sides and corners. Then, following Morris, they bore him as gently as they could up the steps into the Abbey to a large bedroom upon the first floor, where they laid him upon the bed.

Meanwhile, by the industrious ringing of bells as they went, Morris had succeeded in rousing a groom, a page-boy, and the cook. The first of these he sent off post haste for Dr. Charters. Next, having directed the cook to give the foreign sailormen some food and beer, he told the page-boy to conduct them to the Sailors' Home, a place of refuge provided, as is common upon this stormy coast, for the accommodation of distressed and shipwrecked mariners. As he could extract nothing further, it seemed useless to detain them at the Abbey. Then, pending the arrival of the doctor, with the assistance of the old housekeeper, he set to work to examine the patient. This did not take long, for his injuries were obvious. The right thigh was broken and badly bruised, and he bled from a contusion upon the forehead. This wound upon his head seemed also to have affected his brain; at any rate, he was unable to speak coherently or to do more than mutter something about "shipwreck" and "steamer Trondhjem," and to ask for water.

Thinking that at least it could do no harm, Morris gave him a cup of soup, which had been hastily prepared. Just as the patient finished drinking it, which he did eagerly, the doctor arrived, and after a swift examination administered some anaesthetic, and got to work to set the broken limb.

"It's a bad smash—very bad," he explained to Morris; "something must have fallen on him, I think. If it had been an inch or two higher, he'd have lost his leg, or his life, or both, as perhaps he will now. At the best it means a couple of months or so on his back. No, I think the cut on his head isn't serious, although it has knocked him silly for a while."

At length the horrid work was done, and the doctor, who had to return to a confinement case in the village, departed. Before he went he told Morris that he hoped to be back by five o'clock. He promised also that before his return he would call in at the Sailor's Home to see that the crew were comfortable, and discover what he could of the details of the catastrophe. Meanwhile for his part, Morris undertook to watch in the sick-room.

For nearly three hours, while the drug retained his grip of him, the

H. RIDER HAGGARD

patient remained comatose. All this while Morris sat at his bedside wondering who he might be, and what curious circumstance could have brought him into the company of these rough Northmen sailors. To his profession he had a clue, although no sure one, for round his neck the man wore a silver cross suspended by a chain. This suggested that he might be a clergyman, and went far to confirm the broken talk of the French-speaking sailor. Clearly, also, he was a person of some breeding and position, the refinement of his face and the delicacy of his hands showed as much. While Morris was watching and wondering, suddenly the man awoke, and began to talk in a confused fashion.

"Where am I?" he asked.

"At Monksland," answered Morris.

"That's all right, that's where I should be, but the ship, the ship"—then a pause and a cry: "Stella, Stella!"

Morris pricked his ears. "Where is Stella?" he asked.

"On the rocks. She struck, then darkness, all darkness. Stella, come here, Stella!"

A memory awoke in the mind of Morris, and he leant over the patient, who again had sunk into delirium.

"Do you mean Stella Fregelius?" he asked.

The man turned his flushed face and opened his dark eyes.

"Of course, Stella Fregelius—who else? There is only one Stella," and again he became incoherent.

For a while Morris plied him with further questions; but as he could obtain no coherent answer, he gave him his medicine and left him quiet. Then for another half-hour or so he sat and watched, while a certain theory took shape in his mind. This gentleman must be the new rector. It seemed as though, probably accompanied by his daughter, he had taken passage in a Danish tramp boat bound for Northwold, which had touched at some Northumbrian port. Morris knew that the incoming clergyman had a daughter, for, now that he thought of it, he had heard Mr. Tomley mention the fact at the dinner-party on the night when he became engaged. Yes, and certainly she was named Stella. But there was no woman among those who had come to land, and he understood the injured man to suggest that his daughter had been left upon the steamer which was said to have gone ashore upon some rocks; or, perhaps, upon the Sunk Rocks themselves.

Now, the only rocks within twenty miles of them were these famous Sunk Rocks, about six knots away. Even within his own lifetime four vessels had been lost there, either because they had missed, or mistaken, the lightship signal further out to sea, as sometimes happened in a fog such as prevailed this night, or through false reckonings. The fate of all these vessels had been identical; they had struck upon the reef, rebounded or slid off, and foundered in deep water. Probably in this case the same thing had happened. At least, the facts, so far as he knew them, pointed to that conclusion. Evidently the escape of the crew had been very hurried, for they had saved nothing. He judged also that the clergyman, Mr. Fregelius, having rushed on deck, had been injured by the fall of some spar or block consequent upon the violence of the impact of the vessel upon the reef, and in this hurt condition had been thrown into the boat by the sailors.

Then where was the daughter Stella? Was she killed in the same fashion or drowned? Probably one or the other. But there was a third bare possibility, which did no credit to the crew, that she had been forgotten in the panic and hurry, and left behind on the sinking ship.

At first Morris thought of rousing the captain of the lifeboat. On reflection, however, he abandoned this idea, for really what had he to go on beyond the scanty and disjointed ravings of a delirious man? Very possibly the girl Stella was not upon the ship at all. Probably, also, hours ago that vessel had vanished from the eyes of men for ever. To send out the lifeboat upon such a wild-goose chase would be to turn himself into a laughing-stock.

Still something drew his thoughts to that hidden line of reef, and the ship which might still be hanging on it, and the woman who might still be living in the ship.

It was a painful vision from which he could not free his mind.

Then there came to him an idea. Why should he not go to the Sunk Rocks and look? There was a light breeze off land, and with the help of the page-boy, who was sitting up, as the tide was nearing its full he could manage to launch his small sailing-boat, which by good fortune was still berthed near the beach steps. It was a curious chance that this should be so, seeing that in most seasons she would have been by now removed to the shed a mile away, to be out of reach of possible damage from the furious winter gales. As it happened, however, the weather remaining so open, this had not been done. Further, the codlings having begun to run in unusual numbers, as is common upon this coast in late autumn, Morris that very morning had taken the boat out to fish for them, an amusement which he proposed to resume on the morrow in the hope of better sport. Therefore the boat had her sails on board, and was in every way ready for sea.

Why should he not go? For one reason only that he could suggest. There was a certain amount of risk in sailing about the Sunk Rocks in a fog, even for a tiny craft like his, for here the currents were very sharp; also, in many places the points of the rocks were only just beneath the surface of the water. But he knew the dangerous places well enough if he could see them, as he ought to be able to do, for the dawn should break before he arrived. And, after all, what was a risk more or less in life? He would go. He felt impelled—strangely impelled—to go, though of course it was all nonsense, and probably he would be back by nine o'clock, having seen nothing at all.

By this time the injured Mr. Fregelius had sunk into sleep or stupor, doubtless beneath the influence of the second draught which he had administered to him in obedience to the doctor's orders. On his account, therefore, Morris had no anxiety, since the cook, a steady, middle-aged woman, could watch by him for the present.

He called her and gave her instructions, bidding her tell the doctor when he came that he had gone to see if he could make out anything more about the wreck, and that he would be back soon. Then, ordering the page-boy, a stout lad, to accompany him, he descended the steps, and together, with some difficulty, they succeeded in launching the boat. Now for a moment Morris hesitated, wondering whether he should take the young man with him; but remembering that this journey was not without its dangers, finally he decided to go alone.

"I am just going to have a sail round, Thomas, to look if I can make out anything about that ship."

"Yes, sir," remarked Thomas, doubtfully. "But it is rather a queer time to hunt for her, and in this sea-haze too, especially round the Sunk Rocks. Shall I leave the lunch basket in the locker, sir, or take it up to the house?"

"Leave it; it wasn't touched to-day, and I might be glad of some breakfast," Morris answered. Then, having hoisted his sail, he sat himself in the stern, with the tiller in one hand and the sheet in the other. Instantly the water began to lap gently against the bow, and in another minute he glided away from the sight of the doubting Thomas, vanishing like some sea-ghost into the haze and that chill darkness which precedes the dawn.

It was very dark, and the mist was very damp, and the wind, what there was of it, very cold, especially as in his hurry he had forgotten to bring a thick ulster, and had nothing but a covert coat and a thin oil-skin to wear. Moreover, he could not see in the least where he was going, or do more than lay his course for the Sunk Rocks by means of the boat's compass, which he consulted from time to time by the help of a bull's-eye lantern.

This went on for nearly an hour, by the end of which Morris began to wonder why he had started upon such a fool's errand. Also, he was growing alarmed. He knew that by now he should be in the neighbourhood of the reef, and fancied, indeed, that he could hear the water lapping against its rocks. Accordingly, as this reef was ill company in the dark, Morris hauled down his sail, and in case he should have reached the shallows, threw out his little anchor, which was attached to six fathoms of chain. At first it swung loose, but four or five minutes later, the boat having been carried onward into fleeter water by the swift current that was one of the terrors of the Sunk Rocks, it touched bottom, dragged a little, and held fast.

Morris gave a sigh of relief, for that blind journey among unknown dangers was neither safe nor pleasant. Now, at least, in this quiet weather he could lie where he was till light came, praying that a wind might not come first. Already the cold November dawn was breaking in the east; he was able to see the reflection of it upon the fog, and the surface of the water, black and oily-looking, became visible as it swept past the sides of his boat. Now, too, he was sure that the rocks must be close at hand, for he could hear the running tide distinctly as it washed against them and through the dense growth of seaweed that clung to their crests and ridges.

Presently, too, he heard something else, which at first caused him to rub his eyes in the belief that he must have fallen asleep and dreamt; nothing less, indeed, than the sound of a woman's voice. He began to reason with himself. What was there strange in this? He was told, or had inferred, that a woman had been left upon a ship. Doubtless this was she, upon some rock or raft, perhaps. Only then she would have been crying for help, and this voice was singing, and in a strange tongue, more sweetly than he had heard woman sing before.

It was incredible, it was impossible. What woman would sing in a winter daybreak upon the Sunk Rocks—sing like the siren of old fable? Yet, there, quite close to him, over the quiet sea rose the song, strong, clear, and thrilling. Once it ceased, then began again in a deeper, more triumphant note, such as a Valkyrie might have sung as she led some Norn-doomed host to their last battle.

Morris sat and listened with parted lips and eyes staring at the fleecy mist. He did not move or call out, because he was certain that he must be the victim of some hallucination, bred of fog, or of fatigue, or of cold; and, as it was very strange and moving, he had no desire to break in upon its charm.

So there he sat while the triumphant, splendid song rolled and thrilled above him, and by degrees the grey light of morning grew to right and left. To right and left it grew, but, strangely enough, although he never noted it at the time, he and his boat lay steeped in shadow. Then of a sudden there was a change.

A puff of wind from the north seemed to catch the fog and roll it up like a curtain, so that instantly all the sea became visible, broken here and there by round-headed, weed-draped rocks. Out of the east also poured a flood of light from the huge ball of the rising sun, and now it was that Morris learned why the gloom had been so thick about him, for his boat lay anchored full in the shadow of the lost ship Trondhjem. There, not thirty yards away, rose her great prow; the cutwater, which stood up almost clear, showing that she had forced herself on to a ridge of rock. There, too, poised at the extreme point of the sloping forecastle, and supporting herself with one hand by a wire rope that ran thence to the foremast, was the woman to whose siren-like song he had been listening.

At that distance he could see little of her face; but the new-wakened wind blew the long dark hair about her head, while round her, falling almost to her naked feet, was wrapped a full red cloak. Had Morris wished to draw the picture of a Viking's daughter guiding her father's ship into the fray, there, down to the red cloak, bare feet, and flying tresses, stood its perfect model.

The wild scene gripped his heart. Whoever saw the like of it? This girl who sang in the teeth of death, the desolate grey face of ocean, the brown and hungry rocks, the huge, abandoned ship, and over all the angry rays of a winter sunrise.

Thus, out of the darkness of the winter night, out of the bewildering white mists of the morning, did this woman arise upon his sight, this strange new star begin to shine upon his life and direct his destiny.

At the moment that he saw her she seemed to see him. At any rate, she ceased her ringing, defiant song, and, leaning over the netting rail, stared downwards.

Morris began to haul at his anchor; but, though he was a strong man, at first he could not lift it. Just as he was thinking of slipping the cable, however, the little flukes came loose from the sand or weeds in which they were embedded, and with toil and trouble he got it shipped. Then he took a pair of sculls and rowed until he was nearly under the prow of the Trondhjem. It was he, too, who spoke first.

"You must come to me," he called.

"Yes," the woman answered, leaning over the rail; "I will come, but how? Shall I jump into the water?"

"No," he said, "it is too dangerous. You might strike against a rock or be taken by the current. The companion ladder seems to be down on the starboard side. Go aft to it, I will row round the ship and meet you there."

She nodded her head, and Morris started on his journey. It proved perilous. To begin with, there were rocks all about. Also, here the tide or the current, or both, ran with the speed of a mill-race, so that in places the sea bubbled and swirled like a boiling kettle. However skilled and strong he might be, it was hard for one man to deal with such difficulties and escape disaster. Still following the port side of the ship, since owing to the presence of certain rocks he dared not attempt the direct starboard passage, he came at last to her stern. Then he saw how imminent was the danger, for the poop of the vessel, which seemed to be of about a thousand tons burden, was awash and water-logged, but rolling and lifting beneath the pressure of the tide as it drew on to flood.

To Morris, who had lived all his life by the sea, and understood such matters, it was plain that presently she would float, or be torn off the point of the rock on which she hung, broken-backed, and sink in the hundred-fathom-deep water which lay beyond the reef. There was no time to spare, and he laboured at his oars fiercely, till at length, partly by skill and partly by good fortune, he reached the companion ladder and fastened to it with a boat-hook.

Now no woman was to be seen; she had vanished. Morris called and called, but could get no answer, while the great dead carcass of the ship rolled and laboured above, its towering mass of iron threatening to fall and crush him and his tiny craft to nothingness. He shouted and shouted again; then in despair lashed his boat to the companion, and ran up the ladder.

Where could she have gone? He hurried forward along the heaving, jerking deck to the main hatchway. Here he hesitated for a moment;

then, knowing that, if anywhere, she must be below, set his teeth and descended. The saloon was a foot deep in water, which washed from side to side with a heavy, sickening splash, and there, carrying a bag in one hand, holding up her garments with the other, and wading towards him from the dry upper part of the cabin, at last he found the lady whom he sought.

"Be quick!" he shouted; "for God's sake, be quick! The ship is coming off the rock."

She splashed towards him; now he had her by the hand; now they were on the deck, and now he was dragging her after him down the companion ladder. They reached the boat, and just as the ship gave a great roll towards them, Morris seized the oars and rowed like a madman.

"Help me!" he gasped; "the current is against us." And, sitting opposite to him, she placed her hands upon his hands, pressing forward as he pulled. Her slight strength made a difference, and the boat forged ahead—thirty, forty, seventy yards—till they reached a rock to which, exhausted, he grappled with a hook, bidding her hold on to the floating seaweed. Thus they rested for thirty seconds, perhaps, when she spoke for the first time:

"Look!" she said.

As she spoke the steamer slid and lifted off the reef. For a few moments she wallowed; then suddenly her stern settled, her prow rose slowly in the air till it stood up straight, fifty or sixty feet of it. Then, with a majestic, but hideous rush, down went the Trondhjem and vanished for ever.

All round about her the sea boiled and foamed, while in the great hollow which she made on the face of the waters black lumps of wreckage appeared and disappeared.

"Tight! hold tight!" he cried, "or she will suck us after her."

Suck she did, till the water poured over the gunwale. Then, the worst passed, and the boat rose again. The foam bubbles burst or floated away in little snowy heaps; the sea resumed its level, and, save for the floating debris, became as it had been for thousands of years before the lost Trondhjem rushed downward to its depths.

Now, for the first time, knowing the immediate peril past, Morris looked at the face of his companion. It was a fine face, and beautiful in its way. Dark eyes, very large and perfect, whereof the pupils seemed to expand and contract in answer to every impulse of the thoughts within. Above the eyes long curving lashes and delicately pencilled, arched eyebrows, and above them again a forehead low and broad. The chin rounded; the lips full, rich, and sensitive; the complexion of a clear and beautiful pallor; the ears tiny; the hands delicate; the figure slim, of medium height, and alive with grace; the general effect most uncommon, and, without being lovely, breathing a curious power and personality.

Such was the woman whom he had saved from death.

"Oh, how splendid!" she said in her deep voice, and clasping her hands. "What a death! For ship or man, what a death! And after it the great calm sea, taking and ready to take for ever."

"Thank Heaven that it did not take you," answered Morris wrathfully.

"Why?" she answered.

"Because you are still alive, who by now would have been dead."

"It seems that it was not fated this time," she answered, adding: "The next it may be different."

"Yes," he said reflectively; "the next it may be different, Miss Fregelius."

She started. "How do you know my name?" she asked.

"From your father's lips. He is ashore at my house. The sailors must have seen the light in my workshop and steered for it."

"My father?" she gasped. "He is still alive? But, oh, how is that possible? He would never have left me."

"Yes, he lives, but with a broken thigh and his head cut open. He was brought ashore senseless, so you need not be ashamed of him. Those sailors are the cowards."

She sighed, as though in deep relief. "I am very glad. I had made up my mind that he must be dead, for of course I knew that he would never have left me otherwise. It did not occur to me that he might be carried away senseless. Is he—" and she paused, then added: "tell me the worst—quick."

"No; the doctor thinks in no danger at present; only a break of the thigh and a scalp wound. Of course, he could not help himself, for he can have known no more than a corpse of what was passing," he went on. "It is those sailors who are to blame—for leaving you on the ship, I mean."

She shrugged her shoulders contemptuously.

"The sailors! From such rough men one does not expect much. They had little time, and thought of themselves, not of a passenger, whom they had scarcely seen. Thank God they did not leave my father behind also."

"You do not thank God for yourself," said Morris curiously, as he prepared to hoist the sail, for his mind harked back to his old wonderment.

"Yes, I do, but it was not His will that I should die last night. I have told you that it was not fated," she answered.

"Quite so. That is evident now; but were I in your case this really remarkable escape would make me wonder what is fated."

"Yes, it does a little; but not too much, for you see I shall learn in time. You might as well wonder how it happened that you arrived to save me, and to what end."

Morris hesitated, for this was a new view of the case, before he answered.

"That your life should be saved, I suppose."

"And why should it happen that your boat should come to save me?"

"I don't know; chance, I suppose."

"Neither do I; but I don't believe in chance. Everything has its meaning and purpose."

"Only one so seldom finds it out. Life is too short, I suppose," replied Morris.

By now the sail was up, the boat was drawing ahead, and he was seated at her side holding the tiller.

"Why did you go down into the saloon, Miss Fregelius?" he asked presently.

She glanced at herself, and now, for the first time, he noticed that she wore a dress beneath her red cloak, and that there were slippers on her feet, which had been bare.

"I could not come into the boat as I was," she explained, dropping her eyes. "The costume which is good enough to be drowned in is not fitted for company. My cabin was well forward, and I guessed that by wading I could reach it. Also, I had some trinkets and one or two books I did not wish to lose," and she nodded at the hand-bag which she had thrown into the boat.

Morris smiled. "It is very nice of you to pay so much respect to appearances," he said; "but I suppose you forgot that the vessel might come off the rocks at any moment and crush me, who was waiting."

"Oh, no," she answered; "I thought of it. I have always been accustomed to the sea, and know about such things."

"And still you went for your dress and your trinkets?"

"Yes, because I was certain that it wouldn't happen and that no harm would come to either of us by waiting a few minutes."

"Indeed, and who told you that?"

"I don't know, but from the moment that I saw you in the boat I was certain that the danger was done with—at least, the immediate danger," she added.

IX

Miss Fregelius

While Miss Fregelius was speaking, Morris had been staring at the sail, which, after drawing for a time in an indifferent fashion, had begun to flap aimlessly.

"What is the matter?" asked his companion. "Has the wind veered again?"

He nodded. "Dead from the west, now, and rising fast. I hope that your spirit of prophecy still speaks smooth things, for, upon my word, I believe we are both of us in a worse mess than ever."

"Can't we row ashore? It is only a few miles, is it?"

"We can try, but I am afraid we are in for a regular tearer. We get them sometimes on this coast after a spell of calm weather."

"Please give me an oar," she said. "I am used to rowing—of a sort."

So he let down the sail, and they began to row. For ten minutes or so they struggled against the ever-rising gale. Then Morris called to her to ship oars.

"It is no use exhausting ourselves, Miss Fregelius," he said, "for now the tide is on the ebb, and dead against us, as well as the wind."

"What are you going to do?" she asked.

Morris glanced back to where a mile behind them the sea was beginning to foam ominously over the Sunk Rocks, here and there throwing up isolated jets of spray, like those caused by the blowing of a whale.

"I am going to try to clear them," he said, "and then run before it. Perhaps we might make the Far Lightship five and twenty miles away. Help me to pull up the sail. So, that's enough; she can't stand too much. Now hold the sheet, and if I bid you, let go that instant. I'll steer."

A few seconds later the boat's head had come round, and she was rushing through the water at great speed, parallel with the line of the Sunk Rocks, but being momentarily driven nearer to them. The girl, Stella Fregelius, stared at the farthest point of foam which marked the end of the reef.

"You must hold her up if you want to clear it," she said quietly.

"I can't do any more in this wind," he answered. "You seem to know about boats; you will understand."

She nodded, and on they rushed, the ever-freshening gale on their beam.

"This boat sails well," said Stella, as a little water trickled over the gunwale.

Morris made no answer, his eyes were fixed upon the point of rock; only bidding his companion hold the tiller, he did something to the sail. Now they were not more than five hundred yards away.

"It will be a very near thing," she said.

"Very," he answered, "and I don't want to be officious, but I suggest that you might do well to say your prayers."

She looked at him, and bowed her head for a minute or so. Then suddenly she lifted it again and stared at the terror ahead of them with wide, unflinching eyes.

On sped the boat while more and more did tide and gale turn her prow into the reef. At the end of it a large, humpbacked rock showed now and again through the surf, like the fin of a black whale. That was the rock which they must clear if they would live. Morris took the boat-hook and laid it by his side. They were very near now. They would clear it; no, the wash sucked them in like a magnet.

"Good-bye," said Morris instinctively, but Stella answered nothing.

The wave that lifted them broke upon the rock in a cloud of spray wherein for some few instants their boat seemed to vanish. They were against it; the boat touched, and Stella felt a long ribbon of seaweed cut her like a whip across the face. Kneeling down, Morris thrust madly with the boat-hook, and thus for an instant—just one—held her off. His arms doubled beneath the strain, and then came the back-wash.

Oh, heaven! it had swept them clear. The rock was behind, the sail drew, and swiftly they fled away from the death that had seemed certain.

Stella sighed aloud, while Morris wiped the water from his face.

"Are we clear?" she asked presently.

"Of the Sunk Rocks? Yes, we are round them. But the North Sea is in front of us, and what looks like the worst gale that has blown this autumn is rising behind."

"This is a good sea-boat, and on the open water I think perhaps that we ought to weather it," she said, trying to speak cheerfully, as Morris stowed the sail, for in that wind they wanted no canvas.

"I wish we had something to eat," she added presently; "I am so hungry."

"By good luck I can help you there," he answered. "Yesterday I was out fishing and took lunch for myself and the boatman; but the fish wouldn't bite, so we came back without eating it, and it is still in the locker. Shift a little, please, I will get the basket."

She obeyed, and there was the food sure enough, plenty of it. A thick packet of sandwiches, and two boiled eggs, a loaf, and a large lump of cheese for the boatman, a flask of whiskey, a bottle of beer, another of water, and two of soda. They ate up the sandwiches and the eggs, Morris drinking the beer and Stella the soda water, for whiskey as yet she would not touch.

"Now," she said, "we are still provisioned for twenty-four hours with the bread and cheese, the water and the soda which is left."

"Yes," he answered, "if we don't sink or die of cold we shall not starve. I never thought that sandwiches were so good before;" and he looked hungrily at the loaf.

"You had better put it away; you may want it later," she suggested. And he put it away.

"Tell me, if you don't mind," he asked, for the food and the lightening of the strain upon his nerves had made him conversational, "what is that song which you sang upon the ship, and why did you sing it?"

She coloured a little, and smiled, a sweet smile that seemed to begin in her eyes.

"It is an old Norse chant which my mother taught me; she was a Dane, as my father is also by descent. It has come down in her family for many, many generations, and the legend is that the women of her race always sang it or repeated it while the men were fighting, and, if they had the strength, in the hour of their own death. I believe that is true, for she died whispering it herself; yes, it grew fainter and fainter until it ceased with her breath. So, when I thought that my hour had come, I sang it also, for the first time, for I tried to be brave, and wished to go as my forefathers went. It is a foolish old custom, but I like old customs. I am ashamed that you should have heard it. I thought myself alone. That is all."

"You are a very strange young lady," said Morris, staring at her.

"Strange?" she answered, laughing. "Not at all; only I wanted to show those scores of dead people that their traditions and spirit still lived on in me, their poor modern child. Think how glad they must have been to hear the old chant as they swept by in the wind just now, waiting to give me welcome."

Morris stared still harder. Was this beautiful girl mad? He knew something of the old Norse literature and myths. A fantastic vision rose up in his mind of her forebears, scores and hundreds of them gathered at some ghostly Walhalla feast, listening to the familiar paean as it poured from her fearless heart, and waiting to rise and greet her, the last newcomer of their blood, with "*Skoll*, daughter, *skoll!*"

She watched him as though she read his thought.

"You see, they would have been pleased; it is only natural," she said; "and I have a great respect for the opinion of my ancestors."

"Then you are sure they still exist in some shape or form, and are conscious?"

She laughed again. "Of course I am sure. The world of spirits, as I think, is the real world. The rest is a nightmare; at least, it seems like a nightmare, because we don't know the beginning or the end of the dream."

"The old Egyptians thought something like that," said Morris reflectively. "They only lived to die."

"But we," she answered, "should only die to live, and that is why I try not to be afraid. I daresay, however, I mean the same as they did, only you do not seem to have put their thought quite clearly."

"You are right; I meant that for them death was but a door."

"That is better, I think," she said. "That was their thought, and that is my thought; and," she added, searching his face, "perhaps your thought also."

"Yes," he answered, "though somehow you concentrate it; I have never seen things, or, rather, this thing, quite so sharply."

"Because you have never been in a position to see them; they have not been brought home to you. Or your mind may have wanted an interpreter. Perhaps I am that interpreter—for the moment." Then she added: "Were you afraid just now? Don't tell me if you had rather not, only I should like to compare sensations. I was—more than on the ship. I admit it."

"No," he answered; "I suppose that I was too excited."

"What were you thinking of when we bumped against the rocks?" she asked again.

"Well, now that you mention it," he replied, rubbing his forehead with his left hand like a man newly awakened, "I could think of nothing but that song of yours, which you sang upon the vessel. Everything grew dark for an instant, and through the darkness I remembered the song."

"Are you married?" she asked, as though speaking to herself.

"No; I am engaged."

"Then, why—" and she stopped, confused.

Morris guessed what had been in her mind, and of a sudden felt terribly ashamed.

"Because of that witch-song of yours," he answered, with a flash of anger, "which made me forget everything."

She smiled and answered. "It wasn't the song; it was the excitement and struggle which blotted out the rest. One does not really think at all at such moments, or so I believe. I know that I didn't, not just when we bumped against the rock. But it is odd that you should believe that you remembered my song, for, according to tradition, that is just what the chant should do, and what it always did. Its ancient name means 'The Over-Lord,' because those who sang it and those who heard it were said to remember nothing else, and to fear nothing, not even Death our lord. It is the welcome that they give to death."

"What egregious nonsense!" he blurted out.

"I daresay; but then, why do you understand my nonsense so well? Tell me, if you will, of what blood are you?"

"Danish, I believe, in the beginning."

"Oh," she said, laughing, "no doubt that accounts for it. Some forefather of yours may have heard the song of the Over-Lord, perhaps from the lips of some foremother of mine. So, of course, you remembered and understood."

"Such a thing will scarcely bear argument, will it?"

"Of course it won't. I have only been joking all the time, though I do half believe in this old song, as my ancestors did before me. I mean, that as I thought I had to die, I liked to keep up the ancient custom and sing it first. It encouraged my spirits. But where are we going?"

"To where our spirits will need no more encouragement," he answered grimly; "or, at least, I fear it may be so. Miss Fregelius, to drop jests, it is blowing very hard off land; the sea is getting up, and this is but a small boat. We are doing pretty well now, but sooner or later, I fear, and I think it right to tell you, that a wave may poop us and then—"

"There will be an end," said Stella. "Is there anything to be done? Have you any plan?"

"None, except to make the Far Lightship, as I told you; but even if we succeed, I don't know whether it will be possible to get aboard of her unless the sea moderates."

"Won't the lifeboat come out to look for you?" she asked.

He shook his head. "How could they find one tiny sail upon the great ocean? Moreover, it will be supposed either that I have foundered or made some port along the coast. There is the worst of it. I fear that it may be telegraphed everywhere," and he sighed deeply.

"Why?" she asked. "Are you a very important person that they should bother to do that? You see," she added in explanation, "I don't even know your name or where you come from, only that you told me you worked in a shop which," she added reflectively, looking at him, "seems odd."

Even then and there Morris could not help a smile; really this young lady was very original.

"No," he answered, "I am not at all important, and I work in a shop because I am an inventor—or try to be—in the electrical line. My name is Morris Monk, and I am the son of Colonel Monk, and live at the Abbey House, Monksland. Now you know all about me."

"Oh! of course I do, Mr. Monk," she said in some confusion, "how foolish of me not to guess. You are my father's principal new parishioner, of whom Mr. Tomley gave us a full description."

"Did he indeed? What did he say?" he asked idly.

"Do you really want to know, Mr. Monk?"

"Yes, if it is amusing. Just now I shall be grateful for anything that can divert my thoughts."

"And you will promise not to bear malice against Mr. Tomley?"

"Certainly, especially as he has gone away, and I don't expect to see him any more."

"Well, he described your father, Colonel Monk, as a handsome and distinguished elderly gentleman of very good birth, and manners, too, when he chose, who intensely disliked growing old. He said that he thought of himself more than of anybody else in the world, and next of the welfare of his family, and that if we wished to get on with him we must be careful not to offend his dignity, as then he would be quarrelsome."

"That's true enough, or most of it," answered Morris, "a good picture of my father's weak side. And what was his definition of myself?"

"He said that you were in his opinion one of the most interesting people that he had ever met; that you were a dreamer and a mystic; that you cared for few of the things which usually attract young men, and that you were in practice almost a misogynist. He added that, although heretofore you had not succeeded, he thought that you possessed real genius in certain lines, but that you had not your father's 'courtly air,' that was his term. Of course, I am only repeating, so you must not be angry."

"Well," said Morris, "I asked for candour and I have got it. Without admitting the accuracy of his definitions, I must say that I never thought that pompous old Tomley had so much observation." Then he added quickly, to change the subject, since the possible discussion of his own attributes, physical or mental, alarmed him, "Miss Fregelius, you have not told me how you came to be left aboard the ship."

"Really, Mr. Monk, I don't know. I heard a confused noise in my sleep, and when I woke up it was to find myself alone, and the saloon half full of water. I suppose that after the vessel struck, the sailors, thinking that she was going down, got off at once, taking my father, who had been injured and made insensible in some way, with them as he happened to be on deck, leaving me to my chance. You know, we were the only passengers."

"Were you not frightened when you found yourself all alone like that?"

"Yes, at first, dreadfully; then I was so distressed about my father, whom I thought dead, and angry with them for deserting me, that I forgot to be frightened, and afterwards—well, I was too proud. Besides, we must die alone, every one of us, so we may as well get accustomed to the idea."

Morris shrugged his shoulders impatiently.

"You think that I need not talk so much about our mortal end. Well, perhaps under all the circumstances, we may as well keep our thoughts on this world—while it lasts. You have not told me, Mr. Monk, how you came to be sailing about alone this morning. Did you come out to look at the wreck?"

"Do you think that I am mad?" he asked, not without indignation. "Should I make a journey at night, in a November fog, with every chance of a gale coming up, to the Sunk Rocks in this cockle-shell, and alone, merely to look at the place where, as I understood rather vaguely, a foreign tramp steamer had gone down?"

"Well, it does seem rather odd. But why else did you come? Were you fishing? Men will risk a great deal for fishing, I know, I have seen that in Norway."

"Why do you pretend not to understand, Miss Fregelius? You must know perfectly well that I came to look for you."

"Indeed," she answered candidly, "I knew nothing of the sort. How did you find out that I was still on the ship, or that the ship was still above water? And even if you knew both, why should you risk your life just on the faint chance of rescuing a girl whom you never saw?"

"I can't quite tell you; but your father in his delirium muttered some words which made me suspect the truth, and a sailor who could speak a little bad French said that the Trondhjem was lost upon some rocks. Well, these are the only rocks about here; and as the whole story was too vague to carry to the lifeboat people I thought that I would come to look. So you see it is perfectly simple."

"So simple, Mr. Monk, that I do not understand it in the least. You must have known the risks, for you asked no one to share them—the risks that are so near and real;" and, shivering visibly, she looked at the grey combers seething past them, and the wind-torn horizon beyond. "Yet, you—you who have ties, faced all this on the chance of saving a stranger."

"Please, please," broke in Morris. "At any rate, you see, it was a happy inspiration."

"Yes, for me, perhaps—but for you! Oh, if it should end in your being taken away from the world before your time, from the world and the lady who—what then?"

Morris winced; then he said: "God's will be done. But although we may be in danger, we are not dead yet; not by a long way."

"She would hate me whose evil fortune it was to draw you to death, and in life or out of it I should never forgive myself—never! never!" and she covered her eyes with her cold, wet hand and sighed.

"Why should you grieve over what you cannot help?" asked Morris gently.

"I cannot quite explain to you," she answered; "but the thought of it seems so sad."

X

Dawn and the Land

A day, a whole day, spent upon that sullen, sunless waste of water, with the great waves bearing them onwards in one eternal, monotonous procession, till at length they grew dizzy with looking at them, and the ceaseless gale piping in their ears. Long ago they had lost sight of land; even the tall church towers built by our ancestors as beacons on this stormy coast had vanished utterly. Twice they sighted ships scudding along under their few rags of canvas, and once a steamer passed, the smoke from her funnels blowing out like long black pennons. But all of these were too far off, or too much engaged with their own affairs to see the little craft tossing hither and thither like a used-up herring basket upon the endless area of ocean.

Fortunately, from his youth Morris had been accustomed to the management of boats in all sorts of weather, the occupation of sailing alone upon the waters being one well suited to his solitary and reflective disposition. Thus it came about that they survived, when others, less skilful, might have drowned. Sometimes they ran before the seas; sometimes they got up a few square feet of sail, and, taking advantage of a veer in the wind, tried to tack, and once, when it blew its hardest, fearing lest they should be pooped, for over an hour they contrived to keep head on to the waves.

Thus, diversified by some necessary bailing, passed the short November day, long enough for them, till once more the darkness began to gather. They had still some food and drink left; indeed, had it not been for these they would have perished. Most happily, also, with the sun the wind dropped, although for hours the sea remained dangerously high. Now wet and cold were their enemies, worse than any that they had been called upon to face. Long ago the driving spray had soaked them to the skin, and there upon the sea the winter night was very chill.

While the wind, fortunately for them, by comparison a warm one, still blew from the west, and the sea remained tempestuous, they found some shelter by wrapping themselves in a corner of the sail. Towards midnight, however, it got round to the northeast, enough of it to moderate the sea considerably, and to enable them to put the boat about and go before it with a closely reefed sail. Now, indeed, they were bitterly cold, and longed even for the shelter of the wet canvas. Still Morris felt, and Stella was of the same mind, that before utter exhaustion overtook them their best chance for life lay in trying to make the shore, which was, they knew not how far away.

There, then, for hours they cowered in the stern of the boat, huddled together to protect themselves as best they might from the weather, and plunging forward beneath their little stretch of sail. Sleep they could not, for that icy breath bit into their marrow, and of this Morris was glad, since he did not dare relax his watch for an instant. So sometimes they sat silent, and sometimes by fits and starts they talked, their lips close to each other's face, as though they were whispering to one another.

To while away the weary time, Morris told his companion about his invention, the aerophone. Then she in turn told him something of her previous life—Stella was now a woman of four and twenty. It seemed that her mother had died when she was fourteen at the rectory in Northumberland, where she was born. After that, with short intervals, she had spent five years in Denmark, whither her father came to visit her every summer. Most of this time she passed at a school in Copenhagen, going for her holidays to stay with her grandmother, who was the widow of a small landowner of noble family, and lived in an ancient, dilapidated house in some remote village. At length the grandmother died, leaving to Stella the trifle she possessed, after which, her education being completed, she returned to Northumberland to keep house for her father. Here, too, it would seem that her life was very lonely, for the place was but an unvisited coast village, and they were not rich enough to mix much with the few county families who lived anywhere within reach.

"Have you no brothers or sisters?" asked Morris.

Even then, numb as was her flesh with cold, he felt her wince at the question.

"No, no," she answered, "none now—at least, none here. I have—I mean I had—a sister, my twin, but she died when we were seventeen. This was the most dreadful thing that ever happened to me, the thing which made me what I am."

"I don't quite understand. What are you, then?"

"Oh, something very unsatisfactory, I am afraid, quite different from other people. What Mr. Tomley said *you* were, Mr. Monk, a mystic and a dreamer of dreams; a lover of the dead; one who dwells in the past, and—in the future."

Morris did not pursue the subject; even under their strange circumstances, favourable as they were to intimacy and confidences, it seemed impertinent to him to pry into the mysteries of his companion's life. Only he asked, at hazard almost:

"How did you spend your time up there in Northumberland?"

"In drawing a little, in collecting eggs, moths, and flowers a great deal; in practising with my violin playing and singing; and during the long winters in making translations in my spare time of Norse sagas, which no one will publish."

"I should like to read them; I am fond of the sagas," he said, and after this, under pressure of their physical misery, the conversation died away.

Hour succeeded to hour, and the weather moderated so much that now they were in little danger of being swamped. This, indeed, was fortunate, since in the event of a squall or other emergency, in their numbed condition it was doubtful whether they could have found enough strength to do what might be necessary to save themselves. They drank what remained of the whiskey, which put life into their veins for a while, but soon its effects passed off, leaving them, if possible, more frozen than before.

"What is the time?" asked Stella, after a long silence.

"It should be daybreak in about two hours," he said, in a voice that attempted cheerfulness.

Then a squall of sleet burst upon them, and after this new misery a torpor overcame Stella; at least, her shiverings grew less violent, and her head sank upon his shoulder. Morris put one arm round her waist to save her from slipping into the water at the bottom of the boat, making shift to steer with the other. Thus, for a while they ploughed forward—whither he knew not, across the inky sea, for there was no moon, and the stars were hidden, driven on slowly by the biting breath of the winter wind.

Presently she awoke, lifted her head, and spoke, saying:

"We can't last much longer in this cold and wet. You are not afraid, are you?"

"No, not exactly afraid, only sorry; it is hard to go with so much to be done, and—to leave behind."

"You shouldn't think like that," she answered, "for what we leave must follow. She will suffer, but soon she will be with you again, where everything is understood. Only you ought to have died with her, and not with me, a stranger."

"Fate settles these things," he muttered, "and if it comes to that, maybe God will give her strength. But the dawn is near, and by it we may see land."

"Yes, yes,"—now her voice had sunk to a whisper,—"the dawn is always near, and by it we shall see land."

Then again Stella's head sank upon his shoulder, and she slept heavily; nor, although he knew that such slumbers are dangerous, did he think it worth while to disturb her.

The invisible seas hissed past; the sharp wind bit his bones, and over him, too, that fatal slumber began to creep. But, although he seldom exercised it, Morris was a man of strong will, and while any strength was left he refused to give way. Would this dreadful darkness never end? For the fiftieth time he glanced back over his shoulder, and now, he was sure of it, the east grew ashen. He waited awhile, for the November dawn is slow in breaking, then looked again. Heaven be thanked! the cold wind had driven away the clouds, and there, upon the edge of the horizon, peeped up the fiery circle of the sun, throwing long rays of sickly yellow across the grey, troubled surface of the waters. In front of him lay a dense bank of fog, which, from its character, as Morris knew well, must emanate from the reeking face of earth. They were near shore, it could not be doubted; still, he did not wake his companion. Perhaps he might be in error, and sleep, even a death-sleep, is better than the cheatings of disappointed hope.

What was that dim object in front of him? Surely it must be the ruin a mile or so to the north of Monksland, that was known as the Death Church? Once a village stood here, but the sea had taken most of it; indeed, all that remained to-day was this old, deserted fane, which, having been built upon a breast of rising ground, still remained, awaiting its destruction by the slow sap of the advancing ocean. Even now, at times of very high tide, the sea closed in behind, cutting the fabric off from the mainland, where it looked like a forsaken lighthouse rather than the tower and chancel of a church. But there, not much more than a mile away, yes, there it was, and Morris felt proud to think how straight he had steered homewards through that stormy darkness.

The sea was still wild and high, but he was familiar with every inch of the coast, and knew well that there was a spot to the south of the Dead Church, just where the last rood of graveyard met the sand, upon which he could beach the boat safely even in worse weather. For this nook Morris headed with a new energy; the fires of life and hope burnt up in him, giving him back his strength and judgment.

At last they were opposite to the place, and, watching his chance, he put the helm down and ran in upon the crest of a wave, till the boat grounded in the soft sand, and began to wallow there like a dying thing. Fearing lest the back-wash should suck them off into the surf again, he rolled himself into the water, for jump he could not; indeed, it was as much as he could do to stand. With a last effort of his strength he seized Stella in his arms and struggled with her to the sandy shore, where he sank down exhausted. Then she woke. "Oh, I dreamed, I dreamed!" she said, staring round her wildly.

"What?" he asked.

"That it was all over; and afterwards, that I—" and she broke off suddenly, adding: "But it was all a dream, for we are safe on shore, are we not?"

"Yes, thank Heaven!" said Morris. "Sit still, and I will make the boat secure. She has served us a good turn, and I do not want to lose her after all."

She nodded, and wading into the water, with numbed hands he managed to lift the little anchor and carry it ashore in his arms.

"There," he said, "the tide is ebbing, and she'll hold fast enough until I can send to fetch her; or, if not, it can't be helped. Come on, Miss Fregelius, before you grow too stiff to walk;" and, bending down, he helped her to her feet.

Their road ran past the nave of the church, which was ruined and unroofed. At some time during the last two generations, however, although the parishioners saw that it was useless to go to the cost of repairing the nave, they had bricked in the chancel, and to within the last twenty years continued to use it as a place of worship. Indeed, the old oak door taken from the porch still swung on rusty hinges in the partition wall of red brick. Stella looked up and saw it.

"I want to look in there," she said.

"Wouldn't it do another time?" The moment did not strike Morris as appropriate for the examination of ruined churches.

"No; if you don't mind I should like to look now, while I remember, just for one instant."

So he shrugged his shoulders, and they limped forward up the roofless nave and through the door. She stared at the plain stone altar, at the eastern window, of which part was filled with ancient coloured glass and part with cheap glazed panes; at the oak choir benches, mouldy and broken; at the few wall-slabs and decaying monuments, and at the roof still strong and massive.

"I dreamed of a place very like this," she said, nodding her head. "I thought that I was standing in such a spot in a fearful gale, and that the sea got under the foundations and washed the dead out of their graves."

"Really, Miss Fregelius," he said, with some irritation, for the surroundings of the scene and his companion's talk were uncanny, "do you think this an occasion to explore ruins and relate nightmares?" Then he added, "I beg your pardon, but I think that the cold and wet have affected your nerves; for my part, I have none left."

"Perhaps; at least forgive me, I did so want to look," she answered humbly as, arm-in-arm, for she needed support, they passed from the altar to the door.

A grotesque imagination entered the numbed mind of Morris. Their slow and miserable march turned itself to a vision of a bridal procession from the altar. Wet, dishevelled, half-frozen, they two were the bride-groom and the bride, and the bride was a seer of visions, and the bridegroom was a dreamer of dreams. Yes, and they came up together out of the bitter sea and the darkness, and they journeyed together to a vault of the dead—

Thank Heaven! they were out of the place, and above was the sun shining, and, to the right and left, the grey ocean and the purple plough-lands, cold-looking, suggesting dangers and labour, but wholesome all of them, and good to the eye of man. Only why did this woman see visions, and why did he dream dreams? And what was the meaning of their strange meeting upon the sea? And what—

"Where are we going?" asked Stella after a while and very faintly.

"Home; to the Abbey, I mean, where your father lies. Now it is not much more than a mile away."

She sighed; her strength was failing her.

"You had better try to walk, it will warm you," he urged, and she struggled on.

It was a miserable journey, but they reached the house at length, passing first through a street of the village in which no one seemed to be awake. A wretched-looking couple, they stumbled up the steps into the porch, where Morris rang the bell, for the door was locked. The time seemed an age, but at last steps were heard, the door was unbarred, and there appeared a vision of the lad Thomas, yawning, and clad in a nightshirt and a pair of trousers, with braces attached which dangled to the floor.

"Oh, Lord!" he said when he saw them, and his jaw dropped.

"Get out of the way, you young idiot," said Morris, "and call the cook."

It was half-past seven in the evening, that is, dinner time, and Morris stood in the study waiting for Stella, who had announced through the housemaid that she was coming down.

After telling the servants to send for the doctor and attend to his companion, who had insisted upon being led straight to her father's room, Morris's first act that morning on reaching home was to take a bath as hot as he could bear. Then he drank several cups of coffee with brandy in it, and as the office would soon be open, wrote a telegram to Mary, which ran thus:

"If you hear that I have been drowned, don't believe it. Have arrived safe home after a night at sea."

This done, for he guessed that all sorts of rumours would be abroad, he inquired after Mr. Fregelius and Stella. Having learned that they were both going on well and sent off his telegram, Morris went to bed and slept for ten hours.

Morris looked round the comfortable sitting-room with its recessed Tudor windows, its tall bookcases and open hearth, where burned a bright fire of old ship's timbers supported on steel dogs, and thought to himself that he was fortunate to be there. Then the door opened, he heard the housemaid's voice say, "This way please, Miss," and Stella came in. She wore a plain white dress that seemed to fit her very well, though where she got it from he never discovered, and her luxuriant hair was twisted up into a simple knot. On the bosom of her dress was fixed a spray of brilliant ampelopsis leaves; it was her only ornament, but none could have been more striking. For the rest, although she limped and still looked dark and weary about the eyes, to all appearances she was not much the worse for their terrible adventure.

Morris glanced at her. Could this dignified and lovely young lady be that red-cloaked, loose-haired Valkyrie whom he had seen singing at daybreak upon the prow of the sinking ship, or the piteous bedraggled person whom he had supported from the altar in the Dead Church?

She guessed his thought—from the beginning Stella had this curious power of discovering his mind—and said with a smile:

"Fine feathers make fine birds, and even Cleopatra would have looked dreadful after a November night in an open boat."

"Have you recovered?" he asked.

"Yes, Mr. Monk; that is, I don't think I am going to have inflammation of the lungs or anything horrid of the sort. The remedies and that walk stopped it. But my feet are peeling from being soaked so long in salt water, and my hands are not much better. See," and she held them towards him.

Then dinner was announced, and for the second time that day they walked arm-in-arm.

"It seems a little strange, doesn't it?" suggested Morris as he surveyed the great refectory in which they two, seated at the central table, looked so lone and small.

"Yes," she answered; "but so it should, anything quite usual would have been out of place to-day."

Then he asked her how her father was going on, and heard what he had already learned from the doctor, that he was doing as well as could be expected.

"By the way, Mr. Monk," she added; "if you can spare a few minutes after dinner, and are not too tired, he would so much like to see you."

"Of course," answered Morris a little nervously, for he scented a display of fervent gratitude.

After this they dropped into desultory conversation, curiously different from the intimate talk which passed between them in the boat. Then they had been in danger, and at times in the very shadow of Death; a condition that favours confidences since those who stand beneath his wings no longer care to hide their hearts. The reserves which so largely direct our lives are lifted, their necessity is past, and in the face of the last act of Nature, Nature asserts herself. Who cares to continue to play a part when the audience has dispersed, the curtain is falling, and the pay-box has put up its shutters? Now, very unexpectedly these two were on the stage again, and each assumed the allotted role.

Stella admired the room; whereon Morris set to work to explain its characteristics, to find, to his astonishment, that Miss Fregelius had more knowledge of architecture than he could boast. He pointed out certain details, alleging them to be Elizabethan work, to which age they had been credited for generations, whereon she suggested and, indeed, proved that some of them dated from the earlier years of Henry VIII, and that some were late Jacobean. While Morris was wondering how he could combat this revolutionary opinion, the servant brought in a telegram. It was from Mary, at Beaulieu, and ran:

> Had not heard that you were drowned, but am deeply
> thankful that you are saved. Why did you pass a night at sea
> in this weather? Is it a riddle? Grieved to say my father not so
> well. Best love, and please keep on shore.
>
> MARY

At first Morris was angry with this rather flippant message; then he laughed. As he had already discovered, in fact, his anxieties had been quite groundless. The page-boy, Thomas, it appeared, when questioned, had given the inquirers to understand that his master had gone out to fish, taking his breakfast with him. Later, on his non-appearance, he amended this statement, suggesting out of the depths of a fertile imagination, that he had sailed down to Northwold, where he meant to pass the night. Therefore, although the cook, a far-seeing woman who knew her Thomas and hated him, had experienced pangs of doubt, nobody else troubled the least, and even the small community of Monksland remained profoundly undisturbed as to the fate of one of its principal inhabitants.

So little is an unsympathetic world concerned in our greatest and most particular adventures! A birth, a marriage, an inquest, a scandal— these move it superficially, for the rest it has no enthusiasm to spare. This cold neglect of events which had seemed to him so important reacted upon Morris, who, now that he had got over his chill and fatigue, saw them in their proper proportions. A little adventure in an open boat at sea which had ended without any mishap, was not remarkable, and might even be made to appear ridiculous. So the less said about it, especially to Mary, whose wit he feared, the better.

When dinner was finished Stella left the room, passing down its shadowed recesses with a peculiar grace of which even her limp could not rob her. Ten minutes later, while Morris sat sipping a glass of claret, the nurse came down to tell him that Mr. Fregelius would like to see him if he were disengaged. Reflecting that he might as well get the interview over, Morris followed her at once to the Abbot's chamber, where the sick man lay.

Except for a single lamp near the bed, the place was unlighted, but by the fire, its glow falling on her white-draped form and pale, uncommon face, sat Stella. As he entered she rose, and, coming forward, accompanied him to the bedside, saying, in an earnest voice:

"Father, here is our host, Mr. Monk, the gentleman who saved my life at the risk of his own."

The patient raised his bandaged head and stretched out a long thin hand; he could stir nothing else, for his right thigh was in splints beneath a coffer-like erection designed to keep the pressure of the blankets from his injured limb.

"Sir, I thank you," he said in a dry, staccato voice; "all the humanity that is lacking from the hearts of those rude wretches, the crew of the Trondhjem, must have found its home in you."

Morris looked at the dark, quiet eyes that seemed to express much which the thin and impassive face refused to reveal; at the grey pointed beard and the yellowish skin of the outstretched arm. Here before him, he felt, lay a man whose personality it was not easy to define, one who might be foolish, or might be able, but of whose character the leading note was reticence, inherent or acquired. Then he took the hand, and said simply:

"Pray, say no more about it. I acted on an impulse and some wandering words of yours, with results for which I could not hope. There is nothing to thank me for."

"Then, sir, I thank God, who inspired you with that impulse, and may every blessing reward your bravery."

Stella looked up as though to speak, but changed her mind and returned to her seat by the fire.

"What is there to reward?" said Morris impatiently; "that your daughter is still alive is my reward. How are you to-night, Mr. Fregelius?"

XI

A Morning Service

M r. Fregelius replied he was as well as could be expected; that the doctor said no complications were likely to ensue, but that here upon this very bed he must lie for at least two months. "That," he added, "is a sad thing to have to say to a man into whose house you have drifted like a log into a pool of the rocks."

"It is not my house, but my father's, who is at present in France," answered Morris. "But I can only say on his behalf that both you and your daughter are most welcome until you are well enough to move to the Rectory."

"Why should I not go there at once?" interrupted Stella. "I could come each day and see my father."

"No, no, certainly not," said Morris. "How could you live alone in that great, empty house?"

"I am not afraid of being alone," she answered, smiling; "but let it be as you like, Mr. Monk—at any rate, until you grow tired of us, and change your mind."

Then Mr. Fregelius told Morris what he had not yet heard—that when it became known that they had deserted Stella, leaving her to drown in the sinking ship, the attentions of the inhabitants of Monksland to the cowardly foreign sailors became so marked that their consul at Northwold had thought it wise to get them out of the place as quickly as possible. While this story was in progress Stella left the room to speak to the nurse who had been engaged to look after her father at night.

Afterwards, at the request of Mr. Fregelius, Morris told the tale of his daughter's rescue. In the course of it he mentioned how he found her standing on the deck of the sinking ship and singing a Norse song, which she had informed him was an ancient death-dirge.

The old clergyman turned his head and sighed.

"What is the matter?" asked Morris.

"Nothing, Mr. Monk; only that song is unlucky in my family, and I hoped that she had forgotten it."

Morris looked at him blankly.

"You don't understand—how should you? But, Mr. Monk, there are strange things and strange people in this world, and I think that my daughter Stella is one of the strangest of them. Fey like the rest—only a fey Norse woman would sing in such a moment."

Again Morris looked at him.

"Oh, it is an old northern term, and means foreseeing, and foredoomed. To my knowledge her grandmother, her mother, and her sister, all three of them, sang or repeated that song when in some imminent danger to their lives, and all three of them were dead within the year. The coincidence is unpleasant."

"Surely," said Morris, with a smile, "you who are a clergyman, can scarcely believe in such superstition?"

"No, I am not superstitious, and I don't believe in it; but the thing recalls unhappy memories. They have been death-lovers, all of them. I never heard of a case of one of that family who showed the slightest fear at the approach of death; and some have greeted it with eagerness."

"Well," said Morris, "would not that mean only that their spiritual sight is a little clearer than ours, and their faith a little stronger? Theoretically, we should all of us wish to die."

"Quite so, yet we are human, and don't. But she is safe, thanks to you, who but for you would now be gone. My head is still weak from that blow—you must pay no attention to me. I think that I hear Stella coming; you will say nothing to her—about that song, I mean—will you? We never talk of it in my family."

When, still stiff and sore from his adventure in the open boat, Morris went to bed, it was clear to his mind after careful consideration that fortune had made him the host of an exceedingly strange couple. Of Mr. Fregelius he was soon able to form an estimate distinct enough, although, for aught he knew, it might be erroneous. The clergyman struck him as a person of some abilities who had been doomed to much disappointment and suffered from many sorrows. Doubtless his talents had not proved to be of a nature to advance him in the world. Probably, indeed—and here Morris's hazard was correct—he was a scholar and a bookworm without individuality, to whom fate had assigned minor positions in a profession, which, however sincere his faith, he was scarcely fitted to adorn.

The work of a clergyman in a country parish if it is to succeed, should be essentially practical, and this man was not practical. Clearly, thought Morris, he was one of those who beat their wings against the bars with the common result; it was the wings that suffered, the bars only grew a trifle brighter. Then it seemed that he had lost a wife to whom he was attached, and the child who remained to him, although he loved her and clung to her, he did not altogether understand. So it came about, perhaps, that he had fallen under the curses of loneliness and continual apprehension; and in this shadow where he was doomed to walk, flourished forebodings and regrets, drawing their strength from his starved nature like fungi from a tree outgrown and fallen in the forest.

Mr. Fregelius, so thought Morris, was timid and reticent, because he dared not discover his heart, that had been so sorely trampled by Fate and Fortune. Yet he had a heart which, if he could find a confessor whom he could trust, he longed to ease in confidence. For the rest, the man's physical frame, not too robust at any time, was shattered, and with it his nerve—sudden shipwreck, painful accident, the fierce alternatives of hope and fear; then at last a delirium of joy at the recovery of one whom he thought dead, had done their work with him; and in this broken state some ancient, secret superstition became dominant, and, strive as he would to suppress it, even in the presence of a stranger, had burst from his lips in hints of unsubstantial folly.

Such was the father, or such he appeared to Morris, but of the daughter what could be said? Without doubt she was a woman of strange and impressive power. At this very moment her sweet voice, touched with that continual note of pleading, still echoed in his brain. And the dark, quiet eyes that now slept, and now shone large, as her thoughts fled through them, like some mysterious sky at night in which the summer lightning pulses intermittently! Who might forget those eyes that once had seen them? Already he wished to be rid of their haunting and could not. Then her beauty—how unusual it was, yet how rich and satisfying to the eye and sense; in some ways almost Eastern notwithstanding her Norse blood!

Often Morris had read or heard of the bewildering power of women, which for his part hitherto he had been inclined to attribute to shallow and very common causes, such as underlie all animate nature. Yet that of Stella—for undoubtedly she had power—suggested another interpretation to his mind. Or was it, after all, nothing but a variant, one of the Protean shapes of the ancient, life-compelling mystery? And her strange chant, the song of which her father made light, but feared so much; her quick insight into the workings of his own thought; her courage in the face of danger and sharp physical miseries; her charm, her mastery. What was he to make of them? Lastly, why did he think so much about her? It was not his habit where strangers were concerned. And why had she awakened in his somewhat solitary and secluded mind a sympathy so unusual that it seemed to him that he had known her for years and not for hours?

Pondering these things and the fact that perhaps within the coming weeks he would find out their meaning, Morris went to sleep. When he awoke next morning his mood had changed. Somewhat vaguely he remembered his perturbations of the previous night indeed, but now they only moved him to a smile. Their reasons were so obvious. Such exaggerated estimates and thoughts follow strange adventures— and in all its details this adventure was very strange—as naturally as nightmares follow indigestion.

Presently Thomas came to call him, and brought up his letters, among them one from Mary containing nothing in particular, for, of course, it had been despatched before her telegram, but written in her usual humorous style, which made him laugh aloud.

There was a postscript to the letter screwed into the unoccupied space between the date line and the "Dearest Morris" at its commencement. It ran:

> "How would you like to spend our honeymoon? In a yacht in the Mediterranean? I think that would do. There is nothing like solitude in a wretched little boat to promote mutual understanding. If your devotion could stand the strain of a dishevelled and seasick spouse, our matrimonial future has no terrors for your loving Mary."

As Morris read he ceased to laugh. "Yes," he thought to himself, "'solitude in a wretched little boat' does promote mutual understanding. I am not certain that it does not promote it too much." Then, with an access of irritation, "Bother the people! I wish I could be rid of them; the whole thing seems likely to become a worry."

Next he took up a letter from his father, which, when perused, did not entertain him in the least. There was nothing about Lady Rawlins in it, of whom he longed to hear, or thought that he did; nothing about that entrancing personality, the bibulous and violent Sir Jonah, now so meek and lamblike, but plenty, whole pages indeed, as to details connected with the estate. Also it contained a goodly sprinkling of sarcasms and grumblings at his, Morris's, bad management of various little matters which the Colonel considered important. Most of all, however, was his parent indignant at his neglect to furnish him with details sufficiently ample of the progress of the new buildings. Lastly, he desired, by return of post, a verbatim report of the quarrel that, as he was informed, had occurred on the school board when a prominent Roman Catholic threatened to throw an inkstand at a dissenting minister who, *coram populo*, called him the son of "a Babylonian woman."

By the time that Morris had finished this epistle, and two others which accompanied it, he was in no mood for further reflections of an unpractical or dreamy nature. Who can wonder when it is stated that they contained, respectively, a summary demand for the amount of a considerable bill which he imagined he had paid, and a request that he would read a paper before a "Science Institute" upon the possibilities of aerial telephones, made by a very unpleasing lady whom he had once met at a lawn-tennis party? Indeed it would not be too much to say that if anyone had given him the opportunity he would have welcomed a chance to quarrel, especially with the lady of the local Institute. Thus, cured of all moral distempers, and every tendency to speculate on feminine charms, hidden or overt, did he descend to the Sabbath breakfast.

That morning Morris accompanied Stella to church, where the services were still being performed by a stop-gap left by Mr. Tomley. Here, again, Stella was a surprise to him, for now her demeanour, and at a little distance her appearance also, were just such as mark ninety-eight out of every hundred clergyman's daughters in the country. So quiet and reserved was she that anyone meeting her that morning might have imagined that she was hurrying from the accustomed Bible-class to sit among her pupils in the church. This impression indeed was, as it were, certificated by an old-fashioned silk fichu that she had been obliged to borrow, which in bygone years had been worn by Morris's mother.

Once in church, however, matters changed. To begin with, finding it warm, Stella threw off the fichu, greatly to the gain of her personal appearance. Next, it became evident that the beauties of the ancient building appealed to her, which was not wonderful; for these old, seaside, eastern counties churches, relics of long past wealth and piety, are some of them among the most beautiful in the world. Then came the "Venite," of which here and there she sang a line or so, just one or two rich notes like those that a thrush utters before he bursts into full song. Rare as they might be, however, they caused those about her in the church to look at the strange singer wonderingly.

After this, in the absence of his father, Morris read the lessons, and although, being blessed with a good voice, this was a duty which he performed creditably enough, that day he went through it with a certain sense of nervousness. Why he was nervous at first he did not guess; till, chancing to glance up, he became aware that Miss Fregelius was looking at him out of her half-closed eyes. What is more, she was listening critically, and with much intenseness, whereupon, instantly, he made a mistake and put a false accent on a name.

In due course, the lessons done with, they reached the first hymn, which was one that scarcely seemed to please his companion; at any rate, she shut the book and would not sing. In the case of the second hymn, however, matters were different. This time she did not even open the book. It was evident that she knew the words, perhaps among the most beautiful in the whole collection, by heart. The reader will probably be acquainted with them. They begin:

> "And now, O Father, mindful of the love
> That bought us, once for all, on Calvary's tree."

At first Stella sang quite low, as though she wished to repress her powers. Now, as it happened, at Monksland the choir was feeble, but inoffensive; whereas the organ was a good, if a worn and neglected instrument, suited to the great but sparsely peopled church, and the organist, a man who had music in his soul. Low as she was singing, he caught the sound of Stella's voice, and knew at once that before him was a woman who in a supreme degree possessed the divinest gift, perhaps, with which Nature can crown her sex, the power and gift of song. Forgetting his wretched choir, he began to play to her. She seemed to note the invitation, and at once answered to it.

> "Look, Father, look on His anointed face,"

swelled from her throat in deep contralto notes, rich as those the organ echoed.

But the full glory of the thing, that surpassing music which set Monksland talking for a week, was not reached till she came to the third verse. Perhaps the pure passion and abounding humanity of its spirit moved her. Perhaps by this time she was the thrall of her own song. Perhaps she had caught the look of wonder and admiration on the face of Morris, and was determined to show him that she had other music at command besides that of pagan death-chants. At least, she sang up and out, till her notes dominated those of the choir, which seemed to be but an accompaniment to them; till they beat against the ancient roof and down the depth of the long nave, to be echoed back as though from the golden trumpets of the angels that stood above the tower screen; till even the village children ceased from whispers and playing to listen open-mouthed.

> *"And then for those, our dearest and best,*
> *By this prevailing Presence we appeal;*
> *O! fold them closer to Thy mercy's breast,*
> *O! do Thine utmost, for their souls' true weal;*
> *From tainting mischief keep them white and clear,*
> *And crown Thy gifts with strength to persevere."*

It was as her voice lingered upon the deep tones of these last words that suddenly Stella seemed to become aware that practically she was singing a solo; that at any rate no one else in the congregation was contributing a note. Then she was vexed, or perhaps a panic took her; at least, not another word of that hymn passed her lips. In vain the organist paused and looked round indignantly; the little boys, the clerk, and the stout coach-builder were left to finish it by themselves, with results that by contrast were painful.

When Stella came out of church, redraped in the antique and unbecoming fichu, she found herself the object of considerable attention. Indeed, upon one pretext and another nearly all the congregation seemed to be lingering about the porch and pathway to stare at the new parson's shipwrecked daughter when she appeared. Among them was Miss Layard, and with her the delicate brother. They were staying to lunch with the Stop-gap's meek little wife. Indeed, this self-satisfied and somewhat acrimonious lady, Miss Layard, engaged Morris in conversation, and pointedly asked him to introduce her to Miss Fregelius.

"We are to be neighbours, you know," she explained, "for we live at the Hall in the next parish, not more than a mile away."

"Indeed," answered Stella, who did not seem much impressed.

"My brother and I hope to call upon Mr. Fregelius and yourself as soon as possible, but I thought I would not wait for that to have the pleasure of making your acquaintance."

"You are very kind indeed," said Stella simply. "At present, I am afraid, it is not much use calling upon my father, as he is in bed with a broken thigh; also, we are not at the Rectory. Until he can be moved we are only guests at the Abbey," and she looked at Morris, who added rather grumpily, by way of explanation:

"Of course, Miss Layard, you have heard about the wreck of the Trondhjem, and how those foreign sailors saw the light in my workshop and brought Mr. Fregelius to the Abbey."

"Oh, yes, Mr. Monk, and how they left Miss Fregelius behind, and you went to fetch her, and all sorts of strange things happened to you. We think it quite wonderful and romantic. I am writing to dear Miss Porson to tell her about it, because I am sure that you are too modest to sing your own praises."

Morris grew angry. At the best of times he disliked Miss Layard. Now he began to detest her, and to long for the presence of Mary, who understood how to deal with that not too well-bred young person.

"You really needn't have troubled," he answered. "I have already written."

"Then my epistle will prove a useful commentary. If I were engaged to a modern hero I am sure I could not hear too much about him, and," fixing her eyes upon the black silk fichu, "the heroine of the adventure."

Meanwhile, Stella was being engaged by the brother, who surveyed her with pale, admiring eyes which did not confine their attentions to the fichu.

"Monk is always an awfully lucky fellow," he said. "Just fancy his getting the chance of doing all that, and finding you waiting on the ship at the end of it," he added, with desperate and emphatic gallantry. "There's to be a whole column about it in the 'Northwold Times' tomorrow. I wish the thing had come my way, that's all."

"Unless you understand how to manage a boat in a heavy sea, and the winds and tides of this coast thoroughly, I don't think that you should wish that, Mr. Layard," said Stella.

"Why not?" he asked sharply. As a matter of fact the little man was a miserable sailor and suspected her of poking fun at him.

"Because you would have been drowned, Mr. Layard, and lying at the bottom of the North Sea among the dogfish and conger-eels this morning instead of sitting comfortably in church."

Mr. Layard started and stared at her. Evidently this lady's imagination was as vivid as it was suggestive.

"I say, Miss Fregelius," he said, "you don't put things very pleasantly."

"No, I am afraid not, but then drowning isn't pleasant. I have been near it very lately, and I thought a great deal about those conger-eels. And sudden death isn't pleasant, and perhaps—unless you are very, very good, as I daresay you are—what comes after it may not be quite pleasant. All of which has to be thought of before one goes to sea in an open boat in winter, on the remotest chance of saving a stranger's life—hasn't it?"

Somehow Mr. Layard felt distinctly smaller.

"I daresay one wouldn't mind it at a pinch," he muttered; "Monk isn't the only plucky fellow in the world."

"I am sure you would not, Mr. Layard," replied Stella in a gentler voice, "still these things must be considered upon such occasions and a good many others."

"A brave man doesn't think, he acts," persisted Mr. Layard.

"No," replied Stella, "a foolish man doesn't think, a brave man thinks and sees, and still acts—at least, that is how it strikes me, although perhaps I have no right to an opinion. But Mr. Monk is going on, so I must say good-morning."

"Are many of the ladies about here so inquisitive, and the young gentlemen so?"—"decided" she was going to say, but changed the word to "kind"—asked Stella of Morris as they walked homeward.

"Ladies!" snapped Morris. "Miss Layard isn't a lady, and never will be; she has neither birth nor breeding, only good looks of a sort and money. I should like," he added, viciously—"I should like to shut her into her own coal mine."

Stella laughed, which was a rare thing with her—usually she only smiled—as she answered:

"I had no idea you were so vindictive, Mr. Monk. And what would you like to do with Mr. Layard?"

"Oh! I—never thought much about him. He is an ignorant, uneducated little fellow, but worth two of his sister, all the same. After all, he's got a heart. I have known him do kind things, but she has nothing but a temper."

Meanwhile, at the luncheon table of the Stop-gap the new and mysterious arrival, Miss Fregelius, was the subject of fierce debate.

"Pretty! I don't call her pretty," said Miss Layard; "she has fine eyes, that is all, and they do not look quite right. What an extraordinary garment she had on, too; it might have come out of Noah's Ark."

"I fancy," suggested the hostess, a mild little woman, "that it came out of the wardrobe of the late Mrs. Monk. You know, Miss Fregelius lost all her things in that ship."

"Then if I were she I should have stopped at home until I got some new ones," snapped Miss Layard.

"Perhaps everybody doesn't think so much about clothes as you do, Eliza," suggested her brother Stephen, seeing an opportunity which he was loth to lose. Eliza, in the privacy of domestic life, was not a person to be assailed with a light heart, but in company, when to some extent she must keep her temper under control, more might be dared.

She shifted her chair a little, with her a familiar sign of war, and while searching for a repartee which would be sufficiently crushing, cast on Stephen a glance that might have turned wine into vinegar.

Somewhat tremulously, for unless the fire could be damped before it got full hold, she knew what they might expect, the little hostess broke in with—

"What a beautiful singing voice she has, hasn't she?"

"Who?" asked Eliza, pretending not to understand.

"Why, Miss Fregelius, of course."

"Oh, well, that is a matter of opinion."

"Hang it all, Eliza!" said her brother, "there can't be two opinions about it, she sings like an angel."

"Do you think so, Stephen? I should have said she sings like an opera dancer."

"Always understood that their gifts lay in their legs and not in their throats. But perhaps you mean a prima donna," remarked Stephen reflectively.

"No, I don't. Prima donnas are not in the habit of screeching at the top of their voices, and then stopping suddenly to make an effect and attract attention."

"Certainly she has attracted my attention, and I only wish I could hear such screeching every day; it would be a great change." It may be explained that the Layards were musical, and that each detested the music of the other.

"Really, Stephen," rejoined Eliza, with sarcasm as awkward as it was meant to be crushing, "I shall have to tell Jane Rose that she is dethroned, poor dear—beaten out of the field by a hymn-tune, a pair of brown eyes, and—a black silk fichu."

This was a venomous stab, since for a distance of ten miles round everyone with ears to hear knew that Stephen's admiration of Miss Rose had not ended prosperously for Stephen. The poisoned knife sank deep, and its smart drove the little pale-eyed man to fury.

"You can tell her what you like, Eliza," he replied, for his self-control was utterly gone; "but it won't be much use, for she'll know what you mean. She'll know that you are jealous of Miss Fregelius because she's so good looking; just as you are jealous of her, and of Mary Porson, and of anybody else who dares to be pretty and," with crushing meaning, "to look at Morris Monk."

Eliza gasped, then said in a tragic whisper, "Stephen, you insult me. Oh! if only we were at home, I would tell you—"

"I have no doubt you would—you often do; but I'm not going home at present. I am going to the Northwold hotel."

"Really," broke in their hostess, almost wringing her hands, "this is Sunday, Mr. Layard; remember this is Sunday."

"I am not likely to forget it," replied the maddened Stephen; but over the rest of this edifying scene we will drop a veil.

Thus did the advent of Stella bring with it surprises, rumours, and family dissensions. What else it brought remains to be told.

XII

Mr. Layard's Wooing

The days went by with an uneventful swiftness at the Abbey, and after he had once accustomed himself to the strangeness of what was, in effect, solitude in the house with an unmarried guest of the other sex, it may be admitted, very pleasantly to Morris. At first that rather remarkable young lady, Stella, had alarmed him somewhat, so that he convinced himself that the duties of this novel hospitality would prove irksome. As a matter of fact, however, in forty-eight hours the irksomeness was all gone, to be replaced within twice that period by an atmosphere of complete understanding, which was comforting to his fearful soul.

The young lady was never in the way. Now that she had procured some suitable clothes the young lady was distinctly good looking; she was remarkably intelligent and well-read; she sang, as Stephen Layard had said, "like an angel"; she took a most enlightened interest in aerophones and their possibilities; she proved a very useful assistant in various experiments; and made one or two valuable suggestions. While Mary and the rest of them were away the place would really be dull without her, and somehow he could not be as sorry as he ought when Dr. Charters told him that old Mr. Fregelius's bones were uniting with exceeding slowness.

Such were the conclusions which one by one took shape in the mind of that ill-starred man, Morris Monk. As yet, however, let the student of his history understand, they were not tinged with the slightest "arriere-pensee." He did not guess even that such relations as already existed between Stella and himself might lead to grievous trouble; that at least they were scarcely wise in the case of a man engaged.

All he felt, all he knew, was that he had found a charming companion, a woman whose thought, if deeper, or at any rate different to his and not altogether to be followed, was in tune with his. He could not always catch her meaning, and yet that unrealised meaning would appeal to him. Himself a very spiritual man, and a humble seeker after truth, his nature did intuitive reverence to one who appeared to be still more spiritual, who, as he conjectured, at times at any rate, had discovered some portion of the truth. He believed it, although she had never told him so. Indeed that semi-mystical side of Stella, whereof at first she had shown him glimpses, seemed to be quite in abeyance; she dreamed no more dreams, she saw no more visions, or if she did she kept them to herself. Yet to him this woman seemed to be in touch with that unseen which he found it so difficult to weigh and appreciate. Instinctively he felt that her best thoughts, her most noble and permanent desires, were there and not here.

As he had said to her in the boat, the old Egyptians lived to die. In life a clay hut was for them a sufficient lodging; in death they sought a costly, sculptured tomb, hewn from the living rock. With them these things were symbolical, since that great people believed, with a wonderful certainty, that the true life lay beyond. They believed, too, that on the earth they did but linger in its gateway, passing their time with such joy as they could summon, baring their heads undismayed to the rain of sorrow, because they knew that very soon they would be crowned with eternal joys, whereof each of these sorrows was but an earthly root.

Stella Fregelius reminded Morris of these old Egyptians. Indeed, had he wished to carry the comparison from her spiritual to her physical attributes it still might have been considered apt, for in face she was somewhat Eastern. Let the reader examine the portrait bust of the great Queen Taia, clothed with its mysterious smile, which adorns the museum in Cairo, and, given fair instead of dusky skin, with certain other minor differences, he will behold no mean likeness to Stella Fregelius. However this may be, for if Morris saw the resemblance there were others who could not agree with him; doubtless although not an Eastern, ancient or modern, she was tinged with the fatalism of the East, mingled with a certain contempt of death inherited perhaps from her northern ancestors, and an active, pervading spirituality that was all her own. Yet her manners were not gloomy, nor her air tragic, for he found her an excellent companion, fond of children and flowers, and at times merry in her own fashion. But this gaiety of hers always reminded Morris of that which is said to have prevailed in the days of the Terror among those destined to the guillotine. Never for one hour did she seem to forget the end. "'Vanity of vanities,' saith the Preacher"; and that lesson was her watchword.

One evening they were walking together upon the cliff. In the west the sun had sunk, leaving a pale, lemon-coloured glow upon the sky.

Then far away over the quiet sea, showing bright and large in that frosty air, sprang out a single star. Stella halted in her walk, and looked first at the sunset heaven, next at the solemn sea, and last at that bright, particular star set like a diadem of power upon the brow of advancing night. Morris, watching her, saw the blood mantle to her pale face, while the dark eyes grew large and luminous, proud, too, and full of secret strength. At length his curiosity got the better of him.

"What are you thinking of?" he asked.

"Do you wish me to tell you?"

"Yes, if you will."

"You will laugh at me."

"Yes—as I laugh at that sky, and sea, and star."

"Well, then, I was thinking of the old, eternal difference between the present and the future."

"You mean between life and death?" queried Morris, and she nodded, answering:

"Between life and death, and how little people see or think of it. They just live and forget that beneath them lie their fathers' bones. They forget that in some few days—perhaps more, perhaps less—other unknown creatures will be standing above *their* forgotten bones, as blind, as self-seeking, as puffed up with the pride of the brief moment, and filled with the despair of their failure, the glory of their success, as they are to-night."

"Perhaps," suggested Morris, "they say that while they are in the world it is well to be of the world; that when they belong to the next it will be time to consider it. I am not sure that they are not right. I have heard that view," he added, remembering a certain conversation with Mary.

"Oh, don't think that!" she answered, almost imploringly; "for it is not true, really it is not true. Of course, the next world belongs to all, but our lot in it does not come to us by right, that must be earned."

"The old doctrine of our Faith," suggested Morris.

"Yes; but, as I believe, there is more behind, more which we are not told; that we must find out for ourselves with 'groanings which cannot be uttered; by hope we are saved.' Did not St. Paul hint at it?"

"What do you mean?"

"I mean that as our spirit sows, so shall it reap; as it imagines and desires, so shall it inherit. It is here that the soul must grow, not there. As the child comes into the world with a nature already formed, and its blood filled with gifts of strength or weakness, so shall the spirit come into its world wearing the garment that it has woven and which it cannot change."

"The garment which it has woven," said Morris. "That means free will, and how does free will chime in with your fatalism, Miss Fregelius?"

"Perfectly; the material given us to weave with, that is Fate; the time which is allotted for the task, that is Fate again; but the pattern is our own. Here are brushes, here is pigment, so much of it, of such and such colours, and here is light to work by. 'Now paint your picture,' says the Master; 'paint swiftly, with such skill as you can, not knowing how long is allotted for the task.' And so we weave, and so we paint, every one of us—every one of us."

"What is your picture, Miss Fregelius? Tell me, if you will."

She laughed, and drew herself up. "Mine, oh! it is large. It is to reign like that star. It is to labour forward from age to age at the great tasks that God shall set me; to return and bow before His throne crying, 'It is done. Behold, is the work good?' For the hour that they endure it is still to be with those whom I have loved on earth, although they cannot see me; to soothe their sorrows, to support their weakness, to lull their fears. It is that the empty longing and daily prayer may be filled, and filled, and filled again, like a cup from a stream which never ceases."

"And what is that daily prayer?" asked Morris, looking at her.

"O! God, touch me with Thy light, and give me understanding—yes, understanding—the word encloses all I seek," she replied, then, checking herself, added in a changed voice, "Come, let us go home; it is foolish to talk long of such things."

Shortly after this curious conversation, which was never renewed between them, or, at least, but once, a new element entered into the drama, the necessary semi-comic element without which everything would be so dull. This fresh factor was the infatuation, which possibly the reader may have foreseen, of the susceptible, impulsive little man, Stephen Layard, for Stella Fregelius, the lady whose singing he had admired, and who had been a cause of war between him and his sister. Like many weak men, Stephen Layard was obstinate, also from boyhood up he had suffered much at the hands of Eliza, who was not, in fact, quite so young as she looked. Hence there arose in his breast a very natural desire for retaliation. Eliza had taken a violent dislike to Miss Fregelius, whom he thought charming. This circumstance in their strained relations was reason enough to induce Stephen to pay court to her, even if his natural inclination had not made the adventure very congenial.

Therefore, on the first opportunity he called at the Abbey to ask after the rector, to be, as he had hoped, received by Stella. Finding his visit exceedingly agreeable, after a day or two he repeated it, and this time was conducted to the old clergyman's bedroom, upon whom his civility made a good impression.

Now, as it happened, although he did not live in Monksland, Mr. Layard was one of the largest property owners in the parish, a circumstance which he did not fail to impress upon the new rector. Being by nature and training a hard-working man who wished to do his best for his cure even while he lay helpless, Mr. Fregelius welcomed the advances of this wealthy young gentleman with enthusiasm, especially when he found that he was no niggard. A piece of land was wanted for the cemetery. Mr. Layard offered to present an acre. Money was lacking to pay off a debt upon the reading-room. Mr. Layard headed the subscription list with a handsome sum. And so forth.

Now the details of these various arrangements could not conveniently be settled without many interviews, and thus very soon it came about that scarcely a day went by upon which Mr. Layard's dog-cart did not pass through the Abbey gates. Generally he came in the morning and stopped to lunch; or he came in the afternoon and stopped to tea. In fact, or thus it seemed to Morris, he always stopped to something, so much so that although not lacking in hospitality, at times Morris found his presence wearisome, for in truth the two men had nothing in common.

"He must have turned over a new leaf with a vengeance, for he never would give a sixpence to anything during old Tomley's time," remarked Morris to Stella. "I suppose that he has taken a great fancy to your father, which is a good thing for the parish, as those Layards are richer than Croesus."

"Yes," answered Stella with a curious little smile.

But to herself she did not smile; for, if Morris found his visitor a bore, to Stella he was nothing short of an infliction, increased rather than mitigated by numerous presents of hot-house fruit and flowers offered to herself, and entailing, each of them, an expression of thanks verbal or written. At first she treated the thing as a joke, till it grew evident that her admirer was as much in earnest as his nature would permit. Thereon, foreseeing eventualities, she became alarmed.

Unless some means could be found to stop him it was now clear to

Stella that Mr. Layard meant to propose to her, and as she had not the slightest intention of accepting him this was an honour which she did not seek. But she could find no sufficient means; hints, and even snubs, only seemed to add fuel to the fire, and of a perpetual game of hide and seek she grew weary.

So it came about that at last she shrugged her shoulders and left things to take their chance, finding some consolation for her discomfort in the knowledge that Miss Layard, convinced that the rector's daughter was luring her inexperienced brother into an evil matrimonial net, could in no wise restrain her rage and indignation. So openly did this lady express her views, indeed, that at length a report of them reached even Morris's inattentive ears, whereon he was at first very angry and then burst out laughing. That a man like Stephen Layard should hope to marry a woman like Stella Fregelius seemed to him so absurd as to be almost unnatural. Yet when he came to think it over quietly he was constrained to admit to himself that the match would have many advantages for the young lady, whereof the first and foremost were that Stephen was very rich, and although slangy and without education in its better sense, at heart by no means a bad little fellow. So Morris shrugged his shoulders, shut his eyes, continued to dispense luncheons and afternoon teas, and though with an uneasy mind, like Stella herself, allowed things to take their chance.

All this while, however, his own friendship with Stella grew apace, enhanced as it was in no small degree by the fact that now her help in his scientific operations had become most valuable. Indeed, it appeared that he was destined to owe the final success of his instrument to the assistance of women who, at the beginning, at any rate, knew little of its principles. Mary, it may be remembered, by some fortunate chance, made the suggestion as to the substance of the receiver, which turned the aerophone from a great idea into a practical reality. Now to complete the work it was Stella, not by accident, but after careful study of its problem who gave the thought that led to the removal of the one remaining obstacle to its general and successful establishment.

To test this new development of the famous sound deflector and perfect its details, scores of experiments were needed, most of which he and she carried out together. This was their plan. One of them established him or herself in the ruined building known as the Dead Church, while the other took up a position in the Abbey workshop. From these respective points, a distance of about two miles, they tested the machines with results that day by day grew better and clearer, till at length, under these conditions they were almost perfect.

Strange was the experience and great the triumph when at last Morris, seated in the Abbey with his apparatus before him, unconnected with its twin by any visible medium, was able without interruption for a whole morning to converse with Stella established in the Dead Church.

"It is done," he cried in unusual exultation. "Now, if I die to-morrow it does not matter."

Instantly came the answer in Stella's voice.

"I am very happy. If I do nothing else I have helped a man to fame."

Then a hitch arose, the inevitable hitch; it was found that, in certain states of the atmosphere, and sometimes at fixed hours of the day, the sounds coming from the receiver were almost inaudible. At other times again the motive force seemed to be so extraordinarily active that, the sound deflector notwithstanding, the instrument captured and transmitted a thousand noises which are not to be heard by the unobservant listener, or in some cases by any human ear.

Weird enough these noises were at times. Like great sighs they came, like the moan of the breeze brought from an infinite distance, like mutterings and groanings arisen from the very bowels of the earth. Then there were the splash or boom of the waves, the piping of the sea-wind, the cry of curlew, or black-backed gulls, all mingled in one great and tangled skein of sound that choked the voice of the speaker, and in their aggregate, bewildered him who hearkened.

These, and others which need not be detailed, were problems that had to be met, necessitating many more experiments. Thus it came about that through most of the short hours of winter daylight Morris and Stella found themselves at their respective positions, corresponding, or trying to correspond, through the aerophones. If the weather was very bad, or very cold, Morris went to the dead Church, otherwise that post was allotted to Stella, both because it was more convenient that Morris should stay in his laboratory, and by her own choice.

Two principal reasons caused her to prefer to pass as much of her time as was possible in this desolate and unvisited spot. First, because Mr. Layard was less likely to find her when he called, and secondly, that for her it had a strange fascination. Indeed, she loved the place, clothed as it was with a thousand memories of those who had been human like herself, but now—were not. She would read the inscriptions upon the chancel stones and study the coats-of-arms and names of those departed, trying to give to each lost man and woman a shape and character, till at length she knew all the monuments by appearance as well as by the names inscribed upon them.

One of these dead, oddly enough, had been named Stella Ethel Smythe, daughter of Sir Thomas Smythe, whose family lived at the old hall now in the possession of the Layards. This Stella had died at the age of twenty-five in the year 1741, and her tombstone recorded that in mind she was clean and sweet, and in body beautiful. Also at the foot of it was a doggerel couplet, written probably by her bereaved father, which ran:

"Though here my Star seems set,
I know 'twill light me yet."

Stella, the live Stella, thought these simple words very touching, and pointed them out to Morris. He agreed with her, and tried in the records of the parish and elsewhere to discover some details about the dead girl's life, but quite without avail.

"That's all that's left," he said one day, nodding his head at the tombstone. "The star is quite set."

"'I know 'twill light me yet,'" murmured his companion, as she turned away to the work in hand. "Sometimes," she went on, "as I sit here at dusk listening to all the strange sounds which come from that receiver, I fancy that I can hear Stella and her poor father talking while they watch me; only I cannot understand their language."

"Ah!" said Morris, "if that were right we should have found a means of communication from the dead and with the unseen world at large."

"Why not?" asked Stella.

"I don't know, I have thought of it," he answered, and the subject dropped.

One afternoon Stella, wrapped in thick cloaks, was seated in the chancel of the Dead Church attending to the instrument which stood upon the stone altar. Morris had not wished her to go that morning, for the weather was very coarse, and snow threatened; but, anticipating a visit from Mr. Layard, she insisted, saying that she should enjoy the walk. Now the experiments were in progress, and going beautifully. In order to test the aerophones fully in this rough weather, Morris and Stella had agreed to read to each other alternate verses from the Book of Job, beginning at the thirty-eighth chapter.

"'Canst thou bind the sweet influences of Pleiades, or loose the bands of Orion?'" read Stella presently in her rich, clear voice.

Instantly from two miles away came the next verse, the sound of those splendid words rolling down the old church like echoes of some lesson read generations since.

"'Canst thou bring forth Mazzaroth in his season, or canst thou guide Arcturus with his sons?'"

So it went on for a few more verses, till just as the instrument was saying, "'Who hath put wisdom in the inward parts, or who hath given understanding to the heart?'" the rude door in the brick partition opened, admitting a rush of wind and—Stephen Layard.

The little man sidled up nervously to where Stella was sitting on a camp-stool by the altar.

"How do you do?" said Stella, holding out her hand, and looking surprised.

"How do you do, Miss Fregelius? What—what are you doing in this dreadfully cold place on such a bitter day?"

Before she could answer the voice of Morris, anxious and irritated, for as the next verse did not follow he concluded that something had gone wrong with the apparatus, rang through the church asking:

"'Who hath put wisdom in the inward parts, or who hath given understanding to the heart?'"

"Good gracious," said Mr. Layard. "I had no idea that Monk was here; I left him at the Abbey. Where is he?"

"At the Abbey," answered Stella, as for the second time the voice of Morris rolled out the question from the Book.

"I don't understand," said Stephen, beginning to look frightened; "has it anything to do with his electrical experiments?"

Stella nodded. Then, addressing the instrument, said:

"Please stop reading for a while. Mr. Layard is calling here."

"Confound him," came the swift answer. "Let me know when he is gone. He said he was going home," whereon Stella switched off before worse things happened.

Mr. Layard, who had heard these words, began a confused explanation till Stella broke in.

"Please don't apologise. You changed your mind, and we all do that; but I am afraid this is a cold place to come to."

"You are right there. Why on earth do you sit here so long?"

"To work, Mr. Layard."

"Why should you work? I thought women hated it, and above all, why for Monk? Does he pay you?"

"I work because I like work, and shall go on working till I die, and afterwards I hope; also, these experiments interest me very much. Mr. Monk does not pay me. I have never asked him to do so. Indeed, it is I who am in his debt for all the kindness he has shown to my father and myself. To any little assistance that I can give him he is welcome."

"I see," said Mr. Layard; "but I should have thought that was Mary Porson's job. You know he is engaged to her, don't you?"

"Yes, but Miss Porson is not here; and if she were, perhaps she would not care for this particular work."

Then came a pause, which, not knowing what this awkward silence might breed, Stella broke.

"I suppose you saw my father," she said; "how did you find him looking?"

"Oh! better, I thought; but that leg of his still seems very bad." Then, with a gasp and a great effort, he went on: "I have been speaking to him about you."

"Indeed," said Stella, looking at him with wondering eyes.

"Yes, and he says that if—it suits us both, he is quite willing; that, in fact, he would be very pleased to see you so well provided for."

Stella could not say that she did not understand, the falsehood was too obvious. So she merely went on looking, a circumstance from which Mr. Layard drew false auguries.

"You know what I mean, don't you?" he jerked out.

She shook her head.

"I mean—I mean that I love you, that you have given me what this horrid thing was talking about just now—understanding to the heart; yes, that's it, understanding to the heart. Will you marry me, Stella? I will make you a good husband, and it isn't a bad place, and all that, and though your father says he has little to leave you, you will be treated as liberally as though you were a lady in your own right."

Stella smiled a little.

"Will you marry me?" he asked again.

"I am afraid that I must answer no, Mr. Layard."

Then the poor man broke out into a rhapsody of bitter disappointment, genuine emotion, and passionate entreaty.

"It is no use, Mr. Layard," said Stella at last. "Indeed, I am much obliged to you. You have paid me a great compliment, but it is not possible that I should become your wife, and the sooner that is clear the better for us both."

"Are you engaged?" he asked.

"No, Mr. Layard; and probably I never shall be. I have my own ideas about matrimony, and the conditions under which I would undertake it are not at all likely ever to be within my reach."

Again he implored,—for at the time this woman really held his heart,—wringing his hands, and, indeed, weeping in the agony of a repulse which was the more dreadful because it was quite unexpected. He had scarcely imagined that this poor clergyman's daughter, who had little but her looks and a sweet voice, would really refuse the best match for twenty miles round, nor had his conversation with her father suggested to his mind any such idea.

It was true that Mr. Fregelius had given him no absolute encouragement; he had said that personally the marriage would be very pleasing to himself, but that it was a matter of which Stella must judge; and when asked whether he would speak to his daughter, he had emphatically declined. Still, Stephen Layard had taken this to be all a part of the paternal formula, and rejoiced, thinking the matter as good as settled. Dreadful indeed, then, was it to him when he found that he was called upon to contemplate the dull obverse of his shield of faith, and not its bright and shining face, in which he had seen mirrored so clear a picture of perfect happiness.

So he begged on piteously enough, till at last Stella was forced to stop him by saying as gently as she could:

"Please spare us both, Mr. Layard; I have given my answer, and I am sorry to say that it is impossible for me to go back upon my word."

Then a sudden fury seized him.

"You are in love with somebody else," he said; "you are in love with Morris Monk; and he is a villain, when he is engaged, to go taking you too. I know it."

"Then, Mr. Layard," said Stella, striving to keep her temper, "you know more than I know myself."

"Very likely," he answered. "I never said you knew it, but it's true, for all that. I feel it here—where you will feel it one day, to your sorrow"— and he placed his hand upon his heart.

A sudden terror took hold of her, but with difficulty she found her mental balance.

"I hoped, Mr. Layard," she said, "that we might have parted friends; but how can we when you bring such accusations?"

"I retract them," broke in the distracted man. "You mustn't think anything of what I said; it is only the pain that has made me mad. For God's sake, at least let us part friends, for then, perhaps, some day we may come together again."

Stella shook her head sadly, and gave him her hand, which he covered with kisses. Then, reeling in his gait like one drunken, the unhappy suitor departed into the falling snow.

Mechanically Stella switched on the instrument, and at once Morris's voice was heard asking:

"I say, hasn't he gone?"

"Yes," she said.

"Thank goodness! Why on earth did you keep him gossiping all that time? Now then—'Who can number the clouds in wisdom—'"

"Not Mr. Layard or I," thought Stella sadly to herself, as she called back the answering verse.

XIII

Two Questions, and the Answer

At length the light began to fade, and for that day their experiments were over. In token of their conclusion twice Stella rang the electric warning bell which was attached to the aerophone, and in some mysterious manner caused the bell of its twin instrument to ring also. Then she packed the apparatus in its box, for, with its batteries, it was too heavy and too delicate to be carried conveniently, locking it up, and left the church, which she also locked behind her. Outside it was still snowing fast, but softly, for the wind had dropped, and a sharp frost was setting in, causing the fallen snow to scrunch beneath her feet. About half-way along the bleak line of deserted cliff which stretched from the Dead Church to the first houses of Monksland, she saw the figure of a man walking swiftly towards her, and knew from the bent head and broad, slightly stooping shoulders that it was Morris coming to escort her home. Presently they met.

"Why did you not wait for me?" he asked in an irritated voice, "I told you I was coming, and you know that I do not like you to be tramping about these lonely cliffs at this hour."

"It is very kind of you," she answered, smiling that slow, soft smile which was characteristic of her when she was pleased, a smile that seemed to be born in her beautiful eyes and thence to irradiate her whole face; "but it was growing dreary and cold there, so I thought that I would start."

"Yes," he answered, "I forgot, and, what is more, it is very selfish of me to keep you cooped up in such a place upon a winter's day. Enthusiasm makes one forget everything."

"At least without it we should do nothing; besides, please do not pity me, for I have never been happier in my life."

"I am most grateful," he said earnestly. "I don't know what I should have done without you through this critical time, or what I shall—" and he stopped.

"It went beautifully to-day, didn't it?" she broke in, as though she had not heard his words.

"Yes," he answered, "beyond all expectations. We must experiment over a greater distance, and then if the thing still works I shall be able to speak with my critics in the gate. You know I have kept everything as dark as possible up to the present, for it is foolish to talk first and fail afterwards. I prefer to succeed first and talk afterwards."

"What a triumph it will be!" said Stella. "All those clever scientists will arrive prepared to mock, then think they are taken in, and at last go away astonished to write columns upon columns in the papers."

"And after that?" queried Morris.

"Oh, after that, honour and glory and wealth and power and—the happy ending. Doesn't it sound nice?"

"Ye—es, in a way. But," he added with energy, "it won't come off. No, not the aerophones, they are right enough I believe, but all the rest of it."

"Why not?"

"Because it is too much. 'Happy endings' don't come off. The happiness lies in the struggle, you know,—an old saying, but quite true. Afterwards something intervenes."

"To have struggled happily and successfully is happiness in itself. Whatever comes afterwards nothing can take that away. 'I have done something; it is good; it cannot be changed; it is a stone built for ever in the pyramid of beauty, or knowledge, or advancement.' What can man hope to say more at the last, and how few live to say it, to say it truly? You will leave a great name behind you, Mr. Monk."

"I shall leave my work; that is enough for me," he answered.

For a while they walked in silence; then some thought struck him, and he stopped to ask:

"Why did Layard come to the Dead Church to-day? He said that he was going home, and it isn't on his road."

Stella turned her head, but, even in that faint light, not quickly enough to prevent him seeing a sudden flush change the pallor of her face to the rich colour of her lips.

"To call, I suppose; or," correcting herself, "perhaps from curiosity."

"And what did he talk about?"

"Oh, the aerophone, I think; I don't remember."

"That must be a story," he said, laughing. "I always remember Layard's conversation for longer than I want; it has a knack of impressing itself upon me. What was it? Cemetery land, church debts, the new drainage scheme, or something equally entrancing and confidential?"

Under this cross-examination Stella grew desperate, unnecessarily, perhaps, and said in a voice that was almost cross:

"I cannot tell you; please let's talk of something else."

Then of a sudden Morris understood, and, like a foolish man, at once jumped to a conclusion far other than the truth. Doubtless Layard had gone to the church to propose to Stella, and she had accepted him, or half accepted him; the confusion of her manner told its own tale. A new and strange sensation took possession of Morris. He felt unwell; he felt angry; if the aerophone refused to work at all to-morrow, he would care nothing. He could not see quite clearly, and was not altogether sure where he was walking.

"I beg your pardon," he said in a cold voice, as he recovered himself; "it was most impertinent of me." He was going to add, "pray accept my congratulations," but fortunately, or unfortunately, stopped himself in time.

Stella divined something of what was passing in his mind; not all, indeed, for to her the full measure of his folly would have been incomprehensible. For a moment she contemplated an explanation, then abandoned the idea because she could find no words; because, also, this was another person's secret, and she had no right to involve an honest man, who had paid her a great compliment, in her confidences. So she said nothing. To Morris, for the moment at any rate, a conclusive proof of his worst suspicions.

The rest of that walk was marked by unbroken silence. Both of them were very glad when it was finished.

It was five o'clock when they reached the Abbey, so that there were two hours to be spent before it was time to dress for dinner. When she had taken off her things Stella went straight to her father's room to give him his tea. By now Mr. Fregelius was much better, although the nature of his injuries made it imperative that he should still stay in bed.

"Is that you, Stella?" he said, in his high, nervous voice, and, although she could not see them in the shadow of the curtain, she knew that his quick eyes were watching her face eagerly.

"Yes, father, I have brought you your tea. Are you ready for it?"

"Thank you, my dear. Have you been at that place—what do you call it?—the Dead Church, all day?"

"Yes, and the experiments went beautifully."

"Did they, did they indeed?" commented her father in an uninterested voice. The fate of the experiments did not move him. "Isn't it very lonely up there in that old church?"

"I prefer to be alone—generally."

"I know, I know. Forgive me; but you are a very odd woman, my dear."

"Perhaps, father; but not more so than those before me, am I? Most of them were a little different from other people, I have been told."

"Quite right, Stella; they were all odd women, but I think that you are quite the oddest of the family." Then, as though the subject were disagreeable to him, he added suddenly: "Mr. Layard came to see me to-day."

"So he told me," answered Stella.

"Oh, you have met him. I remember; he said he should call in at the Dead Church, as he had something to say to you."

Stella determined to get the conversation over, so she forced the pace. She was a person who liked to have disagreeable things behind her. Drawing herself up, she answered steadily:

"He did call in, and—he said it."

"What, my dear, what?" asked Mr. Fregelius innocently.

"He asked me to marry him, father; I think he told me with your consent."

Mr. Fregelius, auguring the very best from this openness, answered in tones which he could not prevent from betraying an unseemly joy.

"Quite true, Stella; I told him to go on and prosper; and really I hope he has prospered."

"Yes," said Stella reflectively.

"Then, my dear love, am I to understand that you are engaged to him?"

"Engaged to him! Certainly not," she answered.

"Then," snapped out her justly indignant parent, "how in the name of Heaven has he prospered?"

"By my refusing him, of course. We should never have suited each other at all; he would have been miserable if I had married him."

Mr. Fregelius groaned in bitterness of spirit.

"Oh, Stella, Stella," he cried, "what a disappointment!"

"Why should you be disappointed, father dear?" she asked gently.

"Why? You stand there and ask why, when I hear that my daughter, who will scarcely have a sixpence—or at least very few of them—has refused a young man with between seventeen and eighteen thousand pounds a year—that's his exact income, for he told me himself, a most estimable churchman, who would have been a pillar of strength to me, a man whom I should have chosen out of ten thousand as a son-in-law—" and he ceased, overwhelmed.

"Father, I am sorry that you are sorry, but it is strange you should understand me so little after all these years, that you could for one moment think that I should marry Mr. Layard."

"And why not, pray? Are you better born—"

"Yes," interrupted Stella, whose one pride was that of her ancient lineage.

"I didn't mean that. I meant better bred and generally superior to him? You talk as though you were of a different clay."

"Perhaps the clay is the same," said Stella, "but the mind is not."

"Oh, there it is again, spiritual and intellectual pride, which causes you to set yourself above your fellows, and in the end will be your ruin. It has made a lonely woman of you for years, and it will do worse than that. It will turn you into an old maid—if you live," he added, as though shaken by some sudden memory.

"Perhaps," said Stella, "I am not frightened at the prospect. I daresay that I shall have a little money and at the worst I can always earn a living; my voice would help me to it, if nothing else does. Father, dear, you mustn't be vexed with me; and pray—pray do understand that no earthly thing would make me marry a man whom I dislike rather than otherwise; who, at least, is not a mate for me, merely because he could give me a fine house to live in, and treat me luxuriously. What would be the good of such things to me if I knew that I had tarnished myself and violated my instincts?"

"You talk like a book—you talk like a book," muttered the old gentleman. "But I know that the end of it will be wretchedness for everybody. People who go on as you do about instincts, and fine feelings, and all that stuff, are just the ones who get into some dreadful mess at last. I tell you that such ideas are some of the devil's best baits."

Stella began to grow indignant.

"Do you think, father, that you ought to talk to me quite like that?" she asked. "Don't you know me well enough to be sure that I should never get into what you call a mess—at least, not in the way I suppose you mean? My heart and thought are my own, and I shall be prepared to render account of them; for the rest, you need not be afraid."

"I didn't mean that—I didn't mean anything of the sort—"

"I am glad to hear it," broke in Stella. "It would scarcely have been kind, especially as I am no longer a child who needs to be warned against the dangers of the world."

"What I did mean is that you are an enigma; that I am frightened about you; that you are no companion; because your thoughts—yes, and at times your face, too—seem unnatural, unearthly, and separate you from others, as they have separated you from this poor young man."

"I am what I was made," answered Stella with a little smile, "and I seek company where I can find it. Some love the natural, some the spiritual, and each receive from them their good. Why should they blame one another?"

"Mad," muttered her father to himself as she left the room. "Mad as she is charming and beautiful; or, if not mad, at least quite impracticable and unfitted for the world. What a disappointment to me—what a bitter disappointment! Well, I should be used to them by now."

Meanwhile, Morris was in his workshop in the old chapel entering up his record of the day's experiments, which done, he drew his chair to the stove and fell into thought. Somehow the idea of the engagement of Miss Fregelius to Stephen Layard was not agreeable to him; probably because he did not care about the young man. Yet, now that he came to think of it quietly, in all her circumstances it would be an admirable arrangement, and the offer undoubtedly was one which she had been wise to accept. On the whole, such a marriage would be as happy as marriages generally are. The man was honest, the man was young and rich, and very soon the man would be completely at the disposal of his brilliant and beautiful wife.

Personally he, Morris, would lose a friend, since a woman cannot marry and remain the friend of another man. That, however, would probably have happened in any case, and to object on this account, even in his secret heart, would be abominably selfish. Indeed, what right had he even to consider the matter? The young lady had come into his life very strangely, and made a curious impression upon him; she was now going out of it by ordinary channels, and soon nothing but the impression would remain. It was proper, natural, and the way of the world; there was nothing more to be said.

Somehow he was in a dreary mood, and everything bored him. He fetched Mary's last letter. There was nothing in it but some chit-chat, except the postscript, which was rather longer than the letter, and ran:

"I am glad to hear the young lady whom you fished up out of the sea is such an assistance to you in your experiments. I gather from what I hear—although you haven't mentioned the fact—that she is as beautiful as she is charming, and that she sings wonderfully. She must be something remarkable, I am sure, because Eliza Layard evidently detests her, and says that she is trying to ensnare the affections of that squire of dames, her brother Stephen, now temporarily homeless after a visit to Jane Rose. What will you do when you have to get on without her? I am afraid you must accustom yourself to the idea, unless she would like to make a third in the honeymoon party. Joking apart, I am exceedingly grateful to her for all the help she has given you, and, dear, dear Morris, more delighted than I can tell you to learn that after all your years of patient labour you believe success to be absolutely within sight.

"My father, I am sorry to say, is no better; indeed, although the doctors deny it, I believe he is worse, and I see no prospect of our getting away from here at present. However, don't let that bother you, and above all, don't think of coming out to this place which makes you miserable, and where you can't work. What a queer menage you must be at the Abbey now! You and the Star who has risen from the ocean—she ought to have been called Venus—tete-a-tete, and the, I gather, rather feeble and uninteresting old gentleman in bed upstairs. I should like to see you when you didn't know. Why don't you invent a machine to enable people at a distance to see as well as to hear each other? It would be very popular and bring Society to utter wreck. Does the Northern star—she is Danish, isn't she?—make good coffee, and how, oh! how does she get on with the cook?"

Morris put down the letter and laughed aloud. Mary was as amusing as ever, and he longed to see her again, especially as he was convinced that she was really bored out there at Beaulieu, with Mr. Porson sick, and his father very much occupied with his own affairs. In a moment he made up his mind; he would go out and see her. Of course, he could ill spare the time, but for the present the more pressing of his experiments were completed, and he could write up his "data" there. Anyway, he would put in a fortnight at Beaulieu, and, what is more, start to-morrow if it could be arranged.

He went to the table and began a letter to Mary announcing that she might expect to see him sometime on the day that it reached her. When he had got so far as this he remembered that the dressing bell had already rung some minutes, and ran upstairs to change his clothes. As he fastened his tie he thought to himself sadly that this would be his last dinner with Stella Fregelius, and as he brushed his hair he determined that unless she had other wishes, it should be as happy as it could be made. He would like this final meal to be the pleasantest of all their meals, and although, of course, he had no right to form an opinion on the matter, he thought that perhaps she might like it, too. They were going to part, to enter on different walks of life—for now, be it said, he had quite convinced himself that she was engaged—so let their parting memories of each other be as agreeable as possible.

Meanwhile, Stella also had her reflections. Her conversation with her father had troubled her, more, perhaps, than her remarks might have suggested. There was little between this pair except the bond of blood, which sometimes seems to be so curiously accidental, so absolutely devoid of influence in promoting mutual sympathies, or in opening the door to any deep and real affection. Still, notwithstanding this lack of true intimacy, Stella loved her father as she felt that he loved her, and it gave her pain to be forced to cross his wishes. She knew with what a fierce desire, although he was ashamed to express all its intensity, he desired that she should accept this, the first chance of wealthy and successful marriage that had come her way, and the anguish which her absolute refusal must have entailed upon his heart.

Of course, it was very worldly of him, and therefore reprehensible; yet to a great extent she could sympathise with his disappointment. At bottom he was a proud man, although he repressed his pride and kept it secret. He was an ambitious man, also, and his lot had been confined to humble tasks, absolutely unrecognised beyond his parish, of a remotely-placed country parson. Moreover, his family had been rich; he had been brought up to believe that he himself would be rich, and then, owing to certain circumstances, was doomed to pass his days in comparative poverty.

Even death had laid a heavy hand on him; she was the last of her race, and she knew he earnestly desired that she should marry and bear children so that it might not become extinct. And now this chance, this princely chance, which, from his point of view, seemed to fill every possible condition, had come unawares, like a messenger from Heaven, and she refused its entertainment. Looked at through his eyes the position was indeed cruel.

Yet, deeply as she sympathised with him in his disappointment, Stella never for one moment wavered in her determination. Marry Mr. Layard! Her blood shrank back to her heart at the very thought, and then rushed to her neck and bosom in a flood of shame. No, she was sorry, but that was impossible, a thing which no woman should be asked to do against her will.

The subject wearied her, but as brooding on it could not mend matters, she dismissed it from her mind, and turned her thoughts to Morris. Why, she did not know, but something had come between them; he was vexed with her, and what was more, disappointed; she could feel it well enough, and—she found his displeasure painful. What had she done wrong, how had she offended him? Surely it could not be—and once again that red blush spread itself over face and bosom. He could not believe that she had accepted the man! He could never have so grossly misunderstood her, her nature, her ideas, everything about her! And yet who knew what he would or would not believe? In some ways, as she had already discovered, Mr. Monk was curiously simple. How could she tell him the truth without using words which she did not desire to speak? Here instinct came to her aid. It might be done by making herself as agreeable to him as possible, for surely he must know that no girl would do her best to please one man when she had just promised herself to another. So it came about that quite innocently Stella determined to allay her host's misgivings by this doubtful and dangerous expedient.

To begin with, she put on her best dress—a low bodice of black silk relieved with white and a single scarlet rose from the hothouse. Round her neck also, fastened by a thin chain, she wore a large blood-red carbuncle shaped like a heart, and about her slender waist a quaint girdle of ancient Danish silver, two of the ornaments which she had saved from the shipwreck. Her dark and waving hair she parted in the middle after a new fashion, tying its masses in a heavy knot at the back of her head, and thus adorned descended to the library where Morris was awaiting her.

He stood leaning over the fire with his back towards her, but hearing the sweep of a skirt turned round, and as his eyes fell upon her, started a little. Never till he saw her thus had he known how beautiful Stella was at times. Quite without design his eyes betrayed his thought, but with his lips he said merely as he offered her his arm,—

"What a pretty dress! Did it come out of Northwold?"

"The material did; I made it up, and I am glad that you think it nice."

This was a propitious beginning, and the dinner that followed did not belie its promise. The conversation turned upon one of the Norse sagas that Stella had translated, for which Morris had promised to try to find a publisher. Then abandoning the silence and reserve which were habitual to him he began to talk, asking her about her work and her past. She answered him freely enough, telling him of her school days in Denmark, of her long holiday visits to the old Danish grandmother, whose memory stretched back through three generations, and whose mind was stored with traditions of men and days now long forgotten. This particular saga, she said, had, for instance, never been written in its entirety till she took it down from the old dame's lips, much as in the fifteenth century the Iceland sagas were recorded by Snorro Sturleson and others. Even the traditional music of the songs as they were sung centuries ago she had received from her with their violin accompaniments.

"I have one in the house," broke in Morris, "a violin—rather a good instrument; I used to play a little when I was young. I wish, if you don't mind, that you would sing them to me after dinner."

"I will try if you like," she answered, "but I don't know how I shall get on, for my own old fiddle, to which I am accustomed, went to the bottom with a lot of other things in that unlucky shipwreck. You know we came by sea because it seemed so cheap, and that was the end of our economy. Fortunately, all our heavy baggage and furniture were not ready, and escaped."

"I do not call it unlucky," said Morris with grave courtesy, "since it gave me the honour of your acquaintance; or perhaps I may say of your friendship."

"Yes," she answered, looking pleased; "certainly you may say of my friendship. It is owing to the man who saved my life, is it not,—with a great deal more that I can never pay?"

"Don't speak of it," he said. "That midnight sail was my one happy inspiration, my one piece of real good luck."

"Perhaps," and she sighed, "that is, for me, though who can tell? I have often wondered what made you do it, there was so little to go on."

"I have told you, inspiration, pure inspiration."

"And what sent the inspiration, Mr. Monk?"

"Fate, I suppose."

"Yes, I think it must be what we call fate—if it troubles itself about so small a thing as the life of one woman."

Then, to change the subject, she began to talk of the Northumberland moors and mountains, and of their years of rather dreary existence among them, till at length it was time to leave the table. This they did together, for even then Morris drank very little wine.

"May I get you the violin, and will you sing?" he asked eagerly, when they reached the library.

"If you wish it I will try."

"Then come to the chapel; there is a good fire, and it is put away there."

Presently they were in the ancient place, where Morris produced the violin from the cupboard, and having set a new string began to tune it.

"That is a very good instrument," said Stella, her eyes shining, "you don't know what you have brought upon yourself. Playing the violin is my pet insanity, and once or twice since I have been here, when I wanted it, I have cried over the loss of mine, especially as I can't afford to buy another. Oh! what a lovely night it is; look at the full moon shining on the sea and snow. I never remember her so bright; and the stars, too; they glitter like great diamonds."

"It is the frost," answered Morris. "Yes, everything is beautiful to-night."

Stella took the violin, played a note or two, then screwed up the strings to her liking.

"Do you really wish me to sing, Mr. Monk?" she asked.

"Of course; more than I can tell you."

"Then, will you think me very odd if I ask you to turn out the electric lamps? I can sing best so. You stand by the fire, so that I can see my audience; the moon through this window will give me all the light I want."

He obeyed, and now she was but an ethereal figure, with a patch of red at her heart, and a line of glimmering white from the silver girdle beneath her breast, on whose pale face the moonbeams poured sweetly. For a while she stood thus, and the silence was heavy in that beautiful, dismantled place of prayer. Then she lifted the violin, and from the first touch of the bow Morris knew that he was in the presence of a mistress of one of the most entrancing of the arts. Slow and sweet came the plaintive, penetrating sounds, that seemed to pass into his heart and thrill his every nerve. Now they swelled louder, now they almost died away; and now, only touching the strings from time to time, she began to sing in her rich, contralto voice. He could not understand the words, but their burden was clear enough; they were a lament, the lament of some sorrowing woman, the sweet embodiment of an ancient and forgotten grief thus embalmed in heavenly music.

It was done; the echoes of the following notes of the violin fainted and died among the carven angels of the roof. It was done, and Morris sighed aloud.

"How can I thank you?" he said. "I knew that you were a musician, but not that you had such genius. To listen to you makes a man feel very humble."

She laughed. "The voice is a mere gift, for which no one deserves credit, although, of course, it can be improved."

"If so, what of the accompaniment?"

"That is different; that comes from the heart and hard work. Do you know that when I was under my old master out in Denmark, who in his time was one of the finest of violinists in the north of Europe, I often played for five and sang for two hours a day? Also, I have never let the thing drop; it has been the consolation and amusement of a somewhat lonely life. So, by this time, I ought to understand my art, although there remains much to be learnt."

"Understand it! Why, you could make a fortune on the stage."

"A living, perhaps, if my voice will bear the continual strain. I daresay that some time I shall drift there—for the living—not because I like the trade or have any wish for popular success. It is a fact that I had far rather sing alone to you here to-night, and know that you are pleased, than be cheered by a whole opera house full of strange people."

"And I—oh, I cannot explain! Sing on, sing all you can, for to-morrow I must go away."

"Go away!" she faltered.

"Yes; I will explain to you afterwards. But please sing while I am here to listen."

The words struck heavy on her heart, numbing it—why, she knew not. For a moment she felt helpless, as though she could neither sing nor play. She did not wish him to go; she did not wish him to go. Her intellect came to her aid. Why should he go? Heaven had given her power, and this man could feel its weight. Would it not suffice to keep him from going? She would try; she would play and sing as she had never done before; sing till his heart was soft, play till his feet had no strength to wander beyond the sound of the sweet notes her art could summon from this instrument of strings and wood.

So again she began, and played on, and on, and on, from time to time letting the bow fall, to sing in a flood of heavenly melody that seemed by nature to fall from her lips, note after note, as dew or honey fall drop by drop from the calyx of some perfect flower. Now long did she play and sing those sad, mysterious siren songs? They never knew. The moon travelled on its appointed course, and as its beams passed away gradually that divine musician grew dimmer to his sight. Now only the stars threw their faint light about her, but still she played on, and on, and on. The music swelled, it told of dead and ancient wars, "where all day long the noise of battle rolled"; it rose shrill and high, and in it rang the scream of the Valkyries preparing the feast of Odin. It was low, and sad, and tender, the voice of women mourning for their dead. It changed; it grew unearthly, spiritualised, such music as those might use who welcome souls to their long home. Lastly, it became rich and soft and far as the echo of a dream, and through it could be heard sighs and the broken words of love, that slowly fell away and melted as into the nothingness of some happy sleep.

The singer was weary; her fingers could no longer guide the bow; her voice grew faint. For a moment, she stood still, looking in the flicker of the fire and the pale beams of the stars like some searcher returned from heaven to earth. Then, half fainting, down she sank upon a chair.

Morris turned on the lamps, and looked at this fair being, this chosen home of Music, who lay before him like a broken lily. Then back into his heart with a chilling shock came the thought that this woman, to him at least the most beautiful and gifted his eyes had seen, had promised herself in marriage to Stephen Layard; that she, her body, her mind, her music—all that made her the Stella Fregelius whom he knew—were the actual property of Stephen Layard. Could it be true? Was it not possible that he had made some mistake? that he had misunderstood? A burning desire came upon him to know, to know before he went, and upon the forceful impulse of that moment he did what at any other time would have filled him with horror. He asked her; the words broke from his lips; he could not help them.

"Is it true," he said, with something like a groan, "can it be true that you—*you* are really going to marry that man?"

Stella sat up and looked at him. So she had guessed aright. She made no pretence of fencing with him, or of pretending that she did not know to whom he referred.

"Are you mad to ask me such a thing?" she asked, with a strange break in her voice.

"I am sorry," he began.

She stamped her foot upon the ground.

"Oh!" she said, "it hurts me, it hurts—from my father I understood, but that you should think it possible that I would sell myself—I tell you that it hurts," and as she spoke two large tears began to roll from her lovely pleading eyes.

"Then you mean that you refused him?"

"What else?"

"Thank you. Of course, I have no right to interfere, but forgive me if I say that I cannot help feeling glad. Even if it is taken on the ground of wealth you can easily make as much money as you want without him," and he glanced at the violin which lay beside her.

She made no reply, the subject seemed to have passed from her mind. But presently she lifted her head again, and in her turn asked a question.

"Did you not say that you are going away to-morrow?"

Then something happened to the heart and brain and tongue of Morris Monk so that he could not speak the thing he wished. He meant to answer a monosyllable "Yes," but in its place he replied with a whole sentence.

"I was thinking of doing so; but after all I do not know that it will be necessary; especially in the middle of our experiments."

Stella said nothing, not a single word. Only she found her handkerchief, and without in the least attempting to hide them, there before his eyes wiped the two tears off her face, first one and then the other.

This done she held out her hand to him and left the room.

XIV

The Return of the Colonel

Next morning Morris and Stella met at breakfast as usual, but as though by mutual consent neither of them alluded to the events of the previous evening. Thus the name of Mr. Layard was "taboo," nor were any more questions asked, or statements volunteered as to that journey, the toils of which Morris had suddenly discovered he was after all able to avoid. This morning, as it chanced, no experiments were carried on, principally because it was necessary for Stella to spend the day in the village doing various things on behalf of her father, and lunching with the wife of Dr. Charters, who was one of the churchwardens.

By the second post, which arrived about three o'clock, Morris received two letters, one from his father and one from Mary. There was something about the aspect of these letters that held his eye. That from his father was addressed with unusual neatness, the bold letters being written with all the care of a candidate in a calligraphic competition. The stamps also were affixed very evenly, and the envelope was beautifully sealed with the full Monk coat done in black wax. These, as experience told him, were signs that his father had something important to communicate, since otherwise everything connected with his letters was much more casual. Further, to speak at hazard, he should judge that this matter, whatever it might be, was not altogether disagreeable to the writer.

Mary's letter also had its peculiarities. She always wrote in a large, loose scrawl, running the words into one another after the idle fashion which was an index to her character. In this instance, however, the fault had been carried to such an extreme that the address was almost illegible; indeed, Morris wondered that the letter had not been delayed. The stamps, too, were affixed anyhow, and the envelope barely closed.

"Something has happened," he thought to himself. Then he opened Mary's letter. It was dated Tuesday, that is, two days before, and ran:

> Dearest,
>   My father is dead, my poor old father, and now I have nobody but you left in the world. Thank God, at the last he

was without pain and, they thought, insensible; but I know he wasn't, because he squeezed my hand. Some of his last words that could be understood were, 'Give my love to Morris.' Oh! I feel as though my heart would break. After my mother's death till you came into my life, he was everything to me—everything, everything. I can't write any more.

Your loving Mary

"P.S. Don't trouble to come out here. It is no good. He is to be buried to-morrow, and next day I am going 'en retraite' for a month, as I must have time to get over this—to accustom myself to not seeing him every morning when I come down to breakfast. You remember my French friend, Gabrielle d'Estree? Well; she is a nun now, a sub-something or other in a convent near here where they take in people for a payment. Somehow she heard my father was dead, and came to see me, and offered to put me up at the convent, which has a beautiful large garden, for I have been there. So I said yes, for I shan't feel lonely with her, and it will be a rest for a month. I shall write to you sometimes, and you needn't be afraid, they won't make me a Roman Catholic. Your father objected at first, but now he quite approves; indeed, I told him at last that I meant to go whether he approved or not. It seems it doesn't matter from a business point of view, as you and he are left executors of my father's will. When the month is up I will come to England, and we will settle about getting married. This is the address of the convent as nearly as I can remember it. Letters will reach me there."

Morris laid down the sheet with a sad heart, for he had been truly attached to his uncle Porson, whose simple virtues he understood and appreciated. Then he opened his father's letter, which began in an imposing manner:

My Dear Son (usually he called him Morris),

It is with the deepest grief that I must tell you that poor John Porson, your uncle, passed away this morning about ten o'clock. I was present at the time, and did my best to soothe his last moments with such consolations as can be offered by a relative who is not a clergyman. I wished to wire the sad event to you, but Mary, in whom natural grief develops a self-will that perhaps is also natural, peremptorily refused to allow it, alleging that it was useless to alarm you and waste money on telegrams (how like a woman to think of money at such a moment) when it was quite impossible that you could arrive here in time for the funeral (for he wouldn't be brought home), which, under these queer foreign regulations, must take place to-morrow. Also she announced, to my surprise, and, I must admit, somewhat to my pain, that she intended to immure herself for a month in a convent, after the fashion of the Roman faith, so that it was no use your coming, as men are not admitted into these places. It never seems to have occurred to her that under this blow I should have liked the consolation of her presence, or that I might wish to see you, my son. Still, you must not think too much of all this, although I have felt bound to bring it to your notice, since women under such circumstances are naturally emotional, rebellious against the decrees of Providence, and consequently somewhat selfish.

"To turn to another subject. I am glad to be able to inform you—you will please accept this as an official notice of the fact—that on reading a copy of your uncle's will, which by his directions was handed to me after his death, I find that he has died much better off even than I expected. The net personalty will amount to quite 100,000 pounds, and there is large realty, of which at present I do not know the value. All this is left to Mary with the fullest possible powers of disposal. You and I are appointed executors with a complimentary legacy of 500 pounds to you, and but 100 pounds to me. However, the testator 'in consideration of the forthcoming marriage between his son Morris and my daughter Mary, remits all debts and obligations that may be due to his estate by the said Richard Monk, Lieutenant-Colonel, Companion of the Bath, and an executor of this will.' This amounts to something, of course, but I will not trouble you with details at the moment.

"After all, now that I come to think of it, it is as well that you should not leave home at present, as there will be plenty of executor's business to keep you on the spot. No doubt you will hear from your late uncle's lawyers, Thomas and Thomas, and as soon as you do so you had better go over to Seaview and take formal possession of it and its contents as an executor of the will. I have no time to write more at present, as the undertaker is waiting to see me about the last arrangements for the interment, which takes place at the English cemetery here. The poor man has gone, but at least we may reflect that he can be no more troubled by sickness, etc., and it is a consolation to know that he has made arrangements so eminently proper under the circumstances.

Your affectionate father,
Richard Monk

"P.S. I shall remain here for a little while so as to be near Mary in case she wishes to see me, and afterwards work homewards via Paris. I expect to turn up at the Abbey in a fortnight's time or so."

"Quite in his best style," reflected Morris to himself. "'Remits all debts and obligations that may be due to his estate by the said Richard Monk.' I should be surprised if they don't amount to a good lot. No wonder my father is going to return via Paris; he must feel quite rich again."

Then he sat down to write to Mary.

Under the pressure of this sudden blow—for the fact that Mr. Porson had been for some time in failing health, and the knowledge that his life might terminate at any time, did not seem to make it less sudden—a cloud of depression settled on the Abbey household. Before dinner Morris visited Mr. Fregelius, and told him of what had happened; whereon that pious and kindly, but somewhat inefficient man, bestowed upon him a well-meant lecture of consolation. Appreciating his motives, Morris thanked him sincerely, and was rising to depart, when the clergyman added:

"It is most grievous to me, Mr. Monk, that in these sad hours of mourning you should be forced to occupy your mind with the details of an hospitality which has been forced upon you by circumstances. For the present I fear this cannot be altered—"

"I do not wish it altered," interrupted Morris.

"It is indeed kind of you to say so, but I am happy to state the doctor tells me if I continue to progress as well as at present, I shall be able to leave your roof—"

"My father's roof," broke in Morris again.

"I beg pardon—your father's roof—in about a fortnight."

"I am sorry to hear it, sir; and please clear your mind of the idea that you have ceased to be welcome. Your presence and that of Miss Fregelius will lessen, not increase, my trouble. I should be lonely in this great place with no company but that of my own thoughts."

"I am glad to hear you say so. Whether you feel it or not you are kind, very kind."

And so for the while they parted. When she came in that afternoon, Mr. Fregelius told Stella the news; but, as it happened, she did not see Morris until she met him at dinner time.

"You have heard?" he asked.

"Oh, yes," she answered; "and I am sorry, so sorry. I do not know what more to say."

"There is nothing to be said," answered Morris; "my poor uncle had lived out his life—he was sixty-eight, you know, and there is an end."

"Were you fond of him? Forgive me for asking, but people are not always fond—really fond—of those who happen to be their relations."

"Yes, I was very fond of him. He was a good man, though simple and self-made; very kind to everybody; especially to myself."

"Then do not grieve for him, his pains are over, and some day you will meet him again, will you not?"

"I suppose so; but in the presence of death faith falters."

"I know; but I think that is when it should be strongest and clearest, that is when we should feel that whatever else is unreal and false, this is certain and true."

Morris bowed his head in assent, and there was silence for a while.

"I am afraid that Miss Porson must feel this very much," Stella said presently.

"Yes, she seems quite crushed. She was his only living child, you know."

"Are you not going to join her?"

"No, I cannot; she has gone into a convent for a month, near Beaulieu, and I am afraid the Sisters would not let me through their gates."

"Is she a Catholic?"

"Not at all, but an old friend of hers holds some high position in the place, and she has taken a fancy to be quiet there for a while."

"It is very natural," answered Stella, and nothing more was said upon the subject.

Stella neither played the violin nor sang that night, nor, indeed, again while she remained alone with Morris at the Abbey. Both of them felt that under the circumstances this form of pleasure would be out of place, if not unfeeling, and it was never suggested. For the rest, however, their life went on as usual. On two or three occasions when the weather was suitable some further experiments were carried out with the aerophone, but on most days Stella was engaged in preparing the Rectory, a square, red-brick house, dating from the time of George III, to receive them as soon as her father could be moved. Very fortunately, as has been said, their journey in the steamer Trondhjem had been decided upon so hurriedly that there was no time to allow them to ship their heavy baggage and furniture, which were left to follow, and thus escaped destruction. Now at length these had arrived, and the unpacking and arrangement gave her constant thought and occupation, in which Morris occasionally assisted.

One evening, indeed, he stayed in the Rectory with her, helping to hang some pictures till about half-past six o'clock, when they started for the Abbey. As it chanced, a heavy gale was blowing that night, one of the furious winter storms which are common on this coast, and its worst gusts beat upon Stella so fiercely that she could scarcely stand, and was glad to accept the support of Morris's arm. As they struggled along the high road thus, a particularly savage blast tore the hood of Stella's ulster from her head, whereupon, leaning over her in such a position that his face was necessarily quite close to her own, with some difficulty he managed to replace the hood.

It was while Morris was so engaged that a dog-cart, which because of the roar of the wind he did not hear, and because of his position he could not see until it was almost passing them, came slowly down the road.

Then catching the gleam of the lamps he looked up and started back, thinking that they were being run into, to perceive that the occupants of the dog-cart were Stephen and Eliza Layard.

At the same moment Stephen recognised them, as indeed he could scarcely help doing with the light of the powerful lamp shining full upon their faces. He shouted something to his sister, who also stared coldly at the pair. Then a kind of fury seemed to seize the little man; at any rate, he shook his clenched fist in a menacing fashion, and brought down the whip with a savage cut upon the horse. As the animal sprang forward, moreover, Morris could almost have sworn that he heard the words "kissing her," spoken in Stephen's voice, followed by a laugh from Eliza.

Then the dog-cart vanished into the darkness, and the incident was closed.

For a moment Morris stood angry and astonished, but reflecting that in this wind his ears might have deceived him, and that, at any rate, Stella had heard nothing through her thick frieze hood, he once more offered his arm and walked forward.

The next day was Sunday, when, as usual, he escorted Stella to church. The Layards were there also, but he noticed that, somewhat ostentatiously, they hurried from the building immediately on the conclusion of the service, and it struck him that this demonstration might have some meaning. Eliza, whom he afterwards observed, engaged apparently in eager conversation with a knot of people on the roadway, was, as he knew well, no friend to him, for reasons which he could guess. Nor, as he had heard from various quarters, was she any friend of Stella Fregelius, any more than she had been to Jane Rose. It struck him that even now she might be employed in sowing scandal about them both, and for Stella's sake the thought made him furious. But even if it were so he did not see what he could do; therefore he tried to think he was mistaken, and to dismiss the matter from his mind.

Colonel Monk had written to say that he was coming home on the Wednesday, but he did not, in fact, put in an appearance till the half-past six train on the following Saturday evening, when he arrived beautifully dressed in the most irreproachable black, and in a very good temper.

"Ah, Morris, old fellow," he said, "I am very pleased to see you again. After all, there is no place like home, and at my time of life nothing to equal quiet. I can't tell you how sick I got of that French hole. If it hadn't been for Mary, and my old friend, Lady Rawlins, who, as usual, was in trouble with that wretched husband of hers—he is an imbecile now, you know—I should have been back long before. Well, how are you getting on?"

"Oh, pretty well, thank you, father," Morris answered, in that rather restrained voice which was natural to him when conversing with his parent. "I think, I really think I have nearly perfected my aerophone."

"Have you? Well, then, I hope you will make something out of it after all these years; not that it much matters now, however," he added contentedly. "By the way, that reminds me, how are our two guests, the new parson and his daughter? That was a queer story about your finding her on the wreck. Are they still here?"

"Yes; but the old gentleman is out of bed now, and he expects to be able to move into the Rectory on Monday."

"Does he? Well, they must have given you some company while you were alone. There is no time like the present. I will go up and see him before I dress for dinner."

Accordingly Morris conducted his father to the Abbot's chamber, and introduced him to the clergyman. Mr. Fregelius was seated in his arm-chair, with a crutch by his side, and on learning who his visitor was, made a futile effort to rise.

"Pray, pray, sir," said the Colonel, "keep seated, or you will certainly hurt your leg again."

"When I should be obliged to inflict myself upon you for another five or six weeks," replied Mr. Fregelius.

"In that case, sir," said the Colonel, with his most courteous bow, "and for that reason only I should consider the accident fortunate," by these happy words making of his guest a devoted friend for ever.

"I don't know how to thank you; I really don't know how to thank you."

"Then pray, Mr. Fregelius, leave the thanks unspoken. What would you have had us—or, rather, my son—do? Turn a senseless, shattered man from his door, and that man his future spiritual pastor and master?"

"But there was more. He, Mr. Monk, I mean, saved my daughter Stella's life. You know, a block or a spar fell on me immediately after the ship struck. Then those cowardly dogs of sailors, thinking that she must founder instantly, threw me into the boat and rowed away, leaving her to her fate in the cabin; whereon your son, acting on some words which I spoke in my delirium, sailed out alone at night and rescued her."

"Yes, I heard something, but Morris is not too communicative. The odd thing about the whole affair, so far as I can gather, is that he should have discovered that there was anybody left on board. But he is a curious fellow, Morris; those things which one would expect him to know he never does know; and the things that nobody else has ever heard of he seems to have at his fingers' ends by instinct, or second sight, or something. Well, it has all turned out for the best, hasn't it?"

"Oh, yes, I suppose so," answered Mr. Fregelius, glancing at his injured leg. "At any rate, we are both alive and have not lost many of our belongings."

"Quite so; and under the circumstances you should be uncommonly thankful. But I need not tell a parson that. Well, I can only say that I am delighted to have such a good opportunity of making your acquaintance, which I am sure will lead to our pulling together in parish affairs like a pair of matched horses. Now I must go and dress. But I tell you what, I'll come and smoke a cigar with you afterwards, and put you au fait with all our various concerns. You'll find them a nice lot in this parish, I can tell you, a nice lot. Old Tomley just gave them up as a bad job."

"I hope I shan't do that," replied Mr. Fregelius, after his retreating form.

The Colonel was down to dinner first, and standing warming himself at the library fire when Stella, once more in honour of his arrival arrayed in her best dress, entered the room. The Colonel put up his eyeglass and looked at her as she came down its length.

"By Jove!" he thought to himself, "I didn't know that the clergyman's daughter was like this; nobody ever said so. After all, that fellow Morris can't be half such a fool as he looks, for he kept it dark." Then he stepped forward with outstretched hand.

"You must allow me to introduce myself, Miss Fregelius," he said with an old-fashioned and courtly bow, "and to explain that I have the honour to be my son's father."

She bowed and answered: "Yes, I think I should have known that from the likeness."

"Hum!" said the Colonel. "Even at my age I am not certain that I am altogether flattered. Morris is an excellent fellow, and very clever at electrical machines; but I have never considered him remarkable for personal beauty—not exactly an Adonis, or an Apollo, or a Narcissus, you know."

"I should doubt whether any of them had such a nice face," replied Stella with a smile.

"My word! Now, that is what I call a compliment worth having. But I hear the gentleman himself coming. Shall I repeat it to him?"

"No, please don't, Colonel Monk. I did not mean it for compliment, only for an answer."

"Your wish is a command; but may I make an exception in favour of Miss Porson, who prospectively owns the nice face in question? She would be delighted to know it so highly rated;" and he glanced at her sharply, the look of a man of the world who is trying to read a woman's heart.

"By all means," answered Stella, in an indifferent voice, but recognising in the Colonel one who, as friend or foe, must be taken into account. Then Morris came in, and they went to dinner.

Here also Colonel Monk was very pleasant. He made Stella tell the story of the shipwreck and of her rescue, and generally tried to draw her out in every possible way. But all the while he was watching and taking note of many things. Before they had been together for five minutes he observed that this couple, his son and their visitor, were on terms of extreme intimacy—intimacy so extreme and genuine that in two instances, at least, each anticipated what the other was going to say, without waiting for any words to be spoken. Thus Stella deliberately answered a question that Morris had not put, and he accepted the answer and continued the argument quite as a matter of course. Also, they seemed mysteriously to understand each other's wants, and, worst of all, he noted that when speaking they never addressed each other by name. Evidently just then each of them had but one "you" in the world.

Now, the Colonel had not passed through very varied experiences and studied many sides and conditions of life for nothing; indeed, he would himself explain that he was able to see as far into a brick wall as other folk.

The upshot of all this was that first he thought Morris a very lucky fellow to be an object of undoubted admiration to those beautiful eyes. (It may be explained that the Colonel throughout life had been an advocate of taking such goods as the gods provided; something of a worshipper, too, at the shrine of lovely Thais.) His second reflection was that under all the circumstances it seemed quite time that he returned home to look after him.

"Now, Miss Fregelius," he said, as she rose to leave the table, "when Morris and I have had a glass of wine, and ten minutes to chat over matters connected with his poor uncle's death, I am going to ask you to do me a favour before I go up to smoke a cigar with your father. It is that you will play me a tune on the violin and sing me a song."

"Did Mr. Monk tell you that I played and sang?" she asked.

"No, he did not. Indeed, Mr. Monk has told me nothing whatsoever about you. His, as you may have observed, is not a very communicative nature. The information came from a much less interesting, though, for aught I know, from a more impartial source—the fat page-boy, Thomas, who is first tenor in the Wesleyan chapel, and therefore imagines that he understands music."

"But how could Thomas—" began Morris, when his father cut him short and answered:

"Oh, I'll tell you, quite simply. I had it from the interesting youth's own lips as he unpacked my clothes. It seems that the day before the news of your uncle's death reached this place, Thomas was aroused from his slumbers by hearing what he was pleased to call 'hangels a-'arping and singing.' As soon as he convinced himself that he still lingered on the earth, drawn by the sweetness of the sounds, 'just in his jacket and breeches,' he followed them, until he was sure that they proceeded from your workshop, the chapel.

"Now, as you know, on the upstair passage there still is that queer slit through which the old abbots used to watch the monks at their devotions. Finding the shutter unlocked, the astute Thomas followed their example, as well as he could, for he says there was no light in the chapel except that of the fire, by which presently he made out your figure, Miss Fregelius, sometimes playing the violin, and sometimes singing, and that of Morris—again I must quote—'a-sitting in a chair by the fire with his 'ands at the back of 'is 'ead, a-staring at the floor and rocking 'imself as though he felt right down bad.' No, don't interrupt me, Morris; I must tell my story. It's very amusing.

"Well, Miss Fregelius, he says—and, mind you, this is a great compliment—that you sang and played till he felt as though he would cry when at last you sank down quite exhausted in a chair. Then, suddenly realising that he was very cold, and hearing the stable clock strike two, he went back to bed, and that's the end of the tale. Now you will understand why I have asked you this favour. I don't see why Morris and Thomas should keep it all to themselves."

"I shall be delighted," answered Stella, who, although her cheeks were burning, and she knew that the merciless Colonel was taking note of the fact, on the whole had gone through the ordeal remarkably well. Then she left the room.

As soon as the door closed Morris turned upon his father angrily.

"Oh! my dear boy," the Colonel said, "please do not begin to explain. I know it's all perfectly right, and there is nothing to explain. Why shouldn't you get an uncommonly pretty girl with a good voice to sing to you—while you are still in a position to listen? But if you care to take my advice, next time you will see that the shutter of that hagioscope, or whatever they call it, is locked, as such elevated delights 'a deux' are apt to be misinterpreted by the vulgar. And now, there's enough of this chaff and nonsense. I want to speak to you about the executorship and matters connected with the property generally."

Half an hour later, when the Colonel appeared in the drawing-room, the violin was fetched, and Stella played it and sang afterwards to a piano-forte accompaniment. The performance was not of the same standard, by any means, as that which had delighted Thomas, for Stella did not feel the surroundings quite propitious. Still, with her voice and touch she could not fail, and the result was that before she had done the Colonel grew truly enthusiastic.

"I know a little of music," he said, "and I have heard most of the best singers and violinists during the last forty years; but in the face of all those memories I hope you will allow me to congratulate you, Miss Fregelius. There are some notes in your voice which really reduce me to the condition of peeping Thomas, and, hardened old fellow that I am, almost make me feel inclined to cry."

XV

Three Interviews

The next day was a Sunday, and the Colonel went to church, wearing a hat-band four inches deep. Morris, however, declined to accompany him, saying that he had a letter to write to Mary; whereon his father, who at first was inclined to be vexed, replied that he could not be better employed, and that he was to give her his love. Then he asked if Miss Fregelius was coming, but somewhat to his disappointment, was informed that she wished to stay with her father.

"I wonder," thought the Colonel to himself as he strolled to the church, now and again acknowledging greetings or stopping to chat with one of the villagers—"I wonder if they are going to have a little sacred music together in the chapel. If so, upon my soul, I should like to make the congregation. And that pious fellow Morris, too—the blameless Morris—to go philandering about in this fashion. I hope it won't come to Mary's ears; but if it does, luckily, with all her temper, she is a sensible woman, and knows that even Jove nods at times."

After the service the Colonel spoke to various friends, accepted their condolences upon the death of Mr. Porson, and finally walked down the road with Eliza Layard.

"You must have found that all sorts of strange things have happened at the Abbey since you have been away, Colonel Monk," she said presently in a sprightly voice.

"Well, yes; at least I don't know. I understand that Morris has improved that blessed apparatus of his, and the new parson and his daughter have floated to our doors like driftwood. By the way, have you seen Miss Fregelius?"

"Seen her? Yes, I have seen her."

"She is a wonderfully captivating girl, isn't she? So unusual, with those great eyes of hers that seem to vary with the light—"

"Like a cat's," snapped Eliza.

"The light within—I was going to say."

"Oh! I thought you meant the light without. Well, she may be fascinating—to men, but as I am only a woman, I cannot be expected to appreciate that. You see we look more to other things."

"Ah. Well, so far as I am a judge she seemed to me to be pretty well set up in them also. She has a marvellous voice, is certainly a first-class violinist, and I should say extremely well-read, especially in Norse literature."

"Oh! I daresay she is a genius as well as a beauty."

"I gather," said the Colonel with a smile, "that you do not like Miss Fregelius. As my acquaintance with her is limited, would you think me rude if I asked why?"

"How can I be expected to like her, seeing—" and she paused.

"Seeing what, Miss Layard?"

"What, haven't you heard? I thought it was common property."

He shook his head. "I have heard nothing. Go on, pray, this is quite interesting."

"That she led on that silly brother of mine until he proposed to her—yes, proposed to her!—and then refused him. Stephen has been like a crazy creature ever since, moaning, and groaning, and moping till I think that he will go off his head, instead of returning thanks to Providence for a merciful escape."

The Colonel set his lips as though to whistle, then checked himself.

"Under the circumstances, presuming them to be accurately stated, I am not prepared to say who is to be congratulated or who should thank Providence. These things are so individual, are they not? But if one thing is clear, whatever else she is or is not, Miss Fregelius cannot be a fortune-hunter, although she must want money."

"She may want other things more."

"Perhaps. But I am very stupid, I am afraid I do not understand."

"Men, for instance," suggested Eliza.

"Dear me! that sounds almost carnivorous. I am afraid that there are not many about here to satisfy her appetite. Your brother, Morris, the curate at Morton, and myself, if at my age I may creep into that honourable company, are the only single creatures within four miles, and from these Stephen and Morris must apparently be eliminated."

"Why should Morris be eliminated?"

"A reason may occur to you."

"Do you mean because he is engaged? What on earth does that matter?"

"Nothing—in the East—but, rightly or wrongly, we have decided upon a monogamous system; a man can't marry two wives, Miss Layard."

"But he can throw over one girl to marry another."

"Do you suggest that Morris is contemplating this experiment?"

"I? I suggest nothing; all I know is—"

"Well, now, what do you know?"

"If you wish me to tell you, as perhaps I ought, I know this, Colonel Monk, that the other night, when I was driving along the Rectory road, I saw your son, Mr. Monk, kissing this wonderful Miss Fregelius; that is all, and Stephen saw it also, you ask him."

"Thank you; I think I would rather not. But what an odd place for him to choose for this interchange of early Christian courtesies! Also— if you are not mistaken—how well it illustrates that line in the hymn this morning:

"'How many a spot defiles the robe that wraps an earthly saint.'

Such adventures seem scarcely in Morris's line, and I should have thought that even an inexperienced saint would have been more discreet."

"Men always jest at serious things," said Eliza severely.

"Which do you mean—the saints or the kissing? Both are serious enough, but the two in combination—"

"Don't you believe me?" asked Eliza.

"Of course. But could you give me a few details?"

Eliza could and did—with amplifications.

"Now, what do you say, Colonel Monk?" she asked triumphantly.

"I say that I think you have made an awkward mistake, Miss Layard. It seems to me that all you saw is quite consistent with the theory that he was buttoning or arranging the young lady's hood. I understand that the wind was very high that night."

Eliza started; this was a new and unpleasant interpretation which she hastened to repudiate. "Arranging her hood, indeed—"

"When he might have been kissing her? You cannot understand such moderation. Still, it is possible, and he ought to have the benefit of the doubt. Witnesses to character would be valuable in such a case, and his—not to mention the lady's—is curiously immaculate."

"Of course you are entitled to your own opinion, but I have mine."

Suddenly the Colonel changed his bantering, satirical tone, and became stern and withering.

"Miss Layard," he said, "does it occur to you that on evidence which would not suffice to convict a bicyclist of riding on a footpath, you are circulating a scandal of which the issue might be very grave to both the parties concerned?"

"I am not circulating anything. I was telling you privately;" replied Eliza, still trying to be bold.

"I am glad to hear it. I understand that neither you nor your brother have spoken of this extraordinary tale, and I am quite certain that you will not speak of it in the future."

"I cannot answer for my brother," she said sulkily.

"No, but in his own interest and in yours I trust that you will make him understand that if I hear a word of this I shall hold him to account. Also, that his propagation of such a slander will react upon you, who were with him."

"How?" asked Eliza, now thoroughly frightened, for when he chose the Colonel could be very crushing.

"Thus: Your brother's evidence is that of an interested person which no one will accept; and of yours, Miss Layard, it might be inferred that it was actuated by jealousy of a charming and quite innocent girl; or, perhaps, by other motives even worse, which I would rather you did not ask me to suggest."

Eliza did not ask him. She was too wise. As she knew well, when roused the Colonel was a man with a bitter tongue and a good memory.

"I am sure I am the last person who would wish to do mischief," she said in a humble voice.

"Of course, I know that, I know that. Well, now we understand each other, so I must be turning home. Thank you so much for having been quite candid with me. Good morning, Miss Layard; remember me to Stephen."

"Phew!" reflected the Colonel to himself, "that battle is won—after a fashion—but just about forty-eight hours too late. By this time that vixen of a woman has put the story all over the place. Oh, Morris, you egregious ass, if you wanted to take to kissing like a schoolboy, why the deuce did you select the high road for the purpose? This must be put a stop to. I must take steps, and at once. They mustn't be seen together again, or there will be trouble with Mary. But how to do it? how to do it? That is the question, and one to which I must find an answer within the next two hours. What a kettle of fish! What a pretty kettle of fish!"

In due course, and after diligent search, he found the answer to this question.

At lunch time the Colonel remarked casually that he had walked a little way with Miss Layard, who mentioned that she had seen them—i.e., his son and Miss Fregelius—struggling through the gale the other night. Then he watched the effect of this shot. Morris moved his chair and looked uncomfortable; clearly he was a most transparent sinner. But on Stella it took no effect.

"As usual," reflected the Colonel, "the lady has the most control. Or perhaps he tried to kiss her and she wouldn't let him, and a consciousness of virtue gives her strength."

After luncheon the Colonel paid a visit to Mr. Fregelius, ostensibly to talk to him about the proposed restoration of the chancel, for which he, as holder of the great tithes, was jointly liable with the rector, a responsibility that, in the altered circumstances of the family, he now felt himself able to face. When this subject was exhausted, which did not take long, as Mr. Fregelius refused to express any positive opinion until he had inspected the church, the Colonel's manner grew portentously solemn.

"My dear sir," he said, "there is another matter, a somewhat grave one, upon which, for both our sakes and the sakes of those immediately concerned, I feel bound to say a few words."

Mr. Fregelius, who was a timid man, looked very much alarmed. A conviction that the "grave matter" had something to do with Stella flashed into his mind, but all he said was:

"I am afraid I don't understand, Colonel Monk."

"No; indeed, how should you? Well, to come to the point, it has to do with that very charming daughter of yours and my son Morris."

"I feared as much," groaned the clergyman.

"Indeed! I thought you said you did not understand."

"No, but I guessed; wherever Stella goes things seem to happen."

"Exactly; well, things have happened here. To be brief, I mean that a lot of silly women have got up a scandal about them—no, scandal is too strong a word—gossip."

"What is alleged?" asked Mr. Fregelius faintly.

"Well, that your daughter threw over that young ass, Stephen Layard, because—the story seems to me incredible, I admit—she had fallen violently in love with Morris. Further that she and the said Morris were seen embracing at night on the Rectory road, which I don't believe, as the witnesses are Layard, who is prejudiced, and his sister, who is the most ill-bred, bitter, and disappointed woman in the county. Lastly, and this is no doubt true, that they are generally on terms of great intimacy, and we all know where that leads to between a man and woman—'Plato, thy confounded fantasies,' etc. You see, when people sit up singing to each other alone till two in the morning—I don't mean that Morris sings, he has no more voice than a crow; he does the appreciative audience—well, other people will talk, won't they?"

"I suppose so, the world being what it is," sighed Mr. Fregelius.

"Exactly; the world being what it is, and men and women what they are, a most unregenerate lot and 'au fond' very primitive, as I daresay you may have observed."

"What is to be done?"

"Well, under other circumstances, I should have said, Nothing at all except congratulate them most heartily, more especially my son. But in this case there are reasons which make such a course impossible. As you know, Morris is engaged to be married to my niece, Miss Porson, and it is a contract which, even if he wished it, honour would forbid him to break, for family as well as for personal reasons."

"Quite so, quite so; it is not to be thought of. But again I ask—What is to be done?"

"Is that not rather a question for you to consider? I suggest that you had better speak to your daughter; just a hint, you know, just a hint."

"Upon my word, I'd rather not. Stella can be so—decided—at times, and we never seem quite to understand each other. I did speak to her the other day when Mr. Layard wished to marry her, a match I was naturally anxious for, but the results were not satisfactory."

"Still, I think you might try."

"Very well, I will try; and, Colonel Monk, I cannot tell you how grieved I am to have brought all this trouble on you."

"Not a bit," answered the Colonel cheerfully. "I am an old student of human nature, and I rather enjoy it; it's like watching the puppets on a stage. Only we mustn't let the comedy grow into a tragedy."

"Ah! that's what I am afraid of, some tragedy. Stella is a woman who takes things hard, and if any affection really has sprung up—"

"—It will no doubt evaporate with the usual hysterics and morning headache. Bless me! I have known dozens of them, and felt some myself in my time—the headaches, I mean, not the other things. Don't be alarmed if she gets angry, Mr. Fregelius, but just appeal to her reason; she will see the force of it afterwards."

An hour or so later the Colonel started for a walk on the beach to look at some damage which a high tide had done to the cliff. As he was nearing the Abbey steps on his return he saw the figure of a woman standing quite still upon the sands. An inspection through his eyeglass revealed that it was Stella, and instinct told him her errand.

"This is rather awkward," he thought, as he braced himself to battle, "especially as I like that girl and don't want to hurt her feelings. Hullo! Miss Fregelius, are you taking the air? You should walk, or you will catch cold."

"No, Colonel Monk, I was waiting for you."

"Waiting for me? Me! This is indeed an honour, and one which age appreciates."

She waved aside his two-edged badinage. "You have been speaking to my father," she said.

Instantly the Colonel assumed a serious manner, not the most serious, such as he wore at funerals, but still one suited to a grave occasion.

"Yes, I have."

"You remember all that you said?"

"Certainly, Miss Fregelius; and I assume that for the purposes of this conversation it need not be repeated."

She bowed her head, and replied, "I have come to explain and to tell you three things. First, that all these stories are false except that about the singing. Secondly, that whoever is responsible for them has made it impossible that I should live in Monksland, so I am going to London to earn my own living there. And, thirdly, that I hope you will excuse my absence from dinner as I think the more I keep to myself until we go to-morrow, the better; though I reserve to myself the right to speak to Mr. Monk on this subject and to say good-bye to him."

"She *is* taking it hard and she *is* fond of him—deuced fond of him, poor girl," thought the Colonel; but aloud he said, "My dear Miss Fregelius, I never believed the stories. As for the principal one, common sense rebels against it. All I said to your father was that there appears to be a lot of talk about the place, and, under the circumstances of my son's engagement, that he might perhaps give you a friendly hint."

"Oh! indeed; he did not put it quite like that. He gave me to understand that you had told him—that I was—so—so much in love with Mr. Monk that on this account I had—rejected Mr. Layard."

"Please keep walking," said the Colonel, "or you *really* will catch cold." Then suddenly he stopped, looked her sharply in the face, much as he had done to Eliza, and said, "Well, and are you not in love with him?"

For a moment Stella stared at him indignantly. Then suddenly he saw a blush spread upon her face to be followed by an intense pallor, while the pupils of the lovely eyes enlarged themselves and grew soft. Next instant she put her hand to her heart, tottered on her feet, and had he not caught her would perhaps have fallen.

"I do not think I need trouble you to answer my question, which, indeed, now that I think of it, was one I had no right to put," he said as she recovered herself.

"Oh, my God!" moaned Stella, wringing her hands; "I never knew it till this moment. You have brought it home to me; you, yes, you!" and she burst out weeping.

"Here are the hysterics," thought the Colonel, "and I am afraid that the headache will be bad to-morrow morning."

To her, however, he said very tenderly, "My dear girl, my dear girl, pray do not distress yourself. These little accidents will happen in the best regulated hearts, and believe me, you will get over it in a month or two."

"Accident!" she said. "It is no accident; it is Fate!—I see it all now—and I shall never get over it. However, that is my own affair, and I have no right to trouble you with my misfortunes."

"Oh! but you will indeed, and though you may think the advice hard, I will tell you the best way."

She looked up in inquiry.

"Change your mind and marry Stephen Layard. He is not at all a bad fellow, and—there are obvious advantages."

This was the Colonel's first really false move, as he himself felt before the last word had left his lips.

"Colonel Monk," she said, "because I am unfortunate is it any reason that you should insult me?"

"Miss Fregelius, to my knowledge I have never insulted any woman; and certainly I should not wish to begin with one who has just honoured me with her confidence."

"Is it not an insult," she answered with a sort of sob, "when a woman to her shame and sorrow has confessed—what I have—to bid her console herself by marriage with another man?"

"Now that you put it thus, I confess that perhaps some minds might so interpret an intention which did not exist. It seemed to me that, after a while, in marriage you would most easily forget a trouble which my son so unworthily has brought on you."

"Don't blame him for he does not deserve it. If anybody is to blame it is I; but in truth all those stories are false; we have neither of us done anything."

"Do not press the point, Miss Fregelius; I believe you."

"We have neither of us done anything," she repeated; "and, what is more, if you had not interfered, I do not think that I should have found out the truth; or, at least, not yet—till I saw him married, perhaps, when it would have been no matter."

"When you see a man walking in his sleep you do your best to stop him," said the Colonel.

"And so cause him to fall over the precipice and be dashed to bits. Oh! you should have let me finish my journey. Then I should have come back to the bed that I have made to lie on, and waked to find myself alone, and nobody would have been hurt except myself who caused the evil."

The Colonel could not continue this branch of the conversation. Even to him, a hardened vessel, as he had defined himself, it was too painful.

"You said you mean to earn a living in London. How?"

"By my voice and violin, if one can sing and play with a sore heart. I have an old aunt, a sister of my father's, who is a music mistress, with whom I daresay I can arrange to live, and who may be able to get me some introductions."

"I hope that I can help you there, and I will to the best of my ability; indeed, if necessary, I will go to town and see about things. Allow me to add this, Miss Fregelius, that I think you are doing a very brave thing, and, what is more, a very wise one; and I believe that before long we shall hear of you as the great new contralto."

She shrugged her shoulders. "It may be; I don't care. Good-bye. By the way, I wish to see Mr. Monk once more before I go; it would be better for us all. I suppose that you don't object to that, do you?"

"Miss Fregelius, my son is a man advancing towards middle age. It is entirely a point for you and him to decide, and I will only say that I have every confidence in you."

"Thank you," she answered, and turning, walked rapidly down the lonely beach till her figure melted into the gathering gloom of the winter's night. Once, however, when she thought that she was out of eyeshot, he saw her stop with her face towards the vast and bitter sea, and saw also that she was wringing her hands in an agony of the uttermost despair.

"She looks like a ghost," said the Colonel aloud with a little shiver, "like a helpless, homeless ghost, with the world behind her and the infinite in front, and nothing to stand on but a patch of shifting sand, wet with her own tears."

H. RIDER HAGGARD

When the Colonel grew thus figurative and poetical it may be surmised by anyone who has taken the trouble to study his mixed and somewhat worldly character that he was deeply moved. And he was moved; more so, indeed, than he had been since the death of his wife. Why? He would have found it hard to explain. On the face of it, the story was of a trivial order, and in some of its aspects rather absurd. Two young people who happened to be congenial, but one of whom was engaged, chance to be thrown together for a couple of months in a country house. Although there is some gossip, nothing at all occurs between them beyond a little perfectly natural flirtation. The young man's father, hearing the gossip, speaks to the young lady in order that she may take steps to protect herself and his son against surmise and misinterpretation. Thereupon a sudden flood of light breaks upon her soul, by which she sees that she is really attached to the young man, and being a woman of unusual character, or perhaps absurdly averse to lying even upon such a subject, in answer to a question admits that this is so, and that she very properly intends to go away.

Could anything be more commonplace, more in the natural order of events? Why, then, was he moved? Oh! it was that woman's face and eyes. Old as he might be, he felt jealous of his son; jealous to think that for him such a woman could wear this countenance of wonderful and thrilling woe. What was there in Morris that it should have called forth this depth of passion undefiled? Now, if there were no Mary—but there was a Mary, it was folly to pursue such a line of thought.

From sympathy for Stella, which was deep and genuine, to anger with his son proved to the Colonel an easy step. Morris was that worst of sinners, a hypocrite. Morris, being engaged to one woman, had taken advantage of her absence deliberately to involve the affections of another, or, at any rate, caused her considerable inconvenience. He was wroth with Morris, and what was more, before he grew an hour older he would let him have a piece of his mind.

He found the sinner in his workshop, the chapel, making mathematical calculations, the very sight of which added to his father's indignation. The man, he reflected to himself, who under these circumstances could indulge an abnormal talent for mathematics, especially on Sunday, must be a cold-blooded brute. He entered the place slamming the door behind him; and Morris looking up noted with alarm, for he hated rows, that there was war in his eye.

"Won't you take a chair, father?" he said.

"No, thank you; I would rather say what I have to say standing."

"What is the matter?"

"The matter is, sir, that I find that by your attentions you have made that poor girl, Miss Fregelius, while she was a guest in my house, the object of slander and scandal to every ill-natured gossip in the three parishes."

Morris's quiet, thoughtful eyes flashed in an ominous and unusual manner.

"If you were not my father," he said, "I should ask you to change your tone in speaking to me on such a subject; but as things are I suppose that I must submit to it, unless you choose otherwise."

"The facts, Morris," answered his father, "justify any language that I can use."

"Did you get these facts from Stephen Layard and Miss Layard? Ah! I guessed as much. Well, the story is a lie; I was merely arranging her hood which she could not do herself, as the wind forced her to use her hand to hold her dress down."

The thought of his own ingenuity in hitting on the right solution of the story mollified the Colonel not a little.

"Pshaw," he said, "I knew that. Do you suppose that I believed you fool enough to kiss a girl on the open road when you had every opportunity of kissing her at home? I know, too, that you have never kissed her at all; or, ostensibly at any rate, done anything that you shouldn't do."

"What is my offence, then?" asked Morris.

"Your offence is that you have got her talked about; that you have made her in love with you—don't deny it; I have it from her own lips. That you have driven her out of this place to earn a living in London as best she may, and that, being yourself an engaged man"—here once more the Colonel drew a bow at a venture—"you are what is called in love with her yourself."

These two were easy victims to the skill of so experienced an archer. The shaft went home between the joints of his son's harness, and Morris sank back in his chair and turned white. Generosity, or perhaps the fear of exciting more unpleasant consequences, prevented the Colonel from following up this head of his advantage.

"There is more, a great deal more, behind," he went on. "For instance, all this will probably come to Mary's ears."

"Certainly it will; I shall tell her of it myself."

"Which will be tantamount to breaking your engagement. May I ask if that is your intention?"

"No; but supposing that all you say were true, and that it *was* my intention, what then?"

"Then, sir, to my old-fashioned ideas you would be a dishonourable fellow, to cast away the woman who has only you to look to in the world, that you may put another woman who has taken your fancy in her place."

Morris bit his lip.

"Still speaking on that supposition," he replied, "would it not be more dishonourable to marry her; would it not be kinder, shameful as it may be, to tell her all the truth and let her seek some worthier man?"

The Colonel shrugged his shoulders. "I can't split hairs," he said, "or enter on an argument of sentimental casuistry. But I tell you this, Morris, although you are my only son, and the last of our name, that rather than do such a thing, under all the circumstances, it would be better that you should take a pistol and blow your brains out."

"Very probably," answered Morris, "but would you mind telling me also what are the exact circumstances which would in your opinion so aggravate this particular case?"

"You have a copy of your uncle Porson's will in that drawer; give it me."

Morris obeyed, and his father searched for, and read the following sentence: "In consideration of the forthcoming marriage between his son Morris and my daughter Mary, the said testator remits all debts and obligations that may be due to his estate by the said Richard Monk, Lieutenant Colonel, Companion of the Bath, and an executor of this will."

"Well," said Morris.

"Well," replied the Colonel coolly, "those debts in all amounted to 19,543 pounds. No wonder you seem astonished, but they have been accumulating for a score of years. There's the fact, any way, so discussion is no use. Now do you understand? 'In consideration of the forthcoming marriage,' remember."

"I shall be rich some day; that machine you laugh at will make me rich; already I have been approached. I might repay this money."

"Yes, and you might not; such hopes and expectations have a way of coming to nothing. Besides, hang it all, Morris, you know that there is more than money in the question."

Morris hid his face in his hands for a moment; when he removed them it was ashen. "Yes," he said, "things are unfortunate. You remember that you were very anxious that I should engage myself, and Mary was so good as to accept me. Perhaps, I cannot say, I should have done better to have waited till I felt some real impulse towards marriage. However, that is all gone by, and, father, you need not be in the least afraid; there is not the slightest fear that I shall attempt to do anything of which you would disapprove."

"I was sure you wouldn't, old fellow," answered the Colonel in a friendly tone, "not when you came to think. Matters seem to have got into a bit of a tangle, don't they? Most unfortunate that charming young lady being brought to this house in such a fashion. Really, it looks like a spite of what she called Fate. However, I have no doubt that it will all straighten itself somehow. By the way, she told me that she should wish to see you once to say good-bye before she went. Don't be vexed with me if, should she do so, I suggest to you to be very careful. Your position will be exceedingly painful and exceedingly dangerous, and in a moment all your fine resolutions may come to nothing; though I am sure that she does not wish any such thing, poor dear. Unless she really seeks this interview, I think, indeed, it would be best avoided."

Morris made no answer, and the Colonel went away somewhat weary and sorrowful. For once he had seen too much of his puppet-show.

XVI

A Marriage and After

Stella did not appear at dinner that night, or at breakfast next day. In the course of the morning, growing impatient, for he had explanations to make, Morris sent her a note worded thus:

"Can I see you?—M. M."

to which came the following answer:

Not to-day. Meet me to-morrow at the Dead Church at three o'clock.

—Stella

It was the only letter that he ever received from her.

That afternoon, December 23, Mr. Fregelius and his daughter moved to the Rectory in a fly that had been especially prepared to convey the invalid without shaking him. Morris did not witness their departure, as the Colonel, either by accident or design, had arranged to go with him on this day to inspect the new buildings which had been erected on the Abbey Farm. Nor, indeed, were the names of the departed guests so much as mentioned at dinner that night. The incident of their long stay at the Abbey, with all its curious complications, was closed, and both father and son, by tacit agreement, determined to avoid all reference to it; at any rate for the present.

The Christmas Eve of that year will long be remembered in Monksland and all that stretch of coast as the day of the "great gale" which wrought so much damage on its shores. The winter's dawn was of extraordinary beauty, for all the eastern sky might have been compared to one vast flower, with a heart of burnished gold, and sepals and petals of many coloured fires. Slowly from a central point it opened, slowly its splendours spread across the heavens; then suddenly it seemed to wither and die, till where it had been was nothing but masses of grey vapour that arose, gathered, and coalesced into an ashen pall hanging low above the surface of the ashen sea. The coastguard, watching the glass, hoisted their warning cone, although as yet there was no breath of wind, and old sailormen hanging about in knots on the cliff and beach went to haul up their boats as high as they could drag them, knowing that it would blow hard by night.

About mid-day the sea began to be troubled, as though its waves were being pushed on by some force as yet unseen, and before two o'clock gusts of cold air from the nor'east travelled landwards off the ocean with a low moaning sound, which was very strange to hear.

As Morris trudged along towards the Dead Church he noticed, as we do notice such things when our minds are much preoccupied and oppressed, that these gusts were coming quicker and quicker, although still separated from each other by periods of aerial calm. Then he remembered that a great gale had been prophesied in the weather reports, and thought to himself that they portended its arrival.

He reached the church by the narrow spit of sand and shingle which still connected it with the shore, passed through the door in the rough brick wall, closing it behind him, and paused to look. Already under that heavy sky the light which struggled through the brine-encrusted eastern window was dim and grey. Presently, however, he discovered the figure of Stella seated in her accustomed place by the desolate-looking stone altar, whereon stood the box containing the aerophone that they had used in their experiments. She was dressed in her dark-coloured ulster, of which the hood was still drawn over her head, giving her the appearance of some cloaked nun, lingering, out of time and place, in the ruined habitations of her worship.

As he advanced she rose and pushed back the hood, revealing the masses of her waving hair, to which it had served as a sole covering. In silence Stella stretched out her hand, and in silence Morris took it; for neither of them seemed to find any words. At length she spoke, fixing her sad eyes upon his face, and saying:

"You understand that we meet to part. I am going to London to-morrow; my father has consented."

"That is Christmas Day," he faltered.

"Yes, but there is an early train, the same that runs on Sundays."

Then there was another pause.

"I wish to ask your pardon," he said, "for all the trouble that I have brought upon you."

She smiled. "I think it is I who should ask yours. You have heard of these stories?"

H. RIDER HAGGARD

"Yes, my father spoke to me; he told me of his conversation with you."

"All of it?"

"I do not know; I suppose so," and he hung his head.

"Oh!" she broke out in a kind of cry, "if he told you all—"

"You must not blame him," he interrupted. "He was very angry with me. He considered that I had behaved badly to you, and everybody, and I do not think that he weighed his words."

"I am not angry. Now that I think of it, what does it matter? I cannot help things, and the truth will out."

"Yes," he said, quite simply; "we love each other, so we may as well admit it before we part."

"Yes," she echoed, without disturbance or surprise; "I know now—we love each other."

These were the first intimate words that ever passed between them; this, their declaration, unusual even in the long history of the passions of men and women, and not the less so because neither of them seemed to think its fashion strange.

"It must always have been so," said Morris.

"Always," she answered, "from the beginning; from the time you saved my life and we were together in the boat and—perhaps, who can say?—before. I can see it now, only until they put light into our minds we did not understand. I suppose that sooner or later we should have found it out, for having been brought together nothing could ever have really kept us asunder."

"Nothing but death," he answered heavily.

"That is your old error, the error of a lack of faith," she replied, with one of her bright smiles. "Death will unite us beyond the possibility of parting. I pray God that it may come quickly—to me, not to you. You have your life to lead; mine is finished. I do not mean the life of my body, but the real life, that within."

"I think that you are right; I grow sure of it. But here there is nothing to be done."

"Of course," she answered eagerly; "nothing. Do you suppose that I wished to suggest such a treachery?"

"No, you are too pure and good."

"Good I am not—who is?—but I believe that I am pure."

"It is bitter," groaned Morris.

"Why so? My heart aches, and yet through the pain I rejoice, because I know that it is well with us. Had you not loved me, then it would have been bitter. The rest is little. What does it matter when and how and where it comes about? To-day we part—for ever in the flesh. You will not look upon this mortal face of mine again."

"Why do you say so?"

"Because I feel that it is true."

He glanced up hastily, and she answered the question in his eyes.

"No—indeed—not that—I never thought of such a thing. I think it a crime. We are bid to endure the burden of our day. I shall go on weaving my web and painting my picture till, soon or late, God says, 'Hold,' and then I shall die gladly, yes, very gladly, because the real beginning is at hand."

"Oh! that I had your perfect faith," groaned Morris.

"Then, if you love me, learn it from me. Should I, of all people, tell you what is not true? It is the truth—I swear it is the truth. I am not deceived. I know, I know, I *know*."

"What do you know—about us?"

"That, when it is over, we shall meet again where there is no marriage, where there is nothing gross, where love perfect and immortal reigns and passion is forgotten. There that we love each other will make no heart sore, not even hers whom here, perhaps, we have wronged; there will be no jealousies, since each and all, themselves happy in their own way and according to their own destinies, will rejoice in the happiness of others. There, too, our life will be one life, our work one work, our thought one thought—nothing more shall separate us at all in that place where there is no change or shadow of turning. Therefore," and she clasped her hands and looked upwards, her face shining like a saint's, although the tears ran down it, "therefore, 'O Death, where is thy sting? O grave, where is thy victory?'"

"You talk like one upon the verge of it, who hears the beating of Death's wings. It frightens me, Stella."

"I know nothing of that; it may be to-night, or fifty years hence— we are always on the verge, and those Wings I have heard from childhood. Fifty, even seventy years, and after them—all the Infinite; one tiny grain of sand compared to the bed of the great sea, that sea from which it was washed at dawn to be blown back again at nightfall."

"But the dead forget—in that land all things are forgotten. Were you to die I should call to you and you would not answer; and when my time came, I might look for you and never find you."

"How dare you say it? If I die, search, and you shall see. No; do *not* search, wait. At your death I will be with you."

"Whatever happens in life or death—here or hereafter—swear that you will not forget me, and that you will love me only. Swear it, Stella."

"Come to this altar," she said, when she had thought a moment, "and give me your hand—so. Now, before my Maker and the Presences who surround us, I marry you, Morris Monk. Not in the flesh—with your flesh I have nothing to do—but in the spirit. I take your soul to mine, I give my soul to yours; yours it was from its birth's day, yours it is, and when it ceases to be yours, let it perish everlastingly."

"So be it to both of us, for ever and for ever," he answered.

This, then, was their marriage, and as they walked hand in hand away from the ancient altar, which surely had never seen so strange a rite, there returned to Morris an idle fantasy which had entered his mind at this very spot when they landed one morning half-frozen after that night in the open boat. But he said nothing of it; for with the memory came a recollection of certain wandering words which that same day fell from Stella's lips, words at the thought of which his spirit thrilled and his flesh shuddered. What if she were near it, or he were near it, or both of them? What if this solemn ceremony of marriage mocked, yet made divine, had taken place upon the very threshold of its immortal consummation? She read his thought and answered:

"Remember always, far and near, it is the same thing; time is nothing; this oath of ours cannot be touched by time or earthly change."

"I will remember," he answered.

What more did they say? He never could be sure, nor does it matter, for what is written bears its gist.

"Go away first," she said presently; "I promised your father that I would bring no further trouble on you, so we must not be seen together. Go now, for the gale is rising fast and the darkness grows."

"This is hard to bear," he muttered, setting his teeth. "Are you sure that we shall not meet again in after years?"

"Sure. You look your last upon me, on the earthly Stella whom you know and love."

"It must be done," he said.

"It must be done," she echoed. "Good-bye, husband, till that appointed hour of meeting when I may call you so without shame," and she held out her hand.

He took and pressed it; speak he could not. Then, like a man stricken in years, he passed down the church with bent head and shambling feet. At the door he turned to look at her. She was standing erect and proud as a conqueror, her hand resting upon the altar. Even at that distance their eyes met, and in hers, lit with a wild and sudden ray from the sinking sun, he could see a strange light shine. Then he went out of the door and dragged it to behind him, to battle his way homeward through the roaring gale that stung and buffeted him like all the gathered spites and hammerings of Destiny.

This, then, was their parting, a parting pure and stern and high, unsolaced by one soft word, unsweetened by a single kiss. Yet it seems fitting that those who hope to meet in the light of the spirit should make their last farewells on earth beneath such solemn shadows.

And Stella? After all she was but a woman, a woman with a very human heart. She knew the truth indeed, to whom it was given to see before the due determined time of vision, but still she was troubled with that human heart, and weighed down by the flesh over which she triumphed. Now that he was gone, pride and strength seemed both to leave her, and with a low cry, like the cry of a wounded sea-bird, she cast herself down there upon the cold stones before the altar, and wept till her senses left her.

A great gale roared and howled. The waters, driven onwards by its furious breath, beat upon the eastern cliffs till these melted like snow beneath them, taking away field and church, town and protecting wall, and in return casting up the wrecks of ships and the bodies of dead men.

Morris could not sleep. Who could sleep in such an awful tempest? Who could sleep that had passed through such a parting? Oh! his heart ached, and he was as one sick to death, and with him continually was the thought of Stella, and before him came the vision of her eyes. He could not sleep, so rising, he dressed himself and went to the window. High in the heavens swept clean of clouds by the furious blasts floated a wandering moon, throwing her ghastly light upon the swirling, furious sea. Shorewards rushed the great rollers in unending lines, there to break in thunder and seethe across the shingle till the sea-wall stopped them and sent the spray flying upwards in thin, white clouds.

"God help those in the power of the sea to-night," thought Morris, "for many of them will not keep Christmas here."

Then it seemed to his mind, excited by storm and sorrow, as though some power were drawing him, as though some voice were telling him that there was that which he must hear. Aimlessly, half-unconsciously he wandered to his workshop in the old chapel, turned on one of the lamps, and stood at the window watching the majestic progress of the storm, and thinking, thinking, thinking.

While he remained thus, suddenly, thrilling his nerves as though with a quick shock of pain, sharp and clear even in that roar and turmoil, rang out the sound of an electric bell. He started round and looked. Yes; as he thought in all the laboratory there was only one bell that could ring, none other had its batteries charged, and that bell was attached to the aerophone whereof the twin stood upon the altar in the Dead Church. The instrument was one of the pair with which he had carried out his experiments of the last two months.

His heart stood still. "Great God! What could have caused that bell to ring?" It could not ring; it was a physical impossibility unless somebody were handling the sister instrument, and at four o'clock in the morning, who could be there, and except one, who would know its working? With a bound he was by the aerophone and had given the answering signal. Then instantly, as though she were standing at his side in the room, for this machine does not blur the voice or heighten its tone, he heard Stella speaking.

"Is it you who answer me?" she asked.

"Yes, yes," he said, "but where are you at this hour of the night?"

"Where you left me, in the Dead Church," floated back the quick reply through the raving breadths of storm. "Listen: After you went my strength gave out and I suppose that I fainted; at least, a little while ago I woke up from a deep sleep to find myself lying before the alter here. I was frightened, for I knew that it must be far into the night, and an awful gale is blowing which shakes the whole church. I went to the door and opened it, and by the light of the moon I saw that between me and the shore lies a raging sea hundreds of yards wide. Then I came back and threw out my mind to you, and tried to wake you, if you slept; tried to make you understand that I wished you to go to the aerophone and hear me."

"I will get help at once," broke in Morris.

"I beg you," came back the voice, "I beg you, do not stir. The time is very short; already the waves are dashing against the walls of the chancel, and I hear the water rumbling in the vaults beneath my feet. Listen!" her voice ceased, and in place of it there swelled the shriek of the storm which beat about the Dead Church, the rush, too, of the water in the hollow vaults and the crashing of old coffins as they were washed from their niches. Another instant, and Stella had cut off these sounds and was speaking again.

"It is useless to think of help, no boat, nothing could live upon that fearful sea; moreover, within five minutes this church must fall and vanish."

"My God! My God!" wailed Morris.

"Do not grieve; it is a waste of precious time, and do not stir till the end. I want you to know that I did not seek this death. I never dreamed of such a thing. You must tell my father so, and bid him not to mourn for me. It was my intention to leave the church within ten minutes of yourself. This cup is given to me by the hand of Fate. I did not fill it. Do you hear and understand?"

"I hear and understand," answered Morris.

"Now you see," she went on, "that our talk to-day was almost inspired. My web is woven, my picture is painted, and to me Heaven says, 'Hold.' The thought that it might be so was in your mind, was it not?"

"Yes."

"And I answered your thought, telling you that time is nothing. This I tell you again for your comfort in the days that remain to you of life. Oh! I bless God; I bless God Who has dealt so mercifully to me. Where are now the long years of lonely suffering that I feared—I who stand upon the threshold of the Eternal? . . . I can talk no more, the water is rising in the church—already it is about my knees; but remember every word which I have said to you; remember that we are wed—truly wed, that I go to wait for you, and that even if you do not see me I will, if I may, be near you always—till you die, and afterwards will be with you always—always."

"Stay," cried Morris.

"What have you to say? Be swift, the water rises and the walls are cracking."

"That I love you now and for ever and for ever; that I will remember everything; and that I know beyond a doubt that you have seen, and speak the truth."

"Thank you for those blessed words, and for this life fare you well."

For a moment there was silence, or at least Stella's voice was silent, while Morris stood over the aerophone, the sweat running from his face, rocking like a drunken man in his agony and waiting for the end. Then suddenly loud, clear, and triumphant, broke upon his ears the sound of that song which he had heard her sing upon the sinking ship when her death seemed near; the ancient song of the Over-Lord. Once more at the last mortal ebb, while the water rose about her breast, Stella's instincts and blood had asserted themselves, and forgetting aught else, she was dying as her pagan forefathers had died, with the secret ancient chant upon her lips. Yes, she sang as Skarphedinn the hero sang while the flame ate out his life.

The song swelled on, and the great waters boomed an accompaniment. Then came a sound of crashing walls, and for a moment it ceased, only to rise again still clearer and more triumphant. Again a crash—a seething hiss—and the instrument was silent, for its twin was shattered. Shattered also was the fair shape that held the spirit of Stella.

Again and again Morris spoke eagerly, entreatingly, but the aerophone was dumb. So he ceased at length, and even then well nigh laughed when he thought that in this useless piece of mechanism he saw a symbol of his own soul, which also had lost its mate and could hold true converse with no other.

Then he started up, and just as he was, ran out into the raving night.

Three hours later, when the sun rose upon Christmas Day, if any had been there to note him they might have seen a dishevelled man standing alone upon the lonely shore. There he stood, the back-wash of the mighty combers hissing about his knees as he looked seaward beneath the hollow of his hand at a spot some two hundred yards away, where one by one their long lines were broken into a churning yeast of foam.

Morris knew well what broke them—the fallen ruins of the church that was now Stella's sepulchre, and, oh! in that dark hour, he would have been glad to seek her where she lay.

XVII

The Return of Mary

Curiously enough, indirectly, but in fact, it was the circumstance of Stella's sudden and mysterious death that made Morris a rich and famous man, and caused his invention of the aerophone to come into common use. Very early on the following morning, but not before, she was missed from the Rectory and sought far and wide. One of the first places visited by those who searched was the Abbey, whither they met Morris returning through the gale, wild-eyed, flying-haired, and altogether strange to see. They asked him if he knew what had become of Miss Fregelius.

"Yes," he replied, "she has been crushed or drowned in the ruins of the Dead Church, which was swept away by the gale last night."

Then they stared and asked how he knew this. He answered that, being unable to sleep that night on account of the storm, he had gone into his workshop when his attention was suddenly attracted by the bell of the aerophone, by means of which he learned that Miss Fregelius had been cut off from the shore in the church. He added that he ran as hard as he could to the spot, only to find at dawn that the building had entirely vanished in the gale, and that the sea had encroached upon the land by at least two hundred paces.

Of course these statements concerning the aerophone and its capabilities were reported all over the world and much criticised—very roughly in some quarters. Thereupon Morris offered to demonstrate the truth of what he had said. The controversy proved sharp; but of this he was glad; it was a solace to him, perhaps even it prevented him from plunging headlong into madness. At first he was stunned; he did not feel very much. Then the first effects of the blow passed; a sense of the swiftness and inevitableness of this awful consummation seemed to sink down into his heart and crush him. The completeness of the tragedy, its Greek-play qualities, were overwhelming. Question and answer, seed and fruit—there was no space for thought or growth between them. The curtain was down upon the Temporal, and lo! almost before its folds had shaken to their place, it had risen upon the Eternal. His nature reeled beneath this knowledge and his loss. Had it not been for those suspicions and attacks it might have fallen.

The details of the struggle need not be entered into, as they have little to do with the life-story of Morris Monk. It is enough to say that in the end he more than carried out his promises under the severest conditions, and in the presence of various scientific bodies and other experts.

Afterwards came the natural results; the great aerophone company was floated, in which Morris as vendor received half the shares—he would take no cash—which shares, by the way, soon stood at five and a quarter. Also he found himself a noted man; was asked to deliver an address before the British Association; was nominated on the council of a leading scientific society, and in due course after a year or two received one of the greatest compliments that can be paid to an Englishman, that of being elected to its fellowship, as a distinguished person, by the committee of a famous Club. Thus did Morris prosper greatly—very greatly, and in many different ways; but with all this part of his life we are scarcely concerned.

On the day of his daughter's death Morris visited Mr. Fregelius, for whom he had a message. He found the old man utterly crushed and broken.

"The last of the blood, Mr. Monk," he moaned, when Morris, hoarse-voiced and slow-worded, had convinced him of the details of the dreadful fact, "the last of the blood; and I left childless. At least you will feel for me and with me. *You* will understand."

It will be seen that although outside of some loose talk in the village, which indirectly had produced results so terrible, no one had ever suggested such a thing, curiously enough, by some intuitive process, Mr. Fregelius who, to a certain extent, at any rate, guessed his daughter's mind, took it for granted that she had been in love with Morris. He seemed to know also by the same deductive process that he was attached to her.

"I do, indeed," said Morris, with a sad smile, thinking that if only the clergyman could look into his heart he would perhaps be somewhat astonished at the depth of that understanding sympathy.

"I told you," went on Mr. Fregelius, "and you laughed at me, that it was most unlucky her having sung that hateful Norse song, the 'Greeting to Death,' when you found her upon the steamer Trondhjem."

"Everything has been unlucky, Mr. Fregelius—or lucky," he added beneath his breath. "But you will like to know that she died singing it. The aerophone told me that."

"Mr. Monk," the old man said, catching his arm, "my daughter was a strange woman, a very strange woman, and since I heard this dreadful news I have been afraid that perhaps she was—unhappy. She was leaving her home, on your account—yes, on your account, it's no use pretending otherwise, although no one ever told me so—and—that she knew the church was going to be washed away."

"She thought you might think so," answered Morris, and he gave him Stella's last message. Moreover, he told him more of the real circumstances than he revealed to anybody else. He told him what nobody else ever knew, for on that lonely coast none had seen him enter or leave the place, how he had met her in the church—about the removal of the instruments, as he left it to be inferred—and at her wish had come home alone because of the gossip which had arisen. He explained also that according to her own story, from some unexplained cause she had fallen asleep in the church after his departure, and awakened to find herself surrounded by the waters with all hope gone.

"And now she is dead, now she is dead," groaned Mr. Fregelius, "and I am alone in the world."

"I am sorry for you," said Morris simply, "but there it is. It is no use looking backward, we must look forward."

"Yes, look forward, both of us, since she is hidden from both. You see, almost from the first I knew you were fond of her," added the clergyman simply.

"Yes," he answered, "I am fond of her, though of that the less said the better, and because our case is the same I hope that we shall always be friends."

"You are very kind; I shall need a friend now. I am alone now, quite alone, and my heart is broken."

Here it may be added that Morris was even better than his word. Out of the wealth that came to him in such plenty, for instance, he was careful to augment the old man's resources without offending his feelings, by adding permanently and largely to the endowment of the living. Also, he attended to his wants in many other ways which need not be enumerated, and not least by constantly visiting him. Many were the odd hours and the evenings that shall be told of later, which they spent together smoking their pipes in the Rectory study, and talking of her who had gone, and whose lost life was the strongest link between them. Otherwise and elsewhere, except upon a few extraordinary occasions, her name rarely passed the lips of Morris.

Yet within himself he mourned and mourned, although even in the first bitterness not as one without hope. He knew that she had spoken truth; that she was not dead, but only for a while out of his sight and hearing.

Ten days had passed, and for Morris ten weary, almost sleepless, nights. The tragedy of the destruction of the new rector's daughter in the ruins of the Dead Church no longer occupied the tongues of men and paragraphs in papers. One day the sea gave up the hood of her brown ulster, the same that Morris had been seen arranging by Stephen and Eliza Layard; it was found upon the beach. After this even the local police admitted that the conjectures as to her end must be true, and, since for the lack of anything to hold it on there could be no inquest, the excitement dwindled and died. Nor indeed, as her father announced that he was quite satisfied as to the circumstances of his daughter's death, was any formal inquiry held concerning them. A few people, however, still believed that she was not really drowned but had gone away secretly for unknown private reasons. The world remembers few people, even if they be distinguished, for ten whole days. It has not time for such long-continued recollection of the dead, this world of the living who hurry on to join them.

If this is the case with the illustrious, the wealthy and the powerful, how much more must it be so in the instance of an almost unknown girl, a stranger in the land? Morris and her father remembered her, for she was part of their lives and lived on with their lives. Stephen Layard mourned for the woman whom he had wished to marry—fiercely at first, with the sharp pain of disappointed passion; then intermittently; and at last, after he was comfortably wedded to somebody else, with a mild and sentimental regret three or four times a year. Eliza, too, when once convinced that she was "really dead," was "much shocked," and talked vaguely of the judgments and dispensations of Providence, as though this victim were pre-eminently deserving of its most stern decrees. It was rumoured, however, among the observant that her Christian sorrow was, perhaps, tempered by a secret relief at the absence of a rival, who, as she now admitted, sang extremely well and had beautiful eyes.

The Colonel also thought of the guest whom the sea had given and taken away, and with a real regret, for this girl's force, talents, and loveliness had touched and impressed him who had sufficient intellect and experience to know that she was a person cast in a rare and noble mould. But to Morris he never mentioned her name. No further confidence had passed between them on the matter. Yet he knew that to his son this name was holy. Therefore, being in some ways a wise man, he thought it well to keep his lips shut and to let the dead bury their dead.

By all the rest Stella Fregelius was soon as much forgotten as though she had never walked the world or breathed its air. That gale had done much damage and taken away many lives—all down the coast was heard the voice of mourning; hers chanced to be one of them, and there was nothing to be said.

On the morning of the eleventh day came a telegram from Mary addressed to Morris, and dated from London. It was brief and to the point. "Come to dinner with me at Seaview, and bring your father.—Mary."

When Morris drove to Seaview that evening he was as a man is in a dream. Sorrow had done its work on him, agonising his nerves, till at length they seemed to be blunted as with a very excess of pain, much as the nerves of the victims of the Inquisition were sometimes blunted, till at length they could scarcely feel the pincers bite or the irons burn. Always abstemious, also, for this last twelve days he had scarcely swallowed enough food to support him, with the result that his body weakened and suffered with his mind.

Then there was a third trouble to contend with,—the dull and gnawing sense of shame which seemed to eat into his heart. In actual fact, he had been faithful enough to Mary, but in mind he was most unfaithful. How could he come to her, the woman who was to be his wife, the woman who had dealt so well by him, with the memory of that spiritual marriage at the altar of the Dead Church still burning in his brain—that marriage which now was consecrated and immortalised by death? What had he to give her that was worth her taking? he, who if the truth were known, shrank from all idea of union with any earthly woman; who longed only to be allowed to live out his time in a solitude as complete as he could find or fashion? It was monstrous; it was shameful; and then and there he determined that before ever he stood in Monksland church by the side of Mary Porson, at least he would tell her the truth, and give her leave to choose. To his other sins against her deceit should not be added.

"Might I suggest, Morris," said the Colonel, who as they drove, had been watching his son's face furtively by the light of the brougham lamp—"might I suggest that, under all the circumstances, Mary would perhaps appreciate an air a little less reminiscent of funerals? You may recollect that several months have passed since you parted."

"Yes," said Morris, "and a great deal has happened in that time."

"Of course, her father is dead." The Colonel alluded to no other death. "Poor Porson! How painfully that beastly window in the dining-room will remind me of him! Come, here we are; pull yourself together, old fellow."

Morris obeyed as best he could, and presently found himself following the Colonel into the drawing-room, for once in his life, as he reflected, heartily glad to have the advantage of his parent's society. He could scarcely be expected to be very demonstrative and lover-like under the fire of that observant eyeglass.

As they entered the drawing-room by one door, Mary, looking very handsome and imposing in a low black dress, which became her fair beauty admirably, appeared at the other. Catching sight of Morris, she ran, or rather glided, forward with the graceful gait that was one of her distinctions, and caught him by both hands, bending her face towards him in open and unmistakable invitation.

In a moment it was over somehow, and she was saying:

"Morris, how thin you look, and there are great black lines under your eyes! Uncle, what have you been doing to him?"

"When I have had the pleasure of saying, How-do-you-do to you, my dear," he replied in a somewhat offended voice—for the Colonel was not fond of being overlooked, even in favour of an interesting son—"I shall be happy to do my best to answer your question."

"Oh! I am so sorry," she said, advancing her forehead to be kissed; "but we saw each other the other day, didn't we, and one can't embrace two people at once, and of course one must begin somewhere. But, why have you made him so thin?"

The Colonel surveyed Morris critically with his eyeglass.

"Really, my dear Mary," he replied, "I am not responsible for the variations in my son's habit of body." Then, as Morris turned away irritably, he added in a stage whisper, "He's been a bit upset, poor fellow! He felt your father's death dreadfully."

Mary winced a little, then, recovering her vivacity, said:

"Well, at any rate, uncle, I am glad to see that nothing of the sort has affected your health; I never saw you looking better."

"Ah! my dear, as we grow older we learn resignation—"

"And how to look after ourselves," thought Mary.

At that moment dinner was announced, and she went in on Morris's arm, the Colonel gallantly insisting that it should be so. After this things progressed a good deal better. The first plunge was over, and the cool refreshing waters of Mary's conversation seemed to give back to Morris's system some of the tone that it had lost. Also, when he thought fit to use it, he had a strong will, and he thought fit this night. Lastly, like many a man in a quandary before him, he discovered the strange advantages of a scientific but liberal absorption of champagne. Mary noticed this as she noticed everything, and said presently with her eyes wide open:

"Might I ask, my dear, if you are—ill? You are eating next to nothing, and that's your fourth large glass of champagne—you who never drank more than two. Don't you remember how it used to vex my poor dad, because he said that it always meant half a bottle wasted, and a temptation to the cook?"

Morris laughed—he was able to laugh by now—and replied, as it happened, with perfect truth, that he had an awful toothache.

"Then everything is explained," said Mary. "Did you ever see me with a toothache? Well, I should advise you not, for it would be our last interview. I will paint it for you after dinner with pure carbolic acid; it's splendid, that is if you don't drop any on the patient's tongue."

Morris answered that he would stick to champagne. Then Mary began to narrate her experiences in the convent in a fashion so funny that the Colonel could scarcely control his laughter, and even Morris, toothache, heartache, and all, was genuinely amused.

"Imagine, my dear Morris," she said, "you know the time I get down to breakfast. Or perhaps you don't. It's one of those things which I have been careful to conceal from you, but you will one day, and I believe that over it our matrimonial happiness may be wrecked. Well, at what hour do you think I found myself expected to be up in that convent?"

"Seven," suggested Morris.

"At seven! At a quarter to five, if you please! At a quarter to five every morning did some wretched person come and ring a dinner-bell outside my door. And it was no use going to sleep again, not the least, for at half-past five two hideous old lay-sisters arrived with buckets of water—they have a perfect passion for cleanliness—and began to scrub out the cell whether you were in bed or whether you weren't."

Then she rattled on to other experiences, trivial enough in themselves, but so entertaining when touched and lightened with her native humour, that very soon the evening had worn itself pleasantly away without a single sad or untoward word.

"Good night, dear!" said Mary to Morris, who this time managed to embrace her with becoming warmth; "you will come and see me to-morrow, won't you—no, not in the morning. Remember I have been getting up at a quarter to five for a month, and I am trying to equalise matters; but after luncheon. Then we will sit before a good fire, and have a talk, for the weather is so delightfully bad that I am sure I shan't be forced to take exercise."

"Very well, at three o'clock," said Morris, when the Colonel, who had been reflecting to himself, broke in.

"Look here, my dear, you must be down to lunch, or if you are not you ought to be; so, as I want to have a chat with you about some of your poor father's affairs, and am engaged for the rest of the day, I will come over then if you will allow me."

"Certainly, uncle, if you like; but wouldn't Morris do instead—as representing me, I mean?"

"Yes," he answered; "when you are married he will do perfectly well, but until that happy event I am afraid that I must take your personal opinion."

"Oh! very well," said Mary with a sigh; "I will expect you at a quarter past one."

XVIII

Two Explanations

Accordingly, at a quarter past one on the following day the Colonel arrived at Seaview, went in to lunch with Mary, and made himself very amusing and agreeable about the domestic complications of his old friend, Lady Rawlins and her objectionable husband, and other kindred topics. Then, adroitly enough, he changed the conversation to the subject of the great gale, and when he talked of it awhile, said suddenly:

"I suppose that you have heard of the dreadful thing that happened here?"

"What dreadful thing?" asked Mary. "I have heard nothing; you must remember that I have been in a convent where one does not see the English papers."

"The death of Stella Fregelius," said the Colonel sadly.

"What! the daughter of the new rector—the young lady whom Morris took off the wreck, and whom I have been longing to ask him about, only I forgot last night? Do you mean to say that she is dead?"

"Dead as the sea can make her. She was in the old church yonder when it was swept away, and now lies beneath its ruins in four fathoms of water."

"How awful!" said Mary. "Tell me about it; how did it happen?"

"Well, through Morris, poor fellow, so far as I can make out, and that is why he is so dreadfully cut up. You see she helped him to carry on his experiments with that machine, she sitting in the church and he at home in the Abbey, with a couple of miles of coast and water between them. Well, you are a woman of the world, my dear, and you must know that all this sort of thing means a great deal more intimacy than is desirable. How far that intimacy went I do not know, and I do not care to inquire, though for my part I believe that it was a very little way indeed. Still, Eliza Layard got hold of some cock and bull tale, and you can guess the rest."

"Perfectly," said Mary in a quiet voice, "if Eliza was concerned in it; but please go on with the story."

"Well, the gossip came to my ears—"

"Through Eliza?" queried Mary.

"Through Eliza—who said—" and he told her about the incident of the ulster and the dog-cart, adding that he believed it to be entirely untrue.

As Mary made no comment he went on: "I forgot to say that Miss Fregelius seems to have refused to marry Stephen Layard, who fell violently in love with her, which, to my mind, accounts for some of this gossip. Still, I thought it my duty, and the best thing I could do, to give a friendly hint to the old clergyman, Stella's father, a funny, withered-up old boy by the way. He seems to have spoken to his daughter rather indiscreetly, whereon she waylaid me as I was walking on the sands and informed me that she had made up her mind to leave this place for London, where she intended to earn her own living by singing and playing on the violin. I must tell you that she played splendidly, and, in my opinion, had one of the most glorious contralto voices that I ever heard."

"She seems to have been a very attractive young woman," said Mary, in the same quiet, contemplative voice.

"I think," went on the Colonel, "take her all in all, she was about the most attractive young woman that ever I saw, poor thing. Upon my word, dear, old as I am, I fell half in love with her myself, and so would you if you had seen those eyes of hers."

"I remember," broke in Mary, "that old Mr. Tomley, after he returned from inspecting the Northumberland living, spoke about Miss Fregelius's wonderful eyes—at the dinner-party, you know, on the night when Morris proposed to me," and she shivered a little as though she had turned suddenly cold.

"Well, let me go on with my story. After she had told me this, and I had promised to help her with introductions—exactly why or how I forget—but I asked her flat out if she was in love with Morris. Thereon—I assure you, my dear Mary, it was the most painful scene in all my long experience—the poor thing turned white as a sheet, and would have fallen if I had not caught hold of her. When she came to herself a little, she admitted frankly that this was her case, but added—of which, of course, one may believe as much as one likes, that she had never known it until I asked the question."

"I think that quite possible," said Mary; "and really, uncle, to me your cross-examination seems to have been slightly indiscreet."

"Possibly, my dear, very possibly; even Solomon might be excused for occasionally making a mistake where the mysterious articles which young ladies call their hearts are concerned. I tell what happened, that is all. Shall I go on?"

"If you please."

"Well, after this she announced that she meant to see Morris once to say good-bye to him before she went to London, and left me. Practically the next thing I heard about her was that she was dead."

"Did she commit suicide?" asked Mary.

"It is said not; it is suggested that after Morris's interview with her in the Dead Church—for I gather there was an interview though nobody knows about it, and that's where they met—she fell asleep, which sounds an odd thing to do in the midst of such a gale as was raging on Christmas Eve, and so was overwhelmed. But who can say? Impressionable and unhappy women have done such deeds before now, especially if they imagine themselves to have become the object of gossip. Of course, also, the mere possibility of such a thing having happened on his account would be, and indeed has been, enough to drive a man like Morris crazy with grief and remorse."

"What had he to be remorseful for?" asked Mary. "If a young woman chanced to fall in love with him, why should he be blamed, or blame himself for that? After all, people's affections are in their own keeping."

"I imagine—very little, if anything. At least, I know this, that when I spoke to him about the matter after my talk with her, I gathered from what he said that there was absolutely nothing between them. To be quite frank, however, as I have tried to be with you, my dear, throughout this conversation, I also gathered that this young lady had produced a certain effect upon his mind, or at least that the knowledge that she had avowed herself to be attached to him—which I am afraid I let out, for I was in a great rage—produced some such effect. Well, afterwards I believe, although I have asked no questions and am not sure of it, he went and said good-bye to her in this church, at her request. Then this dreadful tragedy happened, and there is an end of her and her story."

"Have you any object in telling it to me, uncle?"

"Yes, my dear, I have. I wished you to know the real facts before they reached you in whatever distorted version Morris's fancy or imagination, or exaggerated candour, may induce him to present them to you. Also, my dear, even if you find, or think you find that you have cause of complaint against him, I hope that you will see your way to being lenient and shutting your eyes a little."

"Severity was never my strong point," interrupted Mary.

"For this reason," went on the Colonel; "the young woman concerned was a very remarkable person; if you could have heard her sing, for instance, you would have said so yourself. It is a humiliating confession, but I doubt whether one young man out of a hundred, single, engaged, or married, could have resisted being attracted by her to just such an extent as she pleased, especially if he were flattered by the knowledge that she was genuinely attracted by himself."

Mary made no answer.

"Didn't you say you had some documents you wanted me to sign?" she asked presently.

"Oh, yes; here is the thing," and he pulled a paper out of his pocket; "the lawyers write that it need not be witnessed."

Mary glanced at it. "Couldn't Morris have brought this?—he is your co-executor, isn't he?—and saved you the trouble?"

"Undoubtedly he could; but—"

"But what?"

"Well, if you want to know, my dear," said the Colonel, with a grave countenance, "just now Morris is in a state in which I do not care to leave more of this important business in his hands than is necessary."

"What am I to understand by that, uncle?" she said, looking at him shrewdly. "Do you mean that he is—not quite well?"

"Yes, Mary, I mean that—he is not quite well; that is, if my observation goes for anything. I mean," he went on with quiet vehemence, "I mean that—just at present, of course, he has been so upset by this miserable affair that for my part I wouldn't put any confidence in what he says about it, or about anything else. The thing has got upon his nerves and rendered him temporarily unfit for the business of ordinary life. You know that at the best of times he is a very peculiar man and not quite like other people.

"Well, have you signed that? Thank you, my dear. By Jove! I must be off; I shall be late as it is. I may rely upon your discretion as to what we have been talking about, may I not? but I thought it as well to let you know how the land lay."

"Yes, uncle; and thank you for taking so much trouble."

When the door had closed behind him Mary reflected awhile. Then she said to herself:

"He thinks Morris is a little off his head, and has come here to warn me. I should not be surprised, and I daresay that he is right. Any way, a new trouble has risen up between us, the shadow of another woman, poor thing. Well, shadows melt, and the dead do not come back. She seems to have been very charming and clever, and I daresay that she fascinated him for a while, but with kindness and patience it will all come right. Only I do hope that he will not insist upon making me too many confidences."

So thought Mary, who by nature was forgiving, gentle, and an optimist; not guessing how sorely her patience as an affianced wife, and her charity as a woman of the world, would be tried within the hour.

From all of which it will be seen that for once the diplomacy of the Colonel had prospered somewhat beyond its deserts. The departed cannot explain or defend themselves, and Morris's possible indiscretions already stood discounted in the only quarter where they might do harm.

Half an hour later Mary, sitting beside the fire with her toes upon the grate and her face to the window, perceived Morris on the gravel drive, wearing a preoccupied and rather wretched air. She noted, moreover, that before he rang the bell he paused for a moment as though to shake himself together.

"Here you are at last," she said, cheerfully, as he bent down to kiss her, "seven whole minutes before your time, which is very nice of you. Now, sit down there and get warm, and we will have a good, long talk."

Morris obeyed. "My father has been lunching with you, has he not?" he said somewhat nervously.

"Yes, dear, and telling me all the news, and a sad budget it seems to be; about the dreadful disasters of the great gale and the death of that poor girl who was staying with you, Miss Fregelius."

At the mention of this name Morris's face contorted itself, as the face of a man might do who was seized with a sudden pang of sharp and unexpected agony.

"Mary," he said, in a hoarse and broken voice, "I have a confession to make to you, and I must make it—about this dead woman, I mean. I will not sail under false colours; you must know all the truth, and then judge."

"Dear me," she answered; "this sounds dreadfully tragic. But I may as well tell you at once that I have already heard some gossip."

"I daresay; but you cannot have heard all the truth, for it was known only to me and her."

Now, do what she would to prevent it, her alarm showed itself in Mary's eyes.

"What am I to understand?" she said in a low voice—and she looked a question.

"Oh, no!" he answered with a faint smile; "nothing at all—"

"Not that you have been embracing her, for instance? That, I understand, is Eliza Layard's story."

"No, no; I never did such a thing in my life."

A little sigh of relief broke from Mary's lips. At the worst this was but an affair of sentiment.

"I think, dear" she said in her ordinary slow voice, "that you had better set out the trouble in your own words, with as few details as possible, or none at all. Such things are painful, are they not—especially where the dead are concerned?"

Morris bowed his head and began: "You know I found her on the ship, singing as she only could sing, and she was a very strange and beautiful woman—perhaps beautiful is not the word—"

"It will do," interrupted Mary; "at any rate, you thought her beautiful."

"Then afterwards we grew intimate, very intimate, without knowing it, almost—indeed, I am not sure that we should ever have known it had it not been for the mischief-making of Eliza Layard—"

"May she be rewarded," exclaimed Mary.

"Well, and after she—that is, Eliza Layard—had spoken to my father, he attacked Mr. Fregelius, his daughter, and myself, and it seems that she confessed to my father that she was—was—"

"In love with you—not altogether unnatural, perhaps, from my point of view; though, of course, she oughtn't to have been so."

"Yes, and said that she was going away and—on Christmas Eve we met there in the Dead Church. Then somehow—for I had no intention of such a thing—all the truth came out, and I found that I was no longer master of myself, and—God forgive me! and you, Mary, forgive me, too—that I loved her also."

"And afterwards?" said Mary, moving her skirts a little.

"And afterwards—oh! it will sound strange to you—we made some kind of compact for the next world, a sort of spiritual marriage; I can call it nothing else. Then I shook hands with her and went away, and in a few hours she was dead—dead. But the compact stands, Mary; yes, that compact stands for ever."

"A compact of a spiritual marriage in a place where there is no marriage. Do you mean, Morris, that you wish this strange proceeding to destroy your physical and earthly engagement to myself?"

"No, no; nor did she wish it; she said so. But you must judge. I feel that I have done you a dreadful wrong, and I was determined that you should know the worst."

"That was very good of you," Mary said, reflectively, "for really there is no reason why you should have told me this peculiar story. Morris, you have been working pretty hard lately, have you not?"

"Yes," he replied, absently, "I suppose I have."

"Was this young lady what is called a mystic?"

"Perhaps. Danish people often are. At any rate, she saw things more clearly than most. I mean that the future was nearer to her mind; and in a sense, the past also."

"Indeed. You must have found her a congenial companion. I suppose that you talked a good deal of these things?"

"Sometimes we did."

"And discovered that your views were curiously alike? For when one mystic meets another mystic, and the other mystic has beautiful eyes and sings divinely, the spiritual marriage will follow almost as a matter of course. What else is to be expected? But I am glad that you were faithful to your principles, both of you, and clung fast to the ethereal side of things."

Morris writhed beneath this satire, but finding no convenient answer to it, made none.

"Do you remember, my dear?" went on Mary, "the conversation we had one day in your workshop before we were engaged—that's years ago, isn't it—about star-gazing considered as a fine art?"

"I remember something," he said.

"That I told you, for instance, that it might be better if you paid a little more attention to matters physical, lest otherwise you should go on praying for vision till you could see, and for power until you could create?"

Morris nodded.

"Well, and I think I said—didn't I? that if you insisted upon following these spiritual exercises, the result might be that they would return upon you in some concrete shape, and take possession of you, and lead you into company and surroundings which most of us think it wholesome to avoid."

"Yes, you said something like that."

"It wasn't a bad bit of prophecy, was it?" went on Mary, rubbing her chin reflectively, "and you see his Satanic Majesty knew very well how to bring about its fulfilment. Mystical, lovely, and a wonderful mistress of music, which you adore; really, one would think that the bait must have been specially selected."

Crushed though he was, Morris's temper began to rise beneath the lash of Mary's sarcasm. He knew, however, that it was her method of showing jealousy and displeasure, both of them perfectly natural, and did his best to restrain himself.

"I do not quite understand you," he said. "Also, you are unjust to her."

"Not at all. I daresay that in herself she was what you think her, a perfect angel; indeed, the descriptions that I have heard from your father and yourself leave no doubt of it in my mind. But even angels have been put to bad purposes; perhaps their innocence makes it possible to take advantage of them—"

He opened his lips to speak, but she held up her hand and went on:

"You mustn't think me unsympathetic because I put things as they appear to my very mundane mind. Look here, Morris, it just comes to this: If this exceedingly attractive young lady had made love to you, or had induced you to make love to her, so that you ran away with her, or anything else, of course you would have behaved badly and cruelly to me, but at least your conduct would be natural, and to be explained. We all know that men do this kind of thing, and women too, for the matter of that, under the influence of passion—and are often very sorry for it afterwards. But she didn't do this; she took you on your weak side, which she understood thoroughly—probably because it was her own weak side—and out-Heroded Herod, or, rather, out-mysticised the mystic, finishing up with some spiritual marriage, which, if it is anything at all, is impious. What right have we to make bargains for the Beyond, about which we know nothing?"

"She did know something," said Morris, with a sullen conviction.

"You think she did because you were reduced to a state of mind in which, if she had told you that the sun goes round the earth, you would quite readily have believed her. My dearest Morris, that way madness lies. Perhaps you understand now what I have been driving at, and the best proof of the absurdity of the whole thing is that I, stupid as I am, from my intimate knowledge of your character since childhood, was able to predict that something of this sort would certainly happen to you. You will admit that is a little odd, won't you?"

"Yes, it's odd; or, perhaps, it shows that you have more of the inner sight than you know. But there were circumstances about the story which you would find difficult to explain."

"Not in the least. In your own answer lies the explanation—your tendency to twist things. I prophesy certain developments from my knowledge of your character, whereupon you at once credit me with second sight, which is absurd."

"I don't see the analogy," said Morris.

"Don't you? I do. All this soul business is just a love affair gone wrong. If circumstances had been a little different—if, for instance, there had been no Mary Porson—I doubt whether anybody would have heard much about spiritual marriages. Somehow I think that things would have settled down into a more usual groove."

Morris did not attempt to answer. He felt that Mary held all the cards, and, not unnaturally, was in a mood to play them. Moreover, it was desecration to him to discuss Stella's most secret beliefs with any other woman, and especially with Mary. Their points of view were absolutely and radically different. The conflict was a conflict between the natural and the spiritual law; or, in other words, between hard, brutal facts and theories as impalpable as the perfume of a flower, or the sound waves that stirred his aerophone. Moreover, he could see clearly that Mary's interpretation of this story was simple; namely, that he had fallen into temptation, and that the shock of his parting from the lady concerned, followed by her sudden and violent death, had bred illusions in his mind. In short, that he was slightly crazy; therefore, to be well scolded, pitied, and looked after rather than sincerely blamed. The position was scarcely heroic, or one that any man would choose to fill; still, he felt that it had its conveniences; that, at any rate, it must be accepted.

"All these questions are very much a matter of opinion," he said; then added, unconsciously reflecting one of Stella's sayings, "and I daresay that the truth is for each of us exactly what each of us imagines it to be."

"I was always taught that the truth is the truth, quite irrespective of our vague and often silly imaginings; the difficulty being to find out exactly what it is."

"Perhaps," answered Morris, declining argument which is always useless between people are are determined not to sympathise with each other's views. "I knew that you would think my story foolish. I should never have troubled you with it, had I not felt it to be my duty, for naturally the telling of such a tale puts a man in a ridiculous light."

"I don't think you ridiculous, Morris; I think that you are suffering slightly from shock, that is all. What I say is that I detest all this spiritual hocus-pocus to which you have always had a leaning. I fear and hate it instinctively, as some people hate cats, because I know that it breeds mischief, and that, as I said before, people who go on trying to see, do see, or fancy that they do. While we are in the world let the world and its limitations be enough for us. When we go out of the world, then the supernatural may become the natural, and cease to be hurtful and alarming."

"Yes," said Morris, "those are very good rules. Well, Mary, I have told you the history of this sad adventure of which the book is now closed by death, and I can only say that I am humiliated. If anybody had said to me six months ago that I should have to come to you with such a confession, I should have answered that he was a liar. But now you see—"

"Yes," repeated Mary, "I see."

"Then will you give me your answer? For you must judge; I have told you that you must judge."

"Judge not, that ye be not judged," answered Mary. "Who am I that I should pass sentence on your failings? Goodness knows that I have plenty of my own; if you don't believe me, go and ask the nuns at that convent. Whatever were the rights and wrongs of it, the thing is finished and done with, and nobody can be more sorry for that unfortunate girl than I am. Also I think that you have behaved very well in coming to tell me about your trouble; but then that is like you, Morris, for you couldn't be deceitful, however hard you might try.

"So, dear, with your leave, we will say no more about Stella Fregelius and her spiritual views. When I engaged myself to you, as I told you at the time, I did so with my eyes open, for better or for worse, and unless you tell me right out that you don't want me, I have no intention of changing my mind, especially as you need looking after, and are not likely to come across another Stella.

"There, I haven't talked so much for months; I am quite tired, and wish to forget about all these disagreeables. I am afraid I have spoken sharply, but if so you must make allowances, for such stories are apt to sour the sweetest-tempered women—for half an hour. If I have seemed bitter and cross, dear, it is because I love you better than any creature in the world, and can't bear to think—So you must forgive me. Do you, Morris?"

"Forgive! I forgive!" he stammered overwhelmed.

"There," she said again, very softly, stretching out her arms, "come and give me a kiss, and let us change the subject once and for ever. I want to tell you about my poor father; he left some messages for you, Morris."

XIX

Morris, the Married Man

More than three years had gone by. Within twelve weeks of the date of the conversation recorded in the last chapter Morris and Mary were married in Monksland church. Although the wedding was what is called "quiet" on account of the recent death of the bride's father, the Colonel, who gave her away, was careful that it should be distinguished by a certain stamp of modest dignity, which he considered to be fitting to the station and fortune of the parties. To him, indeed, this union was the cause of heartfelt and earnest rejoicings, which is not strange, seeing that it meant nothing less than a new lease of life to an ancient family that was on the verge of disappearance. Had Morris not married the race would have become extinct, at any rate in the direct line; and had he married where there was no money, it might, as his father thought, become bankrupt, which in his view was almost worse.

The one terror which had haunted the Colonel for years like a persistent nightmare was that a day seemed to be at hand when the Monks would be driven from Monksland, where, from sire to son, they had sat for so many generations. That day had nearly come when he was a young man; indeed, it was only averted by his marriage with the somewhat humbly born Miss Porson, who brought with her sufficient dowry to enable him to pay off the major portion of the mortgages which then crippled the estate. But at that time agriculture flourished, and the rents from the property were considerable; moreover, the Colonel was never of a frugal turn of mind. So it came about that every farthing was spent.

Afterwards followed a period of falling revenues and unlet farms. But still the expenses went on, with the result, as the reader knows, that at the opening of this history things were worse than they had ever been, and indeed, without the help received from Mr. Porson, must ere that have reached their natural end. Now the marriage of his son with a wealthy heiress set a period to all such anxiety, and unless the couple should be disappointed of issue, made it as certain as anything can be in this mutable world, that for some generations to come, at any rate, the name of Monk of Monksland would still appear in the handbooks of county families.

In the event these fears proved to be groundless, since by an unexpected turn of the wheel of chance Morris became a rich man in reward of his own exertions, and was thus made quite independent of his wife's large fortune. This, however, was a circumstance which the Colonel could not be expected to foresee, for how could he believe that an electrical invention which he looked upon as a mere scientific toy would ultimately bring its author not only fame, but an income of many thousands per annum? Yet this happened.

Other things happened also which, under the circumstances, were quite as satisfactory, seeing that within two years of his marriage Morris was the father of a son and daughter, so that the old Abbey, where, by the especial request of the Colonel, they had established themselves, once more echoed to the voices of little children.

In those days, if anyone among his acquaintances had been asked to point out an individual as prosperous and happy as, under the most favoured circumstances, it is given to a mortal to be, he would unhesitatingly have named Morris Monk.

What was there lacking to this man? He had lineage that in his own neighbourhood gave him standing better than that of many an upstart baronet or knight, and with it health and wealth. He had a wife who was acknowledged universally to be one of the most beautiful, charming, and witty women in the county, whose devotion to himself was so marked and open that it became a public jest; who had, moreover, presented him with healthy and promising offspring. In addition to all these good things he had suddenly become in his own line one of the most famous persons in the world, so that, wherever civilized man was to be found, there his name was known as "Monk, who invented that marvellous machine, the aerophone." Lastly, there was no more need for him, as for most of us, to stagger down his road beneath a never lessening burden of daily labour. His work was done; a great conception completed after half a score of years of toil and experiment had crowned it with unquestionable success. Now he could sit at ease and watch the struggles of others less fortunate.

There are, however, few men on the right side of sixty whose souls grow healthier in idleness. Although nature often recoils from it, man was made to work, and he who will not work calls down upon himself some curse, visible or invisible, as he who works, although the toil seem wasted, wakes up one day to find the arid wilderness where he wanders strown with a manna of blessing. This should be the prayer of all of understanding, that whatever else it may please Heaven to take away, there may be left to them the power and the will to work, through disappointment, through rebuffs, through utter failure even, still to work. Many things for which they are or are not wholly responsible are counted to men as sins. Surely, however, few will press more heavily upon the beam of the balance, when at length we are commanded to unfold the talents which we have been given and earned, than those fateful words: "Lord, mine lies buried in its napkin," or worse still: "Lord, I have spent mine on the idle pleasures which my body loved."

Therefore it was not to the true welfare of Morris when through lack of further ambition, or rather of the sting of that spur of necessity which drives most men on, he rested upon his oars, and in practice abandoned his labours, drifting down the tide. No man of high intelligence and acquisitive brain can toil arduously for a period of years and suddenly cease from troubling to find himself, as he expects, at rest. For then into the swept and garnished chambers of that empty mind enter seven or more blue devils. Depression marks him for its own; melancholy forebodings haunt him; remorse for past misdeeds long repented of is his daily companion. With these Erinnyes, more felt perhaps than any of them, comes the devastating sense that he is thwarting the best instinct of his own nature and the divine command to labour while there is still light, because the night draws on apace in which no man can labour.

Mary was fond of society, in which she liked to be accompanied by her husband, so Morris, whose one great anxiety was to please his wife and fall in with her every wish, went to a great many parties which he hated. Mary liked change also, so it came about that three months in the season were spent in London, where they had purchased a house in Green Street that was much frequented by the Colonel, and another two, or sometimes three, months at the villa on the Riviera, which Mary was very fond of on account of its associations with her parents.

Also in the summer and shooting seasons, when they were at home, the old Abbey was kept full of guests; for we may be sure that people so rich and distinguished did not lack for friends, and Mary made the very best of hostesses.

Thus it happened that except at the seasons when his wife retired under the pressure of domestic occurrences, Morris found that he had but little time left in which to be quiet; that his life in short was no longer the life of a worker, but that of a commonplace country gentleman of wealth and fashion.

Now it was Mary who had brought these things about, and by design; for she was not a woman to act without reasons and an object. It is true that she liked a gay and pleasant life, for gaiety and pleasure were agreeable to her easy and somewhat indolent mind, also they gave her opportunities of exercising her faculties of observation, which were considerable.

But Mary was far fonder of her husband than of those and other vanities; indeed, her affection for him shone the guiding star of her existence. From her childhood she had been devoted to this cousin, who, since her earliest days, had been her playmate, and at heart had wished to marry him, and no one else. Then he began his experiments, and drifted quite away from her. Afterwards things changed, and they became engaged. Again the experiments were carried on, with the aid of another woman, and again he drifted away from her; also the drifting in this instance was attended by serious and painful complications.

Now the complications had ceased to exist; they threatened her happiness no more. Indeed, had they been much worse than they were she would have overlooked them, being altogether convinced of the truth of the old adage which points out the folly of cutting off one's nose to spite one's face. Whatever his failings or shortcomings, Morris was her joy, the human being in whose company she delighted; without whom, indeed, her life would be flat, stale, and unprofitable. The stronger then was her determination that he should not slip back into his former courses; those courses which in the end had always brought about estrangement from herself.

Inventions, the details of which she could not understand, meant, as she knew well, long days and weeks of solitary brooding; therefore inventions, and, indeed, all unnecessary work, were in his case to be discouraged. Such solitary brooding also drew from the mind of Morris a vague mist of thought about matters esoteric which, to Mary's belief, had the properties of a miasma that crept like poison through his being. She wished for no more star-gazing, no more mysticism, and, above all, no more memories of the interloping woman who, in his company, had studied its doubtful and dangerous delights.

Although since the day of Morris's confession Mary had never even mentioned the name of Stella to him, she by no means forgot that such

H. RIDER HAGGARD

a person once existed. Indeed, carelessly and without seeming to be anxious on the subject, she informed herself about her down to the last possible detail; so that within a few months of the death of Miss Fregelius she knew, as she thought, everything that could be known of her life at Monksland. Moreover, she saw three different pictures of her: one a somewhat prim photograph which Mr. Fregelius, her father, possessed, taken when she was about twenty; another, a coloured drawing made by Morris—who was rather clever at catching likenesses—of her as she appeared singing in the chapel on the night when she had drawn the page-boy, Thomas, from his slumbers; and the third, also a photograph, taken by some local amateur, of her and Morris standing together on the beach and engaged evidently in eager discussion.

From these three pictures, and especially from Morris's sketch, which showed the spiritual light shining in her eyes, and her face rapt, as it were, in a very ecstasy of music, Mary was able to fashion with some certainty the likeness of the living woman. The more she studied this the more she found it formidable, and the more she understood how it came about that her husband had fallen into folly. Also, she learned to understand that there might be greater weight and meaning in his confession than she had been inclined to allow to it at the time; that, at any rate, its extravagances ought not to be set down entirely, as her father-in-law had suggested with such extreme cleverness, to the vagaries of a mind suffering from sudden shock and alarm.

All these conclusions made Mary anxious, by wrapping her husband round with common domestic cares and a web of daily, social incident, to bury the memory of this Stella beneath ever-thickening strata of forgetfulness; not that in themselves these reminiscences, however hallowed, could do her any further actual harm; but because the train of thought evoked thereby was, as she conceived, morbid, and dangerous to the balance of his mind.

The plan seemed wise and good, and, in the case of most men, probably would have succeeded. Yet in Morris's instance from the commencement it was a failure. She had begun by making his story and ideas, absurd enough on the face of them, an object of somewhat acute sarcasm, if not of ridicule. This was a mistake, since thereby she caused him to suppress every outward evidence of them; to lock them away in the most secret recesses of his heart. If the lid of a caldron full of fluid is screwed down while a fire continues to burn beneath it, the steam which otherwise would have passed away harmlessly, gathers and struggles till the moment of inevitable catastrophe. The fact that for a while the caldron remains inert and the steam invisible is no indication of safety. To attain safety in such a case either the fire must be raked out or the fluid tapped. Mary had screwed down the lid of her domestic caldron, but the flame still burned beneath, and the water still boiled within.

This was her first error, and the second proved almost as mischievous. She thought to divert Morris from a central idea by a multitude of petty counter-attractions; she believed that by stopping him from the scientific labours and esoteric speculation connected with this idea, that it would be deadened and in time obliterated.

As a matter of fact, by thus emptying his mind of its serious and accustomed occupations, Mary made room for the very development she dreaded to flourish like an upas tree. For although he breathed no word of it, although he showed no sign of it, to Morris the memory of the dead was a constant companion. Time heals all things, that is the common saying; but would it be possible to formulate any fallacy more complete? There are many wounds that time does not heal, and often enough against the dead it has no power at all—for how can time compete against the eternity of which they have become a part? The love of them where they have been truly loved, remains quite unaltered; in some instances, indeed, it is emdued with a power of terrible and amazing growth.

On earth, very probably, that deep affection would have become subject to the natural influences of weakening and decay; and, in the instance of a man and woman, the soul-possessing passion might have passed, to be replaced by a more moderate, custom-worn affection. But the dead are beyond the reach of those mouldering fingers. There they stand, perfect and unalterable, with arms which never cease from beckoning, with a smile that never grows less sweet. Come storm, come shine, nothing can tarnish the pure and gleaming robes in which our vision clothes them. We know the worst of them; their faults and failings cannot vex us afresh, their errors are all forgiven. It is their best part only that remains unrealised and unread, their purest aspirations which we follow with leaden wings, their deepest thoughts that we still strive to plumb with the short line of our imagination or experience, and to weigh in our imperfect balances.

Yes, there they stand, and smile, and beckon, while ever more radiant grow their brows, and more to be desired the knowledge of their perfect majesty. There is no human passion like this passion for the dead; none so awful, none so holy, none so changeless. For they have become eternal, and our desire for them is sealed with the stamp of their eternity, and strengthens in the shadow of its wings till the shadows flee away and we pass to greet them in the dawn of the immortal morning.

Yes, within the secret breast of Morris the flame of memory still burned, and still seethed those bitter waters of desire for the dead. There was nothing carnal about this desire, since the passions of the flesh perish with the flesh. Nor was there anything of what a man may feel when he sees the woman whom he loves and who loves him, forced to another fate, for to those he robs death has this advantage over the case of other successful rivals: his embrace purifies, and of it we are not jealous. The longing was spiritual, and for this reason it did not weaken, but, indeed, became a part of him, to grow with the spirit from which it took its birth. Still, had it not been for a chance occurrence, there, in the spirit, it might have remained buried, in due course to pass away with it and seek its expression in unknown conditions and regions unexplored.

In a certain fashion Morris was happy enough. He was very fond of his wife, and he adored his little children as men of tender nature do adore those that are helpless, and for whose existence they are responsible. He appreciated his public reputation, his wealth, and the luxury that lapped him round, and above all he was glad to have been the means of restoring, and, indeed, of advancing the fortunes of his family.

Moreover, as has been said, above all things he desired to please Mary, the lovely, amiable woman who had complimented him with her unvarying affection; and—when he went astray—who, with scarcely a reproach, had led him back into its gentle fold. Least of all, therefore, was it his will to flaunt before her eyes the spectre from a past which she wished to forget, or even to let her guess that such a past still permeated his present. Therefore, on this subject settled the silence of the dead, till at length Mary, observant as she was, became well-nigh convinced that Stella Fregelius was forgotten, and that her fantastic promises were disproved. Yet no mistake could have been more profound.

It was Morris's habit, whenever he could secure an evening to himself, which was not very often, to walk to the Rectory and smoke his pipe in the company of Mr. Fregelius. Had Mary chanced to be invisibly present, or to peruse a stenographic report of what passed at one of these evening calls—whereof, for reasons which she suppressed, she did not entirely approve—she might have found sufficient cause to vary her opinion. On these occasions ostensibly Morris went to talk about parish affairs, and, indeed, to a certain extent he did talk about them. For instance, Stella who had been so fond of music, once described to him the organ which she would like to have in the fine old parish church of Monksland. Now that renovated instrument stood there, and was the admiration of the country-side, as it well might be in view of the fact that it had cost over four thousand pounds.

Again, Mr. Fregelius wished to erect a monument to his daughter, which, as her body never had been found, could properly be placed in the chancel of the church. Morris entered heartily into the idea and undertook to spend the hundred pounds which the old gentleman had saved for this purpose on his account and to the best advantage. In affect he did spend it to excellent advantage, as Mr. Fregelius admitted when the monument arrived.

It was a lovely thing, executed by one of the first sculptors of the day, in white marble upon a black stone bed, and represented the mortal shape of Stella. There she lay to the very life, wrapped in a white robe, portrayed as a sleeper awakening from the last sleep of death, her eyes wide and wondering, and on her face that rapt look which Morris had caught in his sketch of her, singing in the chapel. At the edge of the base of this remarkable effigy, set flush on the black marble in letters of plain copper was her name—Stella Fregelius—with the date of her death. On one side appeared the text that she had quoted, "O death, where is thy sting?" and on the other its continuation, "O grave, where is thy victory?" and at the foot part of a verse from the forty-second psalm: "Deep calleth unto deep. . . All Thy waves and storms have gone over me."

Like the organ, this monument, which stood in the chancel, was much admired by everybody, except Mary, who found it rather theatrical; and, indeed, when nobody was looking, surveyed it with a gloomy and a doubtful eye.

That Morris had something to do with the thing she was quite certain, since she knew well that Mr. Fregelius would never have invented any memorial so beautiful and full of symbolism; also she doubted his ability to pay for a piece of statuary which must have cost many hundreds of pounds. A third reason, which seemed to her conclusive, was that the face on the statue was the very face of Morris's drawing, although, of course, it was possible that Mr. Fregelius might have borrowed the sketch for the use of the sculptor. But of all this, although it disturbed her, occurring as it did just when she hoped that Stella was beginning to be forgotten, she spoke not a word to Morris. "Least said, soonest mended," is a good if a homely motto, or so thought Mary.

The monument had been in place a year, but whenever he was at home Morris's visits to Mr. Fregelius did not grow fewer. Indeed, his wife noticed that, if anything, they increased in number, which, as the organ was now finished down to the last allegorical carvings of its case, seemed remarkable and unnecessary. Of course, the fact was that on these occasions the conversation invariably centred on one subject, and that subject, Stella. Considered in certain aspects, it must have been a piteous thing to see and hear these two men, each of them bereaved of one who to them above all others had been the nearest and dearest, trying to assuage their grief by mutual consolations. Morris had never told Mr. Fregelius all the depth of his attachment to his daughter, at least, not in actual, unmistakable words, although, as has been said, from the first her father took it for granted, and Morris, tacitly at any rate, had accepted the conclusion. Indeed, very soon he found that no other subject had such charms for his guest; that of Stella he might talk for ever without the least fear that Morris would be weary.

So the poor, childless, unfriended old man put aside the reserve and timidity which clothed him like a garment, and talked on into those sympathetic ears, knowing well, however—for the freemasonry of their common love taught it to him—that in the presence of a third person her name, no allusion to her, even, must pass his lips. In short, these conversations grew at length into a kind of seance or solemn rite; a joint offering to the dead of the best that they had to give, their tenderest thoughts and memories, made in solemn secrecy and with uplifted hearts and minds.

Mr. Fregelius was an historian, and possessed some interesting records, upon which it was his habit to descant. Amongst other things he instructed Morris in the annals of Stella's ancestry upon both sides, which, as it happened, could be traced back for many generations. In these discourses it grew plain to his listener whence had sprung certain of her qualities, such as her fearless attitude towards death, and her tendency towards mysticism. Here in these musty chronicles, far back in the times when those of whom they kept record were half, if not wholly, heathen, these same qualities could be discovered among her forbears.

Indeed, there was one woman of whom the saga told, a certain ancestress named Saevuna, whereof it is written "that she was of all women the very fairest, and that she drew the hearts of men with her wonderful eyes as the moon draws mists from a marsh," who, in some ways, might have been Stella herself, Stella unchristianized and savage.

This Saevuna's husband rebelled against the king of his country, and, being captured, was doomed to a shameful death by hanging as a traitor. Thereon, under pretence of bidding him farewell, she administered poison to him, partaking of the same herself; "and," continues the saga, "they both of them, until their pains overcame them, died singing a certain ancient song which had descended in the family of one of them, and is called the Song of the Over-Lord, or the Offering to Death. This song, while strength and voice remained to them, it is the duty of this family to say or sing, or so they hold it, in the hour of their death. But if they sing it, except by way of learning its words and music from their mothers, and escape death, it will not be for very long, seeing that when once the offering is laid upon his altar, the Over-Lord considers it his own, and, after the fashion of gods and men, takes it as soon as he can. So sweet and strange was the singing of this Saevuna until she choked that the king and his nobles came out to hear it, and all men thought it a great marvel that a woman should sing thus in the very pains of death. Moreover, they declared, many of them, that while the song went on they could think of nothing else, and that strange and wonderful visions passed before their eyes. But of this nobody can know the truth for certain, as the woman and her husband died long ago."

"You see," said Mr. Fregelius, when he had finished translating the passage aloud, "it is not wonderful that I thought it unlucky when I heard that you had found Stella singing this same song upon the ship, much as centuries ago her ancestress, Saevuna, sang it while she and her husband died."

"At any rate, the omen fulfilled itself," answered Morris, with a sigh, "and she, too, died with the song upon her lips, though I do not think that it had anything to do with these things, which were fated to befall."

"Well," said the clergyman, "the fate is fulfilled now, and the song will never be sung again. She was the last of her race, and it was a law among them that neither words nor music should ever be written down."

When such old tales and legends were exhausted, and, outside the immediate object of their search, some of them were of great interest to a man who, like Morris, had knowledge of Norse literature, and was delighted to discover in Mr. Fregelius a scholar acquainted with the original tongues in which they were written, these companions fell back upon other matters. But all of them had to do with Stella. One night the clergyman read some letters written by her as a child from Denmark. On another he produced certain dolls which she had dressed at the same period of her life in the costume of the peasants of that country. On a third he repeated a piece of rather indifferent poetry composed by her when she was a girl of sixteen. Its strange title was, "The Resurrection of Dead Roses." It told how in its author's fancy the flowers which were cut and cast away on earth bloomed again in heaven, never to wither more; a pretty allegory, but treated in a childish fashion.

Thus, then, from time to time, as occasion offered, did this strange pair celebrate the rites they thought so harmless, and upon the altar of memory make offerings to their dead.

XX

STELLA'S DIARY

It seems to be a law of life that nothing can stand completely still and changeless. All must vary, must progress or retrograde; the very rocks in the bowels of the earth undergo organic alterations, while the eternal hills that cover them increase or are worn away. Much more is this obvious in the case of ephemeral man, of his thoughts, his works, and everything wherewith he has to do, he who within the period of a few short years is doomed to appear, wax, wane, and vanish.

Even the conversations of Mr. Fregelius and Morris were subject to the working of this universal rule; and in obedience to it must travel towards a climax, either of fruition, however unexpected, or, their purpose served, whatever it may have been, to decay and death, for lack of food upon which to live and flourish. The tiniest groups of impulses or incidents have their goal as sure and as appointed as that of the cluster of vast globes which form a constellation. Between them the principal distinction seems to be one of size, and at present we are not in a position to say which may be the most important, the issue of the smallest of unrecorded causes, or of the travelling of the great worlds. The destiny of a single human soul shaped or directed by the one, for aught we know, may be of more weight and value than that of a multitude of hoary universes naked of life and spirit. Or perhaps to the Eye that sees and judges the difference is nothing.

Thus even these semi-secret interviews when two men met to talk over the details of a lost life with which, however profoundly it may have influenced them in the past, they appeared, so far as this world is concerned, to have nothing more to do, were destined to affect the future of one of them in a fashion that could scarcely have been foreseen. This became apparent, or put itself in the way of becoming apparent, when on a certain evening Morris found Mr. Fregelius seated in the rectory dining-room, and by his side a little pile of manuscript volumes bound in shabby cloth.

"What are those?" asked Morris. "Her translation of the Saga of the Cave Outlaws?"

"No, Morris," answered Mr. Fregelius—he called him Morris when they were alone—"of course not. Don't you remember that they were bound in red?" he added reproachfully, "and that we did them up to send to the publisher last week?"

"Yes, yes, of course; he wrote to me yesterday to say that he would be glad to bring out the book"—Morris did not add, "at my risk."—"But what are they?"

"They are," replied Mr. Fregelius, "her journals, which she appears to have kept ever since she was fourteen years of age. You remember she was going to London on the day that she was drowned—that Christmas Day? Well, before she went out to the old church she packed her belongings into two boxes, and there those boxes have lain for three years and more, because I could never find the heart to meddle with them. But, a few nights ago I wasn't able to sleep—I rest very badly now—so I went and undid them, lifting out all the things which her hands had put there. At the bottom of one of the boxes I found these volumes, except the last of them, in which she was writing till the day of her death. That was at the top. I was aware that she kept a diary, for I have seen her making the entries; but of its contents I knew nothing. In fact, until last night I had forgotten its existence."

"Have you read it now?" asked Morris.

"I have looked into it; it seems to be a history of her thoughts and theories. Facts are very briefly noted. It occurred to me that you might like to read it. Why not?"

"Yes, yes, very much," answered Morris eagerly. "That is, if you think she will not mind. You see, it is private."

Mr. Fregelius took no notice of the tense of which Morris made use, for the reason that it seemed natural to him that he should employ it. Their strange habit was to talk of Stella, not as we speak of one dead, but as a living individuality with whom they chanced for a while to be unable to communicate.

"I do not think that she will mind," he answered slowly; "quite the reverse, indeed. It is a record of a phase and period of her existence which, I believe, she might wish those who are—interested in her—to study, especially as she had no secrets that she could desire to conceal. From first to last I believe her life to have been as clear as the sky, and as pure as running water."

"Very well," answered Morris, "if I come across any passage that I think I ought not to read, I will skip."

"I can find nothing of the sort, or I would not give it to you," said Mr. Fregelius. "But, of course, I have not read the volumes through as yet. There has been no time for that. I have sampled them here and there, that is all."

That night Morris took those shabby note-books home with him. Mary, who according to her custom went to bed early, being by this time fast asleep, he retired to his laboratory in the old chapel, where it was his habit to sit, especially when, as at the present time, his father was away from home. Here, without wasting a moment, he began his study of them.

It was with very strange sensations, such as he had never before experienced, that he opened the first of the volumes, written some thirteen years earlier, that is, about ten years before Stella's death. Their actual acquaintance had been but brief. Now he was about to complete his knowledge of her, to learn many things which he had found no time, or had forgotten to inquire into, to discover the explanation of various phases of her character hitherto but half-revealed; perhaps to trace to its source the energy of that real, but mystic, faith with which it was informed. This diary that had come—or perhaps been sent to him—in so unexpected a fashion, was the key whereby he hoped to open the most hidden chambers of the heart of the woman whom he loved, and who loved him with all her strength and soul.

Little wonder, then, that he trembled upon the threshold of such a search. He was like the neophyte of some veiled religion, who, after long years of arduous labour and painful preparation, is at length conducted to the doors of its holy of holies, and left to enter there alone. What will he find beyond them? The secret he longed to learn, the seal and confirmation of his hard-won faith, or empty, baulking nothingness? Would the goddess herself, the unveiled Isis, wait to bless her votary within those doors? Or would that hall be tenanted but by a painted and bedizened idol, a thing fine with ivory and gold, but dead and soulless?

Might it not be better indeed to turn back while there was yet time, to be content to dwell on in the wide outer courts of the imagination, where faith is always possible, rather than to hazard all? No; it would, Morris felt, be best to learn the whole truth, especially as he was sure that it could not prove other than satisfying and beautiful. Blind must he have been indeed, and utterly without intuition if with every veil that was withdrawn from the soul of Stella did not shine more bright.

　　　　　　　　　　　　　　　　H. RIDER HAGGARD

Another question remained. Was it well that he should read these diaries? Was not his mind already full enough of Stella? If once he began to read, might it not be overladen? In short, Mary had dealt well by him; when those books were open in his hand, would he be dealing well by Mary? Answers—excellent answers—to these queries sprang up in his mind by dozens.

Stella was dead. "But you are sworn to her in death," commented the voice of Conscience. "Would you rob the living of your allegiance before the time?"

There was no possible harm in reading the records of the life and thoughts of a friend, or even of a love departed. "Yet," suggested the voice of Conscience, "are you so sure that this life *is* departed? Have you not at whiles felt its presence, that mysterious presence of the dead, so sweet, so heavy, and so unmistakable, with which at some time or other in their lives many have made acquaintance? Will not the study of this life cause that life to draw near? the absorption of those thoughts bring about the visits of other and greater thoughts, whereof they may have been, as it were, the seed?"

Anyone who knew its author would be interested to read this human document, the product of an intelligence singularly bright and clear; of a vision whose point of outlook was one of the highest and most spiritual peaks in the range of our human imaginings. "Quite so," agreed the voice of Conscience. "For instance, Mary would be delighted. Why not begin with her? In fact, why not peruse these pages together—it would lead to some interesting arguments? Why pore over them in this selfish manner all alone and at the dead of night when no one can possibly disturb you, or, since you have blocked the hagioscope, even see you? And why does the door of that safe stand open? Because of the risk of fire if anyone should chance to come in with a candle, I suppose. No, of course it would not be right to leave such books about; especially as they do not belong to you."

Then enraged, or at least seriously irritated, by these impertinent comments of his inner self upon himself, Morris bade Conscience to be gone to its own place. Next, after contemplating it for a while as Eve might have contemplated the apple, unmindful of a certain petition in the Lord's Prayer, he took up the volume marked I, and began to read the well-remembered hand-writing with its quaint mediaeval-looking contractions. Even at the age when its author had opened her diary, he noted that this writing was so tiny and neat that many of the pages might have been taken from a monkish missal. Also there were few corrections; what she set down was already determined in her mind.

From that time forward Morris sat up even later than usual, nor did he waste those precious solitary hours. But the diary covered ten full years of a woman's life, during all of which time certainly never a week passed without her making entries in it, some of them of considerable length. Thus it came about—for he skipped no word—that a full month had gone by before Morris closed the last volume and slipped it away into its hiding-place in the safe.

As Mr. Fregelius had said, the history was a history of thoughts and theories, rather than of facts, but notwithstanding this, perhaps on account of it, indeed, it was certainly a work which would have struck the severest and least interested critic as very remarkable. The prevailing note was that of vividness. What the writer had felt, what she had imagined, what she had desired, was all set out, frequently in but few words, with such crystal clearness, such incisive point, that it came home to the reader's thought as a flash of sudden light might come home to his eye. In a pre-eminent degree Stella possessed the gift of expression. Even her most abstruse self-communings and speculations were portrayed so sharply that their meaning could not possibly be mistaken. This it was that gave the book much of its value. Her thoughts were not vague, she could define them in her own consciousness, and, what is more rare, on paper.

So much for the form of the journal, its matter is not so easy to describe. At first, as might be expected from her years, it was somewhat childish in character, but not on that account the less sweet and fragrant of a child's poor heart. Here with stern accuracy were recorded her little faults of omission and commission—how she had answered crossly; how she had not done her duty; varied occasionally with short poems, some copied, some of her own composition, and prayers also of her making, one or two of them very touching and beautiful. From time to time, too—indeed this habit clung to her to the last—she introduced into her diary descriptions of scenery, generally short and detached, but set there evidently because she wished to preserve a sketch in words of some sight that had moved her mind.

Here is a brief example describing a scene in Norway, where she was visiting, as it appeared to her upon some evening in late autumn: "This afternoon I went out to gather cranberries on the edge of the fir-belt below the Stead. Beneath me stretched the great moss-swamp, so wide that I could not discern its borders, and grey as the sea in winter. The wind blew and in the west the sun was setting, a big, red sun which glowed like the copper-covered cathedral dome that we saw last week. All about in the moss stood pools of black, stagnant water with little straggling bushes growing round them. Under the clouds they were ink, but in the path of the red light, there they were blood. A man with a large basket on his back and a long staff in his hand, was walking across the moss from west to east. The wind tossed his cloak and bent his grey beard as he threaded his way among the pools. The red light fell upon him also, and he looked as though he were on fire. Before him, gathering thicker as the sun sank, were shadows and blackness. He seemed to walk into the blackness like a man wading into the sea. It swallowed him up; he must have felt very lonely with no one near him in that immense grey place. Now he was all gone, except his head that wore a halo of the red light. He looked like a saint struggling across the world into the Black Gates. For a minute he stood still, as though he were frightened. Then a sudden gust seemed to sweep him on again, right into the Gates, and I lost sight of that man whom I shall never see any more. I wonder whether he was a saint or a sinner, and what he will find beyond the Gates. A curlew flew past me, borne out of the darkness, and its cry made me feel sad and shiver. It might have been the man's soul which wished to look upon the light again. Then the sun sank, and there was no light, only the wind moaning, and far, far away the sad cry of the curlew."

This description was simple and unpolished as it was short. Yet it impressed the mind of Morris, and its curious allegorical note appealed to his imagination. The grey moss broken by stagnant pools, lonesome and primeval; the dreary pipe of the wildfowl, the red and angry sun fronting the gloom of advancing, oblivious night; the solitary traveller, wind-buffeted, way-worn, aged, heavy-laden, fulfilling the last stage of his appointed journey to a realm of sleep and shadow. All these sprang into vision as he read, till the landscape, concentrated, and expressing itself in its tiny central point of human interest, grew more real in memory and meaning than many with which he was himself familiar.

Yet that description was written by an untrained girl not yet seventeen years of age. But with such from first to last, and this was by no means the best of them, he found her pages studded.

Then, jotted down from day to day, came the account of the illness and death of her twin sister, Gudrun, a pitiful tale to read. Hopes, prayers, agonies of despair, all were here recorded; the last scene also was set out with a plain and noble dignity, written by the bed of death in the presence of death. Now under the hand of suffering the child had become a woman, and, as was fitting, her full soul found relief in deeper notes. "Good-bye, Gudrun," she ended, "my heart is broken; but I will mourn for you no more. God has called you, and we give you back to God. Wait for me, my sister, for I am coming also, and I will not linger. I will walk quickly."

It was from this sad day of her only sister's death that the first real developments of the mystical side of Stella's character must be dated. The sudden vanishing in Gudrun in the bloom of youth and beauty brought home to her the lesson which all must learn, in such a fashion that henceforth her whole soul was tinged to its sad hue.

"Now I understand it all," she wrote after returning from the funeral. "We do not live to die, we die to live. As a grain of sand to the whole shore, as a drop of water to the whole sea, so is what we call our life to the real life. Of course one has always been taught that in church, but I never really comprehended it before. Henceforth this thought shall be a part of me! Every morning when I wake I will remember that I am one night nearer to the great dawn, every night when I lie down to sleep I will thank God that another day of waiting has ended with the sunset. Yes, and I will try to live so that after my last sunset I may meet the end as did Gudrun; without a single doubt or fear, for if I have nothing to reproach myself with, why should I be reproached? If I have longed for light and lived towards the light, however imperfect I may be, why should I be allotted to the darkness?"

Almost on the next page appeared a prayer "For the welfare and greater glory" of her who was dead, and for the mourner who was left alive, with this quaint note appended: "My father would not approve of this, as it is against the rubric, but all the same I mean to go on praying for the dead. Why should I not? If my poor petitions cannot help them who are above the need for help, at least they may show that they are not forgotten. Oh! that must be the bitter part; to live on full of love and memory and watch forgetfulness creeping into the hearts of the loved and the remembered. The priests never thought of it, but there lies the real purgatory."

The diary showed it to be a little more than a year after this that spiritual doubts began to possess the soul of Stella. After all, was she not mistaken? Was there any world beyond the physical? Were we not mere accidents, born of the will or the chance of the flesh, and shaped by the pressure of centuries of circumstance? Were not all religions different forms of a gigantic fraud played by his own imagination upon blind, believing man? And so on to the end of the long list of those questions which are as old as thought.

"I look," she wrote under the influence of this mood, "but everywhere is blackness; blackness without a single star. I cry aloud, but the only answer is the echo of my own voice beating back upon me from the deaf heavens. I pray for faith, yet faith fades and leaves me. I ask for signs, and there is no sign. The argument? So far as I have read and heard, it seems the other way. And yet I do not believe their proofs. I do not believe that so many generations of good men would have fed full upon a husk of lies and have lain down to sleep at last as though satisfied with meat. My heart rises at the thought. I am immortal. I know that I am immortal. I am a spirit. In days to come, unchained by matter, time, or space, I shall stand before the throne of the Father of all spirits, receiving of His wisdom and fulfilling His commandments. Yet, O God, help Thou my unbelief. O God, draw and deliver me from this abyss."

From this time forward here and there in the diary were to be found passages, or rather sentences, that Morris did not understand. They alluded to some secret and persistent effort which the writer had been making, and after one of them came these words, "I have failed again, but she was near me; I am sure that she was very near me."

Then at last came this entry, which, as the writing showed, was written with a shaking hand. "I have seen her beyond the possibility of a doubt. She appeared, and was with me quite a while; and, oh! the rapture! It has left me weak and faint after all that long, long preparation. It is of the casting forth of spirits that it is said, 'This kind goeth not out but by prayer and fasting,' but it is also true of the drawing of them down. To see a spirit one must grow akin to spirits, which is not good for us who are still in the flesh. I am satisfied. I have seen, and I _know_. Now I shall call her back no more lest the thing should get the mastery of me, and I become unfitted for my work on earth. This morning I could scarcely hold the bow of the violin, and its sweetest notes sounded harsh to me; I heard discords among their harmonies. Also I had no voice to sing, and after all the money and time that have been spent upon them, I must keep up my playing and singing, since, perhaps, in the future if my father's health should fail, as it often threatens to do, they may be our only means of livelihood. No, I shall try no more; I will stop while there is yet time, while I am still my own mistress and have the strength to deny me this awful joy. But I have seen! I have seen, and I am thankful, who shall never doubt again. Yet the world, and those who tread it, can never more be quite the same to me, and that is not wholesome. This is the price which must be paid for vision of that which we were not meant to touch, to taste, to handle."

After this, for some years—until it was decided, indeed, that they should move to Monksland—there was little of startling interest in the diary. It recorded descriptions of the wild moorland scenery, of birds, and ferns, and flowers. Also there were sketches of the peasantry and of the gentlefolk with whom the writer came in contact; very shrewd and clever, some of them, but with this peculiarity—that they were absolutely free from unkindness of thought or words, though sometimes their author allowed herself the license of a mitigated satire. Such things, with notes of domestic and parish matters, and of the progress made in her arduous and continual study of vocal and instrumental music, made up the sum of these years of the diary. Then at length, at the beginning of the last volume, came this entry:

"The unexpected has happened, somebody has actually been found in whose eyes this cure of souls is desirable—namely, a certain Mr. Tomley, the rector of a village called Monksland, upon the East Coast of England. I will sum up the history of the thing. For some years I have been getting tired of this place, although, in a way, I love it too. It is so lonely here, and—I confess my weakness—playing and singing as I do now, I should like, occasionally, to have a better audience than a few old, half-deaf clergymen, their preoccupied and commonplace wives, some yeomen farmers, and a curate or two.

"It was last year, though I find that I didn't put it down at the time, that at the concert in aid of the rebuilding of Pankford church I played Tartini's 'Il Trillo del Diavolo,' to me one of the weirdest and most wonderful bits of violin music in the world. I know that I was almost crying when I finished it. But next day I saw in the report in the local paper, written by 'Our Musical Man,' that 'Miss Fregelius then relieved the proceedings with a comic interlude on the violin, which was much appreciated by the audience.' It was that, I confess it—yes, the idiotic remark of 'Our Musical Man,' which made me determine if it was in any way possible that I would shake the dust of this village off my feet. Then, so far as my father is concerned, the stipend is wretched and decreasing.

Also he has never really got on here; he is too shy, too reserved, perhaps, in a way, too well read and educated, for these rough-and-ready people. Even his foreign name goes against him. The curates about here call him 'Frigid Fregelius.' It is the local idea of a joke.

"So I persuaded him to advertise for an exchange, although he said it was a mere waste of money, as nobody in his senses would look at this parish. Then came the wonderful thing. After the very first advertisement—yes, the very first—arrived a letter from Mr. Tomley, rector of Monksland, where the stipend is 100 pounds a year better than this, saying that he would wish to inquire into the matter. He has inquired, he has been, a pompous old gentleman with a slow voice and a single lock of white hair above his forehead; he says that it is satisfactory, and that, subject to the consent of the bishop, etc., he thinks that he will be glad to effect the exchange. Afterwards I found him in front of the house staring at the moorland behind, the sea in front, and the church in the middle, and looking very wretched. I asked him why he wanted to do it—the words popped out of my mouth, I couldn't help them; it was all so odd.

"Then I found out the reason. Mr. Tomley has a wife who is, or thinks she is—I am not sure which—an invalid, and who, I gather, speaks to Mr. Tomley with no uncertain sound. Mr. Tomley's wife was the niece of a long-departed rector who was inducted in 1815, and reigned here for forty-five years. He was rich, a bachelor, and rebuilt the church. (Is it not all written in the fly-leaf of the last register?) Mrs. Tomley inherited her uncle's landed property in this neighbourhood, and says that she is only well in the air of Northumberland. So Mr. Tomley has to come up here, which he doesn't at all like, although I gather that he is glad to escape from his present squire, who seems to be a distinguished but arbitrary old gentleman, an ex-Colonel of the Guards; rather quarrelsome, too, with a habit of making fun of Mrs. Tomley. There's the explanation.

"So just because of the silly criticism of 'Our Musical Man' we are going to move several hundred miles. But is that really the cause? Are these things done of our own desire, or do we do them because we must, as our forefathers believed? Beneath our shouts and chattering they have always heard the slow thunder of the waves of Fate. Through the flare of our straw fires and the dust of our hurrying feet, they could always see the shadow of his black banners and the sheen of his advancing spears, and for them every wayside sign-post was painted with his finger.

"I think like that, too, perhaps because I am all, nearly all, Norse, and we do not shake off the strong and ancient shackle of our blood in the space of a few generations of Christian freedom and enlightenment. Yes, I see the finger of Fate upon this sign-post of an advertisement in a Church paper. His flag is represented to me by Mr. Tomley's white and cherished lock. Assuredly our migration is decreed of the Norns, therefore I accept it without question; but I should like to know what kind of a web of destiny they are weaving for us yonder in the place called Monksland."

XXI

The End of Stella's Diary

A month or two later in the diary came the account of the shipwreck of the Trondhjem and of the writer's rescue from imminent death. "My first great adventure," the pages were headed. They told how her father, with whom ready-money was a scarce commodity, and who had a passion for small and uncomfortable economies, suddenly determined to save two or three pounds by taking a passage in a Norwegian tramp steamboat named the Trondhjem. This vessel, laden with a miscellaneous cargo, had put in at a Northumbrian port, and carried freight consisting of ready-made windows, door-frames, and other wooden house-fittings suited to the requirements of the builders of seaside villas, to be delivered at the rising watering-place of Northwold, upon her way to London. Then followed a description of the voyage, the dirt of the ship, the surpassing nastiness of the food, and the roughness of the crew, whose sailor-like qualities inspired the writer with no confidence.

Next, the diary which now had been written up by Stella in the Abbey where Morris read it, went on to tell of how she had gone to her berth one night in the cabin next to that occupied by her father, and being tired by a long day in the strong sea air had fallen instantly into a heavy sleep, which was disturbed by a nightmare-like dream of shock and noise. This imagined pandemonium, it said, was followed by a great quiet, in the midst of which she awoke to miss the sound of the thumping screw and of the captain shouting his orders from the bridge.

For a while, the writing told, she lay still, till a sense that something was wrong awoke her thoroughly, when she lit the candle which she kept by her berth, and, rising, peeped out into the saloon to see that water was washing along its floor. Presently she made another discovery, that she was alone, utterly alone, even her father's cabin being untenanted.

The rest need not be repeated in detail. Throwing on some garments, and a red cloak of North-country frieze, she made her way to the deck to find that the ship was abandoned by every living soul, including her own father; why, or under what circumstances, remained a mystery. She retreated into the captain's cabin, which was on deck, being afraid to go below again in the darkness, and sheltered there until the light came.

Then she went out, and though the dim, mist-laden dawn crept forward to the forecastle, and staring over the side discovered that the prow of the ship was fixed upon a rock, while her stern and waist, which floated clear, heaved and rolled with every sea. As she stood thus the vessel slipped back along the reef three feet or more, throwing her to the deck, and thrilling her from head to foot with the most sickening sensation she had ever experienced. Then the Trondhjem caught and hung again, but Stella, so she wrote, knew that the end must be near, as the ship would lift off with the full tide and founder, and for the first time felt afraid.

"I did not fear what might come after death," went on the diary, "but I did fear the act of death. I was so lonely, and the dim waters looked so cold; the brown shoulders of the rocks which showed now and again through the surges, so cruel. To be dashed by those cold waters upon those iron rocks till the life was slowly ground out of my body! And my father—the thought of him tormented my mind. Was he dead, or had he deserted me? The last seemed quite impossible, for it would have supposed him a coward, and I was sure that he would rather die than leave me; therefore, as I feared, the first must be true. I was afraid, and I was wretched, and I said my prayers and cried a little, while the cold struck me through the red cloak, and the damp mist made me shiver.

"Then suddenly I remembered that it had not been the custom of my ancestors and countrywomen of the old time to die weeping, and with the thought some of my courage came back. I rose from the deck and stood upon the prow of the ship, supporting myself by a rope, as many a dead woman of my race has done before me in the hour of battle and shipwreck. As I stood thus, believing that I was about to die, there floated into my mind a memory of the old Norse song that my mother had taught me as she learned it from her mother. It is called the 'Song of the Overlord,' and for generations without count on their death-beds has been sung, or if they were too weak to sing, whispered, by the women of my family. Even my mother murmured it upon the day she died, although to all appearances she had become an Englishwoman; and the first line of it,

"'Hail to thee, Sky King! Hail to thee, Earth King!'

were the last words that the gentlest creature whom I ever knew, my sister Gudrun, muttered before she became unconscious. This song it has always been held unlucky to sing except upon the actual approach of death, since otherwise, so goes the old saying, 'it draws the arrow whose flight was wide,' and Death, being invoked, comes soon. Still, for me I believed there was no escape, for I was quite sure from her movements that the steamer would soon come off the rocks, and I had made my confession and said my prayers. So I began to sing, and sang my loudest, pleasing myself with the empty, foolish thought that in some such circumstance as this many a Danish sea-king's daughter had sung that song before me.

"Then, as I sang, a wind began to blow, and suddenly the mist was driven before it like puffs of smoke, and in the east behind me rose the red ball of the sun. Its light fell upon the rocks and upon the waters beyond them, and there to my amazement, appearing and disappearing upon the ridges and hollows of the swell, I saw a man alone in a sailing-boat, which rode at anchor within thirty yards of me. At first I thought that it must be my father, then the man caught sight of me, and I saw his face as he looked up, for the sun shone upon his dark eyes, and knew that he was a stranger.

"He lifted his anchor and called to me to come to the companion ladder, and his voice told me that he was a gentleman. I could not meet him as I was, with my hair loose, and bare-footed like some Norse Viking girl. So I took the risk, for now, although I cannot tell why, I felt sure that no harm would come to him or me, and ran to the cabin, where also was this volume of my diary and my mother's jewels that I did not wish to lose. When at last I was ready after a fashion, I came out with my bag, and there, splashing through the water of the saloon, ran the stranger, shouting angrily to me to be quick, as the ship was lifting off the rock, which made me think how brave it was of him to come aboard to look for me. In an instant he caught me by the hand, and was dragging me up the stairs and down the companion, so that in another minute we were together in the boat, and he had told me that my father was on shore—thank God!—though with a broken thigh."

Then some pages of the diary were taken up with the description of the twenty-four hours which she had spent on the open sea with himself, of their landing, dazed and exhausted, at the Dead Church, and her strange desire to explore it, their arrival at the Abbey, and her meeting with her father. After these came a passage that may be quoted:—

"He is not handsome—I call him plain—with his projecting brow, large mouth, and untidy brown hair. But notwithstanding his stoop and his thin hands, he looks a fine man, and, when they light up, his eyes are beautiful. It was brave of him, too, very brave, although he thinks nothing of it, to come out alone to look for me like that. I wonder what brought him? I wonder if anything told his mind that I, a girl whom he had never seen, was really on the ship and in danger? Perhaps—at any rate, he came, and the odd thing is that from the moment I saw him, and especially from the moment I heard his voice, I felt as though I had known him all my life. Probably he would think me mad if I were to say so; indeed, I am by no means sure that he does not pay me that compliment already, with some excuse, perhaps, in view of the 'Song of the Overlord' and all my wild talk. Well, after such a night as I had spent anyone might be excused for talking foolishly. It is the reaction from never expecting to talk again at all. The chief advantage of a diary is that one may indulge in the luxury of telling the actual truth. So I will say that I feel as though I had known him always; always—and as though I understood him as one understands a person one has watched for years. What is more, I think that he understands me more than most people do; not that this is wonderful, seeing how few I know. At any rate, he guesses more or less what I am thinking about, and can see that there is something in the ideas which others consider foolish, as perhaps they are.

"It is very odd that I, who had made sure that I was gone, should be still alive in this pleasant house, and saved from death by this pleasant companion, to find my father, whom I feared was dead, also living. And all this after I had sung the 'Song of the Overlord!' So much for its ill-luck. But, all the same, my father was rather upset when he heard that I had been found singing it. He is very superstitious, my dear old father; that is one of the few Norse characteristics which he has left in him. I told him that there was no use in being disturbed, since, in the end, things must go as they are fated.

"Mr. Monk is engaged to a Miss Porson. He told me that in the boat. I asked him what he was thinking of when we nearly over-set against that dreadful rock. He answered that he could only think of the song he had heard me singing on the ship, which I considered a great compliment to my voice, quite the nicest I ever had. But he ought to have been thinking about the lady to whom he is engaged, and he understood that I thought so, which I daresay I should not have allowed him to do. However, when people believe that they are going to be drowned they grow confidential, and expose their minds freely. He exposed his when he told me that he thought I was talking egregious nonsense, and I am afraid that I laughed at him. I don't think that he really can love her—that is, as engaged people are supposed to love each other. If he did he would not have grown so angry—with himself—and then turned upon me because the recollection of my old death song had interfered with the reflections which he ought to have offered upon her altar. That is what struck me as odd; not his neglecting to remember her in a moment of danger, since then we often forget everything except some triviality of the hour. But, of course, this is all nonsense, which I oughtn't to write here even, as most people have their own ways of being fond of each other. Also, it is no affair of mine.

"I have seen Miss Porson's photograph, a large one of her in Court dress, which stands in Mr. Monk's laboratory (such a lovely place, it was an old chapel). She is a beautiful woman; large and soft and regal-looking, a very woman; it would be difficult to imagine a better specimen of 'the eternal feminine.' Also, they say, that is, the nurse who is looking after my father says, that she is very rich and devoted to 'Mr. Morris.' So Mr. Morris is a lucky man. I wonder why he didn't save her from a shipwreck instead of me. It would have given an appropriate touch of romance to the affair, which is now entirely wasted upon a young person, if I may still call myself so, with whom it has no concern.

"What interests me more than our host's matrimonial engagements, however, are his experiments with aerophones. That is a wonderful invention if only it can be made to work without fail upon all occasions. I do wish that I could help him there. It would be some return for his great kindness, for it must be a dreadful nuisance to have an old clergyman with a broken leg and his inconvenient daughter suddenly quartered upon you for an unlimited period of time."

The record of the following weeks was very full, but almost entirely concerned—brief mention of other things, such as her father's health excepted—with full and accurate notes and descriptions of the aerophone experiments. To Morris reading them it was wonderful, especially as Stella had received no training in the science of electricity, that she could have grasped the subject thus thoroughly in so short a time. Evidently she must have had a considerable aptitude for its theory and practice, as might be seen by the study that she gave to the literature which he lent her, including some manuscript volumes of his own notes. Also there were other entries. Thus:

"To-day Mr. Stephen Layard proposed to me in the Dead Church. I had seen it coming for the last three weeks and wished to avoid it, but he would not take a hint. I am most sorry, as I really think he cares about me—for the while—which is very kind of him. But it is out of the question, and I had to say no. Indeed, he repels me. I do not even like being in the same room with him, although no doubt this is very fastidious and wrong of me. I hope that he will get over it soon; in fact, although he seemed distressed, I am not vain enough to suppose that it will be otherwise. . .

"Of course, my father is angry, for reasons which I need not set down. This I expected, but he said some things which I wish he had left unsaid, for they made me answer him as I ought not to have done. Fathers and daughters look at marriage from such different standpoints; what is excellent in their eyes may be as bad as death, or in some cases worse to the woman who of course must pay the price. . .

"I sang and played my best last night, my very, very best; indeed, I don't think I ever did so well before, and perhaps never shall again. He was moved—more moved than I meant him to be, and I was moved myself. I suppose that it was the surroundings; that old chapel—how well those monks understood acoustic properties—the moonlight, the upset to my nerves this afternoon, my fear that he believed that I had accepted Mr. L. (imagine his believing that! I thought better of him, and he *did* believe it)—everything put together.

"While I was singing he told me that he was going away—to see Miss Porson at Beaulieu, I suppose. When I had finished—oh! how tired I was after the effort was over—he asked me straight out if I intended to marry Mr. Layard, and I asked him if he was mad! Then I put another question, I don't know why; I never meant to do it, but it came up from my heart—whether he had not said that he was going away? In answer he explained that he was thinking of so doing, but had changed his mind. Oh! I was pleased when I heard that. I was never so pleased in my life before. After all, the gift of music is of some use.

"But why should I have been pleased? Mr. Monk's comings or goings are nothing to me; I have no right to interfere with them, even indirectly, or to concern myself about them. Yet I cried when I heard those words, but I suppose it was the music that made me cry; it has that inconvenient effect sometimes. Well, I have no doubt that he will see plenty of Miss Porson, and it would have been a great pity to break off the experiments just now."

One more extract from the very last entry in the series of books. It was written at the Rectory on Christmas Eve, just before Stella started out to meet Morris at the Dead Church:

"He—Colonel M.—asked me and I told him the truth straight out. I could not help myself; it burst from my lips, although the strange thing is that until he put it into my mind with the question, I knew *nothing*. Then of a sudden, in an instant; in a flash; I understood and I knew that my whole being belonged to this man, his son Morris. What is love? Once I remember hearing a clever cynic argue that between men and women no such thing exists. He called their affection by other names, and said that for true love to be present the influence of sex must be absent. This he proved by declaring that this marvellous passion of love about which people talk and write is never heard of where its object is old or deformed, or even very ugly, although such accidents of chance and time are no bar to the true love of—let us say—the child and the parent, or the friend and the friend.

"Well, the argument seemed difficult to answer, although at the time I knew that it must be wrong, but how could I, who was utterly without experience, talk of such a hard matter? Now I understand that love; the real love between a man and a woman, if it be real, embraces all the other sorts of love. More—whether the key be physical or spiritual, it unlocks a window in our hearts through which we see a different world from the world that we have known. Also with this new vision come memories and foresights. This man whom I love—three months ago I had never seen his face—and now I feel as though I had known him not only all my life, but from the beginning of time—as though we never could be parted any more.

"And I talk thus about one who has never said a tender word to me. Why? Because my thought, is his thought, and my mind his mind. How am I sure of that? Because it came upon me at the moment when I learned the truth about myself. He and I are one, therefore I learned the truth about him also.

"I was like Eve when she left the Tree; knowledge was mine, only I had eaten of the fruit of Life. Yet the taste of it must be bitter in my mouth. What have I done? I have given my spirit into the keeping of a man who is pledged to another woman, and, as I think, have taken his from her keeping to my own. What then? Is this other woman, who is so good and kind, to be robbed of all that is left to her in the world? Am I to take from her him who is almost her husband? Never. If his heart has come to me I cannot help it—for the rest, no. So what is left to me? His spirit and all the future when the flesh is done with; that is heritage enough. How the philosopher who argued about the love of men and women would laugh and mock if he could see these words. Supposing that he could say, 'Stella Fregelius, I am in a position to offer you a choice. Will you have this man for your husband and live out your natural lives upon the strict stipulation that your relationship ends absolutely and forever with your last breaths? Or will you let him go to the other woman for their natural lives with the prospect of that heritage which your imagination has fashioned; that dim eternity of double joy where, hand in hand, twain and yet one, you will fulfil the secret purpose of your destinies?'

"What should I answer then?

"Before Heaven I would answer that I would not sell myself to the devil of the flesh and of this present world. What! Barter my birthright of immortality for the mess of pottage of a few brief years of union? Pay out my high hopes to their last bright coin for this dinner of mingled herbs? Drain the well of faith dug with so many prayers and labours, that its waters may suffice to nourish a rose planted in the sand, whose blooms must die at the first touch of creeping earthly frost?

"The philosopher would say that I was mad; that the linnet in the hand is better than all the birds of paradise which ever flew in fabled tropic seas.

"I reply that I am content to wait till upon some glorious morning my ship breaks into the silence of those seas, and, watching from her battered bulwarks, I behold the islands of the Blest and catch the scent of heavenly flowers, and see the jewelled birds, whereof I dream floating from palm to palm.

"'But if there are no such isles?' he would answer; 'If, with their magic birds and flowers, they are indeed but the baseless fabric of a dream? If your ship, amidst the ravings of the storm and the darkness of the tortured night, should founder once and for ever in the dark strait which leads to the gateways of that Dawn—those gateways through which no traveller returns to lay his fellows' course for the harbours of your perfect sea; what then?'

"Then I would say, let me forswear God Who has suffered me to be deceived with false spirits, and sink to depths where no light breaks, where no memories stir, where no hopes torment. Yes, then let me deny Him and die, who am of all women the most miserable. But it is not so, for to me a messenger has *come*; at my prayer once the Gates were opened, and now I know quite surely that it was permitted to me to see within them that I might find strength in this the bitter hour of my trial.

"Yet how can I choke the truth and tread down the human heart within me? Oh! the road which my naked feet must tread is full of thorns, and heavy the cross that I must bear. I go now, in a few minutes' time, to bid him farewell. If I can help it I shall never see him again. No, not even after many years, since it is better not. Also, perhaps this is weakness, but I should wish him to remember me wearing such beauty as I have and still young, before time and grief and labour have marked me with their ugly scars. It is the Stella whom he found singing at the daybreak on the ship which brought her to him, for whom I desire that he should seek in the hour of a different dawn.

"I go presently, to my marriage, as it were; a cold and pitiful feast, many would think it—these nuptials of life-long renunciation. The philosopher would say, Why renounce? You have some advantages, some powers, use them. The man loves you, play upon his natural weakness. Help yourself to the thing that chances to be desirable in your eyes. Three years hence who will blame you, who will even remember? His father? Well, he likes you already, and in time a man of the world accepts accomplished facts, especially if things go well, as they will do, for that invention must succeed. No one else? Yes; three others. He would remember, however much he loved me, for I should have brought him to do a shameful act. And she would remember, whom I had robbed of her husband, coming into his life after he had promised himself to her. Last of all—most of all, perhaps—I myself should remember, day by day, and hour by hour, that I was nothing more than one of the family of thieves.

"No; I will have none of such philosophy; at least I, Stella Fregelius, will live and die among the upright. So I go to my cold marriage, such as it is; so I bend my back to the burden, so I bow my head to the storm; and throughout it all I thank God for what he has been pleased to send me. I may seem poor, but how rich I am who have been dowered with a love that I know to be eternal as my eternal soul. I go, and my husband shall receive me, not with a lover's kiss and tenderness, but with words few and sad, with greetings that, almost before their echoes die, must fade into farewells. I wrap no veil about my head, he will set no ring upon my hand, perchance we shall plight no troth. So be it; our hour of harvest is not yet.

"Yesterday was very sharp and bleak, with scuds of sleet and snow driven by the wind, but as I drove here with my father I saw a man and a woman in the midst of an empty, lifeless field, planting some winter seed. Who, looking at them, who that did not know, could foretell the fruits of their miserable, unhopeful labour? Yet the summer will come and the sweet smell of the flowering beans, and the song of the nesting birds, and the plentiful reward of the year crowned with fatness. It is a symbol of this marriage of mine. To-day we sow the seed; next, after a space of raving rains and winds, will follow the long, white winter of death, then some dim, sweet spring of awakening, and beyond it the fulness of all joy.

"What is there about me that it would make me ashamed that he should know; this husband to whom I must tell nothing? I cannot think. No other man has been anything to me. I can remember no great sin. I have worked, making the best of such gifts as I possess. I have tried to do my duty, and I will do it to the end. Surely my heart is whole and my hands are clean. Perhaps it is a sin that I should have learned to love him; that I should look to a far future where I may be with him. If so, am I to blame, who ask nothing here? Can I conquer destiny who am its child? Can I read or shape the purpose of my Maker?

"And so I go. O God, I pray Thee of Thy mercy, give me strength to bear my temptations and my trials; and to him, also, give every strength and blessing. O Father, I pray Thee of Thy mercy, shorten these the days of my tribulation upon earth. Accept and sanctify this my sacrifice of denial; grant me pardon here, and hereafter through all the abyss of time in Thy knowledge and presence, that perfect peace which I desire with him to whom I am appointed. Amen."

XXII

THE EVIL GATE

S uch was the end of the diary of Stella.

Morris shut the book with something like a sob. Then he rose and began to tramp up and down the length of the long, lonely room, while thoughts, crowded, confused, and overwhelming, pressed in upon his mind. What a woman was this whom he had lost! Who had known another so pure, so spiritual? Surely she did not belong to this world, and therefore her last prayer was so quickly answered, therefore Heaven took her. Many reading those final pages might have said with the philosopher she imagined that the shock of love and the sorrow of separation had turned her brain, and that she was mad. For who, so such might argue, would think that person otherwise than mad who dared to translate into action, and on earth to set up as a ruling star, that faith which day by day their lips professed.

Yet it would seem after that this "dreamer and mystic" Stella believed in nothing which our religion, accepted by millions without cavil, does not promise to its votaries. Its revelations and rewards marked the extremest limits of her fantasy; immortality of the personal soul, its foundation stone, was the rock on which she built. A heaven where there is no earthly marriage, but where each may consort with the souls most loved and most desired; where all sorrows are forgotten, all tears are wiped away, all purposes made clear, reserved for those who deny themselves, do their duty, and seek forgiveness of their sins—this heaven conceived by Stella, is it not vowed to us in the pages of the Gospel? Is it not vowed again and again, sometimes with more detail, sometimes with less; sometimes in open, simple words, sometimes wrapped in the mystic allegory of the visions of St. John; but everywhere and continually held before us as our crown and great reward? And the rest, such things as her belief in guardian angels, and that it had been given to her mortal eyes to behold and commune with a beloved ghost, is there not ample warrant for them in those inspired writings? Were not the dead seen of many in Jerusalem on the night of fear, and are we not told of "ministering spirits sent forth to do service for the sake of them that shall inherit salvation?" and of the guardian angels, who look continually upon the Father?

Now it all grew clear to Morris. In Stella he beheld an example of the doctrines of Christianity really inspiring the daily life of the believer. If her strong faith animated all those who served under that banner, then in like circumstances they would act as she had acted. They would have no doubts; their fears would vanish; their griefs be comforted, and, to a great extent, even the promptings and passions of their mortality would be trodden under foot. With Stella they would be ready to neglect the temporary in their certainty of the eternal, and even to welcome death, to them in truth, and not in mere convention, the Gate of Life.

Many things are promised to those who can achieve faith. Stella achieved it and became endued with some portion of the promise. Spiritual faith, not inherited, nor accepted, but hard-won by personal struggle and experience; that was the key-note to her character and the explanation of her actions. Yet that faith, when examined into, was nothing exotic; no combination of mysticism and mummery, but one founded upon the daily creed of the English and its fellow churches, and understood and applied to the circumstances of a life which was as brief as it seemed to be unfortunate. This was Morris's discovery, open and obvious enough, and yet at first until he grew accustomed to it, a thing marvellous in his eyes; one, moreover, in which he found comfort; since surely that straight but simple path was such as his feet might follow.

And she loved him. Oh! how she had loved him. There could be no doubt; there were her words written in that book, not hastily spoken beneath the pressure of some sudden wind of feeling, but set down in black and white, thought over, reasoned out, and recorded. And then their purport. They were a paean of passion, but the dirge of its denial. They dwelt upon the natural hopes of woman only to put them by.

"Yet how can I choke the truth and tread down the human heart within me? Oh! the road that my naked feet must tread is full of thorns, and heavy the cross that I must bear. . . So I go to my marriage, such as it is, so I bend my back to the burden, so I bow my head to the storm, and through it all I thank God for what He has been pleased to send me. I may seem poor, but how rich I am who have been dowered with a love that I know to be eternal as my eternal soul."

That was her creed, those were the teachings of her philosophy. And this was the woman who had loved him, who died loving him. Her very words came back, spoken but a few seconds before the end:—
"Remember every word which I have said to you. Remember that we

are wed—truly wed; that I go to wait for you, and that even if you do not see me, I will, if I may, be near you always."

"I go to wait for you. I will be near you always." Here was another inspiration. For three years or more he had been thinking of her as dead. Or rather he had thought of her in that nebulous, undefined fashion in which we consider the dead; the slumberous people who forget everything, who see nothing; who, if they exist at all, are like stones upon the beach rolled to and fro blind and senseless, not of their own desire, but by the waves of a fearful fate that itself is driven on with the strength of a secret storm of Will. And this fate some call the Breath of God, and some the working of a soulless force that compels the universe, past, present, and to be.

But was this view as real as it is common? If Stella were right, if our religion were right, it must be most wrong. That religion told us that the Master of mankind descended into Hades to preach to the souls of men. Did he preach to dumb, ocean-driven stones, to frozen forms and fossils who had once been men, or to spirits, changed, but active and existent?

Stella, too, had walked in the valley of doubt, by the path which all who think must tread; it was written large in the book of her life. But she had not fainted there; she had lived through its thunder-rains, its arid blasts of withering dust, its quivering quicksands, and its mirage-like meadows gay with deceitful, poisonous flowers. At last she had reached the mountain slopes of Truth to travel up them higher—ever higher, till she won their topmost peak, where the sun shone undimmed and the pure air blew; whence the world seemed far away and heaven very near. Yes, and from that heaven she had called down the spirit of her lost sister, and thenceforward was content and sure.

She had called down the spirit of her sister. Was it not written in the pages which she thought that no eye but hers would see?

Well, if such spirits were, hers—Stella's—must be also. And if they could be made apparent, why should not hers share their qualities?

Morris paused in his swift walk and trembled: "I will be near you always." For aught he knew she was near him now—present, perhaps, in this very room. While she was still in life, what were her aspirations? This was one of them, he remembered, as it fell from her lips: "Still to be with those whom I have loved on earth, although they cannot see me; to soothe their sorrows, to support their weakness, to lull their fears." And if this were so; if any power were given her to fulfil her will, whom would she sooner visit than himself?

Stay! That was her wish on earth, while she was a woman. But would she still wish it afterwards? The spirit was not the flesh, the spirit could see and be sure, while the flesh must be content with deductions and hazardings. If she could see, she would know him as he was; every failing, every secret infirmity, every infidelity of heart, might be an open writing to her eyes. And then would she not close that book in horror?

A great writer has said in effect that no man would dare to affront the ears of his fellows—men much worse than himself perhaps—with the true details of his hidden history. Knowing all the truth, they would shrink from him. How much more then at such sights and sounds would a pure spirit, washed clean of every taint of earth, fly from his soiled presence, wailing and aghast? Nay, men are hypocrites, who, in greater or less degree, themselves practice the very sins that shock them, but spirits, knowing all, would forgive all. They are above hypocrisy. If the Lord of spirits can weigh the "dust whereof we are made" and still be merciful, shall his bright messengers trample it in scorn and hate? Will they not also consider the longings of the heart and its uprightness, and be pitiful towards the failings of the flesh? Would Stella hate him because he remained as he was made—as herself she might once have been? Because having no wings with which to rule the air he must still tramp onwards through the foetid, clinging mud of earth?

Oh! how he longed to see her, that he might win her faith; win it beyond all doubt by the evidence of his earthly eyes and senses. "If I die, search and you shall see," she had once said to him, and then added, "No, do not search, but wait." Wait! How could he wait? "At your death I will be with you." Why he might live another fifty years! That book of her recorded thoughts had aroused in him such a desire for the sight, or at least the actual knowledge of her continued being, that his blood was aflame as with a madness. And yet how should he search?

"Stella," he whispered, "come to me, Stella!" But no Stella came; no wings rustled, no breath stirred; the empty room was as the room had been. Its silence seemed to mock him. Those who slept beneath its marble floor were not more silent.

Was he mad that he should claim the power to work this miracle—to charm the dead back through the Gates of Death as Orpheus charmed Eurydice? Yet Stella did this thing—but how? He turned to the volume and page of her diary which dealt with the drawing down of Gudrun. Yes, here she spoke of continual efforts and of "that long, long preparation"—of prayer and fasting also. Here, too, was the whole secret summed up in a dozen words: "To see a spirit one must grow akin to spirits." Well, it could be done, and he would do it. But look further on where she said: "I shall call her back no more, lest the thing should get the mastery of me, and I become unfitted for my work on earth. . . I will stop while there is yet time, while I am still mistress of my mind, and have the strength to deny myself this awful joy."

Was there not a warning in these words, and in those other words: "No, do not search, but wait." Surely they told of risk to him who, being yet on earth, dared to lift a corner of the veil which separates flesh and spirit. "Should get the mastery of me." If he saw her once would he be able to do as Stella did, and by an effort of his will separate himself from a communion so fearful yet so sweet? "Unfitted for my work." Supposing that it did get the mastery of him, would he not also be unfitted for his work on earth?

His work? What work had he now? It seemed to be done; for attending scientific meetings, receiving dividends, playing the country squire's only son and the wealthy host whilst awaiting the title which Mary wished for—these things are not work, and somehow his days were so arranged that he was never allowed to go beyond them. All further researches and experiments were discouraged. What did it matter if he were unfitted for that which he could no longer do? His work was finished. There it stood before him in that box, stamped "Monk's aerophone. The Twin. No. 3412."

No; he had but one ambition left. To pierce the curtain of thick night and behold her who was lost to him; her who loved him as man had been seldom loved.

The fierce temptation struck him as a sudden squall strikes a ship with all her canvas spread. For a moment mast and rigging stood the strain, then they went by the board. He would do it if it killed him; but the task must be undertaken properly, deliberately, and above all in secret. To-morrow he would begin. When he had satisfied himself; when he had seen; then he could always stop.

A few minutes later Morris stood beside his wife's bed. There she lay, in the first perfection of young motherhood and beauty, a lovely, white-wrapped vision with straying golden hair; her sweet, rounded face pink with the flush of sleep, and the long lashes lying like little shadows on her cheek.

Morris looked at her, and his doubts returned. What would Stella say? he thought to himself. It almost seemed to him that he could hear her voice, bidding him forbear; bidding him render unto his wife those things which were his wife's: all honour, loyalty, and devotion. If he entered on this course could he still render them? Was there not such a thing as moral infidelity, and did not such exercises as he proposed partake of its nature? Perhaps, perhaps. On the whole it might be well to put all this behind him.

It was three o'clock, he was tired out, and must sleep. The morning would be a more fitting time to ponder such weighty questions of the unwritten matrimonial law.

In due course, the morning came—indeed, it was not far off—and with it wiser counsels. Mary woke early and talked about the baby, which was teething; indeed, so soon as the nurse was up she sent for it that the three of them might hold a consultation over a swollen gum. Also she discussed the date of their departure to Beaulieu, for again Christmas was near at hand; adding, however, somewhat to Morris's relief, that unless the baby's teeth went on better she really did not think that they could go, as it would be most unwise to take her out of the care of Dr. Charters and trust her to the tender mercies of foreign leeches. Morris agreed that it might be risky, and mentioned that in a letter which he had received from the concierge at Beaulieu a few days before, that functionary said that the place was overrun with measles and scarlatina.

"Morris!" exclaimed Mary, sitting bolt upright in bed, "and you never told me! What is more, had it not been for baby's teeth, which brought it to your mind, I believe you never would have told me, and I might have taken those unprotected little angels and—Oh! goodness, I can't bear to think of it."

Morris muttered some apologies, whereon Mary, looking at him suspiciously through her falling hair, asked:

"Why did you forget to show me the letter? Did you suppress it because you wanted to go to Beaulieu?"

"No," answered Morris with energy; "I hate Beaulieu. I forgot, that is all; because I have so much to think about, I suppose."

"So much? I thought that things were arranged now so that you had nothing at all to think about except how to spend your money and be happy with me, and adore the dear angels—Yes, I think that perhaps the nurse had better take her away. Touch the bell, will you? There, she's gone. Keep her well wrapped up, and mind the draught, nurse.

"No, don't get up yet, Morris; I want to talk to you. You have been very gloomy of late, just like you used to be before you married, mooning about and staring at nothing. And what on earth do you do sitting up to all hours of the morning in that ghosty old chapel, where I wouldn't be alone at twelve o'clock for a hundred pounds?"

"I read," said Morris.

"Read? Read what? Novels?"

"Sometimes," answered Morris.

"Oh, how can you tell such fibs? Why, that last book by Lady What's-her-name which came in the Mudie box—the one they say is so improper—has been lying on your table for over two months, and you can't tell me yet what it was the heroine did wrong. Morris, you are not inventing anything more, are you?"

Here was an inspiration. "I admit that I am thinking of a little thing," he said with diffidence, as though he were a budding poet with a sonnet on his mind.

"A little thing? What little thing?"

"Well, a new kind of aerophone designed to work uninfluenced by its twin."

"Well, and why shouldn't it? Everything can't have a twin—only I suppose there would be nothing to hear."

"That's just the point," replied Morris in his old professional manner. "I think there would be plenty to hear if only I could make the machine sensitive to the sounds and capable of reproducing them."

"What sounds?" asked Mary.

"Well, if, for instance, one could successfully insulate it from the earth noises, the sounds which permeate space, and even those that have their origin upon the surfaces of the planets and perhaps of the more distant stars."

"Great heavens!" exclaimed Mary, "imagine a man who can want to let loose upon our poor little world every horrible noise that happens in the stars. Why, what under heaven would be the use of it?"

"Well, one might communicate with them. Conceivably even one might hear the speech of their inhabitants, if they have any; always presuming that such an instrument could be made, and that it can be successfully insulated."

"Hear the speech of their inhabitants! That is your old idea, but you will never succeed, that's one blessing. Morris, I suspect you; you want to stop at home here to work at this horrible new machine; to work for years, and years, and years without the slightest result. I suppose that you didn't invent that about the measles and the scarlatina, did you? The two of them together sound rather clumsy, as though you might have done so."

"Not a bit, upon my honour," answered Morris. "I will go and get the letter," and, not sorry to escape from further examination, he went.

Whether the cause were Mary's doubts and reproaches, or the infant's gums, or the working of his own conscience,—he felt that a man with a teething baby has no right to cultivate the occult. For quite a long period, a whole fortnight, indeed, Morris steadily refrained from any attempt to fulfil his dangerous ambition to "pierce the curtain of thick night." Only he read and re-read Stella's diary—that secret, fascinating work which in effect was building a wall between him and the healthy, common instincts of the world—till he knew whole pages of it by heart. Also he began a series of experiments whereof the object was to produce an improved and more sensitive aerophone.

That any instrument which the intellect of man could produce would really succeed in conveying sounds which, if they exist at all, are born in the vast cosmic areas that envelope our earth and its atmosphere, he believed to be most improbable. Still, such a thing was possible, for what is not? Moreover, the world itself as it rushes on its fearful journey across the depths of space has doubtless many voices that have not yet been heard by the ears of men, some of which he might be able to discover and record. At the least he stood upon the threshold of a new knowledge, and now a great desire arose in him to pass its doors, if so he might, for who could tell what he would learn or see behind them? And by degrees, as he worked, always with one ulterior object in his mind, his scruples vanished or were mastered by the growth of his longing, till this became his ruling passion—to behold the spirit of Stella. Now he no longer reasoned with himself, but openly, nakedly, in his own heart gave his will over to the achievement of this monstrous and unnatural end.

How was it to be done? That was now the sole dilemma which tormented him—as the possible methods of obtaining the drink he craves, or the drug that gives him peace and radiant visions, torment the dipsomaniac or the morphia victim in his guarded prison. He thought of his instruments, those magic machines with the working of which Stella had been familiar in her life. He even poured petitions into them in the hope that these might be delivered far beyond the ken of man, only to learn that he was travelling a road which led to a wall impassable; the wall that, for the lack of a better name, we call Death, which bars the natural from the spiritual.

Wonderful as were his electrical appliances, innumerable as might be their impalpable emanations, insoluble as seemed the mystery of their power of catching and transmitting sounds by the agency of ether, they were still physical appliances producing physical effects in obedience to the laws of nature. But what he sought lay beyond nature and was subject to some rule of which he did not even know the elements, and much less the axioms. Herein his instruments, or indeed, any that man could make, were as futile and as useless as would be the prayers of an archbishop addressed to a Mumbo-jumbo in a fetish house. The link was wanting; there was, and could be, no communication between the two. The invisible ether which he had subdued to his purposes was still a constituent part of the world of matter; he must discover the spiritual ether, and discover also the animating force by which it might be influenced.

Now he formed a new plan—to reach the dead by his petitions, by the invocation of his own spirit. "Seek me and you shall find me," she had said. So he sought and called in bitterness and concentration of heart, but still he did not find. Stella did not come.

He was in despair. She had promised, and her promise seemed to be broken. Then it was that in turning the pages of her diary he came across a passage that had escaped him, or which he had forgotten. It ran thus:

"In the result I have learned this, that we cannot compel the departed to appear. Even if they hear us they will not, or are not suffered to obey. If we would behold them we must create the power of vision in our own natures. They are about us always, only we cannot see or feel their presence; our senses are too gross. To succeed we must refine our senses until they acquire an aptitude beyond the natural. Then without any will or any intervention on their parts, we may triumph, perhaps even when *they* do not know that we have triumphed."

XXIII

STELLA COMES

Now, by such arts as are known to those who have studied mysticism in any of its protean forms, Morris set himself to attempt communication with the unseen. In their practice these arts are as superlatively unwholesome as in their result, successful or not, they are unnatural. Also, they are very ancient. The Chaldeans knew them, and the magicians who stood before Pharaoh knew them. To the early Christian anchorites and to the gnostics they were familiar. In one shape or another, ancient wonder-workers, Scandinavian and mediaeval seers, modern Spiritualists, classical interpreters of oracles, Indian fakirs, savage witch-doctors and medicine men, all submitted or submit themselves to the yoke of the same rule in the hope of attaining an end which, however it may vary in its manifestations, is identical in essence.

This is the rule: to beat down the flesh and its instincts and nurture the spirit, its aspirations and powers. And this is the end—to escape before the time, if only partially and at intervals, into an atmosphere of vision true or false, where human feet were meant to find no road, and the trammelled minds of men no point of outlook. That such an atmosphere exists even materialists would hesitate to deny, for it is proved by the whole history of the moral world, and especially by that of the religions of the world, their founders, their prophets and their exponents, many of whom have breathed its ether, and pronounced it the very breath of life. Their feet have walked the difficult path; standing on those forbidden peaks they have scanned the dim plains and valleys of the unseen, and made report of the dreams and shapes that haunt them. Then the busy hordes of men beneath for a moment pause to listen and are satisfied.

"Lo, here is Truth," they cry, "now we may cease from troubling." So for a while they rest till others answer, "Nay, *this* is Truth; our teacher told it us from yonder mountain, the only Holy Hill." And yet others fall upon them and slay them, shouting, "Neither of these is Truth. She dwells not among the precipices, but in the valley; there we have heard her accents."

And still from cliff to cliff and along the secret vales echoes the voice of Truth; and still upon the snow-wreathed peaks and across the space of rolling ocean, and even among the populous streets of men, veiled, mysterious, and changeful, her shape is seen by those who have trained themselves or been inspired to watch and hear. But no two see the same shape, and no two hear the same voice, since to each she wears a different countenance, and speaks with another tongue. For Truth is as the sand of the shore for number, and as the infinite hues of the rainbow for variety. Yet the sand is ground out of one mother rock, and all the colours of earth and air are born of a single sun.

So, practising the ancient rites and mysteries, and bowing himself to the ancient law whose primeval principles every man and woman may find graven upon the tablets of their solitary heart, Morris set himself to find that truth, which for him was hid in the invisible soul of Stella, the soul which he desired to behold and handle, even if the touch and sight should slay him.

Day by day he worked, for as many hours as he could make his own, at the details of his new experiments. These in themselves were interesting, and promised even to be fruitful; but that was not his object, or, at any rate, his principal object in pursuing them with such an eager passion of research. The talk and hazardings which had passed between himself and Stella notwithstanding, both reason and experience had taught him already that all instruments made by the hand of man were useless to break a way into the dwellings of the departed. A day might come when they would enable the inhabitants of the earth to converse with the living denizens of the most distant stars; but never, never with the dead. He laboured because of the frame of thought his toil brought with it, but still more that he might be alone: that he might be able to point to his soiled hands, the shabby clothes which he wore when working with chemicals or at the forge, the sheets of paper covered with half-finished and maddening calculations, as an excuse why he should not be taken out, or, worse still, dragged from his home to stay for nights, or perhaps whole weeks, in other places. Even his wife, he felt, would relent at the sight of those figures, and would fly from the odour of chemicals.

In fact, Mary did both, for she hated what she called "smells," and a place strewn with hot irons and bottles of acids, which, as she discovered, if disturbed burnt both dress and fingers. The sight also of algebraic characters pursuing each other across quires of paper, like the grotesque forces of some broken, impish army, filled her indolent mind with a wondering admiration that was akin to fear. The man, she reflected, who could force those cabalistic symbols to reveal anything worth knowing must indeed be a genius, and one who deserved not to be disturbed, even for a tea party.

Although she disapproved deeply of these renewed studies, such was Mary's secret thought. Whether it would have sufficed alone to persuade her to permit them is another matter, since her instinct, keen and subtle as any of Morris's appliances, warned her that in them lay danger to her home and happiness. But just then, as it happened, there were other matters to occupy her mind. The baby became seriously ill over its teething, and, other infantile complications following, for some weeks it was doubtful whether she would survive.

Now Mary belonged to the class of woman which is generally known as "motherly," and adored her offspring almost to excess. Consequently for those weeks she found plenty to think about without troubling herself over-much as to Morris and his experiments. For these same reasons, perhaps, she scarcely noticed, seated as she was some distance away at the further end of the long table, how very ethereal her husband's appetite had become, or that, although he took wine as usual, it was a mere pretence, since he never emptied his glass. The most loving of women can scarcely be expected to consider a man's appetite when that of a baby is in question, or, while the child wastes, to take note whether or no its father is losing flesh. Lastly, as regards the hours at which he came to bed, being herself a sound sleeper Mary had long since ceased to interest herself about them, on the wise principle that so long as she was not expected to sit up it was no affair of hers.

Thus it happened that Morris worked and meditated by day, and by night—ah! who that has not tried to climb this difficult and endless Jacob's ladder resting upon the earth and losing itself far, far away in the blue of heaven above, can understand what he did by night? But those who have stood even on its lowest rung will guess, and—for the rest it does not matter.

He advanced; he knew that he advanced, that the gross wall of sense was wearing thin beneath the attacks of his out-thrown soul; that even if they were not drawn, from time to time the black curtains swung aside in the swift, pure breath of his continual prayers. Moreover, the dead drew near to him at moments, or he drew near the dead. Even in his earthly brain he could feel their awful presence as wave by wave soft, sweet pulses of impression beat upon him and passed through him. Through and through him they passed till his brow ached, and every nerve of his body tingled, as though it had become the receiver of some mysterious current that stirred his blood with what was not akin to it, and summoned to his mind strange memories and foresights. Visions came also that he could not define, to slip from his frantic grasp like wet sand through the fingers of a drowning man. More and more frequently, and with an ever increasing completeness, did this unearthly air, blowing from a shore no human foot has trod, breathe through his being and possess him, much as some faint wind which we cannot feel may be seen to possess an aspen tree so that it turns white and shivers when every other natural thing is still. And as that aspen turns white and shivers in this thin, impalpable air, so did his spirit blanch and quiver with joy and dread mingled mysteriously in the cup of his expectant soul.

Again and again those sweet, yet sickening waves flowed over him, to leave him shaken and unnerved. At first they were rare visitors, single clouds floating across his calm, coming he knew not whence and vanishing he knew not whither. Now they drove in upon him like some scud, ample yet broken, before the wind, till at whiles, as it were, he could not see the face of the friendly, human sun. Then he was like a traveller lost in the mist upon a mountain top, sure of nothing, feeling precipices about him, hearing voices calling him, seeing white arms stretched out to lead him, yet running forward gladly because amid so many perils a fate was in his feet.

Now, too, they came with an actual sense of wind. He would wake up at night even by his wife's side and feel this unholy breath blowing ice-cold on his brow and upon the backs of his outstretched hands. Yet if he lit a candle it had no power to stir its flame; yes, while it still blew sharp upon him the flame of the candle did not move. Then the wind would cease, and within him the intangible, imponderable power would arise, and the voices would speak like the far, far, murmur of a stream, and the thoughts which he could not weigh or interpret would soak into his being like some strange dew, and, soft, soft as falling snow, invisible feet would tread the air about him, till of a sudden a door in his brain seemed to shut, and he woke to the world again.

Every force is subject to laws. Even if they were but the emanations of an incipient madness which like all else have their origins, destinies, and forms, these possessing vapours were a force, which in time Morris, whose mind from a lifelong training was scientific and methodical, accustomed, moreover, to struggle for dominion over elements unknown or imperfectly appreciated, learned to regulate if not entirely to control. Their visits were pleasant to him, a delight even; but to experience this joy to the utmost he discovered that their power must be concentrated; that if the full effect was to be produced this moral morphia must be taken in strong doses, and at stated intervals, sufficient space being allowed between them to give his mental being time to recuperate. Science has proved that even the molecules of a wire can grow fatigued by the constant passage of electricity, or the edge of a razor by too frequent stropping. Both of them, to be effective, to do their utmost service, must have periods of rest.

Here, then, his will came to his aid, for he found that by its strong, concentrated exertion he was enabled both to shut off the sensations or to excite them. Another thing he found also—that after a while it was impossible to do without them. For a period the anticipation of their next visit would buoy him up; but if it were baulked too long, then reaction set in, and with it the horrors of the Pit.

This was the first stage of his insanity—or of his vision.

Dear as such manifestations might be to him, in time he wearied of them; these hints which but awakened his imagination, these fantastic spiced meats which, without staying it, only sharpened his spiritual appetite. More than ever he longed to see and to know, to make acquaintance with the actual presence, whereof they were but the forerunners, the cold blasts that go before the storm, the vague, mystical draperies which veiled the unearthly goddess at whose shrine he was a worshipper. He desired the full fierce fury of the tempest, the blinding flash of the lightning, the heavy hiss of the rain, the rush of the winds bursting on him from the four horizons; he desired the naked face of his goddess.

And she came—or he acquired the power to see her, whichever it might be. She came suddenly, unexpectedly, completely, as a goddess should.

It was on Christmas Eve, at night, the anniversary of Stella's death four years before. Morris and his wife were alone at the Abbey, as the Colonel had gone for a fortnight or so to Beaulieu, just to keep the house aired, as he explained. Also Lady Rawlins was there with her husband, the evil-tempered man who by a single stroke of sickness had been converted into a babbling imbecile, harmless as a babe, and amused for the most part with such toys as are given to babes. She, so Morris understood, had intimated that Sir Jonah was failing, really failing quickly, and that in her friendlessness at a foreign place, especially at Christmas time, she would be thankful to have the comfort of an old friend's presence. This the old friend, who, having been back from town for a whole month, was getting rather bored with Monksland and the sick baby, determined to vouchsafe, explaining that he knew that young married people liked to be left to each other now and again, especially when they were worried with domestic troubles. Lady Rawlins was foolish and fat, but, as the Colonel remembered, she was fond. Where, indeed, could another woman be found who would endure so much scientific discipline and yet be thankful? Also, within a few weeks, after the expected demise of Jonah, she would be wondrous wealthy—that he knew. Therefore it seemed that the matter was worth consideration— and a journey to Beaulieu.

So the Colonel went, and Morris, more and more possessed by his monomania, was glad that he had gone. His absence gave him greater opportunities of loneliness; it was now no longer necessary that he should sit at night smoking with his father, or, rather, watching him smoke at the expense of so many precious hours when he should be up and doing.

Morris and Mary dined tete-a-tete that evening, but almost immediately after dinner she had gone to the nurseries. The baby was now threatened with convulsions, and a trained nurse had been installed. But, as Mary did not in the least trust the nurse, who, according to her account, was quite unaccustomed to children, she insisted upon dogging that functionary's footsteps. Therefore, Morris saw little of her.

It was one o'clock on Christmas morning, or more. Hours ago Morris had gone though his rites, the ritual that he had invented or discovered—in its essence, simple and pathetic enough—whereby he strove to bring himself to the notice of the dead, and to fit himself to see or hear the dead. Such tentative mysticism as served his turn need not be written down, but its substance can be imagined by many. Then, through an exercise of his will, he had invoked the strange, trance-like state which has been described. The soft waves flowing from an unknown source had beat upon his brain, and with them came the accustomed phenomena; the sense of some presence near, impending, yet impotent; suggesting by analogy and effect the misdirected efforts of a blind person seeking something in a room, or the painful attempt of one almost deaf, striving to sift out words from a confused murmur of sounds. The personality of Stella seemed to pervade him, yet he could see nothing, could hear nothing. The impression might be from within, not from without. Perhaps, after all, it was nothing but a dream, a miasma, a mirage, drawn by his own burning thought from the wastes and marshes of his mind peopled with illusive hopes and waterlogged by memories. Or it might be true and real; as yet he could not be certain of its origin.

The fit passed, delightful in its overpowering emptiness, but unsatisfying as all that had gone before it, and left him weak. For a while Morris crouched by the fire, for he had grown cold, and could not think accurately. Then his vital, human strength returned, and, as seemed to him to be fitting upon this night of all nights, he began one by one to recall the events of that day four years ago, when Stella was still a living woman.

The scene in the Dead Church, the agonies of farewell; he summoned them detail by detail, word by word; her looks, the changes of her expression, the movements of her hands and eyes and lips; he counted and pictured each precious souvenir. The sound of her last sentences also, as the blind, senseless aerophone had rendered them just before the end, one by one they were repeated in his brain. There stood the very instrument; but, alas! it was silent now, its twin lay buried in the sea with her who had worked it.

Morris grew weary, the effort of memory was exhausting, and after it he was glad to think of nothing. The fire flickered, the clear light of the electric lamps shone upon the hard, sixteenth-century faces of the painted angels in the ancient roof; without the wind soughed, and through it rose the constant, sullen roar of the sea.

Tired, disappointed, unhappy, and full of self-reproaches, for when the madness was not on him he knew his sin, Morris sank into a doze. Now music crept softly into his sleep; sweet, thrilling music, causing him to open his eyes and smile. It was Christmas Eve, and doubtless he heard the village waifs.

Morris looked up arousing himself to listen, and lo! there before him, unexpected and ineffable, was Stella; Stella as she appeared that night on which she had sung to him, just as she finished singing, indeed, when he stood for a while in the faint moonlight, the flame of inspiration still flickering in those dark eyes and the sweet lips drawn down a little as though she were about to weep.

The sight did not astonish him, at the moment he never imagined even then that this could be her spirit, that his long labours in a soil no man was meant to till had issued into harvest. Surely it was a dream, nothing but a dream. He felt no tremors, no cold wind stirred his hair; his heart did not stand still, nor his breath come short. Why should a man fear so beautiful a dream? Yet, vaguely enough, he wished that it might last forever, for it was sweet to see her so—as she had been. As she had been—yet, was she ever thus? Surely some wand of change had touched her. She was beautiful, but had she worn that beauty? And those eyes! Could any such have shone in the face of woman?

"Stella," he whispered, and from roof and walls crept back the echo of his voice. He rose and went towards her. She had vanished. He returned, and there she was.

"Speak!" he muttered; "speak!" But no word came, only the lovely changeless eyes shone on and watched him.

Listen! Music seemed to float about the room, such music as he had never heard—even Stella could not make the like. The air was full of it, the night without was full of it, millions of voices took up the chant, and from far away, note by note, mighty organs and silver trumpets told its melody.

His brain reeled. In the ocean of those unimagined harmonies it was tossed like a straw upon a swirling river, tossed and overwhelmed.

Slowly, very slowly, as the straw might be sucked into the heart of a whirlpool, his soul was drawn down into blackness. It shuddered, it was afraid; this vision of a whirlpool haunted him. He could see the narrow funnel of its waters, smooth, shining like jet, unspecked by foam, solid to all appearances; but, as he was aware, alive, every atom of them, instinct with some frightful energy, the very face of force—and in the teeth of it, less than a dead leaf, himself.

Down he went, down, and still above him shone the beautiful, pitying, changeless eyes; and still round him echoed that strange, searching music. The eyes receded, the music became faint, and then—blackness.

XXIV

Dreams and the Sleep

The Christmas Day which followed this strange night proved the happiest that Morris could ever remember to have spent since his childhood. In his worldly circumstances of course he was oppressed by none of the everyday worries which at this season are the lot of most—no duns came to trouble him, nor through lack of means was he forced to turn any beggar from his door. Also the baby was much better, and Mary's spirits were consequently radiant. Never, indeed, had she been more lovely and charming than when that morning she presented him with a splendid gold chronometer to take the place of the old silver watch which was his mother's as a girl, and that he had worn all his life. Secretly he sorrowed over parting with that familiar companion in favour of its new eighty-guinea rival, although it was true that it always lost ten minutes a day, and sometimes stopped altogether. But there was no help for it; so he kissed Mary and was grateful.

Moreover, the day was beautiful. In the morning they walked to church through the Abbey plantations, which run for nearly half a mile along the edge of the cliff. The rime lay thick upon the pines and firs—every little needle had its separate coat of white whereon the sun's rays glistened. The quiet sea, too, shone like some gigantic emerald, and in the sweet stillness the song of a robin perched upon the bending bough of a young poplar sounded pure and clear.

Yet it was not this calm and plenty, this glittering ocean flecked with white sails, and barred by delicate lines of smoke, this blue and happy sky, nor all the other good things that were given to him in such abundance, which steeped his heart in Sabbath rest. Although he sought no inspiration from such drugs, and, indeed, was a stranger to them, rather was his joy the joy of the opium-eater while the poison works; the joy of him who after suffering long nights of pain has found their antidote, and perhaps for the first time appreciates the worth of peace, however empty. His troubled heart had ceased its striving, his wrecked nerves were still, his questionings had been answered, his ends were attained; he had drunk of the divine cup which he desired, and its wine flowed through him. The dead had visited him, and he had tasted of the delight which lies hid in death. On that day he felt as though nothing could hurt him any more, nothing could even move him. The angry voices, the wars, the struggles, the questionings—all the things which torment mankind; what did they matter? He had forced the lock and broken the bar; if only for a little while, the door had opened, and he had seen that which he desired to see and sought with all his soul, and with the wondrous harvest of this pure, inhuman passion, that owes nothing to sex, or time, or earth, he was satisfied at last.

"Why did you look so strange in church?" asked Mary as they walked home, and her voice echoed in the spaces of his void mind as words echo in an empty hall.

His thoughts were wandering far, and with difficulty he drew them back, as birds tied by the foot are drawn back and, still fluttering to be free, brought home to the familiar cage.

"Strange, dear?" he answered; "did I look strange?"

"Yes; like a man in a dream or the face of a saint being comfortably martyred in a picture. Morris, I believe that you are not well. I will speak to the doctor. He must give you a tonic, or something for your liver. Really, to see you and that old mummy Mr. Fregelius staring at each other while he murmured away about the delights of the world to come, and how happy we ought to be at the thought of getting there, made me quite uncomfortable."

"Why? Why, dear?" asked Morris, vacantly.

"Why? Because the old man with his pale face and big eyes looked more like an astral body than a healthy human being; if I met him in his surplice at night, I should think he was a ghost, and upon my word, you are catching the same expression. That comes of your being so much together. Do be a little more human and healthy. Lose your temper; swear at the cook like your father; admire Jane Rose's pretty bonnet, or her pretty face; take to horse-racing, do anything that is natural, even if it is wicked. Anything that doesn't make one think of graves, and stars, and infinities, and souls who died last night; of all of which no doubt we shall have plenty in due season."

"All right, dear," answered Morris, with a fine access of forced cheerfulness, "we will have some champagne for dinner and play picquet after it."

"Champagne! What's the use of champagne when you only pretend to drink it and fill up the glass with soda-water? Picquet! You hate it, and so do I; and it is silly losing large sums of money to each other which we never mean to pay. That isn't the real thing, there's no life in that. Oh, Morris, if you love me, do cultivate some human error. It is terrible to have a husband in whom there is nothing to reform."

"I will try, love," said Morris, earnestly.

"Yes," she replied, with a gloomy shake of the head, "but you won't succeed. When Mrs. Roberts told me the other day that she was afraid her husband was taking to drink because he went out walking too often with that pretty widow from North Cove—the one with the black and gold bonnet whom they say things about—I answered that I quite envied her, and she didn't in the least understand what I meant. But I understand, although I can't express myself."

"I give up the drink," said Morris; "it disagrees; but perhaps you might introduce me to the widow. She seems rather attractive."

"I will," answered Mary, stamping her foot. "She's a horrid, vulgar little thing; but I'll ask her to tea, or to stay, and anything, if she can only make you look rather less disembodied."

That night the champagne appeared, and, feeling his wife's eyes upon him, Morris swallowed two whole glasses, and in consequence was quite cheerful, for he had eaten little—circumstances under which champagne exhilarates—for a little while. Then they went into the drawing-room and talked themselves into silence about nothing in particular, after which Morris began to wander round the room and contemplate the furniture as though he had never seen it before.

"What are you fidgeting about?" asked Mary. "Morris, you remind me of somebody who wants to slip away to an assignation, which in your case is absurd. I wish your father were back, I really do; I should be glad to listen to his worst and longest story. It isn't often that I sit with you, so it would be kinder if you didn't look so bored. I'm cross; I'm going to bed. I hope you will spend a pleasant night in the chapel with your thoughts and your instruments and the ghosts of the old Abbots. But please come into my room quietly; I don't like being woke up after three in the morning, as I was yesterday." And she went, slamming the door behind her.

Morris went also with hanging head and guilty step to his accustomed haunt in the old chapel. He knew that he was doing wrong; he could sympathise with Mary's indignation. Yet he was unable to resist, he must see again, must drink once more of that heavenly cup.

And he failed. Was it the champagne? Was it Mary's sharp words which had ruffled him? Was it that he had not allowed enough time for the energy which came from him enabling her to appear before his mortal eyes, to gather afresh in the life-springs of his own nature? Or was she also angry with him?

At least he failed. The waves came indeed, and the cold wind blew, but there was no sound of music, and no vision. Again and again he strove to call it up—to fancy that he saw. It was useless, and at last, weary, broken, but filled with a mad irritation such as might be felt by a hungry man who sees food which he cannot touch, or by a jealous lover who beholds her that should have been his bride take another husband before his eyes, he crept away to such rest as he could win.

He awoke, ill, wretched, and unsatisfied, but wisdom had come to him with sleep. He must not fail again, it was too wearing; he must prepare himself according to the rules which he had laid down. Also he must conciliate his wife, so that she did not speak angrily to him, and thus disturb his calm of mind. Broken waters mirror nothing; if his soul was to be the glass in which that beloved spirit might appear, it must be still and undisturbed. If? Then was she built up in his imagination, or did he really see her with his eyes? He could not tell, and after all it mattered little so long as he did see her.

He grew cunning—in such circumstances a common symptom—affecting a "bonhomie," a joviality of demeanour, indeed, which was rather overdone. He suggested that Mary should ask some people to tea, and twice he went out shooting, a sport which he had almost abandoned. Only when she wanted to invite certain guests to stay, he demurred a little, on account of the baby, but so cleverly that she never suspected him of being insincere. In short, as he could attain his unholy end in no other way, Morris entered on a career of mild deception, designed to prevent his wife from suspecting him of she knew not what. His conduct was that of a man engaged in an intrigue. In his case, however, the possible end of his ill-doing was not the divorce-court, but an asylum, or so some observers would have anticipated. Yet did man ever adore a mistress so fatal and destroying as this poor shadow of the dead which he desired?

It was not until New Year's Eve that Stella came again. Once more enervated and exhausted by the waves, Morris sank into a doze whence, as before, he was awakened by the sound of heavenly music to which, on this night, was added the scent of perfume. Then he opened his eyes—to behold Stella. As she had been at first, so she was now, only more lovely—a hundred times lovelier than the imagination can paint, or the pen can tell. Here was nothing pale or deathlike, no sheeted, melancholy spectre, but a radiant being whose garment was the light, and whose eyes glowed like the heart of some deep jewel. About her rolled a vision of many colours, such hues as the rainbow has fell upon her face and about her hair. And yet it was the same Stella that he had known made perfect and spiritual and, beyond all imagining, divine.

Once more he addressed—implored her, and once more no answer came; nor did her face change, or that wondrous smile pass from her lips into the gravity of her eyes. This, at least, was sure; either that she no longer had any understanding knowledge of his earthly tongue, or that its demonstration was to her a thing forbidden. What was she then? That double of the body which the Egyptians called the *Ka*, or the soul itself, the (preuma), no eidolon, but the immortal *ego*, clothed in human semblance made divine?

Why was there no answer? Because his speech was too gross for her to hearken to? Why did she not speak? Because his ears were deaf? Was this an illusion? No! a thousand times. When he approached she vanished, but what of it? He was mortal, she a spirit; they might not mix.

Yet in her own method she did speak, spoke to his soul, bidding the scales fall from its eyes so that it might see. And it saw what human imagination could not fashion. Behold those gardens, those groves that hang upon the measureless mountain face, and the white flowers which droop in tresses from the dark bough of yonder towering poplar tree, and the jewelled serpent nestling at its root.

Oh! they are gone, and when the flame-eyed Figure smote, the vast, barring, precipices fall apart and the road is smooth and open.

How far? A million miles? No, twenty thousand millions. Look, yonder shines the destined Star; now come! So, it is reached. Nay, do not stop to stare. Look again! out through utter space to where the low light glows. So, come once more. The suns float past like windblown golden dust—like the countless lamps of boats upon the bosom of a summer sea. There, beneath, lies the very home of Power. Those springing sparks of light? They are the ineffable Decrees passing outward through infinity. That sound? It is the voice of worlds which worship.

Look now! Out yonder see the flaming gases gather and cohere. They burn out and the great globe blackens. Cool mists wrap it, rains fall, seas collect, continents arise. There is life, behold it, various and infinite. And hearken to the whisper of this great universe, one tiny note in that song of praise you heard but now. Yes, the life dies, the ball grows black again; it is the carcase of a world. How long have you watched it? For an hour, a breath; but, as you judge time, some ten thousand million years. Sleep now, you are weary; later you shall understand.

Thus the wraith of Stella spoke to his soul in visions. Presently, with drumming ears and eyes before which strange lights seemed to play, Morris staggered from the place, so weak, indeed, that he could scarcely thrust one foot before the other. Yet his heart was filled with a mad joy, and his brain was drunken with the deep cup of a delight and a knowledge that have seldom been given to man.

On other nights the visions were different. Thus he saw the spirits of men going out and returning, and among them his own slumbering spirit that a vast and shadowy Stella bore in her arms as a mother bears a babe.

He saw also the Vision of Numbers. All the infinite inhabitants of all the infinite worlds passed before him, marching through the ages to some end unknown. Once, too, his mind was opened, and he understood the explanation of Evil and the Reason of Things. He shouted at their glorious simplicity—shouted for joy; but lo! before he rose from his chair they were forgotten.

Other visions there were without count. Also they would mix and fall into new patterns, like the bits of glass in a kaleidoscope. There was no end to them, and each was lovelier, or grander, or fraught with a more sweet entrancement, than the last. And still she who brought them, she who opened his eyes, who caused his ears to hear and his soul to see; she whom he worshipped; his heart's twin, she who had sworn herself to him on earth, and was there waiting to fulfil the oath to all eternity; the woman who had become a spirit, that spirit that had taken the shape of a woman—there she stood and smiled and changed, and yet was changeless. And oh! what did it matter if his life was draining from him, and oh! to die at those glittering feet, with that perfumed breath stirring in his hair! What did he seek more when Death would be the great immortal waking, when from twilight he passed out to light? What more when in that dawn, awful yet smiling, she should be his and he hers, and they twain would be one, with thought that answered thought, since it was the same thought?

There is much that might be told—enough to fill many pages. It would be easy, for instance, to set out long lists of the entrancing dreams which were the soul speech of the spirit of Stella, and to some extent, to picture them. Also the progress of the possession of Morris might be described and the student of his history shown, step by step, how the consummation that in her life days Stella had feared, overtook him; how "the thing got the mastery of him," and he became "unfitted for his work on earth!" How, too, his body wasted and his spiritual part developed, till every physical sight and deed became a cause of irritation to his new nature, and at times even a source of active suffering.

Thus an evil odour, the spectacle of pain, the cry of grief, the sight of the carcases of dead animals, to take a few examples out of very many, were agonies to his abnormal, exasperated nerves. Nor did it stop there, since the misfortune which threatened Stella when at length she had succeeded in becoming bodily conscious of the presence of the eidolon of her sister, and "heard discords among the harmonies" of the rich music of her violin, overtook him also.

Thus, for instance, in the scent of the sweetest rose at times Morris would discover something frightful; even the guise of tender childhood ceased to be lovely in his eyes, for now he could see and feel the budding human brute beneath. Worse still, his beautiful companion, Mary, fair and gracious as she was, became almost repulsive to him, so that he shrank from her as in common life some delicate-nurtured man might shrink from a full-bodied, coarse-tongued young fishwife. Even her daily need of food, which was healthy though not excessive, disgusted him to witness,—he who was out of touch with all wholesome appetites of earth, whose distorted nature sought an alien rest and solace.

Of Mary herself, also, it might be narrated how, after first mocking at the thought and next thrusting it away, by degrees she grew to appreciate the reality of the mysterious foreign influence which reigned in her home. It might be told how in that spiritual atmosphere, shedding its sleepy indolence, her own spirit awoke and grew conscious and far-seeing, till impressions and hints which in the old days she would have set aside as idle, became for her pregnant with light and meaning. Then at last her eyes were opened, and understanding much and guessing more she began to watch. The attitude of the Colonel also could be studied, and how he grew first suspicious, then sarcastic, and at last thoroughly alarmed, even to his ultimate evacuation of the Abbey House, detailed at length.

But to the chronicler of these doings and of their unusual issues at any rate, it appears best to resist a natural temptation; to deny the desire to paint such closing scenes in petto. Much more does this certainty hold of their explanation. Enough has been said to enable those in whom the spark of understanding may burn, to discover by its light how much is left unsaid. Enough has been hinted at to teach how much there is still to guess. At least few will deny that some things are best abandoned to the imagination. To attempt to drag the last veil from the face of Truth in any of her thousand shapes is surely a folly predoomed to failure. From the beginning she has been a veiled divinity, and veiled, however thinly, she must and will remain. Also, even were it possible thus to rob her, would not her bared eyes frighten us?

It was late, very late, and there, pale and haggard in the low light of the fire, once again Morris stood pleading with the radiant image which his heart revealed.

"Oh, speak! speak!" he moaned aloud. "I weary of those pictures. They are too vast; they crush me. I grow weak. I have no strength left to fight against the power of this fearful life that is discovered. I cannot bear this calm everlasting life. It sucks out my mortality as mists are sucked up by the sun. Become human. Speak. Let me touch your hand. Or be angry. Only cease smiling that awful smile, and take those solemn eyes out of my heart. Oh, my darling, my darling! remember that I am still a man. In pity answer me before I die."

Then a low and awful cry, and Morris turned to behold Mary his wife. At last she had seen and heard, and read his naked heart. At last she knew him—mad, and in his madness, most unfaithful—a man who loved one dead and dragged her down to earth for company.

Look! there in his charmed and secret sight stood the spirit, and there, over against her, the mortal woman, and he—wavering—he lost between the two.

Certainly he had been sick a long while, since the sun-ray touched the face of the old abbot carved in that corner of the room to support the hammer beam. This, as he had known from a child, only chanced at mid-summer. Mary was bending over him, but he was astonished to find that he could sit up and move. Surely, then, his mind must have been more ill than his body.

"Hush!" she said, "drink this, dear, and go to sleep."

It was a week after, and Morris had told her all, the kind and gentle wife who was so good to him, who understood and could even smile as he explained, in faltering, shame-heavy words. And he had sworn for her sake and his children's sake, that he would put away this awful traffic, and seek such fellowship no more.

Nor for six months did he seek it; not till the winter returned. Then, when his body was strong again, the ravening hunger of his soul overcame him, and, lest he should go mad or die of longing, Morris broke his oath—as she was sure he would.

One night Mary missed her husband from her side, and creeping down in the grey of the morning, she found him sitting in his chair in the chapel workshop, smiling strangely, but cold and dead. Then her heart seemed to break, for she loved him. Yet, remembering her promises, and the dust whereof he was made, and the fate to which he had been appointed, she forgave him all.

The search renewed, or the fruit of some fresh discovery—what he sought or what he saw, who knows?—had killed him.

Or perhaps Stella had seemed to speak at last and the word he heard her say was *Come!*

This, then, is the end of the story of Stella Fregelius upon earth, and this the writing on a leaf torn from the book of three human destinies. Remember, only one leaf.

Note About the Author

H. Rider Haggard (1856–1925), also known as Sir Henry Rider Haggard, was an English novelist and scholar. He was educated at Ipswich Grammar School and studied with a private tutor in London. Later, Haggard would travel to South Africa where he worked as a governor's assistant. Upon his return to England, he began writing fiction and nonfiction about his experiences abroad. This led to a successful publishing career which included the novels, *King Solomon's Mines* (1885) and *Allan Quatermain* (1887).

A Note from the Publisher

Spanning many genres, from non-fiction essays to literature classics to children's books and lyric poetry, Mint Edition books showcase the master works of our time in a modern new package. The text is freshly typeset, is clean and easy to read, and features a new note about the author in each volume. Many books also include exclusive new introductory material. Every book boasts a striking new cover, which makes it as appropriate for collecting as it is for gift giving. Mint Edition books are only printed when a reader orders them, so natural resources are not wasted. We're proud that our books are never manufactured in excess and exist only in the exact quantity they need to be read and enjoyed.

Discover more of your favorite classics with Bookfinity™.

- Track your reading with custom book lists.
- Get great book recommendations for your personalized Reader Type.
- Add reviews for your favorite books.
- AND MUCH MORE!

Visit **bookfinity.com** and take the fun Reader Type quiz to get started.

Enjoy our classic and modern companion pairings!

Classic & Modern

Printed in the USA
CPSIA information can be obtained
at www.ICGtesting.com
JSHW022321140824
68134JS00019B/1218